I0460404

THE DARKEST CORNERS

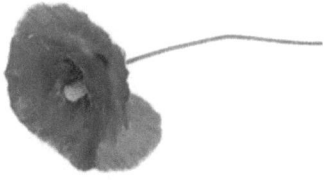

SYDNEY JAMESSON

First Published by S. J. Publishing, 2018
Copyright© Sydney Jamesson, 2018

Cover Design: https://www.michelecatalanocreative.com/
Proof reading & Editing: Marie Piquette
Formatting: Ava Manello

This book is a work of fiction. The characters in
this book have no existence outside the imagination
of the author, and have no relations to anyone bearing
the same name or names. Any resemblance to real
persons, living or dead is purely coincidental.
Likewise, places and incidents are used fictitiously
Or exist within the public domain.

EBooks are not transferable. All rights reserved.
No part of this publication may be reproduced,
copied, scanned, stored in a retrieval system,
recorded or transmitted, in any form or by any
means, without the prior written permission
of the publisher.

sjpublishing@virginmedia.com
ISBN – 978-09575850-6-5

KEEP IN TOUCH

If you would like to keep up to date with exclusive news, giveaways and new publications from Sydney Jamesson, join her mailing list: http://eepurl.com/50ANT

Communicate with her via her Website: http://www.sydneyjamesson.com/

THE DARKEST CORNERS

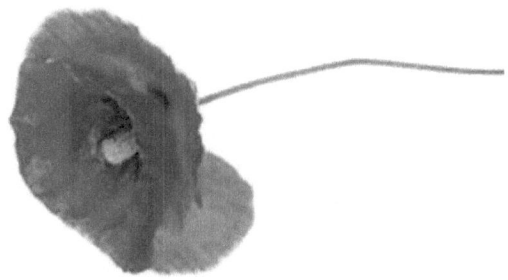

After surviving a life changing event, celebrated artist Maxwell Grant has not touched a paintbrush or a woman in four years. During that time, he has tormented himself over an unspeakable act he dare not admit to, even to himself.

His one chance at redemption comes through a journal left behind by Harriet Harper, a mysterious woman in his night school class.

Shocked by what he reads about her tortured existence, he becomes obsessed by her and falls headfirst into a dangerous game of *he said, she said*, not knowing who to believe—who to trust.

When a dangerous character from Harriet's past appears, events take a turn for the worse and he must say and do whatever necessary to save his sanity and, more importantly, his four-yea-old daughter, Poppy.

Some secrets never get to see the light of day; others are just waiting to be uncovered … with shocking consequences.

PRAISE FOR THE DARKEST CORNERS

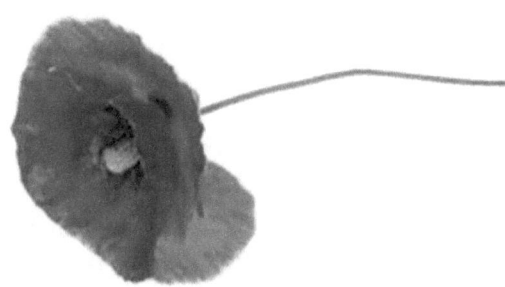

"The Darkest Corners is every bit the psychological thriller the title implies, but there is also a fair dose of romance to balance out the angst. The story is well-constructed and written, and all the characters are richly drawn and complex. This is a great read for those who enjoy suspense. I recommend this book to anyone looking for a bit of excitement in their next read." ~ *Jennifer Locklear, Bestselling Author*

"An incredibly well written story with so many twists and turns. I love Max and think I'd like to keep him!" ~ *Lisa Hobman, Bestselling Author*

"I had to read The Darkest Corners in one sitting and couldn't put it down until I finished it in the early hours, gripped by the story. This is a five-star roller coaster of emotions, twists, and turns." ~ *Ava Manello, Author*

"MIND HANGOVER! Not since GONE GIRL have I enjoyed a book so much! Absolutely amazing plot line you will not easily forget." ~ *As you wish Reviews*

"The writing throughout was exquisite and I couldn't put this book down; it was heartfelt, dramatic, scary and romantic. This page-turner of a psychological thriller isn't just gripping, it's heart-stopping. This is the best thriller I've read this year." ~ *Kindle Friends Forever*

"The Darkest Corners had me hanging on the edge, from the first word and I never wanted to let go." ~ *Once Upon A Book Blog*

"What a mind bender! The Darkest Corners is thrilling, filled with lies, deceit, love, family, loss and shocking events!" ~ *The Book Obsessed Momma Blog*

"Wow! If first impressions are anything to go by, then Sydney Jamesson has become a 1Click author for us! We were blown away by the uniqueness, the creativity, the depth and the vividly splendid writing. The unpredictability kept us on our toes, the emotional aching was felt deep within us as we ventured into the human frailty, with each word eliciting compassion as we uncovered weaknesses and strengths of the characters." *Totally Booked Blog.*

"The Darkest Corners is amazing - a dark, sexy and twisted story! The characters have sucked me in and have made me feel what they felt. You won't want to miss this heartfelt tale. This is definitely a top read for 2018." ~ *Flavory-Savory Reads*

"Two characters who have both suffered life changing events called out to my heart. I love when authors have you question every move, every comment, everybody! ~ *A Woman and Her Book Blog*"Another wonderful book written by Sydney Jamesson about love, loss, and healing that will have you losing sleep because you need to find out what happens next!" ~ *Beyond the Covers Blog*

"Amazing! This slow burning tale of Max, an artist who can no longer paint and Harriet, a young woman escaping a troubled past captured me from the get-go. This story is fabulously written with more twists and turns than the A30 in Cornwall!" ~ *Beyond Books Blog*

DEDICATION

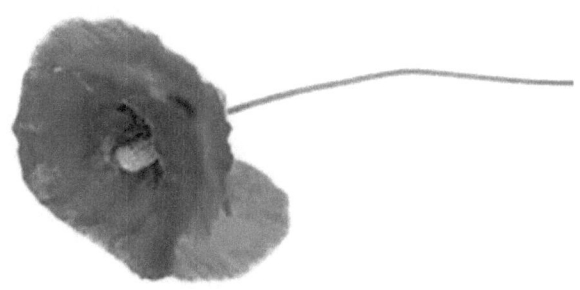

TO THOSE WHO MEAN THE MOST TO ME: BARRY, JENNA,

AARON, LEO, ETHAN, MUM AND DAD

"REJOICE WITH YOUR FAMILY IN THE BEAUTIFUL LAND

OF LIFE." – ALBERT EINSTEIN

PROLOGUE

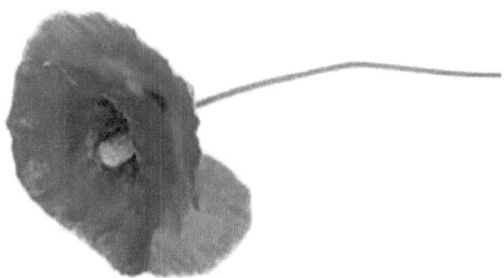

In my dream, I'm drifting in a sea of red daubed with morning mist encircling me like strands of angel hair.

From beneath the undulating waves an outstretched hand reaches out to me. It's a woman's left hand with a slender wrist and delicate fingers. On the third finger rests a wedding band and a diamond solitaire.

I recognise them both.

Rather than take hold of the hand, I frantically propel myself backward, away from it like a helpless swimmer trying to steer clear of danger. Panicking, I look about me for dry land, a single point to focus my attention on, but there is nothing.

Only blackness.

The wind whips up the waves and they begin to rise; red rivulets with icicle white peaks cover the hand, dissolve and dribble between rigid fingers like blood oozing from an open wound.

I begin to tire.

Unable to tread water for a minute longer I start thrashing about, gasping and gulping as the sea rises like a crimson beast. It overwhelms me; drags me under until only my solitary, outstretching hand is visible.

In an instant, I am gone.

The last sound I hear is my garbled, desperate cry for help … and forgiveness.

CHAPTER ONE

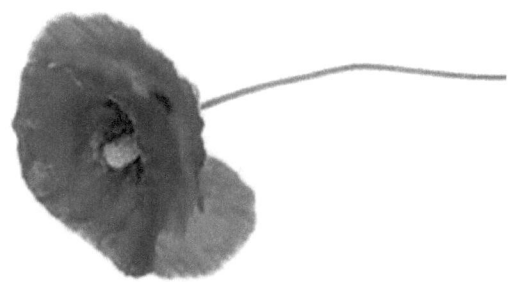

I RECOILED FROM SLEEP like a spring freeing itself from the constraints of a cramped space. I imagined muscles contracting, tendons tearing, disjointed bones held together by saturated flesh.

Perspiration coated my skin, trickled down my breastbone: evidence of my nightly descent into the abyss where my memories lived—witnesses to my fall from grace.

I used to be the early riser, the alarm clock clicker with no desire to snooze. I was 'the one to watch,' 'the man of the hour.'

But all that changed in a single stroke.

In daylight, the combined weight of guilt and regret pressed down upon me to the point of suffocation; breathing was difficult, getting out of bed even harder.

I dragged my sorry arse out of bed at eleven o'clock to the sound of cartoons playing on the TV. Poppy had been able to operate the TV for months and—I hate myself for saying it—even at three-years-of-age she new better than to wake an insomniac with a hangover until her tiny tummy rumbled in need of a pre-lunch snack.

That autumnal, Wednesday morning began like any other. I was treated to the usual trampoline-style greeting; a pyjama-clad pygmy bouncing on my bed amid roaring laughter, landing on me like a ton of bricks.

Time to get up.

Having cleared my jumble-sale mound of clothes from the bedroom floor, sponged the odour of last night's scotch from my skin, and refreshed my breath with mouthwash, I made my way into the kitchen. My hair was still damp on the back of my neck and my beard a bushy mound of wiry hair in need of cultivation, but other than that, I was half decent.

On the worktop sat an empty breakfast bowl and a small puddle of milk, the tell-tale signs of Poppy's early breakfast. I had never been a breakfast person but coffee I could handle—lots of it—before facing another day.

Standing barefoot in sweats, a T-shirt and a moth-eaten, woollen sweater, I checked my to-do list. My tragic life had become no more than a series of pink Post-it notes attached to a fridge door, flanked on one side by puppy pics and lop-sided Polly Pocket people on the other. I gave them a passing glance: I had no room in my life for multi-coloured midgets.

The steaming brew helped to clear my head and the list of three items scrawled on the Post-it note the previous night gave my life some kind of order.

1pm meeting Lance

I had no idea what it was about but I hoped it was not anything serious. Lance Nelson had been the principal at Eastwick College for eight years. He was the one who put in a good word for me when they needed an art teacher for their night class. He has been a good friend over the years; easy to like and fun to be around, if, one day, I should be in the market for some fun, that is. He said, "Maxwell Grant, this is your chance to return to the land of the living…"

Like I said, he's a funny guy.

Bottles

Ah, yes. God forbid I should have forgotten to dispose of the remains of last night's party for one from the prying eyes of my forty-five-year-old, part-time housekeeper, Mary McCafferty; a rotund, apron-wearing woman. A cross between Mrs. Doubtfire and The Madonna—a force of nature: reliable, steadfast and saintly, when she was not cussing. She came jet-propelled into our home two years ago intending to "sort us out," regarding me as an emotional invalid in desperate need of assistance.

She's a perceptive woman.

From day one, her presence stirred the air, created a kind of tornado wherever she positioned herself; tidying the house, sorting laundry, ironing, cooking—she did it all *without so much as a murmur*, is what I'd like to say, but it would be a lie.

My ears burned the entire time.

I was the thorn in her side, the one who had her muttering expletives and yet, if it were not for her, I'd have been knee deep in beer bottles and Poppy would have been living off pizza and ice-cream.

Her shoulders were as broad as her accent and I made a point of keeping out of her way for fear of being rebuked for my lack of parental skills. She once said, "Misery is the coward's curse. A brave man smiles in the face of despair and marches on." A pearl of wisdom from Irish folklore that had traversed the decades, maybe from the Battle of the Boyne when her Catholic ancestors came face to face with a larger, better-equipped, and better-skilled adversary.

I know how they felt.

So why keep her? Why tolerate her contempt?

Well, even in my desensitised state I knew that it was not contempt at all. No more than a shamrock-coloured imitation. In her eyes, my ineptitude had no limits; this I deduced from the litany of Irish expletives that usually left her mouth like cannonballs, seldom reaching their target but potentially hurtful if they were actually fired with intent. She displayed a coarse form of compassion for our tragic circumstances and, for that, I accepted her muttering insults and remained an "eejit,"
until such time as my simmering sadness either boiled dry or I ceased to be exactly that.

Poppy, on the other hand, could do no wrong. She was her "pumpkin," helping around the house, holding a duster, a dishcloth or a wooden spoon. I was tempted to point out that Poppy should have a greater goal in life than 'tending house;' if she had half her mother's brains and my temperament, she would want to set her sights significantly higher.

Yet, when I saw Poppy perched on a stool covered in flour, a tea towel wrapped around her waist, her fingers sticky with a creamy mixture destined to become a sponge cake or a scone, I bit my tongue. On those occasions, Poppy's sweet laughter grated on my ears; it was a cross between hiccups and a high pitched chuckle that, for a split second, had me thinking Hope, her mother, had come back to me. I was not fool enough to believe it, but desperate enough to stand outside the door and torture myself with it.

Car Service

And so my day began.

The previous night, I had begun a thirty-week stretch of what I like to call 'community service'—a session of self-inflicted servitude. The thought of having to teach a class of students with little or no aptitude for art depressed the hell out of me.

Finding a parking space near the main entrance to the college is a nightmare at the best of times. On a Tuesday night in a rainstorm, it was impossible. I parked two rows back and told Poppy to wait for me to open her door so we could make the dash for cover together.

But did she listen?

No.

She got it into her head that it was a race. She ran off between parked cars, around night class attendees and out of sight. I was panic-stricken. I had visions of her stepping out in front of a car, slipping, falling, breaking an arm. I already considered myself the worst father in the world. To have that witnessed would have made the fact public knowledge, and I did not need that kind of publicity.

Thankfully, she was unharmed when I caught up with her, offering one of her playful smiles to the dishevelled man skidding and cursing as he emerged from behind the curtain of rain.

"Daddy!"

"What the hell?" I called out, focusing my attention on an unremarkable young woman holding Poppy's hand. It was her hair that struck me first, dark brown with curls, lots of curls, dripping ringlets around her shoulders and face. It was not until I was face to face with her that I became aware of the intensity of her stare: blue eyes held my attention, so dark and depthless, with large irises that appeared almost black against the clear whites.

I peeled the rain-stained satchel from across my body and swung it in the direction of the car park. "I've been looking for you. I'm wet through…"

"I won!" Poppy exclaimed, beaming, her nose glossy with raindrops. "You need to give me a prize."

I stepped under the canopy and shook my dripping hair, looking more like a dog returning from a swim than a teacher about to direct a class. "A prize for running off? You must be joking."

The young woman released Poppy's hand. "Your daughter made it here in record time. We were waiting for you to show."

Looking left and right at us, Poppy nodded enthusiastically.

"She said it was a race. She won, fair and square. You owe her a prize." Realising she might have been presuming too much, Poppy's companion coughed and attempted to rearrange her bedraggled hair behind her ears.

"And who are you?" I demanded sternly, unimpressed by her assertion. "Her bloody agent?"

"No. Just a friend." Even though she was taken aback by my outburst, she could not conceal her amusement. I swear her mouth twitched.

"Okay." I reached down to take hold of Poppy's hand. "Say goodbye to your friend, Poppy. We have to get inside. I need to dry off." Prompted by a tug, Poppy moved inside the college with me, stopping to turn, wobble, and wave goodbye. I sensed the woman was still watching us as we disappeared down the corridor: one bad-tempered night school art teacher and a ball of squeaking pink plastic.

My students piled into classroom 106, looking expectant and cheerful—a cross section of society with nothing better to do on a Tuesday night in October than seek out a miracle worker. I wanted to say, *Don't expect me to conjure up talent from nothing. This is a pencil in my hand not a bloody wand.* But I did not, not even when, an hour later, I was handed their puerile offerings. A more talentless bunch you could never wish to meet—bar one.

I know talent when I see it, and I saw it in a woman called Harriet Harper, Poppy's new friend.

Refocusing my thoughts on the mail sitting on my desk in my office, I felt my cheeks flush and waited for my embarrassment to abate and the memory to fade. I was not only rude and ungrateful to the woman who had stood waiting for me with Poppy but, later on, I made a bigger fool out of myself. In my glorious, middle-class, sexist state of mind, I assumed *Harry* was a talented *male*, even scoped the room looking for him.

Miss Harper must have found my little pantomime very amusing. It was not until I checked the register that I realised *he*, Harry, was a *she*—an outspoken she, as it happens. That *she* was the one person to stay behind to speak up at the end of the session; *she* who attempted to put me in my place with a few home truths.

"You'd better have something nice to say next week, Mr. Grant, or you won't have a class to teach."

Being me, I eyed her with derision and remarked, "Why would I say anything nice if there's nothing worth complimenting? I'm not here to stroke people's egos."

Boldly, she continued, "I know that. But you *are* here to teach us to become better artists and if people are too scared to even try because you'll rip them to pieces, then you're the failure. You've failed us—not the other way round."

I laughed, mockingly. "Oh, dear. Are you upset because I said something unflattering about your sketch? Did you want me to say you have talent?" I iced my insult with a sickly-sweet smile; it peeped out from behind my beard like a sliver of white frosting.

In response, she threw her rucksack over her shoulder. "You already did."

She was pissed—I could tell—but, even though she was seething, she held her tongue, showing an impressive amount of self-restraint under the circumstances. She turned her back on me and left, knowing I would check the register—I did.

That was the start of my second year of teaching art to night school students. I should qualify that with the word, 'mature.' There was no one there under twenty-five and some as old as sixty, I would guess from their gait and the width of their waistbands.

I was half hoping that bedraggled, purple-clad woman would return to my class; no I *hoped,* there was no 'half' about it. I suspected she could, potentially, be a gleaming

8

oasis in the frigid desert that had become my world—my art world. On second thought she could have turned out to be a pain in the ass.

Either way, I had every reason to assume *Harry* would return for round two. She had left a journal behind; thick and worn and yellowed about the edges like a book of secrets, unlocked and unread.

After a night of introspection, I made the decision to temper my mood with good grace, or at least good manners—there was no excuse for rudeness. If my wife had taught me anything, it was that.

Poppy had been awake for hours and had become bored and weary. Her face had taken on that sorrowful mien of the neglected child having spent too many hours alone with no more than imaginary friends and tiny teacups.

She found me in my office. I spun around in my chair and stretched out a hand. "Come and sit on my knee and tell me what you've been up to."

She snuggled against my chest and poked her fingers through my knitted sweater. "I had a tea party with my Pollys and we drank juice."

I felt the warmth of her body against mine. "Sounds like you had fun. Was there music?"

She looked up at me, unsure of my question. "Cartoon music."

"Ah. We can do better than that. Should I put on some real music?"

She nodded. "Mummy's music."

While she fiddled with my cuff I closed my eyes tight, pictured *Mummy* stretched out on the sofa, her head resting in my lap, my hand on her stomach feeling it rise and fall to the rhythm of Poppy's prenatal paso-doble. It would be four years in December since she left us and not a day had gone by when I had not wished I could have gone back, done things differently.

Regret's a bitch.

It took me a couple of seconds to find my voice and form a sentence. "Okay. Let's go and listen together. I'll read the paper and you can take a nap before Mary gets here."

She jumped down. I grabbed my Kindle and headed for the lounge.

Her mother's fifties playlist was already on in the background when she appeared with her tatty pink blanket and her favourite teddy tucked under her arm.

I lifted her onto the sofa. "All set?"

She nodded and buried her face into her teddy while I tucked her up. This was our midday ritual, one of many I depended on to add some shape to my day—much like numbered dots on a page you join up in the hope of creating a recognisable outline.

It was our time to be still, to take a moment to reflect, in my case. I brushed my hand across her hair; it was the same silky texture as her mother's—but for the knots her father had forgotten to brush out—the same rich, brown colour, streaked with shards of golden chestnut. Her mother's curls complimented her hazel eyes; wild eyes that flashed like brown amethysts when she smiled and appeared luminescent when she laughed. When Hope was around I had my very own firework display, morning, noon and night.

I missed the pyrotechnics.

From the first meeting, Hope triggered my senses, and made me see things differently, and feel emotions so intense I thought my heart would burst. My wife was the rarest of creatures: a mixture of mind reader and muse. But, best of all, she was mine … until the time came for her to leave.

I closed my eyes once more, not wanting to go back but unable to move forward. I was stuck in limbo, and it was all my own doing. I pictured Hope's beautiful face, and there she was—my reason to wake up in the morning.

My reason to breathe.

In need of a distraction I returned my hand to my Kindle.

"Sweet dreams, baby girl."

CHAPTER TWO

"OH, YOU MADE IT then?"

Lance Nelson pushed back his chair and stood behind his desk like the principal he is. As hard as he pretended to be pissed that I was late, I could tell by his smirk that he was pleased I'd made an appearance. Many times before, I'd let him down when the thought of leaving the house had made me want to dig a ditch and throw myself in it.

"I thought you said one fifteen." I checked my watch. "There I was thinking I was fashionably early."

He reached over to shake my hand. "Don't give me that shit! You've never been fashionably early in your life. Take a seat."

I threw down my leather satchel, still damp from the previous night's downpour, and sunk into the comfortable club chair in front of him.

He removed his glasses and looked behind me the way you do when you're expecting a twosome. "Did you bring Poppy with you?"

"Yes. I've left her outside colouring-in with your charming secretary while we chat. I don't want to subject her to your fucking bad language." I smirked.

He laughed, not in the least bit slighted by my suggestion. "That's probably for the best."

I noticed the pile of paperwork on his desk. "You've got your hands full."

"Yeah. Last minute applications keep coming in." He flicked through the stack of pages. "We've only got fifteen minutes, so I'd better get down to business."

I folded my arms across my chest. "Be my guest. Are you going to offer me a raise?"

"Yeah, right. Like you need the money…" The minute his tactless comment hit the airways, he regretted letting it fly.

There was an awkward silence.

"Fuck! Take no notice of me. I'm an insensitive bastard. I didn't mean…"

"Forget it. Just get to the point, Lance. Then you can get back to your pile of shit, okay?" I massaged my beard roughly, in no mood for money talk.

He put the top on his pen and placed it horizontally on his desk. "Look, Maxwell, the point is, I've been asked to have a quiet word with you."

Maxwell?

"No raise, then," I stated with a sneer.

"I'm afraid not, my friend. Only a warning."

I settled my back into the chair. "Warn away."

"Okay." He reached for a file out of his top draw. Inside it were what looked like typed letters or reports. "Last year you took a night school class here, correct?"

"Correct."

"To start with there were twelve people in the class and by the end of it there were eight. Is that correct?"

I rolled my eyes. "You've got the figures right there in front of you. Why bother asking me?"

"I'm just making sure we're both on the same page, Max, because I have four formal complaints. Remember those?" He held them up for me to see.

"No. I don't remember *those*, and why would I?" I huffed, becoming more unsettled by the minute. "You're the one keeping score. I just teach them how to fucking paint, those who can hold a brush, that is."

"Some of the more … mature students aren't very talented. People who come to night classes aren't looking to get qualified. If they were any good, they'd have gone to college decades earlier. They come here for different reasons."

"Oh yeah?"

"Yeah, to get out of the house, to socialise and make friends."

I shook my head. "I'm not running a fucking social club."

"You're not. You're an artist—and a damn good one, Max. The only famous artist I know who doesn't actually paint…"

"You know I can't. And you know why," I reminded him, picking at the balls of wool on my cuff.

"I do."

"And those that can't—teach. Isn't that what they say?"

He would not let it drop. "Sure. But why don't you at least—"

"No! We're not going there. I. Don't. Paint. Get it?"

"But—"

"But nothing! I haven't picked up a brush in almost four years. Not since Poppy was born. And I *never* will. So back the fuck off!" Without realising, I'd stood up, I was pacing, shouting at my best friend.

I fell back into the chair and rested my head in my hands. Slowly, I met his worried stare. "Look. I'll do my best to be nice. I'll say nice things to these nice, talentless people and we'll all have a jolly good time. Okay?"

"Okay." He returned my folder to his drawer. "This is just between us. I'm giving you the heads-up, that's all. If we get *one* more formal complaint then you're out, and there won't be a thing I can do about it." He stood and came around the table, resting his hand on my shoulder. "Look, I know what you've been through. You think your life's shit right now, but it needn't be."

Outside there was the sound of Poppy's laughter. I snickered, closed my eyes and shook my head. "That daughter of mine has great timing."

His grip on my shoulder increased a split second before he removed it. "You've got the cutest kid, Max." He rested on the edge of his desk, facing me. "I'd give my right arm for a daughter like her, and that's no lie."

"What about Renee? She wants children, doesn't she?" I asked, nodding in the direction of the framed photograph on his desk. Renee: a striking blond with a cover girl smile and a permanent tan.

13

"Yes, but she's still got a bee in her bonnet about moving to the States. She wants to move to where there's sunshine every bloody day. You know what she's like…" He sighed, seeming weary of it all.

"Getting pregnant would change all that. Hope stayed out of the sun for most of her pregnancy. She said an increase in body temperature could affect the baby in the first three months; something to do with weight and IQ, I think."

He was taken by surprise, and so was I by my willingness to share the recollection.

"I didn't know that. Best if we keep that to ourselves or it'll be just the two of us until death us do part." He managed a grin and so did I.

It had been a while since my wife's name had left my lips in daylight. Those haunting hours between dusk and dawn when I was left alone with my memories were the worst—a kind of living hell. I'd find myself calling out to her through an alcohol-induced fog, hoping that by some miracle she'd come back to me.

Then I'd wake and the nightmare would continue.

I straightened up and took a couple of leisurely strides over to the window. Outside, the sun was shining, reflecting off parked cars, dust-free after the previous night's storm. There were groups of people carrying satchels and rucksacks returning from the library, hurrying to their next class, all except one, strolling toward the building I was in.

I tipped up my head and leaned into the sash window. "Isn't that Harriet Harper?" I asked, breaking our momentary silence.

Lance joined me by the gleaming pane of glass. "Who?" He focused on the figure moving into view. "I haven't a clue."

I found my attention unwavering. "Is she taking classes here?"

He shrugged his shoulders. "How would I know?"

"The fact that she's here in your bloody college carrying a satchel could be some kind of clue, don't you think?"

"I don't know *every* student personally." He left me standing alone. "Anyway, how do *you* know her?"

"She's attending my art class, and she looked after Poppy when she ran off."

He laughed out loud. "What? Poppy ran off? Why?"

I held up my hands. "She thought it was a race…"

"Who won?"

"It wasn't a race," I insisted. "It was raining. We made a dash for the door—"

"Who won?" he probed, expecting an answer the second time of asking.

"Who do you think? She was the one with the nonslip shoes." Even I could not resist the temptation to smirk.

"And she ran off into the arms of one of my students…"

"It wasn't like that. And, anyway, she's not a student—"

"I though you said she was, what with her carrying a satchel and all—"

"Fuck you, Lance. I mean she wasn't a kid. She was older, smarter, straight-talking."

He nodded as if he was on the receiving end of a secret. "I get the picture."

"I doubt that." I sighed. Having dug myself into a hole, I prepared to leave. "I'd better get going. I don't want Poppy overstaying her welcome."

"No chance of that. She's a sweet kid." He placed a brotherly hand on my back. "Why don't you two come over for lunch on Sunday? It might do Renee good to see how cute she is. Who knows, seeing you two together might get her body clock ticking?"

I shook my head, unconvinced. "Don't hold your breath. She likes to travel too much and babies are like puppies; they're not only for Christmas—"

"They're for life."

"Right. And that includes *all* the holidays."

"I can live with that," he said with a smile of resignation. "Better still, why don't you invite your student friend—who isn't a student—to come with you?"

"Yeah, right," I huffed. "I don't know who the hell she is and even if I did I wouldn't ask her to Sunday dinner with two of my oldest friends. Anyway, the next class isn't until next Tuesday. That's if she turns up…"

He returned to his spot behind his desk. "Don't give me that *if she turns up* bullshit. She'll be there, you wait and see." He checked his watch. "Your time's up, my friend."

I reached for the door handle. "I'll leave you to do what you do best…"

He didn't miss a beat. "And that would be?"

I had my back to him as I opened the door. "Damned if I know."

He pulled one of the files off the pile and began flicking through it. I turned to receive his farewell comment but, without looking up, he flipped me the bird.

I left his office smiling. My smile lingered when I saw Poppy kneeling up on a cushion against a small coffee table in the waiting area, humming one of her mother's songs and colouring in what looked like a vase of flowers, not unlike the one I instructed my class to draw. The colours were brighter and the flowers were more alive and uplifting in fluorescent pink and yellow—a stark reminder of the joy *I* once felt when I had a pencil or a paintbrush in my hand.

"Look, Daddy," she called out on seeing me. "Look at the pretty flowers." She held up the book for me to see her handy work.

I managed to hold onto my smile for a few more seconds. "Well done, Poppy. You've done a great job. Put your colours away now. Say bye to Christine and thank her for letting you stay here with her while Daddy had a chat with Uncle Lance."

Obediently, she tossed her colours into her pencil case, placed it in her Polly Pocket rucksack and dragged it across the floor toward me. "*I* want to say bye to Uncle Lance."

"Okay. But be quick because he's really busy." I lifted her up until she was at my eye level. She tapped on the glass behind which Lance was sitting, talking to someone on the phone. She waved and blew him half a dozen kisses. He waved and blew a kiss in return. When we turned, Christine, his secretary, was standing behind us smiling. She was treated to a beaming smile and rewarded Poppy with a sweet.

Taking Lance's advice, I gave Christine a broad smile. "I must say, you look very nice today, Christine."

She folded her arms and tapped her right foot. "Are you trying to be bloody funny?"

I leant back. "No, of course not. I was just…"

She turned her back on me en route to her desk. I could sense her eyes rolling just from the angle of her head.

"What? No sweet for me?" I asked, rediscovering my inner grouch.

She looked at me from above the rim of her glasses and, saying nothing, began to swivel in her office chair

I was almost out in the corridor when I felt Poppy's hand in mine. With her other

16

hand she held the sweet aloft. "You can have *my* sweetie, Daddy."

I gave her hand a squeeze. "It's okay. I was only teasing Christine. You have your sweetie. You deserve it."

She popped the fruit gum into her mouth. "Are we going home?" she mumbled hopping from one leg to the other.

"No. We can't."

"Why?"

Together we stepped out of the dreary sandstone building into the sunlight. I breathed deeply and explained, "Because, we have to pick up your prize."

Her eyes widened; her pretty face was aglow with expectation. "Yay! What can I choose?"

"Anything, as long as it isn't in pink," I declared, playfully.

The glow faded almost as quickly as it had appeared, replaced instead by a downturned smile. "But, Daddy, pink is the best colour in the world."

"You could be right, but it's not the *only* colour in the world."

"But I want a purse..." She formed her lips into a pout.

"You're three years old. What do you need a purse for?"

She considered her answer. "To keep my pennies in."

"What pennies?" We paused before crossing the road. The car park was within walking distance.

Swinging my hand, she explained, "The pennies the fairies leave."

I was afraid to ask, but I did anyway. "Where do these fairies leave the pennies?"

"On the carpet in your bedroom; sometimes they're dirty and sometimes they're shiny. I like the shiny ones best."

I understood. I just wished I did not.

When I stumbled into bed, half-cut, wriggling out of my jeans, loose change must have fallen out of my pockets. Most nights I was too far gone to notice. At least *fairies* was a better explanation than the real one.

"Okay. A purse it is, then. Won't you think about getting one in a different colour?"

Unwavering, she shook her head and kicked at a small stone with her Wellington boots.

I exhaled. "For an artist's daughter you have a very limited palette."

"What's a palette?" she asked, raising herself up onto her toes.

"It's a collection of paints in different colours."

"Does it have pink?" she asked, sweetly.

"Not as such. You have to mix red with white to make pink."

"I can do that." Her hand left mine as we approach my car, a VW beetle in petrol blue—a leftover from the early days that I'd not had the heart to part with.

In the time it took to open my door and throw down my satchel, she had disappeared. I called out, "Poppy? Don't play hide and seek in the car park, it's dangerous."

I looked under and around the car, then left and right for a little girl in a pink dress and Wellington boots. Not fifty yards away, I spotted her. She was not alone. Leaning over her was a petite brunette dressed in a purple dress and a black leather jacket, looking considerably less waterlogged than she did the night before and considerably more attractive.

There was no concealing her surprise when she saw me; her cheeks flushed, her eyes darted from side to side. I hoped I was managing to disguise my surprise a little better.

"I seem to have lost a daughter," I shouted, heading in their direction.

When I joined them, Poppy slid her hand into mine and sought Miss. Harper's with the other. "I'm here, Daddy. Can't you see me?"

"I can now, but you keep disappearing and running into Miss Harper, these days." I caught her adult friend smiling. "Maybe you should let me know where you'll be tomorrow, Miss Harper, so I won't panic when Poppy goes astray."

Her eyes widened and she smiled. "I'll be right here, Mr. Grant. I just called into Admin to drop a cheque off. What's your excuse?"

"I teach here, remember?"

"During the day?" She sounded surprised.

"God no! I can just about manage two hours on a Tuesday night. Spending any longer than that with the artistically challenged could result in all kinds of misdemeanours."

Soft laughter erupted from her mouth like an effervescent drink; it rippled between the three of us, creating sound waves that warmed the after-noon air. She tipped her head to the side. "Oh. I believe you."

"And what about you? Are you taking art classes?"

"No. Psychology."

"Disappointing…"

She looked unsure of my intimation. "For those in need of therapy?"

"No, of course not. For the art world," I stated, noticing her cheeks flush that delicate rose pink once again: she was not used to receiving compliments. Either that or I made her nervous. I had that effect on people.

Poppy tugged my hand. "This is my friend, Harry, Daddy. She's a lady."

"Yes, I worked that out for myself, thank you, Poppy."

Harriet smirked, as we shared the joke.

"I found that out last night. Harry *is* in fact a lady, and a talented artist—or she could be one day."

Poppy looked up at me. "Like you, Daddy?"

I shook my head and huffed at the suggestion. "Sure. Like me."

Her attention shifted to Harry. "Do you know you have to mix red and white together to make pink?"

The sudden shift in topic took me by surprise. I gave her hand a gentle squeeze. "I think Harry knows already, Poppy. She—"

"Your dad's right," Harry, interjected. "I *did* know that. But do you know you have to mix red and blue together to make purple?" She slipped her satchel off her shoulder and showed it to Poppy. It was purple with a pink trim. Poppy's eyes were on stalks; she was enamoured by the damn thing.

"I *didn't* know that." Poppy turned to me. "Did you know that, Daddy?"

"Yes. I did." I checked my watch. It was beginning to feel like conversation overload for me—first Mary, then Lance, and now this. My beard itched, I found myself shuffling my feet. Needing to get back to my self-imposed solitude, I moved things along. "Maybe your prize should be some paints. That way you'll be able to mix your own colours."

Turning our encounter into a game of Show-and-Tell, Poppy lifted her rucksack off her back. "Yours is purple and pink and mine is pink and purple." She looked positively euphoric.

Harriet bent down to take a closer look at her rucksack, mirroring her rapture. "You're right. The set of paints sounds like a great idea. Your daddy can get you lots of paper too. What do you think?"

"Yes! Yes! Can we get them today, Daddy? Can we?" she pleaded, childish anticipation turning her face into a picture of innocence.

There was my cue. "Sure. Get your bag and say goodbye to Harry."

Still at Poppy's height, Harry arranged her rucksack on her back. Unexpectedly, she found herself on the receiving end of a tight hug. Poppy wrapped her arms around her neck like a human scarf; in response Harriet enveloped her tiny body. I had never seen Poppy so taken with someone before. Seeing this innocent declaration of friendship caused a lump of something hard to form in my throat; it was a vision of what might have been if circumstances had been different.

If I'd...

I couldn't allow my mind to go there.

Poppy rarely came into contact with women—except Mary—and to see her like that with someone she barely knew, tugged at even my frosted heartstrings.

Harriet tucked a curl behind Poppy's right ear. "Go get your prize, sweetie, and get your daddy to pick up some hair slides and a couple of hair bobbles for you. You'll need to keep your hair out of your eyes when you're painting."

In no need of prompting, Poppy spun around. "Okay. Let's go." She looked left then right and made a dash for the car, calling out, "Bye, Harry."

We both watched her leave. "Tell me, Harriet ... why is it that whenever we meet, I end up with a shopping list?"

Harry shrugged her shoulders, slipped her hands into her jacket pockets and rocked back on her heels. "Such a lovely daughter deserves a treat now and again."

I nodded in agreement. "She does. Should I bring my wallet to class on Tuesday evening?"

"That depends..."

"On what?"

"Who makes it to the front door first," she said, making me want to smile in response. But that was something I'd gotten out of the habit of doing; facial muscles circling my mouth were in need of a workout and I was in no fit state to reciprocate with an actual smile. In response, I simply tipped my head and returned to our conversation. "Oh. I'm hoping she'll give me a head start."

She giggled. "I wouldn't count on it. If there's a prize at stake, she'll be like a bullet out of a gun." She checked her phone. "I'll leave you to your shopping. I don't want to miss my bus."

"Ah…"

Squeezing between two parked cars, she called out, "See you next week. I'll be waiting by the door with a stopwatch." She kept walking, not stopping to turn back. I watched her walk all the way to the end of the road until she disappeared around the corner.

It took the cries of an impatient child to shake me free of my reverie.

Sensing I was being watched, I scanned the car park and then the administration offices we had left about fifteen minutes before. Standing at one of the windows was a familiar figure. Having observed our encounter with Harriet, Lance was watching and grinning. He waved and blew me a kiss. Before returning to my car, I flipped him the bird.

My seatbelt clicked in position. At the same time my phone rang in my pocket.

Poppy took hold of my arm. "Daddy! Your phone."

"I know. It's only Uncle Lance. I'll call him back later. Is your seatbelt fastened?" I asked my excitable passenger.

She tugged at the strap across her chest. "Yes. Let's go! What will we do if they don't have paints?"

I turned onto the main road and picked up speed. "We'll get the pink purse."

"I don't want a pink purse. I want paints…"

I sensed a sulk coming on. "I know. But you said before that you wanted a purse to keep your pennies in, and if they don't have paints…"

She bounced up in her seat, causing me to veer to the left as I stretched out an arm

21

to keep her in her seat. "Sit still, Poppy. I'm trying to drive."

"Guess what? I don't need paints." Her hand rested on my arm once more. "I can use *your* paints. You have paints at home. I've seen them in the room with the big windows."

"Those aren't little girls' paints, Poppy…"

"Who has those paints?"

I hesitated. "I did."

"You don't use them."

"I know, but…"

Her excitement peaked. "Is there red and white?"

"Of course there's red and white."

She wriggled in her seat. "Yay! I can have a purse."

I remained silent, blindsided by the undeniable logic of a three-year-old. To say she looked gleefully happy would have been an understatement; her cheeks were flushed with excitement and had become the colour of strawberry ice-cream; her wide hazel eyes appeared to be backlit.

She stepped from the car and skipped into the toy store. A yard or so behind her, I paused, noticing the way my sweater had become tattered around the collar and cuffs. I saw a man reflected in the shop window and didn't recognise him—a vagrant who had been wandering through the wilderness and become lost and disoriented.

Cheerful couples were leaving a nearby clothes store, holding hands, wrapped up in one another. A pain brought on by jealousy caused my chest to tighten. I used to have what they had. I took it for granted, assumed it was just another part of my life without realising it was the *best* part.

As I entered the toy store, Poppy was nowhere to be seen. Thanks to the suggestions from her new friend, my daughter was sitting crossed-legged rummaging through not pink, but purple purses; then came the picking of hair slides and bobbles in matching shades.

We returned to the car, our spirits lifted by the simple act of purchasing childish things. Poppy sank her hands into a plastic carrier bag, pulled out her precious bits and pieces to accompanying gasps. Watching her was like a lesson in parenting. She was almost four and had never owned a hair slide or a bobble.

How had I missed that?

"Look, Daddy. They're *sooo* pretty." She folded back my right hand and filled my palm with strips of crystals and tiny flowers in all kinds of colours, pink and purple, mostly. "You choose." She raised her head, looking up to me through piercing orbs, more green than brown.

I inspected each item, twisted them between my finger and thumb. "Mmm. It's hard to decide. Which would you like to try first?"

She literally trembled with excitement. "This one!"

It was the least ornate of the lot, a modest row of daisies. Exactly what her mother would have chosen. I tugged on my lip. "That's the perfect choice."

She returned all but the matching pair she had chosen to the bag, leaving the strips of decorated metal in my palm like open wounds. Without asking, she leaned and placed her head above the gear stick, waiting for me to slot them into her hair. I held down her overgrown fringe, and as best I could, slipped the first and then the second slide into her hair, left and right.

"Can I see?" she asked. "I want to see!"

I flipped down the sun visor and helped her balance on the passenger seat. "Can you see, now?"

She replied with a smile and a slow-motion nod. Before I could brace myself, she bounced over to me, wrapped her arms around my neck and kissed my left cheek, giggling when my beard tickled her chin.

"Thank you, Daddy."

I swallowed hard. "You're welcome. Every little girl deserves a treat once in a while."

She sat back in her seat, troubled by something, surely not hair slide related.

"What's wrong?"

Her lips puckered. "I have my purse, but my pennies are at home."

I shrugged away concern. "That's okay. You can get them later."

"But I want them now."

"What for? You can't have anything else." I turned the key in the ignition.

"But I want to buy *you* something." Her hand rested on mine. "Next time will be a long time away."

She was right, of course. We never went shopping *together*. "Okay. What do you want to buy me?" I asked, anticipating a return visit to Toy Land.

She pointed over at the clothes shop where young, marble-faced mannequins were decked out in jeans and sweaters with matching scarves.

I started to laugh. "You want to buy me clothes?"

She nodded with exaggerated readiness. "Yes!" She fumbled for the door handle and, before I could say *hold your horses,* she was waiting impatiently outside the store.

Hand in hand we trotted inside, stopping at the first mirror we saw to check the hair slides. I expected her to run off, in search of more childish things, but no. Her excited cries of, "Try this one!" competed with the background music and won.

One hour and fifteen minutes later we left the store ladened with bags full of new clothes and shoes for us both—early Christmas presents, we called them. On the way home we sang along to songs on the radio, played I Spy and guessed what Mary had made us for dinner.

"I can guess," Poppy said, fingering her new slides.

I suspected where the conversation was going. "If you guess right, you get an extra helping," I answered refusing to fall into her trap. "Were you expecting a prize?"

She nodded. "Can I choose?"

"Don't you think you've had enough treats for a while?" I fixed her with a serious stare.

"I want to come with you to paint at the big school where Uncle Lance is."

I felt the skin tightening between my eyes as I frowned with disbelief. "You mean the night class?"

She nodded, hopefully.

"I took you last week. You helped arrange flowers."

"Yes. But I want to paint." She was adamant.

"We didn't paint, Poppy. We drew."

She became suddenly animated. "I can draw."

24

"I know you can, but it's a class for grown-ups. I don't think they allow little girls in there. I'm sorry." I parked up and took my eyes off the road to witness her disappointment.

"But I'll be good," she muttered.

I rested my hand on her hair. "I know you will." I removed the key from the ignition and considered the best way of concluding the conversion without souring what had been a special day for us both. "Tell you what I'll do. I'll have a word with Uncle Lance and see what he says, okay?"

Her smile formed slowly, optimism returning, her cheerful expression restored. "I think Uncle Lance will let me."

"What makes you say that?" This I had to hear.

"Because he went like this today." She kissed her right hand and blew the kiss in my direction.

Her ingenuous deduction caused me to smile. "Right. He did exactly that. He's a pushover, all right."

When we entered our home, we were met with the aroma of meatballs and spaghetti. Before I'd even placed down my bags, Poppy was skipping around me.

"I won. I won."

"Good guess, smarty pants." The look on her face told me I'd been stitched up. She must have known before discussing the prize.

I called out. "Why did you choose the night class? You could have chosen anything?"

She returned, collecting her bag of hair accessories from the coffee table, took a purple bobble from the bag and raised it for me to see. "This is for Harry."

"Ah." And I did see. Harriet Harper had made an impression on both of us with her innocuous remarks and suggestions. Only a self-absorbed fool would deny it.

I strolled into my office, checked my laptop for emails and was about to lower the lid when I caught sight of the weary-looking journal on my desk. I had not mentioned it today when we had run into Harry. Had I forgotten?

No. I had not forgotten.

Was there a part of me that wanted to hear her thoughts, the ones she kept to herself, the ones she did not dare to whisper to anyone?

Only every aching bone in my body…

The meatballs were good; bath time was better. Poppy and I counted out 'pennies' she had salvaged from my drunken bouts and had stored in an empty biscuit tin Mary had given her. They amounted to fourteen pounds and thirty-two pence. I considered it an insufficient gauge of my fluctuating mental state these past four years. I expected there to be a sack full of change.

Poppy dropped the shiniest coins into her purse, in preparation for our next shopping day, gave me another grateful hug and crawled into bed. Her new hair slides were laid out along her bedside table, like matches, ready for the next day.

I could count the number of good times I'd had since her birth on one hand. One hand was used up after our day spent shopping, and I was ready to move onto hand number two.

As if being led by a force over which I had no control, I entered my office like a man playing heave-ho with an imaginary rope. I picked up Harriet's journal and returned to the lounge. Sitting on the sofa with a single lamp to the left of me illuminating the pages, I turned to the beginning feeling guiltless. I was strangely excited at the prospect of making a discovery, even a little afraid of what I might find, but knowing that whatever secrets I stumbled upon would remain untold.

Harriet Harper had already changed two lives for the better. Perhaps this was the beginning of something beautiful? God knows, I longed for it.

I turned to the first page…

CHAPTER THREE

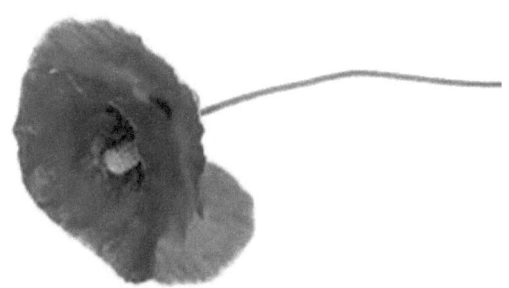

THIS IS THE JOURNAL OF HARRIET HARPER

FORWARD MOTION

IN ALL MY TWENTY-THREE years I've never had reason to keep a journal. I consider myself a self-starter, a lucky person … correction, I considered myself a lucky person.

By some strange quirk of fate, I have become stranded on an island populated by strangers. The strangest of all is the man I have lived with for the past six years.

I ask myself daily…

At what point do you say enough is enough?

Is it when a relationship breaks down? When the love has gone? Or when you feel you're losing yourself to the point that you think you may be vanishing, left to wander this planet ghostlike; your skin faded grey and bruised, your spirit blackened and broken…?

That's not living. It's a living death.

It's hard to believe that such a popular prom king and queen could end up dethroned and on the scrap heap; that after being together for eight years, I should fear for my life and be running away from my first and only love— from the life we've made.

If someone had told me that one day I'd have to leave everything behind and start over, I wouldn't have believed them. But that's exactly what I'm doing.

The time has come to pick up the pieces, throw them in a suitcase and begin again. Now that I'm free of the internal combustion of a failed relationship I can forge ahead on all cylinders. Each new idea comes to me like a breath of fresh air, sea air ... air I take into my lungs deeply before exhaling slowly, savouring it as if it might be my last.

Everything I have been through, everything I have done has brought me here. I'm going to reinvent myself: work hard, take a course, meet someone, fall in love...

But to do that I have to free myself of my past, write it out of me: see it in black and white. Maybe if I can tear it up, burn it and scatter the ashes to the wind, I'll be able to move on. I have to try.

TO SAY I WAS surprised by what I read would be an understatement. I was not oblivious to the chaotic nature of some relationships and the modern predisposition toward short-lived affairs, heavy on the sex and light on commitment. No, it was not that. It was the intensity of her voice; the spark of defiant determination that permeated the first page that had me reaching for my drink and settling my glasses on my nose.

I pictured her as she had appeared in class: black leather jacket, torn jeans, a kind of devil-may-care attitude that can be both endearing and irritating at the same time; a young woman who drifted from day to day with little to worry about other than whether to have a tuna or cheese sandwich for lunch—I was way off the mark.

I had assumed she would have nothing of interest to write in a journal. That having picked it up and read the first page, I would become bored and toss it to one side with the intention of returning it to her the following Tuesday, pretending it had been in a drawer all the time.

That was not what happened.

I had to laugh at myself. I was never any good when it came to reading people— observing, yes, sketching, of course. But when it came to sorting the good from the bad, the worthy from the unworthy, I turned to Hope. She saw through people, past the clothes, the bravado, the bullshit and everything in between, which was just as well as I had my head in the clouds most of the time, daydreaming, seeing the world in water colours or muted shades; measuring time in brush strokes.

Hope had a curious nature; as she looked out upon the world wide-eyed and open-hearted, I looked within, closed-off, self-absorbed and blind to the magnificence of it all, while at the same time, oblivious of the perils that were the inevitable bedfellows of celebrity and wealth.

I see them now on every corner.

There was a time when, like Harriet Harper, *I* wanted to run, to pack a bag, leave and never look back. I almost did.

Alone and grieving, I considered allowing Hope's parents to take care of Poppy, to raise her as their daughter. Seeing her there in the hospital so helpless, a small, motherless bundle, terrified me. I could have walked away.

I did not.

Almost four years ago, I had to dig deep, contain the fear shredding my confidence and get through, because some days that's all it was—getting through.

During that first month when I'd held Poppy in my arms, I trembled, so scared I would drop her, feed her the wrong formula, dress her too warmly… and changing those nappies! Jesus Christ! The bloody smell had me keeling over.

Some days I fell to my knees, overwhelmed by what could only be described as a baptism in fire. But I'd do it all again in a heartbeat. I made the right decision, the only possible decision any father could make—to raise her as best I could.

Harriet also ventured into the unknown. It takes a special kind of fear to force a person to leave behind what they once loved the most; to consider the unknown a better option than facing up to what you have come to know as your family.

I had to know why.

I kicked off my jeans, my T-shirt, and climbed into bed. It was going to be a long night.

SYDNEY JAMESSON

HARRIET – FREEDOM

I BROKE A FINGERNAIL this morning trying to cram all my worldly possessions into a large suitcase. I did it with the fervour of a woman about to embark upon an adventure: the prospect of making a bolt for freedom, starting over and becoming someone else, made me giddy.

I stood before the bathroom mirror, filled a glass with frothing water and took a large mouthful. I gulped. It gurgled and settled in the back of my throat like phlegm. With the help of gravity and a hard swallow, it landed in my stomach like a melted snowflake. Internally chilled, I continued with my mission.

Three months in the planning and only thirty minutes to execute my great escape meant having everything prepped and ready to go: toiletries assembled, clothes ironed and matched in the bottom of my wardrobe—shoes alongside; nightwear and underwear freshly laundered and placed to the left in my top drawer, coats lint-free, taxi booked.

Nothing forgotten.

Flouting house rules I was wearing my coat and outdoor shoes, leather boots to keep my feet dry, too large to pack. Cursing out loud, I dragged my suitcase to the bottom of the stairs, its wheels skidding on the carpet with the weight. I stored it in the cupboard underneath, out of sight. I couldn't be caught absconding. I knew only too well the kind of 'accidental' injuries that would result from attempting to make such a daring escape—the kind that could not be put down to clumsiness. There would be a visit to the hospital, an investigation, questions would be asked—some of a personal nature. I would have to lie, again.

Quivering at the thought, I reached up and retrieved the roll of twenty-pound notes I'd been hiding in a peanut butter jar.

With trembling hands, I stuffed it into the inside pocket of my handbag along with my passport for safekeeping. I had an hour before the ten thirty-six train left Camden Road station, on its way to Brighton. If everything went to plan, I would arrive in plenty of time to smarten myself up in preparation for an interview. I had arranged it a month ago while in hospital and only my nurse and trusted friend Trish knew about it.

30

I bit the inside of my cheek and paced in the hallway like a caged animal, one of those bears you see at the zoo rocking back and forth, eyes darting, contemplating a breakout.

With nothing better to do until the taxi arrived, I entered the lounge—every surface was polished. I had dusted the previous night and removed every trace of myself from the house while Sam had been out with his friends. I'd remembered to top-up the water in the vase on the mantelpiece knowing that with me gone there would be no one to see to the white roses and lisianthus. There was no reason why they should be left to wither and die prematurely.

I stroked the velvet petals and recalled a time when Sam used to buy me flowers just because I had popped in his head while he was filling up the car with fuel or had stopped off to buy a bottle of wine on the way home. He said I was like a song in his head; a chorus that prompted all kinds of memories—all good.

But all good things…

As the days had turned into months and the months into years, those rose-tinted memories seemed to move further away, to change colour and lose their clarity; to become little more than distant images in back to front binoculars. In the nine years we had known each other there had been plenty of 'good times,' I had to give him that.

Sam wouldn't understand why I had left when I had so much going for me—I had us. But, as for us … our love *had* died prematurely, and no amount of nurturing or cultivation would keep it alive. Anyway, he'd be more preoccupied with the whereabouts of the cash I was about to withdraw from our bank account than with where I'd gone. There wasn't much, but most of what was there, I'd earned and we had been happy to spend living the good life, creating memories. Besides, he had his savings account that he assumed I didn't know about.

He wouldn't starve.

When you hear about a relationship ending, you think of it as a gradual thing: a long-suffering ordeal that ends tragically for both parties. To some extent, it was like that with us. Like milk turning sour overnight in a sweltering room, there was no precise point at which it became contaminated and unpalatable—it just did.

Maybe it was the adrenalin, but I actually had a vile taste in my mouth like post-puke saliva or the metallic tang of blood, like my spirit—no, my entire body—was becoming rancid. I'd become embittered and this was its way of telling me that I didn't have to suffer in silence. I had to go while I could still walk away.

In a spare moment, I thought about composing a farewell note. I even reached for a pen: *Don't bother looking for me…* Or perhaps, *It's over!* Or even a simple, *Goodbye, Jane.*

Then, I reconsidered.

That's not my style. I've never been sentimental, and melodrama just didn't seem to fit the occasion. I decided to leave him a wordless message. I placed my keys in the tray on the telephone table by the front door—it spoke volumes: *I've gone. I'm not coming back. Over and out.*

I jumped like a scolded cat when my phone buzzed, announcing the arrival of the taxi. I hauled my case to the front door, down the step and onto the drive, pausing to give the driver time to open the boot.

My heart raced as an uncustomary cocktail of fear and excitement flooded my veins. I wanted to savour it, to feel its invigorating force, if only for a minute or two. But time was a luxury I couldn't afford. I took a gulp of cold air knowing it would be one of the last from the place I used to call home. I looked toward the lawn which had become no more than an undulating bed of clover, extending my gaze to the border, where, again the odds, daffodil heads had speared through in search of sunlight, their cheerful brilliance refusing to be confined in mulch and weeds.

In an instant, one of those good times came to me in a flash: weren't we called 'the golden couple' once upon a time? We were.

Not anymore. Our relationship had lost its sparkle; it had become tarnished and lackluster like the eternity ring on the middle finger of my left hand.

I looked out across our unexceptional garden for the final time, my eyes drawn once more to the splashes of golden yellow, acknowledging the daffodils' steadfast determination to make their presence felt. I considered it a good omen—that and a break in the clouds above the rooftops. It was never going to be clear skies all the way, I knew that, but all I needed was the prospect of brighter days to spur me on—that, and a purpose. If something as delicate as a daffodil could weather every storm, so could I.

The taxi driver hauled my case into the boot with a mighty heave, while I returned inside for my handbag. I stood in the doorway noticing how my shadow appeared elongated on the carpet, ending where a small, stubborn stain had remained despite my scrubbing; it was brownish in colour, the colour of stale red wine or blood—my blood.

I slammed the front door behind me and sat in the backseat of the taxi. I looked straight ahead. I didn't look back.

Why would I? Harriet Jane Harper didn't live there anymore.

CHAPTER FOUR

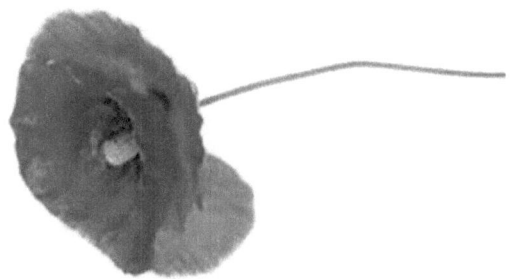

I PLACED THE JOURNAL on the pillow to my right, deep in thought, disbelieving that unassuming young woman I had met just over twenty-four hours ago could have lived such a life. It occurred to me that her life experiences had shaped her into an uncompromising, plain-spoken woman. No wonder she took it upon herself to speak up; to say what needed to be said to an arrogant, insensitive sod like me.

In my mind's eye, I pictured her sitting nervously on that ten thirty-six train to Brighton, venturing into the unknown, starting over—alone—having experienced … who knows what?

At least I had a home to come back to; one Hope and I had designed together with an architect, shaping our ideas into something tangible and practical, reflecting both our personalities: my need for privacy and light, Hope's need for satin cushions, storage and space for us to grow as a family. We had created our own piece of heaven, blissfully unaware that fate would see to it that she did not get to experience it for more than a couple of months.

And there was Harriet, courageously moving on, which is more than I had done.

As bad as it appeared—stealing a look into Harriet's world, her private thoughts, her fears and aspirations—I could not help myself. Sure, her world was alien to me; the landscape was foreign, unrecognisable, but her emotions and sense of displacement were not. We had both loved passionately, and been forced to inhabit an unfamiliar world, forever altered.

I trotted back into the lounge, topped up my drink and threw in a couple of ice cubes.. Glass in hand I headed to bed, stopping to check in on Poppy first. She was sleeping; gentle wisps of air escaped her lips as she dreamed of more precious trinkets, shopping trips, and colouring books awash with fluorescent shades that reflected a world filled with laughter and love—exactly where she belonged.

I COULDN'T SLEEP.

Two brief encounters, and there I was allowing a young woman I barely knew to invade my psyche. Without even trying, Harriet had caused a chain reaction: what started out as annoyance and mild curiosity had morphed into something inexplicably provocative.

My skin was warm and prickly, as if it had been scrubbed clean. After my four-year hiatus, my entire body was throbbing. I turned on the bedside lamp, knocking my glasses to the floor, still trembling from what I assumed was a panic attack, or was it arousal? It had been so long since I'd felt something so visceral and unexpected, it was hard to tell. Whatever it was, there was no way I was going back to sleep.

I put Harriet's journal to one side, deciding to ration out the entries. The last thing I needed was to become obsessed by it—by her. In hindsight, if I'd known how reading about her life was going to affect me and *my* life, I might have thought twice about opening what was turning into Pandora's Box.

Then again, I wonder what would have become of me if I had not opened it and turned the pages, devouring her words like a starving man.

At least I was lucid enough to notice that the glass of scotch I'd poured was still there by the lamp, its contents luminescent in the light cast from beneath the shade. If nothing else, my liver was grateful for her disclosures.

Mildly anesthetized by the alcohol in my veins, I longed for sleep, but it came in waves, angry tidal waves that stirred my soul and stole my breath. Like so many nights before, I began to feel ensnared, sandwiched between those browbeating buddies,

Loneliness and Guilt. They were at their most potent in the hours between dusk and dawn, terrorising me with images from my past that I was still in no shape to confront. From the bottom of a glass they stared back at me, insistent and unforgiving.

My nightmare was always the same; it involved a bloodied hand reaching out to me. No matter how I fought I could not escape it. I could not see whose hand it was, but I knew the name of the phantom who haunted all my dreams. I just could not bring myself to say it out loud.

I woke, disorientated, drowning in perspiration.

Biting back frustration, I swallowed what was left of the elixir, inviting it to numb my senses, needing the deadening effect that it alone could produce in my body, in my mind.

I didn't want to think.

I didn't want to feel.

I wanted to forget. Not only *my* past but Harriet's too for a couple of hours, at least.

All I had wanted to do was to step out of my shoes and into those of a free-spirited human being for a day or two, without dragging my heels or stumbling over obstacles only I could see.

In my desperation, I assumed Harriet was that person. I had her all mapped out.

She was at least six years younger than me. Her life was filled with parties, dates with twenty-something bartenders with a penchant for homemade wine and staying up all night watching boxed sets of *The Walking Dead* or *Game of Thrones*.

With every new entry I was being drawn in deeper. I bent down to pick up her journal, snatching my glasses from beneath the bed where they had landed. I decided I should do no more than flick through the pages to the very last entry, like a teenage boy about to fail a maths assignment; going straight to the answers without even trying to solve the problem.

But ... that would be cheating.

Harriet was clearly a woman of many parts, an enigma with hidden depths and a past that I could either descend into, at my peril, or walk away from. She had fallen in love, experienced the joy of devotion, and yet, she'd ended up alone—like me.

So, taking a deep breath, I dived in...

HARRIET - LEAVING HOME

THE TRAIN LEFT CAMDEN Road Station on time at ten thirty-six. Within seven minutes I was struggling once more with an uncooperative suitcase containing all my worldly possession, trying not to rap the ankles of small children and suited men with their eyes on vibrating phones.

Forty-five minutes later, I was seated aboard the eleven twenty to Brighton. Having cleansed my lungs of foul air, I felt the colour returning to my cheeks; my veins were besieged by an invigorating mixture of exhilaration and nervous tension. My mind was awash with questions…

Had I forgotten anything?

Had Sam noticed my keys in the dish on the hall table?

He had no reason to think anything was out of the ordinary. It was Monday, a working day. I'd be at work, assisting Doctor Mendes with his administrative chores as far as he knew. Doctor Mendes wouldn't miss me either. I'd taken a week's holiday. It had been booked a month ago.

No one would miss me, at least not until dinner time.

In the rush, I hadn't checked my phone or slipped the new Sim card into it—my final act of detachment. I did so immediately, not wanting to be traced or found.

I'd assumed that my carriage would be empty, free of noise and the usual bustle of rush-hour commuters. I was wrong. I was on the train to Gatwick Airport.

There had been at least twenty students on the platform beside me in Victoria Station, but with so much on my mind, I hadn't wondered why. They had appeared like tortoises on speed, weighed down by colourful shells decorated with stainless steel mugs and dangling straps. Faced with at least ten of them in my carriage, I speculated that they were on a gap year about to visit famous cities, sleep in overcrowded hostels, sample local delicacies, doze on long distance train journeys, discovering things about themselves along the way.

I turned to the scenery changing before my eyes; long, drawn out shadows cast by tall buildings and warehouses melted away. As the sun broke through the clouds, I blinked, unaccustomed to blinding sunlight spearing through the murky autumn sky. The urban sprawl morphed into a suburban landscape; terraced properties turned into semi-detached houses slotted around grandiose detached mansions of enviable proportions; a couple even had trampolines, one had a swimming pool covered with an enormous russet rug of leaves and twigs.

Lulled into restfulness by the rocking motion, I dozed. The sounds of chatter and laughter faded until they became no more than a muffled hum. I was only sleeping for twenty minutes, but long enough for me to dream. Images came and went, only one was static—Sam. I felt his clammy, masculine hand around my neck, his other hand gripping my arm, his body pressed up against mine: suffocation, submission, suppression.

I woke with a start in the foetal position, my face pressed up against the window, my knees balancing unsteadily on the seat. Hoping no one had noticed, I straightened out my legs, tidied my jacket and T-shirt and sat bolt upright, blinking away the memory.

Somewhere between the mass exodus at Gatwick Airport and my final destination, Jane became Harriet. I had been Jane Harper all of my life up until that moment and changing it was part of my plan to reinvent myself. I marked the occasion with coffee and a blueberry muffin courtesy of the on-board guard pushing a trolley down the aisle.

Like everyone, I've undergone a few transformations but that was my chance to truly be myself, to let the real me shine through the masquerade that had characterised my life for so long. I recalled the words on a beer mat I had turned between my fingers a few months previously.

"Be yourself; everyone else is taken." Oscar Wilde

It made me smile. It would be a while before I'd answer to the name of Harriet or Harry, but that was okay. The new me would have a new name and, besides, that was the name on my job application.

Silently, I practised my interview entrance. "Hello, I'm Harriet Harper. Nice to meet you." It had a ring to it. The alliteration helped and I much preferred it to 'Plain Jane' as I'd been called so many times by my former boyfriend.

By twelve fifteen I was walking through Brighton train station; it was bright and spacious with a high roof. I tipped back my head to take in the crisscross metalwork, felt my smile broadening and squinted, dazzled by sunlight. It hurt my eyes but lifted my spirits—it felt like the beginning of something promising.

I'd made it that far and there would be no turning back. I had a reservation at the nearby Ibis Hotel and had seven days in which to find myself a job and a place to live—the clock was ticking.

I THREW BACK THE remains of my scotch and wished I had brought the bottle into the bedroom with me. I was thirsty. I'd been taking in air in short, uneasy breaths unsure of what was going to happen next, and my mouth had become parched. In need of a drink, I jumped out of bed and strolled into the bathroom. I rinsed out the glass and filled it with foaming water until it was icy cold against my fingers. I knocked it back, my ears throbbing with the memory of Harriet's train journey, the rumbling engine and the screeching of brakes as it reached its destination.

I was there with her—starting over. Even her nightmare felt real. She had not gone into much detail about Sam; she didn't have to. Clearly, he was a brute.

I slipped back between the sheets, deciding not to read any more. It was making for uncomfortable bedtime reading; besides, it was almost three in the morning and Poppy would be rising in four hours, bright-eyed, ears pricked for any sound of life coming from my bedroom.

The duvet felt snug around my neck, but the far side of the bed was like a frozen tundra inhabited by a shapeless ghost I could not reach out to or escape from. The spaces Hope once occupied were less formidable in sunlight; the sound of movement in the house made life bearable, but at night the deafening sound of my own breathing was enough to scare me shitless.

I tried not to gasp, taking in oxygen through my nose, controlling my diaphragm until it rose and fell rhythmically, and my anxiety eased. Most nights I sedated myself with a bottle, but that night felt like a turning point; I had come across a juncture where I could either go back, resuming 'normal' service, or take a tremulous step forward in a new direction.

I realised I had not learned to live without Hope. Unlike Harriet, I had not bought a metaphorical train ticket and made a conscious decision to start over. I'd stayed exactly where I was four years ago. I'd been pig-headed, assumed I could cope. I was not the kind of man who asked for help, never had, and was not prepared to change the habit of a lifetime. Friends and family had been there for me—for us—but pride had prevented me from taking them up on offers of help and support.

As I stretched out, looking into the darkness enveloping my bed, I considered the possibility of change, a change in the way I lived my life—a change in me.

If Harriet had battled her way through the worst kind of adversity and started over, maybe I could.

That was the first positive idea I'd had in … I couldn't remember how long.

The sense of empowerment that single thought brought with it was imperceptible to anyone but me; a pebble on a beach which could so easily have been kicked to one side, but a stepping stone in the right direction if I could keep my balance long enough to make use of it.

I closed my eyes and allowed my mind to wander to Brighton Beach where Hope and I used to walk hand in hand, her hair spiralling out like Medusa's snakes, her laughter snatched away by the sea breeze, the heels of her boots sinking into the pockets of sand and grit that had amassed between the undulating stones.

In an involuntary movement, I reached out to catch her as she tripped, roused from my memory by the coldness of the sheets on her side of the bed. Tears stung the corners of my eyes and my fingers closed into a defiant fist.

Unexpectedly, the synapses in my fuddled brain fired, and in a moment of mental clarity a cogent thought came to me: I had to fight harder for a better life for Poppy and me. I knew I'd never get over losing the love of my life, but could I learn to live again without her?

I folded my arms into my chest and started to doze, hearing the plop, plop of pebbles as they skimmed the retreating tide on Brighton Beach.

CHAPTER FIVE

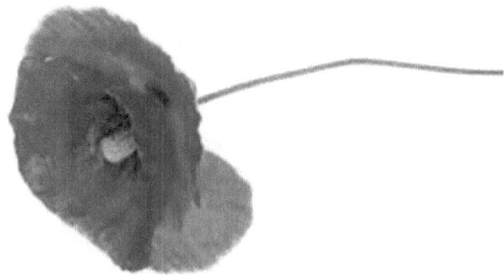

I COULD NOT REMEMBER the last time I'd seen Poppy before nine in the morning in her pyjamas sitting crossed legged on the carpet watching TV. In one hand she had a breakfast bowl brimming with cereal, in the other, a spoon which she held up to her open mouth as if caught in a freeze frame.

"Morning, Poppy," I called out cheerfully, watching the milk drip from the spoon into the bowl as she turned her head to watch me cross the room. I found myself counting, anticipating the pattering of her feet on the polished tiles.

She appeared beside me on the count of nine. I was stood by the sink, filling up a glass jug with water, needing several shots of caffeine to get me going. She stood motionless by my right thigh, saying nothing, merely looking up at me in wonder. What a humbling experience that was, one I would never forget, a dumbstruck daughter feeling the need to pat my leg, making sure I was really there.

"Would you like a drink of something?" I asked balancing the jug of water.

She moved with me and tugged on my right trouser leg. "What are you doing, Daddy?"

"Making coffee and seeing if there's any bread for toast." I opened the top cupboard doors before noticing she had her right arm raised. I followed the line of her tiny forefinger. "There's bread in the freezer?"

She nodded. "Mary puts it in there."

"Ah." I pulled back the freezer door and—lo and behold—there was a pre-sliced, wholemeal loaf. "Do you want some toast?"

She leaned against my leg, making a connection that had been a long time coming—too long. I needed it, maybe even more than she did. I placed my right hand on her head reaffirming our bond, feeling her tousled hair soft and warm against my fingers.

Four slices of frozen bread clicked into the toaster, giving me all the time I needed to explain. Resting one knee on the tiled floor so we could be face to face, I pushed her hair back off her shoulders and looked into bright hazel eyes glistening with a mixture of surprise and suppressed delight.

"I know we haven't had breakfast together for a while, but that's going to change. I'll be getting up earlier from now on and…" I was about to say, *smartening up and drinking less,* but, seeing her smile caused words to solidify in my throat. It felt as if someone had tied me down and held a mirror in front of me, refusing to release me until I swore to face up to my responsibilities.

And there she was, inches away from me.

"We're going to do lots of new things together. Won't that be fun?" I asked, in no need of a response.

Poppy visibly radiated happiness; the disbelief in her eyes moments earlier had been replaced by a childlike exuberance and unconditional acceptance of my belated promise. I hugged her gently and placed a kiss on her cheek. Much to my surprise, she reached for my right hand and wrapped her little finger around mine.

"Pinkie promise," she said, assuming I understood the significance of the act.

I did not. But so expectant was she of my response that I repeated after her, "Pinkie promise," forever bound to be the father she deserved.

With my paternal pledge made, I rose from the floor and lifted out the singed toast, making exaggerated "ow" sounds and throwing the slices in the air when they were too hot to handle. I turned to ask her about marmalade, only to find that she had vanished.

There I was making breakfast and preparing to circle that day in red ink on the calendar, and my pledge partner was nowhere to be seen. I wasn't expecting a standing ovation, but I assumed she would stick around for burnt offerings.

I carried breakfast for two into the lounge on a tray, feeling like an underdressed waiter, not knowing where to place the tray. Seeing Poppy's half-eaten bowl of cereal on the far side of the room, I opted for the sofa, and arranged the breakfast paraphernalia neatly on the coffee table. I lifted a mug of steaming coffee to my lips but it never quite reached them. A pretty little girl appeared in a pink party dress and pink Wellington boots, her hair was brushed—in a fashion—and two beaded pink hair slides were slotted either side of her forehead.

It was a grand entrance; she was both my leading lady and my appreciative breakfast companion. Best of all, she was my daughter.

"Look at you. Are you off to a party?"

She hopped onto the sofa beside me, her legs horizontal; her boots almost touching the edge of the coffee table. "I've come to *your* party, Daddy."

I laughed. "Oh, I'm not having a party. It's just breakfast. Be careful it might be hot. Blow on it." I handed her a Polly Pocket mug, half filled with a hot, caramel coloured beverage that was more milk than coffee.

She took it in both hands and blew, causing it to ripple. "It's *like* a birthday party."

I took a bite of toast. "It is? In what way?"

"When I'm four..." Her eyes widened at the idea. "When I'm four, you can come to *my* party."

"Thank you. It's only a couple of months away. I'm looking forward to it," I reassured her. "But, like I said, Poppy, it's just us and this is only breakfast."

She shook her head, making her whole body shake. "No, Daddy, this is number one day. You pinkie promised." She was emphatic, to the point that I had to take the cup from her hands for fear she would spill its contents.

It took me all of five seconds to decipher her meaning. She didn't have the vocabulary to communicate it clearly but she wanted to be understood; she wanted me to see her happiness, and for her, happiness was pink coloured with bows on.

I understood perfectly.

Me being there was cause for celebration, it signalled the start of some-thing; not becoming one year older, but something very similar to a three-year-old little girl.

I had always been her father, in her eyes there was no other, and she loved me in spite of my inadequacies. I had taken her love for granted, and to be honest, she had known nothing but negligence on my part. Having me there in the morning, eating breakfast together was like receiving a birthday present, one that would keep on giving … if I kept my promise.

Enjoying the luxury of having her father's attention, Poppy unveiled her drawings for my inspection. They were scattered around the lounge like fallen leaves in many colours and many sizes; some were pages torn out of colouring books, others were hand-drawn images on sheets of paper taken from my office. With Poppy's hand in mine, I examined them, treated to a commentary, of sorts.

A few minutes in, I felt the muscles in my throat constricting and my vision blurring. Right there in black and white, pastel shades or vivid fluorescent pinks was Poppy's life set out plainly for all to see. She pointed out the characters she had drawn, stick-like representations, recognisable only by the colour of their clothes and hair colour. Not surprisingly, she appeared in most of them, instantly identifiable by the pink attire and L-shaped wellington boots that featured on most of her self-portraits. Mary was a visible presence, tall and imposing, a powerful adult figure wearing a blue apron.

And then there was me.

In my absence, I had become no more than a make-believe character on the periphery of her compositions, a dark-clothed figure with long hair and a downturned smile. I don't know what touched a nerve first, the blobs of tears she had drawn on my face or the fact that I was a ghostlike presence watching over her but not actively engaging.

"That's you, Daddy?"

My heart sank. It descended to rock bottom as she chronicled the events she had depicted without malice or ill-feeling toward me. Her voice was light-hearted and her mood buoyant, uncompromised by her blunt clarifications intended to be innocent observations but, nevertheless, poignant enough to cut me to the quick.

"Look! You have tears."

52

She swept us along as if on a voyage of self-discovery—which is exactly what it was for me. With each new image, her mood brightened, uplifted by flashes of memories that came and went like fireflies caught in a jar.

The last two drawings, her most recent creations, were noticeably different—shockingly so. Naturally, she was the central image but, on one side of her was a figure clearly recognisable as me, and on the other, a smaller, female figure wearing a purple dress with brown hair.

"This isn't like the others," I commented. "Who's this?" I knew the answer before she could announce it.

"It's Harry," she explained. "And that's you. See? You have a smiley face."

I laughed quietly. "I see that. And why am I smiling?"

She lifted the picture in both hands, pressed it against her lips and kissed the figure in the purple dress. "Because…" She paused to think through her answer. Not wanting to rush her, I folded my arms, happy to wait for as long as was necessary for her to construct a sentence that conveyed her intended meaning.

"Harry has found us," she exclaimed, smiling gleefully, as if that was the only possible explanation.

Taken aback by her declaration, I couldn't help but show my surprise. My eyes widened and air rushed into my mouth. "That's a funny thing to say, Poppy. I don't think Harry has been looking for us…"

She shook her head, not accepting my dismissive answer.

"She's just someone who has joined my art class; someone who can draw a bit and likes the colour purple. I know you like her, but—"

Before I could finish the sentence, she had turned her back on me and was gathering up her artwork. I wanted to finish by saying, *"But don't become too fond of her, because she might not be the person you think she is…"* but I didn't get the chance.

Assuming our exchange of ideas had ended, I returned to the kitchen for more coffee. With a mug in one hand and the other hand resting on the countertop, I replayed our conversation. It wasn't long before my mood altered and the cheerfulness of breakfast time was replaced by something less celebratory.

I had inadvertently introduced a woman into our lives without knowing anything about her and my perceptive daughter, two months away from her fourth birthday, had intuited something that I had been impervious to.

But that was not entirely true.

I was the one who had stayed up half the night reading her journal and then spent the other half thinking about what I had read. I was the one who had been reminded of my parental responsibilities and crawled from my bed earlier than usual, with a clear head, made breakfast and reintroduced myself to my daughter.

That was all me. Wasn't it?

I rinsed out my coffee cup, loaded the breakfast crockery in the dishwasher and made my way to my bedroom, preparing to read a little more from Harriet's journal. With no prior engagements, I had nothing but time on my hands. For some inexplicable reason, my heart was beating to a different drum, a lively rhythm that made me want to throw caution to the wind and read on, hoping to discern what Poppy had perceived instinctively.

I longed to know about Harriet's past, how she and Sam had met and what it was about him that had attracted her in the first place. Was he like me, awkward, impatient, intolerant? Or was he more Prince Charming than devil's advocate? I flicked through the pages, knowing the answers were all there. All I had to do was read.

CHAPTER SIX

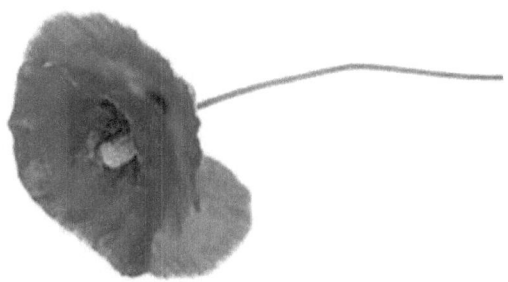

HARRIET - THE EARLY YEARS

I MADE IT.

I'm curled up in a ball on my bed in a hotel room in Brighton on a Monday afternoon feeling like a snake that has shed its skin: I've been reborn. I feel alive, the way I did when I was a schoolgirl discovering her first and only love.

I was fifteen when I met Samuel James Reynolds for the first time and, even then I knew he was going to be mine. It wasn't fate; well, not in the stargazing, horoscopic sense of the word. In those days, I believed you made your own destiny. It wasn't until eight years later I found out that sometimes Fate fucks you over.

I can picture it now, my friend Rita's New Year's Eve party, a theatrical backdrop like something out of *La La Land*: twinkling lights, dashing young men and blossoming girls in party frocks, high heels, and me, ripe for the picking. I was inexperienced. What did I know about attracting a boy's attention?

I was like a ballerina: I had the shoes and the outfit, but my lack of balance and fear of the spotlight were serious stumbling blocks. I was not going to become Margot Fonteyn overnight, so I decided to let my red dress do the talking until I felt comfortable enough to speak for myself. The dress said: "Hey, I'm here. I exist. I deserve to be noticed."

And it worked!

It got me noticed—noticed by Sam, the most popular boy in school. He had his pick of the bunch and stalked the room, craving something sweet after a Christmas filled with flaming cedar and ginger spice.

He chose me, the girl in the red dress.

Up until the second he saw me, I existed on the periphery, observing cliques in corners sharing secrets and rumours. At the time, I had no idea what it was about him that drew my eye, why he had the girls licking gloss from their lips as if tasting the air with their tongue, or why I wanted him so badly. I know now.

He oozed sex appeal—he reeked of it. We were all at an age when sex stopped being a naughty word. It was more like the Holy Grail, that out of reach pinnacle girls lied about, most boys bragged about and I had spent nights wondering about.

When he spoke, Sam was every teenage girl's fantasy come to life, and when he smiled … when he smiled at *you*, every part of you south of the border stirred.

I think I handled myself pretty well; pretending I had no idea who he was turned out to be a stroke of genius, as he had no idea that I even existed. I put it down to my ballerina masquerade and the dress. I was gift-wrapped—an echappé just waiting to happen.

Sam held my hand and walked me home just after midnight to the accompaniment of car horns and crackling fireworks, which I imagined were celebrating our newly formed relationship and not the incidental start of a new year. What started out as a smooch under the stars became a constellation of kisses—just as I knew it would. He found my mouth with his and claimed it with a hunger that left me gasping.

Obscured by an oak tree with naked branches we kissed and raised our eyes to the clouds when the boom of rockets signalled another blinding explosion of colour. In the flashes that illuminated his face, he was dazzling, handsome beyond words.

Sam was a couple of months older than me and a foot taller; the good-looking guy the girls loved to flirt with and the boys wanted to be friends with. Fawning females made themselves available to him, made all kinds of offers that would have been hard for any hot-blooded fifteen-year-old to resist—but resist he did.

After eight months of dating we became the golden couple; he had chiselled features and a mop of blond hair, and I had blond highlights to match. In the early days, I was at ease with him, happy to bask in the glow emanating from his golden aura.

Then came my sixteenth birthday.

I look back on that time and can't help but smile. Much to everyone's surprise, Jane Harper had grown four inches taller, acquired breasts; she had a trim waist and her crystal-blue eyes framed in jet black mascara were bewitching—they said.

The extent of my transformation became undeniable; the auburn-haired little girl with freckles who had been happiest on the back row for most of her life had become a new and improved version of her former self.

Sam said he could look into my eyes all day, every day; they reminded him of holidays spent by the sea under summer skies with nothing to do other than lounge about and rest between ballgames and buffet lunches.

He could be quite the poet.

In my final year at school I was named Carnival Queen. One blistering hot day in May I perched on my throne in my diamante-encrusted gown, surrounded by nymphs and fresh-cut flowers. Sometimes when I close my eyes I can still see the hand-painted, paper wings fluttering around me, feel the glitter on my fingers, catch the fragrance of rose petals mixed with the smell of diesel fuel from the truck that made me want to throw-up when it slowed. I didn't, of course, I soldiered on, smiled and waved until I had to step from my carriage and become a commoner once more.

For most of my school years, I was invisible. No one saw me coming, but Sam did, and he was the only one I cared about. He held my hand in the dinner queue, waited for me after school, took me to the cinema to see *Harry Potter*. Sam walked me home, kissed me goodnight, introduced me to fumbling foreplay and passionate sex, and two years later suggested we move in together.

Way back, I used to think summer nights were magical. I imagined beautiful people like us leaping into taxis, pretty young women wearing high heels, short dresses and self-assured smiles illuminated by lip-gloss, believing their evening would end with a kiss, or something more.

I was that young woman.

If someone had said that eight years later I'd fear for my life and be forced to run away from my first and only love, from the life we had made, I wouldn't have believed them.

READING HARRIET'S JOURNAL WAS turning into therapy.

She recounted events with such clarity, while my memories swayed like reeds in a stream going this way and that, caught up in the ebb and flow of a life-force more potent than my own. Sometimes it felt as if they were entangled, interwoven like frayed ends of a rope that had been tying me down for years. Other times, it seemed as if too many ends had been left unsecured, making it impossible to weather each ensuing storm.

When I met Hope I knew I'd come home. She was my anchor and my inspiration; she kept me grounded while encouraging me to dream big, to believe that my talent was worthy of recognition.

Almost fifteen years ago, I met Hope Chambers during another beer-fuelled night in the student union bar at Warwick University. The place was crowded and noisy, but above the pandemonium, the disputes about who wrote what and when, the ordering of pints and the throwing back of shots, a solitary voice rang out. It was not the voice of an angel, far from it. It was the voice of my future wife.

I knew it, instinctively, even without seeing her. There was something familiar about the cadence of it that matched my own. Something in her contentious comments and her unwillingness to be swayed that reminded me of myself. I imagined the sparks we could generate simply by being in the same room together, not to mention the same bed.

When I turned to look at her up close, all I saw was a tumbling mane of chestnut-coloured hair and an assortment of male admirers, their faces turned to her adoringly. I liked being able to eavesdrop, to listen in on her assertions, to hear about what she had read and what she was studying. I pretended to be reading amusing texts on my phone but, really, I was laughing at her protestations when a member of her group denounced Renoir for being, "Heavy handed."

My friends threw back pints; I sipped mine in no hurry to stifle my senses. I was a second year art student who seldom left those premises alone and that night would be no different, only this time I'd be leaving with the woman I'd be spending the rest of my life with.

I continued to watch my chestnut-haired art critic, rising out of my chair when she grabbed her bag and moved away from the table.

My mark disappeared. I cursed, scanned the crowd and caught sight of her entering the ladies washroom. When she made an appearance, I'd be right there waiting for her like a damn stalker.

She appeared like a vision, initially side-on then facing me. I was willing her to notice me, to look in my direction—just once. That's all I would need, a passing glance.

No such luck. I was invisible to her—just another face in the crowd.

From listening to her conversations, I knew she had a brain and was not afraid to use it. I found that endearing and a turn-on. Having discovered she was beautiful too, I was smitten.

Watching her walk away, I wanted to spin her around and ask, "What will become of us?" I didn't dare.

I found a spot where I could stand, unseen, and watch her speak. I didn't need to hear her words; they were lost in the melee of masculine voices and laughter. As long as I could see her smile in the mirror, I was content.

Having overdosed on her, I turned away, caught the attention of a barman and ordered a pint. I slumped over the countertop, contemplating my next move, struggling to come up with a credible plan.

As if touched by the hand of God, I felt someone grab my right shoulder and spun around to push them away. Instead I turned to face them, lost my balance and felt my spine pressed up against the bar.

Up close, Hope was even more beautiful; clean-faced, bright eyes illuminated by overhead lights with a smile I never wanted to share with another living soul.

"My God. For someone with a reputation as long as my arm, you certainly take your time. What are you waiting for, a formal invitation?"

Seeing only her, I brushed a chestnut curl from her cheek and answered, "We're going to be spending the rest of our lives together. There's no rush. I want the night we meet to be unforgettable: something to tell our children about."

"It will be," she said, taking the weight of my cheek in the palm of her hand.

I was so close I could inhale her feminine fragrance; a hypnotic mixture that reminded me of summer holidays, running through long grass, picking wild flowers. "I've been watching you all night," I confessed easily.

"I've been watching *you,* watching me all night." Her smile broadened. "What's your name?"

"Maxwell Grant, Max. And you?" I reached down to take her hand in mine.

"Hope Chambers."

I placed a soft kiss on her knuckles. "Hope Chambers, you're the woman of my dreams."

She laughed. "You're bloody good, I'll give you that. Is this how you charm the ladies, with great pick-up lines?"

"No. It's not a pick-up line. It's a fact." There was no doubt about it. "Look into my eyes and tell me what you see."

She tilted her head, angled it slightly, creating shadow on one side of her face. "You're very intense, Maxwell Grant."

"So are you. What do you see?"

She paused, thinking through her answer as if her life depended on it. "I see that you're an honest man. Will you be a good husband?"

I felt my brows lift reflectively. "Define *good.* "

"The kind of man who loves unconditionally, and completely? A man who's kind to animals and old people, and wants children and a house in the country? A man who will die for me and knows the difference between fucking and making love." She paused to take a breath. "Are you that man?"

Overwhelmed by the gravity of her multi-faceted question, I took her expectant face in my hands and kissed her softly. When we separated, air left our bodies; vapour, dispersed around our flushed faces like a heat wave. "Yes. Yes. Yes. Yes. Yes," I whispered, finding my voice.

"Then you're the man for me," she stated, unequivocally.

"I am." I laughed at her powers of deduction. "Do you want to get out of here and talk some more about art?"

She paused, pretending she had to think twice about her answer. "Hell, no."

I felt her hand in mine, our fingers slotted side by side, knitted together for posterity. "What then?"

With me in tow, she moved toward the exit, parting the merrymakers as if wielding an imaginary scythe.

Once outside, we buttoned our coats and turned to face each other. Hope was first to speak.

"We have to make plans for our future. You're going to be famous one day, Maxwell Grant, and the sooner we find out what it is you're good at, the better." She slipped her arm in mine and we strolled through campus grounds.

She regaled me with tales from her childhood, her teenage years, moving around the world with her father's job, and her aspirations. She was an artist too, but unlike me she leant toward digital art forms. I called her a philistine, she called me pretentious. Our playful repartee was constant, the blending of voices, the melding of two hearts— unification.

With every new discovery that night, I was falling in love with her; cracks and fissures in the pavement served as measurements of space and time. When I looked back, they were barely visible; our pasts had been erased. That night would stay with us long after it had ended, written in stone—a forever memory.

By the time we reached the house I shared with four other guys, we had ironed out the creases of our histories until they were laid out before us like colourful picnic blankets.

Once inside my bedroom, we had to navigate through the wreckage of an existence driven by self-indulgence. We stepped over sketches, discarded clothes, pizza boxes and empty bottles of beer. My unmade bed was an island of white lost in the sea of floating debris. While Hope removed the bedding, I riffled through drawers for clean sheets, gurgling with embarrassment but excited at the prospect of spending the night with her.

Everything depended on finding those clean sheets.

We had entered the bar alone that night, but left together; spent the night together, held each other tightly having made love patiently, deliberately, cherishing every touch and every word. When we fell asleep encircled by the serenity of the afterglow, I repeated what Hope had said.

"I'm the kind of man who loves unconditionally, and completely; a man who's kind to animals and old people, and wants children and a house in the country; a man who will die for you and knows the difference between fucking and making love."

I had come so close to being *that* man—the man she deserved. What a tragedy that we should have been parted eleven years later.

Why?

Because, it turned out, I was not the man she thought I was.

At university and the years that followed, we were inseparable. I called my future wife a *hopeless* romantic—our private joke.

When she was not singing along to love songs, she was tearing out pages from home decorating magazines: homely settings filled with cushions, Persian rugs and oak furniture—a stark contrast to our one room bedsit with a makeshift kitchen.

We could have lived better, eaten better, but for me and my insistence that I needed time to paint, to create something that would be our one-way ticket to success—it was just a matter of time before I was discovered. I was self-absorbed and believed it; more importantly, so did she.

While she worked full time as PA to an upcoming graphic designer, I would stay home and perfect my art. Portraits were my thing; capturing Hope's essence and transposing it into a realistic representation could take days, sometimes weeks.

The seasons skipped by; the years came and went. and we survived on her wage while I painted and perfected my craft. On a reveal day one morning in June six years ago, I tried not to stare as she began her ritual: she dressed for the occasion, styled her hair, applied two squirts of her favourite perfume, placed two glasses of cheap wine on the dining table and waited for me to lift the dust cover like a magician exposing something miraculous.

She tipped her head left then right, covered her mouth with her right hand and turned to me, wide-eyed. Overwhelmed by what she saw, her eyes became puddles muddied with emotion. "I love it," she said. "You're a wonderful artist, Maxwell Grant. This has to be the one."

And it was.

I carried her portrait across London to a small gallery in Camden with an expectant heart, my veins pulsating with self-belief and optimism. My 'hopeless' muse had inspired me once again to create something of beauty.

At the age of thirty, I had my first exhibition: it received press coverage, it attracted good reviews, I sold paintings. I was commissioned to paint more. I became, 'The one to watch.'

Just in time for Christmas, we moved out of our shoebox into an airy loft in Peckham while our house was being built. We sung along to those soppy love songs, flicked through magazines together and looked to the future with a shared belief that we were two of the luckiest people alive. We visited our house as often as possible and marvelled at the speed with which it was taking shape, just as we had imagined it.

When Easter came around just over four years ago, we moved in. I carried her, then pregnant with Poppy, over the threshold, believing we had come through the hard times and could settle into a life together without financial constraints or complications.

And then the bottom dropped out of my world, making it impossible for me to even consider painting again. Many times since that night I've thought about us finding each other, being drawn to our reflections by some kind of gravitational pull, so sure that we belonged together. What was it about Hope that had me so convinced about our congruity, and why was Hope in no doubt as to our compatibility?

I couldn't say.

My wife had a word for it, that fusion of our souls could be only *one* thing—Kismet. I teased her and said she had made it up; it was no more than a play on words, k*iss-me*, a way of getting me to kiss her when some kind of coincidence occurred in our lives. The joke was on her because I would have kissed her anyway.

My daydream was broken by the sound of the television being turned on in the lounge. Poppy was switching channels looking for something that took her fancy.

That was my cue.

If I could get her to swap her party clothes for a casual outfit, we'd go for a walk. I'd had enough flashbacks for one day.

CHAPTER SEVEN

LATER THAT AFTERNOON, I took Poppy by the hand, intending to walk around the lake, introducing her to the world that existed beyond the picket fence visible from the full-length windows.

For a moment, I faltered on the first step, noticing how slimy and unsafe the wooden decking had become over the years; unsightly green streaks of moss and mould had collected between the cracks, creating a series of parallel lines where there was once smooth, varnished wood.

Tightening my grip on Poppy's hand I stepped tentatively. "Be careful, keep hold of my hand. The wood's slippery."

"Okay," Poppy answered, matching her steps to mine. She had seldom been out into the back garden and was just happy to be exploring. It was a brave new world to her: for me it was like delving into a dark fairy-tale populated by shadows and demons from my past.

Even the air was unfamiliar. Gone was the fragrance of floribunda, instead my nostrils were filled with an overpowering odour of saturated soil and rotting leaves that squelched beneath our feet. It was nothing like I had remembered.

There was a time when Hope would slip into her gardening clothes and dive in: pruning and planting seeds, placing pots while I painted, oblivious of her horticultural pursuits. She loved the house and turned it into a home, inside and out. That was her talent.

My moment of reminiscence was broken by an unexpected tug on my hand. "Ew! Look, Daddy! What is it?" Poppy let go of my hand to inspect something moving on what remained of the path.

I bent down to look. "It's a snail." I picked it up by its shell. "See, it lives in a shell. That's its home."

She edged away, catching sight of the slimy creature. "Why is it so ... so gooey?"

I shrugged my shoulders. "I'm not sure. Maybe to help it to stick to things."

"Like rocks and trees?" she asked, curiously.

"Yes. I suppose so." I returned it to the path. Immediately it began to crawl away, leaving a silver trail.

"Look! It's having a wee-wee."

I smirked. "It's not weeing. It's just slimy. It leaves a trail." I was about to explain how every act, no matter how insignificant, leaves a trail or a trace of having taken place, when she reached for my hand ready to continue our exploration into that strange and wondrous place. "They're not very nice but you get them in gardens like this. In fact, French people eat them."

She began to laugh and looked up at me disbelieving my claim. "You told a joke."

Our adventure continued. "No, it's true."

"I'm asking Mary." She shook her head.

"You can ask Mary. Maybe she'll make them for dinner for us…"

"No! I don't want them." She stuck out her tongue to show just how much she hated the idea of sampling escargot. "I won't eat them."

I shook my head in agreement. "Me neither."

When we reached the gate, I turned to reflect on how far we had walked. Behind us, the house was only a hundred yards or so back, but from that distance it looked stark and imposing, squat and commanding; silver framed, a single storey formally constructed. More like a solitary house of correction than a residential home. The expanse of glass Hope and I had insisted on to take in the view and the light appeared like a mirrored wall reflecting the leaden sky and smoky clouds passing over our heads.

The structure seemed lifeless, without colour and so out of place against the bottle green backdrop that I wondered whatever had possessed us to have it built there, miles from anywhere.

Beyond the picket fence a canvas of green foliage and rippling water held our attention. From their vantage points, blackbirds watched us unseen, macabre silhouettes: boisterous banshees with yellow beaks.

Poppy was like a spring about to uncoil; she wanted to skip and gallop off into the undergrowth but it was much too dangerous to let her run freely. There were divots and pools of inky water deceptively deep, and of course the lake was only a matter of yards away.

Keeping the deep, dark woods to our right, we walked as far as the jetty. Moored alongside it was a small rowing boat. It had become an abandoned vessel into which branches and twigs had fallen, carried by the wind. What was once a bobbing splash of colour had become a semi-circle of bleached-out wood with gloss paint flaking off in places. It's a wonder it was still afloat.

Poppy looked up at me. "Can we go in the boat, Daddy?"

I shook my head. "Not today. It needs to be cleaned out and repainted before we can go out on the lake in it."

She swung a foot in its direction. "I like boats."

Our eyes met. "Really? What kind of boats do you like?"

She pointed at the rowing boat.

"But it's a mess." I let go of her hand and attempted to untie the frayed rope that attached it to the jetty. "Stay right there. Let me try something."

She remained in one spot, tipping her head to see what I was up to. "What are you doing?"

"I'm going to see if I can drag it out of the water to inspect the damage," I said breathlessly, as the wooden object glided smoothly out of the water onto the reeds in response to my two handed heaves.

Poppy joined me on the bank. "Is it broken? Can you mend it?"

I turned to face her. "Me? I don't know how to mend it, Poppy."

She took hold of one of the twigs wedged into the seat. "You have paints."

I tipped the boat over, leaving its contents amassed beneath it in a saturated mound. With it turned upside down the extent of weather and water damage was apparent and miraculously superficial. It was as if it had been protected from the worst of the weather by the jetty and its contents, creating a water-tight barrier.

Poppy wafted the twig around like a magic wand.

"Put that down, you'll get splinters," I called out. She tossed it back into the water. I wiped the dirt from her hands. "I don't have the right kind of paints to repaint it, but I could get some. There's only one problem…"

She looked at me, fearing the worst, waiting to hear the extent of *that* problem.

"I'll need some help. You know, with the painting of it, deciding on colours. That kind of thing."

"I can help, Daddy! I can draw it and we can make colours." Her Wellington boots made a squelching sound as she danced on the spot the way she did when she simply could not contain her excitement.

"Umm…" I rocked the small boat back and forth with my boot. "I suppose we could work on it together. It will be hard work, though."

Her face took on a look of fierce determination as if to say, *I'm not afraid of hard work*. Her eyes moved across the vessel assessing the damage, her lips pressed tightly together. She had no words, but her expression was enough.

I picked up the length of rope and gave it a tug. "Let's get it back to the house so we can start to clean it up." I handed her the end of the rope. "You take the end and I'll get this part." I threw the rope over my right shoulder and bent forward, taking the strain. At first it did not move but once I found my momentum it seemed to glide along behind us on the wet grass.

Poppy held her length of the rope tightly and pulled it against my hand—making my task twice as difficult—but so excited to be helping that I didn't have the heart to tell her to let go. She fiddled with the lock on the gate and managed to open it with minimal instruction. I had to turn the boat onto its side to get it through the gate, aided by my industrious daughter. The undulating carpet of green made the transporting of the boat to the storage shed beneath the house harder than I thought it would be.

Out of breath and perspiring, I stretched my left hand out onto the wall to take in mouthfuls of air. Poppy looked up at me; her breathing was laboured, her nose had that kind of pinched look she got when she was having trouble inhaling. In the upheaval, her pink bobble hat had shifted on her head and fallen down, almost covering her left eye, but she was not bothering to straighten it.

"We made it!" I said between gasps. "Well done. Are you okay?"

She nodded and looked down at her dirty hands then up again at me, her mouth open, her eyes wide and fearful. She was about to have an asthma attack and I had forgotten her inhaler.

I swept her up in my arms, slipping and sliding along the decking and headed inside. Her tiny body was becoming rigid, her breathing no more than a series of wheezing, whistling sounds serious enough to have me running through the house in the direction of the kitchen where one of her inhalers was kept.

"You're okay, Poppy. Just keep taking deep breaths. Daddy's getting your inhaler." I sat her down on the countertop and pulled open the medical drawer. With shaking hands, I placed the mask over her mouth and attached the inhaler, pressing down the button to fill the tube with powder.

"Okay, take a deep breath, nice and slowly." With her eyes fixed on mine she took a breath. The wheezing continued. After around ten seconds I pressed down the inhaler to give her another dose. She grabbed my free hand and took the chemicals into her lungs once more. I could see her chest straining to absorb it. After ten more seconds I did the same again, willing her to breathe, holding my own breath between puffs.

I waited.

I reached for the phone. I was ten seconds away from calling an ambulance.

Only when the colour began to return to her cheeks and her grip on my hand loosened, did I exhale completely.

"There you go." I wrapped my arms around her, too afraid to squeeze tight but desperate to feel her taking in air normally. "You're such a brave girl." I pulled off her bobble hat, which had attached itself to her forehead, sweeping up her fringe. With the attack over, we both needed to smarten ourselves up.

I slipped off her coat and hung it over the handle on the kitchen door, then pulled off her pink Wellington boots. Usually she would object, but seeing them muddied and covered in wet leaves, she did not protest.

I rinsed them under the tap. "There you go. As good as new. Let's leave them there to dry off." She nodded her head and forced a smile. I approached her and rearranged her hair slides as best I could. "I'm sorry you were poorly. I should have taken your inhaler out with us. I will next time."

She kissed my cheek. "It's okay, Daddy. I helped you get the boat."

I kissed her forehead. "Yes. You did. I couldn't have done it without you."

Sensing she had me in an apologetic mood, she seized the moment. "Can I choose the colour of the boat?"

I should have seen it coming, but I didn't even flinch when I was sucker punched. "I think so. But please don't say pink," I pleaded.

She chuckled and reminded me, "Pink is the best colour in the world!"

"Not when it comes to boats, it isn't," I answered. "It will frighten the fish away."

That was something she had not considered. By the look on her face she was re-evaluating her colour choice. "What colour was it before?"

I turned away from her, allowing a memory of her mother and I out on the lake to enter my consciousness. It appeared like ripples on a pond and expanded as the finer details took shape: me cursing and struggling with the oars, trying to get some semblance of a rhythm going, her mother settling her hand across her stomach laughing, her other hand holding onto the side of the rocking boat.

I faced her. "I can't remember, Poppy. When your mummy and I went in it, I only saw her." That momentary flashback caught me off guard. I had become very good at blocking out the memories, good and bad—my sanity depended on it. But now that memory had been raised from the depths of my consciousness, and it would never be repressed again.

She waited for me to find a solution, and I had one.

"I have a couple of photographs of the boat…"

Hopefulness returned to her face; patches of rose pink on her cheeks and a tight-lipped smile. "And Mummy?"

I nodded my head. "Yes, and Mummy."

Poppy outstretched her arms, ready to be lifted down. I lowered her to the floor and handed her a tumbler of water. She drank half of it, handed back the cup and shot off like a speedboat, swerving around the kitchen door into the lounge at a rate of knots.

I was slower to get back on my feet. I peeled off my coat from a body now wet with perspiration caused by a mixture of physical excursion and sheer terror. The failing father had revealed himself once more. Without thinking, I had introduced my daughter to almost every possible trigger for her asthma: cold weather, mould spores, a change of air, even pollen. I had allowed her to become excited, exert herself and then forgotten to take her inhaler out with us.

Who does that?

I dragged off my coat, soiled boots and entered the lounge. Poppy was sitting on the sofa; on her lap was her sketchpad and on her right side her pencil case. She was humming and drawing our boat, readying herself for my session of Show-and-Tell.

I turned the key in the cabinet in my office and lifted out a photo album dated four years ago. It felt heavy, weighted down by memories and regret. From the other room I heard my name being called.

"Daddy!" A brief pause. "Daddy!"

That was my cue. I locked the cabinet and held the photo album in both hands like a gift, a sacred offering, a way of seeking forgiveness from a little girl to whom I had given a pinkie promise.

I closed the door behind me. "I'm coming…"

Later that night, too distracted to watch the news, to do or read anything, I took an old friend to bed. Jim Beam had accompanied me before and seemed perfectly suited to the occasion. The Devil's Cut went down smoothly, one chilled glass after another.

There I was thinking I was in control. I had our outing all planned in my head yet I forgot one thing. That single indispensable thing that could have ended my daughter's life.

What if we had gone out in the boat?

What if I couldn't get hold of her inhaler in time and she stopped breathing?

What if…?

Left alone with my shame I wandered around the house in no particular direction becoming less lucid with every mouthful. I staggered into my office, blurry-eyed, and leaned against the door frame. As if to knock some sense into me, I tapped my head against the architrave once, twice, three times.

What the fuck's wrong with you? Can't you do anything right?

I had no answers, only more questions.

Do you want her to fucking die?

I shook my head left and right and tried to contain my tears. The guilt that tore at my heart also had me by the throat. Barely able to catch my breath, I switched off the light and staggered to bed, stopping to take a peek at Poppy who was sleeping soundly, although I could still hear a faint wheeze in her throat as she exhaled.

Swaying and cursing, I tore at my jeans. I heard coins falling from my pockets mimicking my teardrops, creating pebbledash on the carpet, a glistening mass alongside the bed. I jeered. Poppy would be quick to gather up the booty left behind by benevolent fairies and *I* would be the one left counting the number of ways I had failed as a husband and as a father.

I slipped between the sheets, descending like a drowning man into nothingness.

CHAPTER EIGHT

I WOKE TO THE sound of an annoying hum outside my bedroom door. It took a few minutes for my world to solidify, for my senses to become more acute, to register the sound of someone vacuuming, before making the connection between the vacuum cleaner and Mary.

"Shit!"

Her being there meant it was past midday. I was still in bed. I had not checked on Poppy.

I had not showered and got myself together and, more worryingly, I had not cleared away the previous night's incriminating evidence.

I swung my legs out of bed, taking care to hold onto my head with one hand while an orchestra played. Someone was crashing cymbals in there and keeping time with the base drum vibrating in my temples. I had the hangover from hell.

Having showered, dressed and downed a pint of water, I emerged from my bedroom being careful not to appear too hungover. The house was empty. There was no sound of life: no TV playing and no Irish folksongs leaving the lips of a cheerful housekeeper and her apprentice.

Had Mary taken Poppy to the hospital? Had she had another asthma attack? I quickened my pace. In the kitchen there was a note propped up against the coffee machine. It read:

> *We're in the garden. Poppy said you took her out and dragged a rowing boat out of the lake. I'm assuming that's why you're sleeping in and why she's still wheezy. Mary.*

I wanted to believe that was what she thought but I knew it was not. She had tidied away the ice tray, put the empty bottle in the trash, hung up our clothes from our outing and put away Poppy's inhaler that I had left out in the kitchen—just in case. Maybe she had even sensed the fear still hanging in the air like a bad smell.

I assumed all of this because of the box of Ibuprofen she had used to prop-up the note. I threw back a couple of tablets with two gulps of strong coffee and managed to keep a croissant down before heading toward the glass window overlooking the garden.

There they were kneeling by the path, both wearing pink rubber gloves, picking out weeds and leaves from around what was left of an overgrown flower bed. All this time Mary had been itching to get out there, but she had held back; for the past two years she had been waiting for my signal. Yesterday I had given her just that, and she had not wasted any time responding to it.

I was not up to gardening: for one, the sun hurt my eyes, and two, I was happy to let them have their time together to catch up on their news—Mary's new cat, Poppy's new boat. They had lots to talk about.

I returned the photo album to my office, locked it away for safekeeping, but not before removing a small, framed picture of Hope. I returned it to its old position on my desk and took a step back to look at it. I had taken the photograph a year or so after we had met on a weekend away to Stratford-Upon-Avon. We had visited the Bard's home, had a pub lunch and were strolling by the river Avon when we stumbled upon a small duckling walking around in circles, obviously distressed at having become lost and parted from its mother.

Without thinking, Hope took it in her hands and carried it over to the water's edge, speaking to it softly as she did so. The minute its feet touched the water it was off, in search of its family. I had my phone in my hand and took a couple of pictures, the best of which I had framed. Hope was looking back at me over her shoulder and smiling. It was not a wide smile, more intimate than that, but in the late afternoon sun she appeared illuminated; her hair was a fiery halo and her eyes shone not so much with happiness but with something more intense.

It was the look of love.

Having that photo on my desk caused a stabbing pain in my heart but it was not life threatening, more like a twinge you feel when you're unfit and have run for the first time, using muscles which have been resting for too long. Having Hope back in my life was turning into a workout. I was learning to feel again, and I knew that for a while I would be in pain, I would suffer, but it would be worth it in the end—I had to believe that.

I returned to my bedroom to find an unmade bed; my clothes strewn across the carpet but all my loose change gone. Not only was my daughter smart, she could move with stealth. I tossed the clothes into the wash basket, straightened my bed and picked up Harriet's journal off the bedside table.

For an instant I considered putting it into a bag, ready to return to her in our next class. I had enough on my mind without delving into her past like a peeping Tom.

I decided to read just a little more. Her life was far from ordinary, finding out about her was enthralling and we did seem to have some things in common. With time on my hands I returned to it, eager to know what had become of the *golden couple...*

HARRIET - TWENTY-ONE TODAY

WHAT A DIFFERENCE IT made having the whole day, Saturday, to celebrate my twenty-first birthday: getting up late, lunch with my parents, dinner with Sam.

He woke me up to say, 'Happy Birthday, Jane,' before he left for work, kissed my forehead, and placed my card on the bedside table. He was delivering locally so promised to be home in plenty of time to shower and change into something more suited to a cosy, birthday dinner for two—or that's what I thought it was going to be.

You see, Sam was not the kind of man who liked to drag his heels when it came to making arrangements. He liked to get jobs done: the house, the car, putting up a Christmas tree, sorting out milestone events in our lives. When in company, usually male company, he liked to call it, 'taking the bull by the horns.' What he meant was taking charge because 'the little lady couldn't be trusted to organise anything.'

That was his way.

We all have our little foibles and that was one of his—one of many, I might add— that I was discovering, because that's what happens when you start looking closely; you get to see the mechanics at work, the cogs and components that keep the cerebral wheels turning.

At seven thirty sharp, we walked hand in hand into Lucciano's on the high street, and by seven thirty-three were surrounded by a crowd of people we had known for years: family, friends, neighbours—the place was packed. It was a surprise party for me, and I couldn't have been more surprised if someone had handed me a winning lottery ticket. I had no idea Sam had planned anything other than dinner and I was thrilled to be the one in the spotlight.

Or so everyone thought.

What I assumed would be an intimate, candle-lit dinner for two turned into a buffet with a DJ. Loud, stomach-heaving bass lines bounced off the walls, people bunched together on a tiny dance floor, dipping their shoulders to the beat. I circulated the room, thanking everyone for their gifts and cards while Sam huddled in a side bar with his buddies, throwing back shots and slugging pints. I watched what I was drinking, knowing someone would have to get him home.

That would be me—the birthday girl.

At the time I was too taken aback to stop and think *why*. Why he had gone to so much trouble when he knew we were saving up for a new car and a holiday; when he knew that all I wanted was an intimate meal for two, especially as he'd started driving long distances and was only spending four nights out of seven at home.

I know I sound like an ungrateful bitch—I had no reason to find fault. Everything I wanted was laid out in front of me like enamelled, mosaic tiles on a table top, nothing mismatched or out of place. When friends looked at us they saw a couple who were *right for each other*, school sweethearts who would be together forever.

And that's exactly what Sam wanted them to think.

Looking back, I realise that nothing he did was for me, or done out of love. It was all part of the act of appearing to be the quintessential, perfect partner; the chief breadwinner, the game changer, the man other women compared their partners and husbands to; the model to which other men aspired. Super Sam—the gold medal holder when it came to being Mr. Right.

So ended my birthday party; pushing Sam into a taxi, removing his shoes, getting him into bed, trying unsuccessfully to fight him off when he insisted on giving me a belated birthday kiss which was never intended to be *just* a kiss.

But that's okay because there was no one there to witness his *magnanimous* gesture or to see the bruises beaded around the tops of my arms, or the finger-long red lines caressing my chin.

Only me.

And so was my life, and his disintegration. Each gash tore at his gilded veneer, revealing the most crushing of truths—he didn't love me.

He had never loved me.

From day one, I had believed I had staged our first meeting and our relationship—set the time, the place, the date—left nothing to chance. In reality, he had been playing me. The games he played became more brutal when he lost his job. It was the beginning of the end for us.

One night, thinking he was under the legal limit after two pints, he came to the rescue of a drunken friend and took charge of his car keys. Fifteen minutes later Sam was swerving across the road to avoid a careless pedestrian, wrapping the car *he* was driving around a lamp post. Three passengers in the back suffered whiplash and his front seat passenger required an emergency operation to save his right leg.

Naturally, the police breathalysed him, discovered he was just over the legal limit, and without a moment's hesitation, fined him nine hundred pounds and banned him from driving for a year. Being a delivery man, recently promoted to senior driver, responsible for special consignments as far away as Brighton in the south and Bedford in the north, and the proud recipient of an expense account and a company van, he was—to put it mildly—fucked!

He had never had a desk job. In fact he loved driving; he loved cars, vans … literally anything on four wheels. Minus his beloved van, he quickly went off the rails. I became the sole provider. He didn't take that well; every gender stereotype he had going for him was being turned on its head and he was the wrong kind of man to embrace a subordinate role.

Most nights he'd be sitting in front of the TV when I returned from work, flicking through channels, taking nothing in, his concentration overshadowed by his craving for booze.

In the early stages he used to hate himself for becoming a slave to the bottle.

Over a three-month period the self-hatred went the way of the ice in his glass until only denial remained. He found a new freedom, a new religion; he became a disciple, falling with devotion onto his knees more times than I cared to count. The 'golden' boy I knew was thrown out with the cans, the empty bottles and broken glasses. I had to face facts—I was living with an alcoholic.

No matter how hard I tried, there was no miracle cure for what he had. Alcoholism is a debilitating illness; the pain it causes the victim, and everyone involved is immeasurable—I discovered that first-hand.

Every day, his desires would be filled with images of beer, spirits, wine—anything to drown his sorrows, while mine surfaced like flotsam waiting to be claimed. By seven thirty he'd be on the road to rack and ruin. I'd be the passenger buckling up for the ride, and the inescapable collision with the back of a hand or a fist.

You might think I'm making too much of it. I thought so too until one night, one terrible tear-stained night, he held me down with the force of a dozen men, demanding sex; his face flushed, coated in perspiration, liquor leaking from his pores like machine oil, covering his body in a slick layer of glistening grease.

I yelled, "Get off me! I don't want you." I felt his grip tighten on my wrists, held fast above my head.

"You don't want *me*?" he roared like a demon. I was petrified. I'd never encountered *that* Sam before, only seen flashes of it. "You think I haven't thought the same a hundred times over...." His spit speckled my cheeks. "... about plain Jane who had never been kissed?"

I yelled into his face. "Let me go!"

"No! You've made your fucking bed. Now you get to lie in it—with me." He lowered his hands to the hem of my nightgown and raised it, his eyes never leaving mine. I was terrified, too terrified to even scream. All I could manage was a whimper.

I turned my face to the wall and did what I had to do. I escaped in my mind to happier times, a weekend break and the one place I knew he would never find me: The Uffize Gallery, in Florence.

We're on a city break with friends. I've found myself in Piazza della Signoria, surrounded by tourists and art lovers admiring Michelangelo's David and The Nettuno by Ammannati. The sculptures are fascinating and the artistic fervour coming off the swarming tourists is sweeping me along to the gallery.

He forced my legs apart

My heart is uplifted by the splendour of it all. I want to play hopscotch on the checkered, marble floor, shake the hands of the generals and greet the ancient rulers with a rebellious smile.

He tore at my nightgown, stripping me. I felt exposed, inanimate.

I've come face to face with a gorgon; a wooden shield with the face of a woman— she's extraordinary: it's Medusa. It's so dramatic, almost as if the artist has painted her just when her head has been severed; her silent scream and shocked eyes capture her expression of disbelief; the moment at which she realises she isn't invincible after all.

He fumbled with clumsy fingers and fucked me with little or no regard for my feelings. I was no more than an orifice into which he could thrust and ejaculate.

When he had quietened and his grunts and groans had become wheezy growls, I rolled over onto my side. I wept inside. This wasn't the first time he had raped me and it wouldn't be the last. I opened my mouth and cried silently, mirroring Medusa's expression. Like her, I wasn't invincible, I could be hurt and, if I didn't do something soon, I too would perish.

I had to accept that what I had seen through my fifteen-year-old eyes was a fantasy; something I had craved and been desperate to hold on to. It was laughable and so fucking tragic at the same time.

Sam's Oscar-winning performance was coming to an end and it would only be a matter of time before the curtain fell on his production with the force of a guillotine. And what then? Would I be written out of his script completely?

I couldn't let that happen.

The next day I set up a secret bank account and started syphoning off money, nothing excessive, nothing that would be noticed. From that point on I did without my morning Starbucks latte and chocolate muffin. I ate more fruit, had a yogurt for lunch and walked whenever I could. The funny thing was, I started to feel better, lighter in every way, more agile, more of a participant, less of a victim.

Death by brow beating and bullying was not an option. I chose life.

I TOSSED MY GLASSES onto the bed and rubbed the bridge of my nose, trying to come to terms with Harriet's last entry. To look at her, you would never guess she had been through so much.

I wondered what Sam had done since she had left him? Had he fallen apart or realised what a bastard he had been and turned himself around? I was intrigued enough to Google him. Was he as Harriet had described him, blond, broad shouldered with a boyish charm? More or less.

He came up on my first search, larger than life on Facebook, complete with a profile picture that reminded me of a young Brad Pitt. I checked out his photos, scanning each one for any trace of moody poses or malcontent. He seemed happy enough, no more so than with his drinking buddies. The Prince of Argyll Pool Team held an oversized trophy aloft, smiling ruddy-faced men in football shirts bearing the pub's name. I zoomed in, believing that, if push came to shove, I'd be able to look into his eyes and perceive the depths of his depravity.

I speculated as to his accent; would he be well-spoken or a typical cockney bloke. I even played around with the idea of meeting him, man to man. I'd string him along, just for the hell of it. Find out what made him tick, push his buttons and, when he attempted to retaliate, beat the shit out of him. I could do that.

While Mary cleaned Poppy up after an afternoon spent weeding, I ordered marine paint in red, white and blue and primer, a sander, sandpaper and hand tools to carry out the repair of our rowing boat. It took me an hour to research the products—what did I know about boat paint—and another hour to place orders with Poppy sat on my knee in my office, switching her attention between pizza, paint pots and her mother's photograph.

I told her the story of the lost duckling for the first time, giving her an overdue insight into what it was I loved so much about her mother. I resigned myself to the fact that the story was bound to become a classic—a bedtime favourite. Retelling it meant I would be able to see Hope in my mind's eye. What a pleasing thought. Knowing someone had looked at me like that, at least once, was life affirming. I must have done something right to have deserved the love of such a wonderful woman.

Poppy and I worked on the boat on Saturday, on Sunday took a trip out to choose flowers for the garden. I retrieved a rucksack from the wardrobe, threw in a book on flowers, hand wipes, two biscuits, a bottle of water and, of course, Poppy's inhaler.

Being busy over the weekend had meant that I had no time to think of myself; not once had I considered my inadequacies. I simply got on with things. Poppy and I had a good time in the garden. Best of all, she considered me a boat builder par excellence. As well as her being easily pleased, that might have had something to do with the fact that I was the only one able to read the instructions on the tins of paint.

CHAPTER NINE

THE NEXT DAY, I left Mary and Poppy planting. I'd arranged to meet Lance for a late lunch at the Dog and Duck, not to get out of the house but to ask for advice. Regardless of the question, he'd offer advice minus the bullshit—he'd give it to me straight.

I was reading the newspaper on my Kindle when he arrived, smartly turned out in a casual suit jacket and dark blue trousers, brandishing a battered briefcase and a look of surprise. "I don't believe my eyes. Maxwell Grant early! It's unheard of." He sat across from me with his back to the bar. "Did Mary throw you out?"

I sneered and shook my head. "Nope. I got here on time, all by myself."

He threw back a couple of mouthfuls of warm beer, wiped his mouth on the back of his hand and continued. "Then I don't know whether I should be worried or flattered. What's going on?"

I picked up the menu and raised my eyes. "I'm in need of some advice."

"Off who?"

"You! You stupid sod." I pointed a finger in his direction. "Who else would I ask for advice?"

"Since when did *you* need advice off anyone? You've always done your own thing." He held up his hand to the waitress. "Give us a couple of minutes, please."

"I'm a free spirit. You know that," I stated, anticipating a friendly riposte.

He sat back in his chair and laughed. "Is that what you are? More like a stubborn bastard."

I couldn't deny it. "That too."

He scanned the menu. "I'm having the ham, eggs and chips. It'll make a nice change from Renee's nouveau cuisine."

"She's a *great* cook," I said indignantly. "You don't know when you're well off."

Decision made, he returned the menu to the table. "I suppose so, but you can't beat a good ham and eggs."

"True. I'll have the same." The waitress took our order and left us to get back to our conversation. "Look," I began. "Something's happened and I don't want you to jump to conclusions, but..." I paused.

"But?"

"But I think I might want to do something ... something you might find—how should I put it—reckless?"

"Reckless? You mean reckless in terms of your career?" He took a breath. "Like painting something risqué?"

"No. Besides, I don't have a career." I unfolded my napkin, playing for time. "More like confronting someone about something they've done."

He leaned forward and rested his chin in his right hand. "Does someone owe you money?"

I shook my head emphatically. "No Nothing like that. More to do with helping a friend out..."

"You have friends now!" He looked startled. "Since when?"

I shrugged my shoulders. "I know it's hard to believe."

"Of course not! You being such a socialiser..." His mouth lifted a little in the left side, creating a kind of lopsided smile.

He knew me well, or at least thought he did. "I'll have you know I've been getting out and about. Poppy and I are restoring a boat..."

78

He held off taking a sip to ask, "What kind of boat?"

"A rowing boat. The one we used to take out on the lake, remember?"

He nodded. "Sure. A lifetime ago. Does it still float?" His right eyebrow rose as an unconscious sign of his approval.

"Just about. It needs sanding down and a lick of paint, but after that it'll be good to go." I took the meal from the waitress and folded the napkin over my knee. "I told Poppy we'd go out in it once it's repaired."

"Lucky girl. Sounds like you're making progress." He didn't mean in terms of my nautical skills.

He popped a slice of ham into his mouth and chewed it slowly, savouring the flavour. I did the same. "So, what do you want advice about? Where to get rowing lessons?"

I felt my shoulders slump. "Of course not, smart ass, I can bloody row. It's something else…"

He held a mouthful of food on his fork. "Okay. Can I eat while I listen?"

"Sure." I placed down my knife and fork. "Suppose you found out that someone— a friend—had been badly treated."

He continued to cut the ham into chewable pieces. "Badly treated how?"

"Terrorised, verbally abused, beaten up … raped."

He raised his head slowly and swallowed, before asking, "Raped? Who the hell do you know who's been raped?"

"I'm hypothesizing…"

"Bullshit!" He returned to his irresistible meal.

"Bear with me." I considered how I might reword the question. "What if you found out that someone you knew had been treated like that? What would you do?" I began cutting up food while he considered his answer.

"It depends…"

"On what?"

"If they were a close friend, or a friend of a friend. If they told you personally, then you could report it."

"Who to?"

He shrugged. "The police."

It was more complicated than that. "But what if it happened a couple of years ago and they hadn't told anyone?"

He reconsidered. "Then you could be a shoulder to cry on, I suppose."

"A shoulder to cry on? That's it?"

He placed down his knife and fork. "What do you want me to say? Go find the fucker who raped her and beat the shit out of him?"

I took a few seconds longer than I should have to respond, inadvertently giving my intentions away.

He started nodding. "That's it isn't it? You want to go after him, don't you?"

I shook my head. "I didn't say that."

"You don't have to. It's written all over your face." He took a sip of beer. "Look I know what a righteous bastard you are, and I also know how guilty you feel about what happened to Hope. You've always blamed yourself, even though there was nothing you could have done. Now you get a woman coming to you with a sob story about some son-of-a-bitch who's raped her, and you want to be the one to come to her rescue." He patted his mouth with the napkin. "I get it, but this has *nothing* to do with you, Max. She should never have told you, not knowing what you've been through."

He had it all wrong. "She didn't tell me—not as such."

"Then how do you know she was raped?"

I rubbed at my beard with my right hand, thinking through the pros and cons of confessing; should I tell him the truth, or should I string him along? Explain how I had become absorbed in Harriet's journal, how she was a student in my night school class I barely even knew?

Just thinking those words was bad enough: I didn't dare say them out loud. "I heard it through a third party."

He lifted his eyes from his meal long enough to give me a sceptical glance. "I don't know what you're up to, and I think it's great that you and Poppy are bonding through your boat project. Truly, I'm happy for you both. It's about time. But this? It's too much and you playing vigilante could backfire on you. You want my advice? Then here it is." Wanting to hold my attention, he moved his half empty pint of beer to one side and faced me squarely. "Stay out of it!" He picked up the dessert menu. "Now, do they do a sponge pudding here? I'm in the mood for custard."

While Lance agonised over Eton Mess or Syrup sponge pudding with custard, I thought through what he had said. It was good advice, no more than I would have expected from a trusted friend. In reality, I didn't hear one well-intentioned word he'd said. I was already invested.

Everything I had heard about Samuel James Reynolds caused my blood to boil. I'd met his sort before: the two-faced fraud with a sadistic streak concealed behind a shiny, irresistible veneer. I wanted to meet him, face to face, not only because of what Harriet had said he had done to her but to see the man and his menacing malignity for myself.

A therapist would likely have a name for what I was going through: transference, interdependence, post-traumatic embitterment disorder, even a kind of personal catharsis.

Maybe all of them.

On the way home I began hatching a plan. In the past week I had begun two new projects, two more than I had even *wanted* to consider in the past four years, and all because of a woman I had met only twice: such was the impression she had made on me and my boat building daughter.

I arrived home unable to get within fifty feet of my own front door. Piled six feet high like a miniature, black pyramid was a mound of compost that I had *not* ordered. Mary appeared from the side of the house, accompanied by the sound of a squeaking wheelbarrow and a little girl with a familiar pair of pink, oversized rubber gloves.

"Where the hell's all this come from?" I asked, tipping my thumb over my shoulder in the direction of the steaming heap.

"The garden centre," Mary answered, sweeping past me. "You needed compost so rather than struggle with bags I ordered two tonnes of it, and this." She rocked the empty wheelbarrow from side to side. "Grab a shovel." She passed a shovel to me and picked up one herself.

Poppy held a small spade aloft and waited for me to get started.

"I'm not really dressed for…"

Mary would hear none of it. "By the grace of God almighty, we'll get it done in a flash if we all get stuck-in." She sunk her spade into the compost with a satisfying thud, leaving a wedge like space for me to follow suit.

Following orders, I tossed a moist slice of it into the wheelbarrow, careful not to cover Poppy's hands as she sliced with her spade, breaking up the clods.

It was not easy work; in fact, it felt like hard labour, especially on top of a large lunch and two pints of beer. By the end of it, I had blisters forming on the palm of my right hand, but when all that was left was a few dusty specks of soil on the drive I looked on with a sense of achievement. Little did I know that we were only half done; we had yet to spread it around the back garden.

We worked solidly for three hours until the sun descended, leaving an autumn wind behind; leaves on semi-naked trees rustling, branches cracking and swaying like flaying phantoms.

The three of us ate a hearty stew with chunks of bread torn apart with hands glowing from over washing. Poppy's nails were clean and trimmed. Mine were jagged and dirty, framed by minute traces of soil. There was a time when the dark stains would have been paint, or charcoal.

Those were the days…

So much had changed. Only then did the prospect of change feel like progress, and even that came with an aching back.

CHAPTER TEN

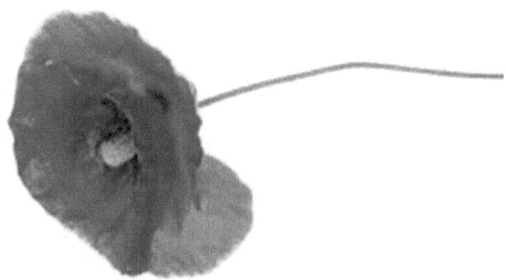

I ARRIVED EARLY TO prepare for my Tuesday art class.

As luck would have it, I was looking and feeling better than I had for a long time. Even though it was a pitiful excuse for actual teaching, I did look as if I was a part of the human race, and not some washed-out hippie who had just returned from a humanitarian mission.

From my appearance last week, I dare say some of the more astute students had been able to deduce that I was 'wifeless'—a single parent. I must have looked like a man on the verge of a precipice, teetering on the edge, maintaining my balance but fighting off the temptation to freefall.

That would have been a fair description.

Also, from the way I'd been interacting—or failing miserably to do so—it must have been obvious that I was not used to being around people. I had lost the ability to read non-verbal clues. You have to mingle to fine-tune those kinds of skills and I'd been atoning for my sins for the past four years in virtual isolation. If a person failed to vocalise what they wanted or didn't make some kind of visual gesticulation, I didn't respond. I see that now. People misinterpreted my reactions, or lack of, and put them down to arrogance or being too self-absorbed to care what people thought of me. The former was a miscalculation; the latter was nearer the mark. It took an unassuming young woman with a penchant for purple dresses and black boots to draw my attention to my social ineptitude and, once alerted to the fact, do something about it.

Still wearing my coat, I was taking great pains to align an old oil lamp and an oil-stained cloth on a stool in preparation for the arrival of my twelve disciples. I say twelve, but I knew it would take a minor miracle to have them *all* return for more verbal flagellation after last week's barrage of insults.

I didn't turn around, even though I was conscious of someone entering the room. From over by the door I heard the scraping of one of the easels along the floor.

"Oh shit!"

I turned to witness Harriet gripping her rucksack with one hand like a babe in arms, while the other had hold of the easel in question.

Too late.

My concentration had been shattered. I moved away from the lamp.

"Sorry about that," she said, holding up her spare hand apologetically. "Are you putting the finishing touches to your display?"

"Composition," I replied unconsciously, giving the lamp a sideways glance.

"I stand corrected." She threw down her rucksack and wandered over to take a closer look at it. "That looks hard to draw, what with all the angles and the folds in the cloth…"

"Not really. It's not any harder than the flowers you drew last week." I sat back on the corner of my desk, gripped it with both hands and eyed her with an artist's eye. If I had been holding a camera, it would have been on zoom, too close for comfort by the way Harriet was fiddling with her leather jacket, wrapping it around her body like a bullet-proof vest. She took a breath as if preparing to break the awkward pause that I had inadvertently created with my tetchy response and what must have come across as an unnerving leer.

"Okay, I'll give it a go, as long as you promise not to tear it to pieces if I make a mess of it. This is my night off, you know, and I've come here for some light relief."

I almost smiled. Five minutes in and we were having a friendly face-off. I was grateful for the fact that she couldn't read me; what with my beard and my social ineptitude I gave little away. I looked at her profile through squinting eyes that I tried to soften so as not to appear too threatening and waited for her to speak. Having read a little of her diary, I knew a few things about her: one being that she was a runaway and she didn't need a bastard like me ruining her day. I offered her a *nice* response. "I'll handle you, and the rest of the students, with the utmost care." I purposefully lowered my voice until it was barely more than a whisper.

She couldn't hide her surprise. She had a face that was absent of expression lines: no frowns, no wrinkles around the eyes—although I suspect she had done more than her fair share of crying—and *no* laughter lines. The giveaway was her eyes; they were bright blue, alert, almost crystal like and in response to my comment they were wide and expectant.

Even me, with my lack of emotional intelligence, could tell that she wasn't used to being spoken to softly—not by a man. Her cheeks were the colour of Poppy's plastic raincoat—a delightful pink that it would take more white than red to create.

She feigned nonchalance and folded her arms across her chest. "Good to know. Nice to see that someone got out of bed on the right side this morning…"

I interjected before she got carried away with her observation. "Could be. Then again I could be acting on some good advice I received from a new friend."

She reached out her hand. "In that case..."

"We meet again, Harry."

She smiled. "Yes, we do."

I shook her hand, shocked by how cold it was; her fingers were like icicles clinging to my skin. It had been a while since I'd held a woman's hand. I'd forgotten the texture, the size… I had become so used to Poppy's that I'd developed a soft grip. I must have seemed quite limp-wristed. I cracked the ice a little more. "Maxwell. Max to my friends."

"Nice to meet you, Max." She gave me a warm, ice-melting smile, wide but toothless. She cast her eyes around the room, appearing to look for someone. "Who won the race tonight, by the way?"

"Who do you think?" I released my hand and looked up to acknowledge the other members of the class as they entered the room apprehensively; some were mumbling others were trying to slip in unnoticed. "What can I say? All I saw was a flash of pink."

I smirked, sharing the joke.

She chuckled in response. "She's really motivated. How's she getting on with the paints?"

As a reflex action I bit the corner of my mouth, nibbling on my beard. "She hasn't painted anything yet. She's been using pencils, highlighters and crayons. I'll have to sort out an apron and some paper, probably a tablecloth as well. It might turn out to be an expensive hobby if I have to redecorate and buy her a new wardrobe." I shook my head feigning annoyance. Inside I was smiling, but she couldn't have known that, given the newness of our friendship; in the same way she couldn't have known how hard it was for me to put the past behind me.

I tried to keep my eyes on anything but her, afraid that she, a fellow sufferer, would see the guilt that lived like a tormentor behind them. Every day, when I looked in the mirror, I came face to face with a man with secrets a plenty who saw the world through dark pools of sadness.

She raised her head and for an instant I thought I saw the same watery tones—not quite. Her sadness was blue and deep like the ocean, but no less woeful for its brilliance.

For a split second, she appraised me coolly and didn't look away when I caught her in the act. It was as if she was seeing me for the first time, seeing something new in me that she hadn't noticed before—my dark soul perhaps…

She positioned herself behind her easel, slipping off her leather jacket to reveal a purple T-shirt with the words, 'Let there be light' on it—maybe a surreptitious nod to her previous life when she was overshadowed by a dark and deadly partner with a nasty streak and a masculine ego that was easily dented.

I hoped her optimism was contagious.

From what I could tell, she seemed intact—a survivor with no tell-tale symptoms of a broken woman: nervousness, apprehension, introversion.

None of the above.

I was no expert on the subject of abused women but, in my humble opinion, she looked just fine—there were no *visible* scars. She didn't appear to be plagued by self-doubt either. Why would she be? She had master-minded her escape from hell, freed herself from the grasp of a fiend and started over, all on her own.

Up close, I considered Harry naturally pretty. She wore little if any eye make-up; perhaps the rosy tinge on her cheeks was natural too, but no one had lips that glossy. Like me, she had made an effort to look presentable.

Granted, she was different, even I could see that. Her love of all things purple and black was a fashion statement, surely, and not an indication of her state of mind or a personality defect. I only had to look at Poppy. Was there ever a day when she didn't wear something pink—usually her Wellington boots—come rain or shine? Why would she not? That small act of self-determination made her happy, and pink *was*, 'the best colour in the world.'

It was of greater importance to me that she was talented, and because of it, I convinced myself that was why I enjoyed having her in my class. It had nothing to do with knowing more about her than I had known about anyone, other than my wife, of course.

With my expectations indelibly printed on the minds of my students in the first lesson, they were eager to get started. Last week there were twelve: twelve had become ten. Two more than I expected—masochists one and all; grown-ups who had developed thick skins over the years, thick and water-tight. I was convinced that nothing I could say would seep through deep enough to touch a nerve.

Sticks and stones…

Having cleared half a dozen easels away to make room for the remaining ten, I had created more space; the room was less cluttered, and I could see each student and they could see me.

Suspecting I had been listening to their pre-class chitchat, they moved quietly around, positioning themselves, waiting for instructions. I removed my coat, preparing to face them, taking a moment to reshape my expression, softening the sullen frown and pained look I had cultivated over time.

I drew my hand across my hair, smoothing out the windswept flicks around my ears. I swept around the room, allowing my eyes to meet theirs momentarily, resisting a reflex action to call out, *"So, what are you waiting for? Pick up your pencils and draw!"*

I bit back the urge to spit out spiteful words, to bully or chastise them for simply turning up. They had paid good money to be there and it was my duty to help them develop what little talent they had or, in Harriet's case, to help her realise her potential.

Discreetly, I checked her out from various angles, watching the glow from the strip lights play with her hair, creating bands of auburn streaks she unselfconsciously slipped behind her ears. I saw how she bit her lip and squinted, aligning the lamp, determined to get the proportions right. She was strong-minded, unwavering, visibly refusing to be beaten by my challenge.

I liked that about her.

When I least expected it, I felt her eyes on me, giving *me* the once over. She had a keen eye for detail and my new, matching clothes and scuff-free shoes didn't go unnoticed. I still had the threadbare sweater Hope had bought me as a birthday present washed and folded in a drawer; there was no way I would ever part with it. And the jeans with worn knees and creases in all the wrong places that I had lived in for weeks would still have their day—just not *that* day.

I felt more like my old self than I had for longer than I could remember.

I could teach, and I could learn what it was to be alive and not feel bad about moving on; three steps forward, two steps back until I found my momentum and could stand tall, unaided. Maybe then, just maybe, I could face up to the fact that Hope was gone, gone but not forgotten. She lived on in our daughter, Poppy, in every tangled ringlet, in every innocent smile and especially in her eyes—puddles of leopard-coloured light that reminded me not only of what I had lost, but of what she had given me—a piece of her.

Much to my surprise, the little girl in question entered the classroom earlier than expected, her pink rucksack attached to her back like a snail's shell. She let go of Debbie's hand, the woman running the flower arranging class, and bounded over to me. I couldn't disguise my surprise, and my lips formed into a smile behind my beard.

"She wanted to come," Debbie said with a shrug.

"Thanks, Debbie." I stooped down to peel the rucksack from her back. "Hey you, I though you liked helping the ladies arrange the flowers?"

"I want to draw. You said I could draw. It was my prize." She wriggled out of her coat and handed it to me as if she had already decided she was going to stay.

Oblivious of the ten students hiding behind easels, listening to her every word, she looked up at me pleadingly. "Can I draw, Daddy?"

"Well, I'm not sure." I rubbed the bristles on my chin thoughtfully, turning my response into a performance piece. "I think you need to do some work first," I stated, causing my ten students to glance over at each other; some rolled their eyes, others simply shook their heads, taken aback by my lack of parental kindness. "Little girls can't attend this class…"

Poppy grabbed my hand and sandwiched it between hers as if in prayer. "Please Daddy, please…"

I tutted, raised my head to see all ten observers looking on disapprovingly. I had played the game for long enough. "All right then, but first you'll have to go round with this." I handed her an empty tin from which the pencils had been taken, and a pencil sharpener. "Go around the room and sharpen everyone's pencils. If you've done a good job, then I'll set up an easel and you can draw."

Poppy danced on the spot, her pink Wellington boots tapping out a merry beat on the wooden floor. "I'll do the best job, Daddy."

"Good. Start over there and work your way around. Tell the students your name and be very polite. Okay?"

"Okay."

Following the line of my finger she skipped over to the right, lightening the atmosphere a little more with every sugar-coated introduction. Her appearance unsettled me at first, seemed to reflect badly on my lack of readiness and professionalism. In fact, it did the opposite. If anything, Poppy endorsed it with every turn of every pencil.

She is her mother's daughter, after all.

There was muted chatter that seemed to give the room a kind of heart-warming hum. I looked up but didn't return Harry's half smile. Instead, I turned away, busying myself with papers on my desk, unwilling or unable to accept her unspoken acknowledgement of my fatherly conduct. Even I knew that little children love to help, love to be given jobs but also needed to learn that things that matter, things they wanted, had to be earned. Poppy's laughter was proof enough that I had got it right, for once, with a little guidance from a young woman who was starting to show me that the wind of change was blowing and would continue to blow whether I fought against it or not. Perhaps the time had come to … not embrace it, exactly, but to allow it to pass through me, to carry me along.

All I had to do was let it.

I positioned myself at the front of the class, on the outside looking in for a change. The invisible wall I had created around myself and Poppy was starting to develop cracks, chinks through which strangers could peer through and see me up close. I knew perfectly well what was happening. My demonstrative daughter was breaking down barriers with her laughter and animated chitchat.

I looked on with only my thoughts for company but, when I glanced down, I was shocked to see the plain sheet of paper on my desk was covered in scratches and pencil marks: the beginning of a drawing. The outline was of Poppy; each line recorded a movement, the tap-dancing steps made by her boots—up and down, the outstretching of her arm to hand back needle-sharp pencils—right and left.

I threw down the pencil half expecting my fingers to be scorched—punishment for creative thinking and believing I could pick up where I had left off four years ago. I had no right to assume my restitution was complete.

What was I thinking?

I rubbed my palms together, creating warmth with the friction, giving myself time to compose myself. Thankfully, no one seemed to notice my momentary lapse. I stood up and paced in the direction of the first easel to my right, still shaken but capable of offering my opinion about what I saw taking shape.

Before I opened my mouth, three words popped in my head. I had said to Lance, 'I'll be nice.' I hadn't forgotten. Keeping my promise and putting my sombre self to one side, I would attempt to be exactly that.

I sensed each student tensing as I approached, taking a step back, hoping to distance themselves from what they assumed would be a scathing critique of their best efforts.

I looked closely and pondered, pointed out weaknesses, resisted the urge to laugh or tear up sheets. Instead, I moved from one to the other but not before saying something nice. In terms of artistic content and appraisal, my parting utterances were no more than platitudes but enough to bring a smile to their faces.

Job done. Promise kept. Even though what I was doing went against my better judgement. On the up-side, I *was* boosting their confidence and, in return, was being thanked for giving them the benefit of my expertise.

Expertise?

They had no idea who I was. I could have said I was Paul Gauguin's great grandson and they would have gone for it. Having said that, not everyone was eager to create something of worth: Harry had other ideas—she wasn't drawing at all.

Behind her easel, positioned on a high stool sat Poppy, pencil in hand following her instructions. She was so engrossed she didn't notice me standing by her side. I was about to make her aware of my presence when I felt Harry's hand on my arm. She shook her head and continued to offer praise and more instructions.

"That's right. You're doing a great job, Poppy. Look carefully and tell me, which side needs more shading?"

In response Poppy tapped the drawing. "There."

"Yes. Can you make it a bit darker where the shading needs to be?"

Poppy nodded, leaned in, and got to work.

Walking into this scene unprepared as I was made me feel as if I'd been ambushed; my authority as teacher-in-charge was being usurped—I had lost control. Irrationally, I wanted to take back what was mine. I couldn't just hand it over without some kind of fight. "Poppy, would you like me to set up an easel for you? Harry would like to finish off her drawing—"

Harry intervened before I could finish my sentence. "I'm happy to let Poppy help me. Your daughter has a good eye."

I couldn't argue with that and simply nodded, looking for an escape route. It came in the form of a time check. I glanced at my watch and called out, "You have fifteen minutes. Then you'll need to turn your easels around so we can all take a look."

Realising they were running out of time, my students switched their attention from me and returned to their drawing—including Harry, not to work on it herself but to further instruct her prodigy.

"Perfect," she commented. "Would you like to have a go at the top of the lamp? I'll help you if you get stuck."

Poppy looked up at Harry, noticing me for the first time. "Look, Daddy, I'm drawing."

I drew my hand over her hair. "I can see that, Poppy. Keep going … you're doing really well." Following Harry's lead was not so bad, not when it was rewarded with a giddy smile.

I leaned over to Harry. "You didn't have to let her work on your drawing."

She shrugged. "I know. I wanted her to. I gave her an outline to follow, that's all. I can always draw the lamp from memory for homework, Mr. Grant."

I snickered. "So, it's Mr. Grant now?"

She returned my smile. "Well, I don't want to be accused of slacking or not following orders."

I shook my head. "I'm not giving any orders. It's a night class and we both know you can do this kind of thing in your sleep." I pointed at the drawing, noticing Poppy's hesitance.

Harry had too. She moved her easel a little to the right to improve Poppy's view. "See how the handle is thin and shiny and the lamp is thick and dark?"

Poppy nodded.

"That means you can draw the handle gently using the tip of your pencil. You can press harder for the other parts, like this." She drew two parallel lines on the bottom of the sheet.

Poppy understood and was eager to get back to work.

I left them to it.

Fifteen minutes later, I called time. Each student turned their easel to face the front of the class and arranged their chairs in a wide arc to face them. Poppy joined them cheerfully, being a fully-fledged student; she folded her arms over her dress, leaned back in her chair and let her legs dangle, her boots at least six inches from the floor.

I regarded each drawing in turn, passing comments to which they responded with modest smiles and applause—it was all very civilised.

When I came to Poppy's, I paused, thinking through my appraisal. It was the work of a child, obviously, and what I was about to say could boost or shatter her confidence. I walked up to the easel, mimicking the posture of a bona fide art critic, folding one arm across my chest, nursing my chin in my free hand. It was staged for Poppy's benefit. I knew it and so did my audience.

There was silence. It was as if time was standing still. All eyes were on me. "As we can tell, this isn't complete, but from what I can see, the linear contours lend themselves to…"

Harry caught my eye. She was drawing her hand across her throat with an invisible knife over and over again. She tipped her head to Poppy sitting next to her, communicating something that it took me a matter of seconds to decipher.

Of course. My sophisticated appraisal was going over the head of the one person I was directing it at. I started over. "Also, from the neat lines, here and here, we can see that the artist has tried really hard. I especially like the way the handle has been drawn with a little hook on it, ready to be picked up…"

I heard the words as they left my mouth and inwardly cringed.

What was I saying?

I was saying all the right things in a language Poppy could understand, and that's all that mattered. Even the other students were nodding in agreement—most of them were parents too.

Poppy's face was a picture. She was glowing with pride, and so was I.

"It's a grand effort. Well done, Poppy."

To my surprise, she covered her face in her hands to hide her embarrassment. She was not used to being in the spotlight and was actually blushing—she was the star of the show. In fact, from the moment she had clip-clopped into the classroom, she had been exactly that.

Harry lifted a colouring book from her rucksack and indicated that I should take it from her.

I held it aloft. "And in recognition of…"

Harry frowned once more.

I did a retake. "For the best work tonight, the first prize goes to…"

Ben did a drumroll on his chair.

"Poppy Grant. Come and get your prize."

More applause followed. The evening was turning into quite an event. Never more so than when Harry lifted Poppy from her chair and she ran toward me, as Harry had described, *like a bullet from a gun,* right into my arms. I lifted her up and set her on my right hip.

"Congratulations, Poppy. This is for you. Would you like to say a few words?" I assumed she would prefer not to, but it was my night for making bad calls and she nodded.

A moment's hesitation, but then, willed on by the congregation, she tucked a strand of hair behind her ear and addressed them. "Thank you for being my friends, and Harry for letting me help and showing me how to draw." She blew Harry a kiss and accepted one in return.

Before I could lower her to the floor, she turned her attention to me. "And thank you for being the best daddy in the world." She planted a wet kiss on my cheek, wrapped her arms around my neck and held on tight. I was too shocked to respond but *was* able to manufacture a tight-lipped smile; quelling mounting emotion, wishing her mother was around to see her daughter in all her glory.

As if reading my mind our audience offered watery smiles, fished out tissues from pockets and bags and dabbed their eyes. I turned to Harry to thank her, but she was looking elsewhere, returning chairs to their original places at the back of the room. I couldn't let her go without thanking her. The explosion of emotion we had all experienced was of her making. It had turned a collection of disparate people into a single group of like-minded individuals.

Poppy shot off to show her new 'friends' her prize. Seizing the moment, I approached Harry. "That was very well orchestrated." I paused, hoping what I was about to say would be recognised as genuine appreciation. "Thank you, Harry."

"You're welcome." She smiled softly. "It worked out better than expected, to be honest, and you were so good with her."

I tipped my head, acknowledging the compliment. "I'm learning."

"Yes, you are." She removed Poppy's drawing from the easel and carried it over to my desk, noticing my semi-conscious attempt at drawing. "You were sketching?"

Embarrassed by my meagre effort, I shrugged it off. "No. Not really."

She nodded in the direction of my desk. "What's that?"

"I was doodling, that's all." I covered it over with sheets of unused paper.

She rearranged her bag on her shoulder for comfort. "You doodle very well."

"Thanks." I looked up to acknowledge other students leaving and waving

"Great class…"

"See you next week…"

"Thanks, Max…"

Harry watched them leave. "Looks like you'll be having a full house next week."

"Yeah. That's a first." Nervously, I chewed my beard at the corner of my mouth.

Harry folded her arms, settling herself. "I looked you up, you know. You don't exist. Not as an artist *or* as a teacher."

She caught me off guard. "I don't?"

"No. And yet, I have the feeling that you can do this…" She swept her arm around the room. "… this drawing stuff, and probably painting too, with one hand tied behind your back. And, if that's the case, it makes me wonder why you're here teaching a night class when you could be with real artists or showcasing your own work." She shook her head. "Anyway, don't mind me. I'm just the curious sort, that's all." She turned to leave. "See you next week."

Before she could about turn, I placed my hand on her arm. "M.G. Chambers."

She looked puzzled. "Who's that?"

"That's who I was before…" I held back. She knew the who. She could find out the why for herself. "Before I reverted back to my real name: Maxwell Grant."

"Ah." She smiled appreciatively. "I'll check you out."

"Feel free." Telling her my name as an artist was a gamble, but the least I could do, particularly as I knew so much about her. "Just keep it to yourself, okay?"

"Will do." Before leaving, she scanned the room one last time. "Say goodbye to Poppy for me."

"Of course."

When everyone had left, I folded away the few remaining easels left standing and placed the drawings into a drawer over by the window. "You all set?" I asked Poppy, watching her slip her arm into her coat.

"Yep."

I picked up her rucksack, my satchel, switched off the lights and locked the door behind us. Holding Poppy's hand, I led us out into the car park. There was an autumnal nip in the air and a dampness that caused windscreens to mist over. Poppy jumped into the passenger seat and quickly belted up, seemingly in a hurry to head home.

Feeling her eyes on me, I turned to face her. "What?"

"I like Harry," she declared impulsively.

"Good. She seems nice." I pulled out onto an empty road and hit the accelerator, assuming our conversation regarding Miss Harper had ended as abruptly as it has started.

True to form, I was wrong.

"Do *you* like Harry, Daddy?" I felt her eyes burrowing through my cheek.

"Sure. Like I said, she seems nice." I had no words to explain *how* I felt about Harry, least of all to my pre-school passenger.

Poppy folded her arms in that, exaggerated *I have a secret* pose of hers.

"What now?"

"She likes you." She rubbed her boots together, making an annoying squeaking sound.

I ignored it and kept my eyes on the road. She had me—hook, line and sinker. I had to know by what powers of deduction she had come to that conclusion. "What makes you say that?"

She shrugged her shoulders.

"You don't have to tell me but remember our *no secrets* rule?"

She nodded and explained. "Because she said you didn't look sad."

I glanced at her disbelievingly. "And that's it?"

"Daddy! It's a *big* thing," she insisted, rocking back into her seat.

I parked up, pulled the key out of the ignition and blew out a hot gust of air. "Women … I swear you speak a different language."

96

Poppy jumped out of the car and stomped off. Once inside she left me to turn on lights and lamps adding a cosy ambiance to our home. In the time it took me to slip off my satchel and remove my coat, she had appeared beside me. In one hand were two sheets of paper with pictures she had drawn.

Taking me by the hand, she led me over to the dining table, climbed onto a chair and kneeled up to explain the significance of her two drawings. I was getting used to her visual representations of our lives but was weary and in no mood for her childish ramblings. "It's almost nine thirty, Poppy. You should be fast asleep in bed. What is it you're showing me?"

She poked her tiny forefinger at an image on the sheet of paper nearest to me. "See! Sad Daddy."

The drawing was not recent, maybe a few months old. She had drawn a man in black with wild curly hair and a wild curly beard; his mouth was downturned, and on either side of his eyes were blue droplets.

My head fell. I rubbed at the back of my neck, easing the knots, contemplating my demise. Was I really such a forlorn figure?

"Okay, I see sad Daddy." Almost too scared to look, I focused my attention on the second drawing. It was only a couple of days old. I could tell that by the inclusion of the rowing boat in the foreground. Poppy was on one side of it. I was on the other. I was wearing dark clothes—no change there—what had changed was my face; my hair and beard appeared to have been tamed but more important than that, I had a u-shaped mouth—I was smiling.

Poppy leaned over, placing her elbows on the table. "Look, Daddy. You're not sad."

"I see that, Poppy. Not as sad as I used to be. You've shown that really well. And look how happy *you* are too."

"Yes!" She smiled broadly and wrinkled up her eyes in a comical way.

I lifted her down. "You have your new colouring book to look forward to tomorrow. Go and get your PJ's on I'll be in, in five minutes."

It was hard to believe my life was being documented by a three-year-old—two months away from her fourth birthday. For all of her life Mary and I had been her world, and here she was so intuitive when I had given her so little to learn from.

I gathered up her pictures, stopping to take a last look at my cheerful self. Poppy had used the right colours for the boat and had even tried to recreate the photo I had shown her—with one shocking modification.

The figure in the boat had been altered.

Swathed in ribbons of blue colour, Hope's ruby red smock had been transformed and revised.

It was purple.

CHAPTER ELEVEN

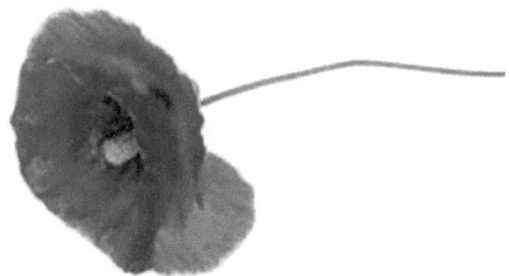

I WAS IN NO rush to find an alcohol fuelled escape from the day's events, not when the evening had been so much fun. I made a cup of hot chocolate and trundled off to bed around eleven, mug in one hand, Harry's journal in the other.

I had second thoughts about continuing. It was turning into one woman's account of her descent into a world of domestic violence and humiliation. Had I not read enough, visualised enough? Was it time to walk away before its contents became too disturbing?

It was meant to be private, and knowing that, knowing it was an honest account from someone I knew and liked, was making me feel again, and that scared me. I said I would never let myself do that again—become so attached to a person that the thought of living without them left me emotionally wrecked. I had detached myself from the world—from people. It was safer for my sanity that way: not caring, not feeling had worked for me; isolation had kept me lucid when melancholy had brought me to the edge of despair. And yet, there I was reading every line, allowing Harriet's accounts to flood my consciousness; like powerful amphetamines her words were triggering feelings that were as familiar to me as a foreign language I once spoke fluently, a form of emotional intelligence that had been rejected was being awakened.

It's true. I did feel uncomfortable reading it but I was unable to stop myself—I was at the point of no return. Any discomfort I was feeling was minimal in comparison to what she had gone through. If Harriet had taken the time to write her story down, the least I could do was take the time to read it.

Before I started reading. I removed my glasses and reconsidered my decision to tell her who I used to be. Was it pride that made me spurt out the name associated with my artistic accomplishments and financial gain? What did I care if she knew the old me or not?

I laughed at my naiveté. I was out of practice; she had played me, gotten me to spill the beans with that comment about teaching with one hand tied behind my back. She was right, of course—I fell for it. A well placed fragment of flattery and I was handing over pieces of my past to her like a jigsaw puzzle.

Getting to know *her* up close was one thing—the way she saw through me, forcing me to do the right thing with Poppy then going on to reveal my deepest secret—but getting to know her through the pages of her journal was another. I was in a unique position, being able to see into her past. Discovering how a brow-beaten young girl could grow into a determined woman with a good heart was turning into a revelation.

It hit me in a flash. The effect she was having on everyone around her—Poppy and myself included—was not accidental. She was extraordinary.

I returned my glasses to the bridge of my nose, removed the bookmark and took a deep breath.

HARRIET - DARK DAYS

THINGS GOT WORSE.

It got so bad that after working all day, I would sit in my car outside our house allowing the minutes to fall away like water from a dripping tap—it was torture. My quickening breath and beating heart worked in unison with my fingers tapping out a subconscious SOS on the steering wheel. To pass the time, I'd scroll through photos on my phone, using the memories they stirred to bolster my confidence; convincing myself that night would be different—it never was.

Three months into his unemployment Sam had established a routine, of sorts: he got up late, searched for jobs, checked emails, read through rejections and padded around the house in his bathrobe at a loose end, his pride preventing him from contacting his former colleagues to ask for help.

By the time I walked through the front door, his mind was awash with alcohol and his vision impaired; he saw me as an object to vent his anger on. Five minutes in, the dripping water had turned into a torrent, wearing away what little confidence I had amassed during the day.

The perpetual grinding down had all the elements of emotional abuse; every comment loaded with innuendo and insults about how I looked, what I said and, more disturbingly, how I had brought about his catastrophic collapse. He lost all sense of purpose and, seeing no way out, turned to the seedier side of business to redefine himself.

One night I came home to a house barely recognisable. From the outside, it looked unchanged, but anyone entering it would have thought they were witnessing the aftermath of a break-in: papers strewn everywhere, boxes tipped up, his satellite navigation devices plugged into an extension cable on the coffee table. I wanted to turnabout, walk away, and could easily have done that if it hadn't been for his insistence that I make dinner. He'd been busy all day—doing what I wouldn't find out until months later when just the thought of it would fill me with revulsion.

I wanted no part of it.

On the plus side, his new venture involved him spending more time out of the house at night leaving me to plot and plant the virtual seeds of my escape. Having the house to myself was one thing, having to withstand his return was another. It was on such a night when a potentially deadly attack brought about injuries that would change my life forever.

For as long as I live, I will never forgive him for what he did.

Two months into my twenty-third birthday, I discovered I was pregnant. Our child had not been conceived out of love. To call what he did to me lovemaking would be a lie: it felt like rape—it was rape.

Most times I could escape his brutality by revisiting holiday destinations I remembered with great fondness: the Eiffel Tower on my twentieth birthday, the Coliseum in Rome bathed in golden sunlight, the splashes of watercolours in The Rodeo Museum in Turkey or, in those moments of desperation, I took strength from the Parthenon in Athens; replacing the feel of chafing sheets against my burning cheek with that of cold, white stone. Sam could hurt me, but he would never reach that part of me where my memories lived—I was always safe there.

I made the decision not to tell him straight away about the baby, secretly hoping my period would come, a week or two late.

It didn't.

When I thought the time was right and his mood tolerant, I broke the news. Since he had started earning cash in hand, he had been less unpredictable. Even though the money he received for his dishonourable pursuits helped to cover the cost of our bills, I hated dirtying my hands with it. His powerlessness was a thing of the past, but bad habits are hard to break.

One alcohol-drenched night he came home late, waking me up at two in the morning with his noisy return. My body tensed with every creaking step as he climbed the stairs, swaying, cursing, calling my name. It was a rerun of the previous Friday night, the only difference being that he fell asleep on the sofa downstairs. That terrifying night, I was not to be that lucky.

He burst through the bedroom door, half tumbling, half staggering. Pretending to be in a deep sleep, I didn't dare to move; I was a block of ice, cold to the touch and inanimate. He threw back the covers and clambered on top of me—a stinking, dead weight with one intention.

While he fiddled with his belt, I slid from beneath him onto the bedroom carpet and crawled on all fours toward the bathroom. There was a lock on the door, and I knew that if I could bolt it and put my back against the door, I could escape him. He would become angry, I knew that, kick the door, pound on it with his fists but eventually, when the booze had numbed all his senses, he would fall to his knees, lurch sideways onto the carpet and sleep it off.

I made it to the bathroom but, when I climbed to my feet, he came behind, picked me up and threw me onto the bed as if I was a sack of rubbish. I scrambled off it and made it as far as the hall. We tussled, I pushed him off with my hands not realising how close I was to the top step. I lost my footing and fell. I didn't stop falling until I reached the bottom step by the hallway.

When I came round, I was chilled to the bone, in a state of shock and I hurt all over. The metallic taste of blood flooded my mouth and leaked onto the carpet, creating a tell-tale mark of our struggle. I lay there until the bright, eye-piercing sunlight of a new day roused me. My legs were twisted beneath me, my arms flung wide like featherless wings. I was rigid and scared to move.

I started at my toes and worked my way up. I could wiggle them; my ankles were stiff but they moved. I could move my legs. I remember thinking, A*t least I'm not paralysed. I can still run.*

When I pulled my arms into my body, my chest hurt, my hips throbbed and the slightest movement of my neck caused my head to spin.

With great difficulty, I attempted to stand, keeping hold of the bannister with one hand and my head with the other. I made it as far as the hall mirror. It's hard to describe what I saw. I say *what* because it wasn't a *who*; that battered thing with a busted lip, a black eye and bruised patches peeping through a torn nightgown wasn't me. It couldn't be me.

But it was.

I dragged myself up the stairs. It took a monumental effort. Halfway, I stopped to pant away the pain before continuing my climb. I bypassed the bedroom, powered on by the reassuring sound of Sam's snoring. I locked myself in the main bathroom and ran a bath. When the bubbles were almost touching the rim, I slipped off my shredded nightdress and clambered in.

I don't know how long I lay there soaking, dipping my head beneath the water from time to time, feeling the sting of warm water on my lip and wincing. I woke to the sound of someone on the landing.

Sam was on the other side of the door listening.

And so was I.

I patted myself dry, unwilling to look in the mirror. Seeing just how broken I was would bring me to my knees and I refused to do that ever again. I had said that so many times before, but that was the final straw.

I dragged a clean bathrobe out of the cupboard and tentatively slipped in one arm after the other. I opened the door and gasped when I saw Sam still standing there. He had showered and dressed, and if it wasn't for the fine lines that exploded in his eyes like red veins in marble, there would have been little—if any—evidence of the previous night's drunken rampage and his brutal assault on my body.

I attempted to move past him, but he took hold of my arm. I winced. There was not a part of me that didn't hurt—even breathing was difficult.

"Let go of me. I need to get dressed," I said, barely recognising my own voice.

He released his grip and followed me into the bedroom. "Why? Where are you going?"

I looked up at him. "Where do you think? I'm going to Accident and Emergency. I need to be checked out."

"It's just a few bruises. A couple of days in bed and you'll be fine." Dismissively, he began picking up his clothes from the carpet. "It was an accident. You slipped and fell. I didn't push you."

"No? And why do you think I ended up on the top of the stairs in my nightdress in the middle of the night? You attacked me. Twice!" I cried, my lips smarting as I formed the words.

He shrugged away blame. "So, I admit I got a bit rough, and I get carried away sometimes, but if you weren't so fucking frigid, then I wouldn't have to, would I?"

I couldn't believe my ears. I was the one who had come within a hair's breadth of losing my life and there he was holding me responsible. "Have you any idea what you've done? You could have killed me."

He tossed a hairbrush onto the bed. "Take it from me, Jane. If I'd wanted you dead, you'd *be* dead. Tidy yourself up." From downstairs he called up to me, "I'll bring you a cup of tea. That should cheer you up."

I was struck dumb. He had completely detached himself from his actions and, if that wasn't bad enough, he didn't give a damn about my injuries. And was what he had said about wanting me dead … was that a threat?

I dressed as quickly as possible, keeping my expression of pain to a minimum, conserving my strength. It was a warm day and I was able to wriggle into a pair of panties and a cotton dress, but still found it hard to insert my arms into the sleeves without contorting my face. I settled for slip-on shoes; bending was out of the question.

I was about to make my way downstairs when our eyes met. He was standing at the bedroom door, a mug of tea in one hand and a box of Ibuprofen in the other. "Nice dress. I thought you were going back to bed." He threw the box onto the bed. "Take a couple of these and sleep it off. You don't want to be seen looking like that, for Christ's sake."

"I hurt all over, Sam. There might be internal injuries. I need X-rays, scans…"

He took me by the arm. "You'll be okay. Drink your tea. You'd be on your knees if you had an internal injury, blood spurting out of your mouth…" He wrinkled his nose in disgust. "Put your feet up, you'll bounce back in no time." He sat me down and removed my shoes before swinging my feet up onto the bed. "How would it look, you turning up looking like that? We've only just started to get back on our feet. The last thing we need is strangers sticking their noses into our business." He puffed up my pillows and pushed me back into them. "There you go." He pulled the duvet up around my chin, drew the bedroom curtains and left.

Too weak to stand up to him, I sipped my tea, swallowed two painkillers and closed my eyes not knowing if I would live to see another day.

IT WAS NOT UNTIL I had reached the very last word that I realised my mouth was agape. In her earlier entries Harry had been less explicit. That had changed. Sam had changed. He had become a monster and someone I wanted to … to inflict pain upon.

He was the inflexible cord that was woven into her journal, like razor wire tearing apart everything it touched.

Harry's journal rested on the bedside table beside me. Through her written words I was able to hear her voice and sift through her recollections like ashes left behind after a camp fire—irrefutable evidence of a relationship that had burnt itself out.

I lay in the dark, eyes wide, looking up at the ceiling as I had done so many times before, so absorbed in my own inner struggle that I couldn't see or feel anything else. That night, all I could think about was Harry, the image of her suffering, her battered body. Her helplessness made me want to jump in a car and present myself before him—someone his own size. Not a petite woman whose only mistake had been loving him.

I didn't sleep well. I walked into the lounge the next morning to see Mary dusting, feeling dry-mouthed and lethargic. I cleared my throat. "Mary, are you doing anything on Friday night?"

She could not have looked more startled if I had asked for her hand in marriage. "Friday? Oh, let me check my diary, Max." She lifted a dog-eared notepad out of her apron pocket and pretended to flick through the pages. "Looks like I have a free night. What did you have in mind?"

I had only one thing in mind: meeting Samuel James Reynolds, but I dare not tell her that. "I've been invited to a small, informal gathering in London and I was thinking of going. Would you be willing to babysit Poppy?"

Her surprise morphed into a broad smile. "Well, would you believe it? Himself is going out of the house to a party!"

"It's not a party, it's more—"

"There's no need to explain." She wafted her duster in my direction. "You feeling well enough to start socialising is a thing of beauty, to be sure. And I get to spend some time with the little 'un."

"So that's a yes, then?" I grinned.

"Of course, it is." She was about to return to her work then stopped. "Does Poppy know?"

I shook my head. "No. Not yet. I'll go and tell her. Would you prefer to stay here or have her stay with you?"

She rested her chin in her hand. "As she's never left the house at night, better I stay here, I think. One step at a time…"

"I agree. You can take the guest bedroom. Just let me know what you need." I gave her a grateful smile.

"Don't you be worrying about me. I'll bring some popcorn over and we can watch TV, even play a game. I do love a game of pontoon."

My tight-lipped smile widened. I had considered my housekeeper to be many things—a card shark was not one of them. "Pontoon? I don't think Poppy will be up for that."

She raised her hands dramatically. "I'll have you know she beats me every time. I can't tell you the bags of sweets I've lost to her. She's as bright as a button, and that's no a word of a lie." She let a fine spray of polish cover the coffee table and attacked it with her duster, humming as she worked.

I went in search of Poppy, half expecting to find her gobbling sweets and shuffling cards. That was not the case.

She had her back to me when I entered her room quietly, not purposely light-footed to catch her out, but to see her simply being herself. She was sat at her desk, her boot-clad feet swinging back and forth like pendulums, her head nodding to a song in her head as she drew.

"Poppy," I said quietly. "Guess who's coming to stay over on Friday while I go meet some friends?"

She jumped down and came over to me, clearly surprised.

"Guess who?"

The answer came to her slowly, but when it did her eyes were alight with joy. She did her usual tap dance on the spot and announced, "Harry!"

I pulled back, not wanting to disappoint her. There was no easy way to break it to her. "No, of course not. Mary is staying over. Won't that be fun?"

Her smile drooped and became a downturned arc. "But Mary comes here all the time."

"She does, but she never stays over," I pointed out. I could see Poppy listening but not hearing my words. "Harry never stays over."

She was not going to make it easy for me. "She doesn't. But that's because we don't know her. I wouldn't leave you with someone I don't know."

She was emphatic. "But you *do* know her, Daddy. She's your friend and she likes you. And you like her, you said so."

I felt cornered. "I did. But you can still like someone and not know them well enough to leave your daughter with them." I scratched at my beard. "I'll tell Mary not to bother."

Poppy returned to her desk.

"It's a shame, because she was going to bring popcorn and cards." I watched as Poppy stopped colouring. "I'll go and tell her." I left the room.

On entering the lounge, Mary could be seen cleaning the dining table. I was about to cancel our arrangement when I felt a tug on my right hand. "Mary…"

"No, Daddy! No!" Poppy whispered, wrapping both her hands around my hand. "Don't tell Mary."

I put one knee on the floor and bent down to Poppy's height. "Don't tell her what?"

"I want her to stay," she implored, turning my face to hers. "Don't say no popcorn and cards, Daddy."

I tried not to laugh. "Why not?"

"Just don't."

I kissed her forehead. "Okay. I won't. Just don't eat too many sweets, even if they are your prize for winning." She heard the word *winning* and knew what I meant. "I'd put the drawings to one side if I were you and concentrate on your sums."

She laughed. "I know my sums, Daddy."

"You do." I didn't take my eyes off her; she was everything her mother wished for and so much more. "You're a very clever girl, Poppy Grant, and I love you." I couldn't remember the last time I had said those words. It had to be four years—minus a couple of months—the day her mother left us: the last three words I uttered to my wife. The ease with which they came from my mouth shocked me, but not as much as it shocked Mary. She actually crossed herself, appearing thankful for something—probably a minor miracle.

Poppy's response was less spiritual and more spontaneous. She wrapped her arms around my neck. "I love you too, Daddy."

I stood, my chest expanding with a powerful cocktail of paternal emotion and pride, watching her scoot off, back to her room. Mary's eyes were on me the entire time.

"What do you want for dinner?" she asked, busily returning ornaments to their designated places.

Why was she asking? She never bothered to ask me. "I don't know. What do you usually prepare for us on Wednesday?"

"Wednesday is usually pasta night," she said, unable to meet my eyes.

I turned in the direction of my office. "Pasta it is, then." I pushed the office door open, still trying to fathom out why I was being consulted about food preparation. What date was it?

I checked the calendar on my laptop, slumping in my chair when the significance of the date hit me with the force of an uppercut. It was our wedding anniversary: fifteen years of marriage—eleven with Hope, the last four with no more than her memory to hold on to.

I focused on her photograph on my desk until she became no more than a blur. My heart ached, my eyes stung, my desiccated throat hurt as I reflected ... our marriage had been fluid, transforming: fresh water I gulped down, taking for granted its regenerative powers. I had given nothing in return.

I struggled to speak. "Forgive me, Hope."

That evening the three of us ate pasta as usual: lasagne with extra sauce and extra cheese, just the way we liked it. In the background Hope's 1950's playlist was on repeat as a kind of tribute. I marked the day by sharing anecdotes: happy times before Poppy's birth, our university days, the pokey bedsit we lived in. Poppy was so wrapped up in my remembrances I had to stop speaking and urge her to, "Eat up."

As best I could, I devoted the night to Poppy's mother and our experiences, and although it felt good to bring her back to life for my fellow diners, at the end of it I felt melancholic and tearful. The celebration was well intentioned, but I had yet to ask Mary how she knew.

I had discovered her plan to teach Poppy the finer points of gaming and card playing, I didn't want her adding detective to her list of skills.

CHAPTER TWELVE

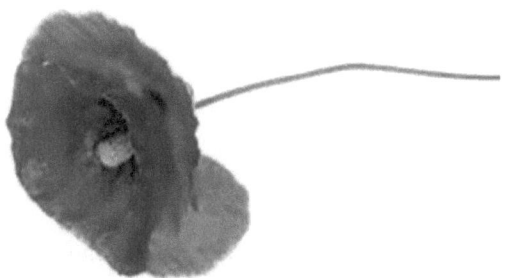

FORTUNATELY, MY MOOD HAD improved by Friday morning. The two glasses of red wine I'd had with dinner seemed to have numbed my senses, coaxing me to sleep even after such a stressful day.

When I entered the lounge at eight thirty in search of strong coffee, I caught sight of Poppy sitting cross-legged over by the floor-to-ceiling window facing the garden.

She turned her head to me. "Mary says he can't come in." She traced the outline of a fluffy head on the glass with her finger.

It wasn't until I approached her that I noticed the kitten. "She's right."

Her shoulders slumped as she sighed. "But, Daddy, he's sooo cute."

I folded my arms and took a long look at the pair of them, inches apart, separated by a transparent wall. "He's lovely, but we can't have a cat in the house."

Her mood brightened. "I could go out. Can I?" Her pleading eyes met mine.

"You know you can't. We've been spending a lot of time outside working on the boat. You need to stay inside today."

She rested her elbows on her knees, folding into herself. She looked as small and as vulnerable as the kitten, and just as cute. "He's hungry," she muttered.

I eyed him looking for signs of malnutrition. There were none. "He looks well-fed to me, and look, he even has a bell on his fancy collar. His owners bought that collar for him so he doesn't get lost."

Tiny paws scratched at the glass. "He *could* be lost."

I shook my head. "I doubt it. Cats never stray too far from their home."

She raised her head, inspecting the newly planted garden, the woods on the right, the lake and the open space beyond. Not a house in sight.

"If he got here than he'll be able to find his way back," I reassured her.

"How?"

I tipped my head in the direction of the garden. "Animals like cats and dogs leave their scent wherever they go. They can follow it."

"In the rain?" she asked curiously.

She did have a point. I didn't know the answer and bluffed my way through. "Yes. They have a good sense of smell." I beckoned her away from the glass. "Come on. If you leave him, he'll go straight home."

"Okay..." Reluctantly, she uncrossed her legs and stood, both hands pressed against the glass, a frosted circle where her nose had touched the transparent divide. One step at a time, she backed away, waving goodbye. The kitten walked in a circle and meowed so loudly, I thought she would fold.

She didn't.

Since employing Mary and having a special air filter installed throughout the house to keep the dust down, there had been an improvement in the frequency of Poppy's asthma attacks, but out there in the big, wide world, there would be no end of triggers. Having had my parenting skills tested only a few days before, and severely reprimanded myself for my recklessness, I was in no mood to take a chance, no matter how cute that kitten was.

Stepping over Poppy's work-in-progress comprising of jigsaw pieces the size of Ritz crackers, I made straight for my office. The sound of rain on glass alerted me to the arrival of the storm. When I glanced over to the window, there was no sign of our visitor. I smiled with relief, knowing there would be no medical emergency that day, which was just as well. I was planning on driving into London, The Prince of Argyll pub in Camden, to be precise, in search of a monster. The last thing I needed was to be worrying about a wheezy daughter.

On the drive to Camden, I constructed a persona Sam would be drawn to: a single guy struggling to get back on his feet after a messy divorce, no mention of Poppy or my past, merely a variation of the truth.

I was Max, a fellow delivery man based in Brighton; I covered the southeast coast and once a week, on a Friday, came up to north London to make a special delivery. I claimed expenses and stopped over, preferring to have a couple of pints than drive back the same day.

It was all very plausible. He would have no idea of who I was or how he had appeared on my radar. I was there to satisfy my curiosity. Nothing more. I wasn't looking to make friends.

Harry had said he was a natural blond—that made spotting him in The Prince of Argyll pub easier than I had anticipated. Like me, he was around six foot, a couple of inches taller than his drinking buddies scattered around the pool table. He was an easy mark wedged between shaven heads and mops of dark brown curls: king of the hill, a snow-covered summit rising out of an unfamiliar landscape.

His bomber jacket was petrol blue, a nice match with his jeans and suede boots. He knew how to dress and oozed self-confidence; from his posture alone, he struck me as a man who was used to being noticed. His profile was striking too: a Roman nose, cleft chin—more movie star than mere mortal.

Even at twenty-eight he still had that boyish appeal Harry had mentioned. It must have given him the edge at school, guaranteed him an easy ride as a teenager: bright blue eyes and a contagious smile the opposite sex couldn't help but be drawn to—he had it all.

I watched him from the bar and observed that he was more of a listener than a talker. I viewed that as a possible complication, one that free beer might solve; whether that would be enough to have him confess his crimes was unlikely—too much to hope for.

I was under no illusions: he was a shrewd character with a dark side, but I didn't let that small detail get in the way. I had made the decision to seek him out, believing I had him all figured out, dispelling the notion that behind that cool exterior there might be a ticking time bomb, needing only the smallest of jolts to set it off.

It had not crossed my mind that jolt might be me.

He noticed me almost at the same time I noticed him. I even thought I detected a slight flicker of recognition. His eyes grazed over me like a predatory creature, taking in the smallest detail: the cut of my jacket, my height, the half empty pint glass in my right hand. I almost expected him to raise his head and sniff the air.

He didn't acknowledge me but I knew instinctively that he had made a mental note of my presence and it wouldn't be long until we connected. I felt my pulse quicken in anticipation and leaned on the bar, feeling like human bait laid out for his delectation, positioned between beer mats and discarded menus for pub grub.

I finished my pint, leaving a single mouthful in the glass, and waited for him to approach the bar with an order of drinks for his fellow team mates who were too busy discussing the finer points of big balls and bad breaks to notice their glasses were empty.

I didn't have to wait for long.

"Same again, Mick," he ordered, pointing at the four empty glasses.

I moved to my right a fraction, giving him more space to stand while his pints were being pulled.

"Thanks. I've not seen you in here before." Now we were within touching distance, he gave me the once over.

"First time. Seems like a friendly place." I held out my hand. "Max."

He shook my hand. "Sam. You any good at pool, Max?"

"Not really. I'm out of practice." I caught the barman's eye and indicated another pint. "I used to play but my ex-wife wasn't keen so I gave it up. That and my car…" I fed him a line. It seemed to strike a familiar chord.

"Tell me about it. My misses did a runner. Cleared me out. That's love for you…"

I held up my pint. "Cheers to that."

He disappeared with two pints and returned for the remaining two. "Why don't you

114

come and join us? No pressure. Take a couple of shots if you like. You've got to be better than Stu. He's standing in for Reg. His wife went into labour this morning."

I turned to face his group of friends. "That's a good excuse."

"Yeah. Poor sod's been firing blanks for the past six years. Finally hit the target." He laughed, mockingly. "Anyway, come over when you're ready."

He strode away from the bar.

I marvelled at the speed with which he had sought me out and then invited me into his group. Contrary to what I'd expected, he was incredibly affable and hardly the monster I had envisaged. I didn't take him up on his offer of a game of pool. I was there to check him out.

I'd done what I set out to do.

Now when I read Harriet's journal, I'd be able to picture him and, with some thoughtful scheming and a large helping of good luck, might be able to put a dent in that *golden boy* image of his.

Either way I was not intending to meet him again, not socially.

But, best laid plans…

I arrived home on Saturday morning to cartoons, a daughter with sticky fingers and a plate of pancakes. There was still the whiff of popcorn in the air left over from the previous night's convivial card playing. While ballads played on the radio, Mary wafted about the house carrying laundry with Poppy skipping behind in her PJ's. I felt like a spare wheel on a bicycle and made myself scarce until the excitement of having had a sleepover died down.

In my office, I thumbed through Harry's journal and prepared to read more, keeping the image of Sam fixed in my mind's eye. Turns out, he was not the archetypal *monster* I had envisaged—he was just a man. Knowing that was like adding fire to what was becoming a simmering cauldron of premeditation.

Leaning back in my leather chair, I read, eager to find out what had become of Harriet after her beating and her shocking fall.

HARRIET - STOLEN DAYS

IF IT HAD NOT been for the glimmer of hope that came from the unearthly glow of a street lamp outside my window, I'd have assumed I was dead. By some miracle, I was still alive and was not lying in limbo waiting to be claimed.

Maneuvering out of bed was a case of mind over matter, brought on by the stabbing pains coming from a bloated bladder. That pain superseded all others and was enough to have me sprinting to the en-suite bathroom. Once I had relieved myself, I was reminded of what had happened. It came back to me in waves: aching, throbbing, stinging waves of pain that made it hard to breathe.

Trying to keep noise to a minimum, I closed the door and took a passing glance at myself in the full-length mirror. My pretty summer dress was so creased it looked like it had just come out of the washing machine, and my blond hair was tangled and frizzy. I hadn't dried it or even combed it after my bath, so desperate was my need to dress and make my escape.

On closer inspection, the woman in front of me was deathly pale, except for the bruises visible around her right eye and cheek; they looked as if they had been dabbed on with a brush, unsightly greyish-blue blobs and blotches circling her eye which was, thankfully, uninjured.

I saw the weakness in the woman; she was fragile and easily wounded, and yet, there she was, grateful for small mercies—how pathetic.

I hated her.

I splashed my face with cold water trying to rouse myself, to lift the fog encircling my mind. I had slept so heavily waking up was a struggle, as was every movement. As best I could, I crept out of the bathroom and made it to the stairs, gripping the bannister, pausing to inspect the pool of dried blood the size of a dinner plate on the hall carpet. I knew I would have to clean it up and sneered at the indignity of it all.

The kitchen was as Sam had left it: cluttered with pots, cutlery and beer cans. I gave the kettle a shake and switched it on hoping a mug of tea would bring some kind of normality to my war-torn existence. As I reached out for the tea caddy, I noticed a box of tablets. They were not Ibuprofen, the box was different. I flipped it over and realised they were travel sickness tablets. I was puzzled. Why were they out?

When I read the directions and the warning, I had my answer.

May cause drowsiness. Do not drive or operate machinery.

That explained my mussy head. In his twisted logic, Sam had drugged me, either wanting to ease my pain by knocking me out or, more worryingly, to make sure I was too doped-up to attempt an *escape.* If that was the case, his plan had worked.

I sipped my tea cautiously, wincing every time the mug touched my bottom lip, considering not only why I had been drugged but for how long. I had no idea what day it was. I looked around for my bag, I knew Sam had brought it downstairs with him when he put me to bed. I swiped my phone.

It wasn't Saturday, or Sunday…

It was Monday morning.

In the blink of a swollen eye, I had lost two days of my life. No, they had been *stolen*—stripped from me, along with every scrap of love I held in my heart for Samuel James Reynolds.

THE MORE I READ, the more I was affected by Harry's suffering and the hopelessness of her position. She had come so close to death, her situation was becoming perilous. It's a wonder she ever got out of there alive.

I was shell-shocked. But not too far gone to admit that I was becoming obsessed by her; not in a creepy, menacing way but as a friend, an admirer…as a potential partner. I loved her spirit, and I found her understated beauty utterly captivating.

With the grotesque image of her clotted blood still vivid in my mind, I read on, hoping her recovery would be swift and her escape even swifter. Little did I know what tragedies the fates had in store for her.

HARRIET - BREAKING FREE

I RETURNED TO WORK on Wednesday, still worse for wear but feeling as if I could join the land of the living. To spare me the embarrassment of having to come up with an explanation for my injuries, Sam had called work and explained how I had been mugged on Friday night on my way home from work. How I'd been beaten and thrown to the ground—left for dead.

Oh, the irony of it.

He even bought me a new purse to make my story plausible. Apparently, the police had been notified, come to the house, taken a statement, and later found my bag and purse minus cash and cards.

I had to give it to him, he had thought of everything. All I had to do was play along. What else could I do?

I was in no state to leave him and start a new life … but given time, I would be.

As the weeks progressed, Sam became everything I grew to fear and despise in a man. It went both ways, it seemed. My little quirks he once loved became annoying and provocative: singing around the house, lounging about in my PJ's on a Sunday, staying up late listening to music...

It was a long list.

Even though I had a good job, I longed to fill my days with something more worthwhile. I was smart but lacked education; ambitious, but without much formal training. When people spoke, I listened. I was hungry for knowledge. I made mental notes for the day when I could use them to show my understanding or produce them as evidence for a prosecution.

But I didn't get the chance.

Just staying alive was a feat in itself. I had to accept the fact that I wasn't going anywhere. All escape routes were closed to me.

To preserve my physical and mental well-being, I became passive in every sense of the word. Rough, irregular edges that seemed to spur him into action were flattened out, leaving a smooth, ornamental figure. I believed he had ruined me, and I was worthless and unlovable.

Through a combination of bad luck and bad timing on my part, and bad behaviour on Sam's, I became suicidal.

For weeks, I played around with the idea of suicide. Who wouldn't under the circumstances? The *what if*'s and the *why nots* of the pitiful process were on repeat in my head like a chorus of black birds: harbingers of my premeditated death.

Left alone one Friday night, I reflected on the chasm that had formed between the person I was and the person I *thought* I was. My persona had been manhandled as an artist might a ball of clay, pulling it this way then that way, to achieve the desired shape and texture—that was me.

It took his sociopathic behaviour to wake me up to three undeniable facts.

One: I had been designed to his personal specification, but there was always the possibility that I could change.

Two: I was his possession and that's why he believed he could do whatever he wanted to me.

Three: If things stayed as they were, I would be dead within the year.

Once I accepted that, I could plan for my future unhampered by pangs of guilt or blame. He would *never* change. That meant I had to, even if it came at a price.

Before he returned home, the monster inside him shaken and stirred into wakefulness, I came to a decision. I faced the hall mirror and spat out my declaration like venom, "I'm leaving you! You can beat me but, in the end, you'll never fucking win!" With an acrid aftertaste stinging my tongue, I headed up to bed.

CHAPTER THIRTEEN

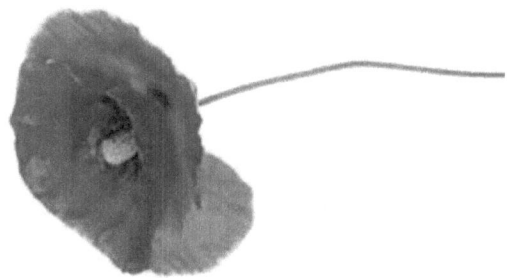

I CALLED OUT, "BRAVO!" Then looked around to see if anyone had heard me.

I placed down Harry's journal, but not before rereading her spirited declaration. I envisioned grabbing hold of Sam by the lapels on his blue bomber and screaming into his face: "You tried to break her but you didn't, you fucker! She got away from you and you'll never get your hands on her."

With increasing delight, I returned to the kitchen for something to quench my thirst. It was only one in the afternoon but having read Harry's last entry I felt the need to celebrate her imminent emancipation from her demon.

I returned with a bottle of beer and a couple of biscuits, still hot from the oven … and Poppy in tow.

"What are you doing, Daddy?" she asked sliding onto my knee.

"I'm reading."

She picked up the journal. "Is it a story?" The pages fanned open between her hands.

"Kind of. More of an autobiography."

"What's an *auto bigraffy*?" she asked, looking into my face for an explanation she could understand.

"It's when a person writes about their life, what they've done, who they've met…"

She ran her fingers over the handwritten words. "Are there animals?"

I shook my head. "I don't think so."

The journal fell onto the desk with a gentle thud. "I like animal stories, or stories about princesses and fairies."

I lifted her down onto her feet. "I know. Maybe we can read one of those stories later."

"Okay. I'll get a book." She scooted off with not so much as a goodbye.

I heard the patter of her boots on the tiled floor, the familiar clip clop all the way to her bedroom. With a smile on my face, I finished off the biscuits, taking a moment to dust the crumbs off the journal before continuing. I had so many expectations.

I wanted Harry to pack her bags that very minute and make a dash for the nearest train station, to keep running and never look back. Of course, I knew it was not going to b that simple...

HARRIET - DOWN AND OUT

THERE ARE TIMES WHEN you stop what you're doing to take stock and ask yourself,

What's the point?

What's the purpose of my so-called life?

I found myself doing just that at least twice a day. The minute I would stop working, I would drift off and begin wishing I was someone else, because being anyone else had to be better than being me.

Even with my newfound resolve to not let Sam win, I struggled to find the silver lining amid the dark cloud that hung over me, believing I had very little to show for an unremarkable life. My one saving grace was that I had a tiny baby growing inside me. I would mother a child.

But, just when you think things can't get any worse—they do.

In the three weeks after the 'mugging' I had kept myself busy. I was domesticity personified: I became the obedient wife and did anything to stay out of Sam's way, day and night, giving him no reason to beat or berate me. I swallowed my pride and put my baby first.

His disreputable enterprise expanded, making it necessary for him to go out most nights. The money he made from it meant we didn't have to worry when my next payday was. Best of all, 'being flushed,' as he called it, went some way toward restoring his beleaguered reputation. If his peers had known what he was up to, they would have torn a strip off him. But, like so much of what Sam got up to behind closed doors, it wasn't revealed, and his golden boy status remained intact.

I knew the truth: he was a charlatan, and a good one at that.

He liked to flash his cash and even bought me gifts, the *spoils of war*, he called them: ornaments and trinkets, mostly, occasionally small pieces of jewellery—all second hand, of course.

I even Googled one of the items: a china teacup and saucer beautifully hand painted with an inscription on the underside of the cup. It turned out to be a collector's item worth £250. I knew there was not a chance in hell that he had paid £250 for it; it had to be either a fake or stolen property. The same could be said for the crystal vase, the silver letter opener and the paperweight with a red flower trapped for eternity in frosted glass.

I must admit, I grew to love them all, not because he had given them to me as gifts, but because each had a story to tell: they had all belonged to people who were happier than me, at least in my versions of their stories they were.

On a dismal day in September that became a universal truth.

I had managed to keep my pregnancy a secret for eight weeks and had endured the usual bout of morning sickness without anyone putting two and two together—particularly Sam as he never heard my alarm go off at seven.

That Monday morning, I woke feeling unwell, and nibbled on a dry cracker in an attempt to stave off nausea. I drove to work but felt so dizzy on the walk to the surgery

I thought I might faint.

Noticing how pale I was, my friend Moira rushed over to me. She sat me down and insisted the nurse take my blood pressure. Concerned by my condition, she called the doctor immediately. I decided to confide in him, explained my symptoms and that I was almost two months into my pregnancy.

That decision saved my life.

The pain in my stomach became excruciating, making me double up and call out all the way to the Accident and Emergency department at the University College Hospital. Everything seemed to happen so quickly, and the morphine they gave me helped to numb the pain, but it did little to reassure me that the life growing inside me would survive.

When I came round, I was in a small side room with one other woman of a similar age to me. She was barefooted and a pitiful figure in her oversized hospital gown; the sadness etched on her face needed no explanation—she had 'lost' her baby. I feared it would only be a matter of time before I wore the same expression.

I waited three hours for the consultant obstetrician to break the news. In that time, I flicked through a magazine, refused lunch, asked for more pain relief and slept. When he did arrive, I was barely conscious. He spoke of a cornual pregnancy. I had no idea what it was and what had gone wrong. I asked questions and still the language tied me in knots. He asked if I had fallen or slipped in the past few weeks and I shook my head, like always. He patted my hand and said I didn't need to know the finer details—there would be time enough for discussing the procedure. All I needed to know was that my condition was rare and had been potentially life threatening.

As hard as he tried to soften the blow of losing what he referred to as *pregnancy tissue,* considering an underdeveloped speck of life unworthy of being called *baby*, it became clear that I was lucky to be alive. During surgery he had discovered that I had a bicornuated uterus. He described it as being heart shaped.

Imagine the irony.

The *gestational sac,* as it had become in his medical jargon—I still heard *baby*— had shifted from my womb and become lodged in my uterus in the cornual region.

Taking into account my blood loss and the level of trauma sustained, he had no alternative but to perform a hysterectomy. I didn't understand too much of what he said but that single, earth-shattering word that came before, "I'm so sorry," needed no translation.

I looked over at the woman in the bed opposite me. She sat on the edge of it looking out of the window, her skin the colour of her off-white gown, her hands shredding paper tissues.

"What's your name?" I called over to her, watching her body jolt at the unexpected sound of my voice.

"Ruth," she answered. As if in slow motion, she turned her head to me. "My baby died," she whispered, pure grief distorting her features and turning her eyes into glossy grey marbles.

"I'm so sorry, Ruth." Fighting back tears, I asked. "How far along were you?"

Her tormented stare settled on the glass. "Five months. This time two days ago she was kicking…" Finding it impossible to carry the weight of her grief, she slumped over onto the bed, her tears puddling on the pillow.

"That's so sad." It truly was. She had felt that tiny being move inside her one minute, and the next—it was gone. I'd not known what it was like to transcend the ordinary, to become a miracle maker. I knew the life growing inside me was no more than a collection of cells, but it was life and it lived long enough for me to fall in love with it—my one and only creation, the Devil's seed but my salvation. It had been taken from me along with any possibility of ever giving birth to another.

My body had been broken and I couldn't keep my baby safe.

I slipped under the crisp, white sheet, pulled it over my head like a shroud, held my breath for as long as I could, and longed to die.

SOFTLY, I PLACED HARRY'S journal on my desk, resting my right hand on the faded blue cover like a man stumbling across the Jupiter Stone. Initially, I'd seen the amalgamation of our two souls as an act of comfort for her in the writing of a journal and for me in the reading of it—a kind of bond carved out of despair and empathy. So moved was I by Harry's entry, I felt the need to do something—anything.

Like a guilty man in the dock, I prepared to swear an oath of allegiance, not to my God or my country, but to a purple-clad, young woman I barely knew. Of course, my oath bore no intrinsic value; no one was there to see it, document it and hold it over me like the lightning sword. It was just for me, something to hold on to, to anchor me in place when life's rough seas tossed me this way or that and sharp rocks that appeared out of the dark night pierced my guilty soul.

For four years I'd been drowning in abject misery. Inadvertently, Harriet had shown me what it was to breathe again, as she obviously had. Like her, I had lazed in bed and longed for Death to claim me, held my breath until my lungs burned and purple dots appeared before my eyes.

Like her, I'd sought answers:

What's the point?

What's the purpose of my so-called life?

She had been dragged down and faced some of the worst challenges imaginable and still managed to reach for the light. And now it was my turn to do the same—to do the right thing. I wanted to do for her what I had not done for Hope and, through an act of compassion, seek retribution.

She was giving me a second chance.

When I stood, a shower of crumbs fell to the floor. I grabbed a sheet of paper, brushed them onto it and tossed it into the waste paper bin. Even that insignificant gesture was revealing. I was starting to notice the smallest of details; how Mary was introducing light, noise and activity back into the house, how Poppy was familiarising me with her world of colour and creativity, a world I had not been aware of a month ago. The virtual blindfold that had prevented me from seeing the beauty in my life had been removed and my sight restored, giving me a better sense of who I was.

And then there was Harry.

Knowing she would pull through her operation gave me hope. In spite of everything she had endured, she found strength within her to breathe again, then again, then again… I had no way of telling what route my life would take; as hard as I might try to take control, as I had always done in the past, there would be unpredictable twists and turns, but I recognised that I was learning to face up to whatever came my way.

When I raised my head, it was to see Poppy standing in the doorway, one hand clutching a cookie, the other grappling with an oversized book. Through chocolate-coated lips came the words, "Story time, Daddy."

I nodded. "Yes, it is." I slipped Harry's journal into the top drawer. "I'll see you in the lounge. Make sure you wipe your hands, you don't want to give those fairies dirty faces."

She grinned and spun around, her boots squeaking like caged mice.

CHAPTER FOURTEEN

IT WAS TOO WINDY to take our newly restored boat out on the lake on Sunday. Autumn was upon us, appearing like an unwanted guest. Her overbearing presence caused ripples and waves to form on the lake and turned the trees into howling giants.

Fearing that Poppy might be blown over or swept away in a whirlwind, we stayed indoors, threw down a sheet and worked on the oars. I scraped away the chipped varnish, sanded the lengths of wood until they were smooth and splinter free and Poppy applied the wood preserver. Because of the fumes, I made her wear a paper mask I had bought for her.

At first she protested, not because of the discomfort, but more to do with her not being able to chat while wearing it. I pretended not to be able to understand her muffled ramblings and, becoming frustrated, she flicked it off her mouth and nose, wearing it like a comical helmet.

"You look like a baby unicorn," I remarked with a sideways glance.

"I don't want to be a unicorn," she protested. "I want to paint. This is not paint. It has no colour." She held her brush out in front of my face. "Look!"

I chuckled. "That's because it's something you put on to protect the wood, so it doesn't fall apart after being in the water for a long time. You don't want to be stuck out on the lake with no oars, do you?"

She considered my question. "You could go in the water and pull the boat."

I gave her a startled look. "Me? Why me."

"Because I'm only three—nearly four—and I can't swim." She resituated the mask over her nose and mouth and continued to apply the preserver.

She did have a point. I *would* have to get into the water and drag the boat to shore, and she *could not* swim a stroke. "You're right. We'll have to get you swimming lessons."

She did not need to remove the mask for me to see her smile; it showed in her sparkling eyes and in her brushstrokes.

"Once the preserver dries, we can put the varnish on. Won't that be fun?"

She repositioned her unicorn horn. "Is it pink?" she asked playfully.

I ruffled her hair. "Nope. It has no colour but it's shiny!" I raised brows, in an attempt to generate some degree of excitement.

Her shoulders sagged resignedly. Mumbling something I was not meant to hear she flicked her mask back into position and got on with the job.

I did the same while making a mental note to Google local swimming pools. If I was going to put Poppy's safety first, I would have to become her swimming instructor.

I smiled as I passed the second oar over to Poppy, not because it was the first time I had seen her roll her eyes, but I was visualising Mary's expression when I asked her if she had come across a pair of swimming trunks when putting my laundered clothes away.

After her day of rest, Mary bounded into the kitchen at midday eager to begin her working week with the usual mixture of elbow grease and hot air. She tipped her nose to the ceiling—I knew why.

"For the love of God, what's that smell?"

It was the turpentine I had used to clean our brushes, and although I had made a point of taking them down to the workshop, the pungent smell remained. "It's turps, Mary. It was too stormy to go outside yesterday so we painted the oars indoors, on a sheet." I tipped my head over to the door off the kitchen. "I've left the brushes downstairs."

"Good. I thought I recognised it." She bypassed me in the direction of the kitchen window and flung it open. "It's enough to give Poppy an attack, so it is."

"She wore a face mask and was perfectly fine. We might be able to take the boat out in a couple of days if the weather improves." I watched her pull out her basket of cleaning materials from under the sink. "You're quite welcome to join us."

"In that little boat?" She held her left hand to her chest melodramatically. "I won't set foot in it. Not for all the tea in China."

I walked alongside her into the lounge. "Why not? It doesn't leak."

She shook her head, so vigorously the band holding her ponytail loosened a little. Seeing that she had my attention, she paused to explain. "I know the boat's ship-shape and you wouldn't take our Poppy out in it if you were going to get your feet wet. As for myself, I'm afraid of boats, especially the little ones." She placed the basket on the floor and took out a duster. For the first time, she was about to reveal something about herself; not because she had been holding back, but because I had the good grace to listen.

"When I was eleven, we moved to Limerick. I would spend the summer holidays with my friends. We'd pack up a few sandwiches and a bottle of pop and head off into the woods. We'd tell each other stories and follow the trail all the way to the lake on the north side. It was a hot summer, hot enough to melt the tarmac on the road. We wanted to cool off, so we made our way to the water's edge. The boys rolled up their trousers and we tucked our dresses into our knickers." She grappled with her skirt, demonstrating what she assumed would be something unfamiliar to me. "The trouble was the ground was wet, like a bog, and so slippery you couldn't make it to the lake. Patrick, he was in my class, he spotted a boat a couple of yards away. It must have belonged to one of the fishermen. He wasn't around so we didn't think he'd mind us taking it out onto the lake, splash our faces, that kind of thing."

"So, you did go in the boat?" I pulled out one of the dining chairs to sit on and listened to her story.

"Ay. All six of us did." She crossed herself. "And what a mistake that was."

"What happened?"

"Well, we all took off our shoes, climbed in. Two of the bigger boys rowed us out to the middle. We were having a grand time, laughing and splashing. Then Patrick decided to go for a swim. He dropped over the side, bobbed up and down and swam around. Everything was fine."

"Did he get a cramp?"

"No. Nothing like that. Boys being boys they decided to race each other, us in the boat and him like an Olympic swimmer heading back to the shore. Oh, we did laugh. All that splashing, all the heave-hoeing and then as if struck down, Patrick disappeared."

"Where had he gone?" I asked leaning back into the chair.

She exhaled. "We didn't know. We thought he was messing around, he was like that. Then he appeared, thrashing around and spinning like a whirling dervish as if the water itself had got a hold of him." She covered her mouth. "We never saw him again. The boys were too afraid to go into the water, so they ran for help and the police came. For two days they looked for him. On the third day they were about to give up when they came across his body."

"Christ!" I shook my head. "What had happened to him?"

"They said it was the reeds. He'd got himself all tangled up in them and the more he twisted and turned, the tighter they held onto him. They had to cut the poor boy free." She squirted a coating of polish onto the duster. "His mother was heartbroken, and I swore I would never go in a little boat just in case I fell out."

I nodded, understanding her reasoning. "I see. I'll make sure no one falls out, Mary. In fact there's something I wanted to ask you about…"

"If it's about Friday night, no need. I'm free." She began buffing the glass.

"Thank you, that's kind of you but it wasn't about that. I wondered if you'd seen a pair of trunks anywhere. You know, in my drawers or in one of the storage boxes…?"

"Trunks! Don't be thinking of taking Poppy in that there lake for a swim…"

I shook my head. "I wouldn't dream of it. I'm going to take her for swimming lessons today."

"Lessons? At the swimming baths? With you?"

There was that look I had anticipated. Sheer surprise mixed with a suppressed smile.

"Well, I'll be…" She threw down the duster. "I did see a pair a couple of years ago

132

in your bottom drawer. They're probably moth-eaten by now."

"Great. I'll go look, and…" I turned on my heels. "Does Poppy have a bathing suit?" I knew it was a longshot.

"That poor child didn't hardly set foot out of the front door until a month ago, now look at her; she's going to art classes, painting boats and having swimming lessons with yourself. If that's not something to sing about, I don't know what is…"

I smiled warmly and exited quickly before she found her voice.

Not surprisingly the trunks were a size too small. I could tell that just from holding them up; also the colour had faded to a smoky grey and the elastic was threadbare. I needed something with more coverage, more suited to a man of my age.

"Poppy," I called. "Grab your coat, we're going shopping."

She appeared carrying two bath towels, weighing as much as she did. "Where did you get them from?"

She pointed over in the direction of Mary. "Are we going shopping again?"

"Yes. We can't go swimming in our birthday suits! Go get your coat." I pulled out a small sports bag from the back of the wardrobe, stuffed the towels in and shrugged on my jacket. I spotted my car keys on the coffee table along with two bottles of body wash, shampoo, a hairbrush, and Poppy's inhaler. I threw them in the bag.

Mary kept her eyes on me. "Don't forget to brush her hair while it's wet. And remember to buy her some arm bands and a rubber ring or she'll sink like a bucket of mud."

"Right. Good idea, thanks." I started to Google swimming baths.

"The best one is Saint Luke's. Get there for three thirty, there's swimming classes, so you can enroll her or get in with her." She gave me a wink.

"Right. I'll put it into my phone." If I sounded unsure of myself, it's because I was. What started out as an idea was turning into a military operation.

First things first, I made sure Poppy was all buckled up before moving out of the drive. "All set?" She nodded and fiddled with her dress. "What's wrong?"

"I'm scared."

I stopped the car before reaching the main road. "What about?"

"The water getting me." She sat bolt upright.

She had heard Mary's story. It must have been terrifying for a small child. All that dragging down... "Were you listening to Mary's story?"

Her eyes widened as she nodded.

"Don't worry. There are no reeds in the swimming pool. I'll get you a rubber ring too."

She tapped her arms.

"Yes, and arm bands." I rested my hand on her head. "Poppy, I love you and I will never let anyone hurt you—ever!"

She held out her right hand to me, her little finger extended like a tiny twig. "Pinkie promise."

I wrapped my little finger around hers. "Pinkie promise."

Reassured, she set back in her seat and wiggled her feet. I hit the accelerator.

"Daddy?" There was a question brewing.

"Yes, Poppy."

She turned to face me. "What's a birthday suit?"

CHAPTER FIFTEEN

I MADE A SPECIAL effort to tidy myself up for my Tuesday night art class: trimmed my beard, did what I could with my hair, even squirted my neck with some expensive cologne Hope had bought me. I convinced myself I was not getting ready to meet a woman, but that idea only lasted until that woman burst through the door carrying several shopping bags, and called out, "Sorry. The damn bus was late."

Harry looked fresh-faced and glowing as if she had been running. She had straightened her hair and the curls that used to bounce off her shoulders had been replaced by auburn ribbons that tumbled in delicate waves.

When she removed her leather jacket, there was the familiar purple dress but it was unlike the ones she had worn before: this was fitted. It showed off her figure to perfection and ruched in all the right places. I tried not to look too closely for too long.

Harry saw the composition I had arranged and did a double take. It was a China teacup on a saucer and a tea towel haphazardly tossed to the side of it. When her eyes met mine, I assumed she would smile; she did in response to *my* smile but, while mine could barely suppress the thrill of seeing her again, I couldn't help but notice that hers masked sadness.

The China cup and saucer stirred up old memories. A similar gift had been given to her by Sam. It was a bad idea. She was so unsettled I actually thought she would leave; she sat, then stood and swapped one pencil for another. It was painful to watch. It was not until Poppy entered the room and she was able to redirect her attention that she seemed more like herself.

I had already set up a small easel for Poppy and positioned it in front of a stool, next to Harry. I'd had time to draw a rough outline for her and, predictably, she was in a hurry to get started. She tossed her coat over the nearest chair and raised her arms for me to lift her onto the stool.

"Okay, take your time. Think about the shading like Harry taught you and try to include the pattern. Call me over if you need any help."

She nodded and leaned in. I could not have been more proud. What a talented and industrious daughter my wife had blessed me with.

Ninety minutes later, it was pencils down. I could see an improvement in their drawings. Some of the pencil strokes were even executed with accuracy and confidence. I was eager to view all the finished articles with one exception. Harry had found the exercise extremely difficult, so much so that her drawing lacked the flair and panache shown previously.

When I came to pass comment, I decided to be nice—nothing to do with the promise I had made to Lance—more to do with feeling thoroughly ashamed of myself. I had purposely thrown her off balance by venturing into forbidden territory. Her past was a well-kept secret that I couldn't possibly admit to knowing anything about. To apologise would be a sure fire way of disclosing my disloyalty.

I pressed on, finding something positive to say about her work, but there was so little to comment on that I moved on to Poppy's. I praised her for her effort and use of colour, but I was not going to award a prize; she had to learn that you have to practise and work a lot harder to come first in contests, and that being cute wouldn't always be enough.

Having spooked Harry, I assumed the night would end abruptly for her. Amid habitual handclapping Ben would be named the night's best student, then Harry would grab her coat and slip quietly away. Thankfully, I was wrong.

Unbeknown to me it was Halloween. While Alison explained what it was to Poppy, and I diffused talk of ghosts and evil spirits with references to fairy-tales and pagan rituals in an attempt to stave off nightmares, Harry began lifting an array of confectionary from her shopping bags as a magician would a rabbit out of a hat.

Inside each box was a selection of Halloween cakes and biscuits that caused quite a commotion and a crowd to form around my desk. We marvelled at the skill with which the fangs and fake blood had been piped onto biscuits covered in black icing. Harry pushed a particularly grotesque cat with fiery red eyes in my direction, making us chuckle at the voiceless insinuation.

Poppy's mouth was wide open and her eyes were on stalks; she had never seen multi-coloured biscuits, and certainly not chalk white, ghostly shaped gingerbread men. Gleefully she snapped off one leg then the other and proceeded to march her dismembered biscuit across her knees amid raucous laughter.

We scattered a little, some were sitting others were standing: twelve individuals, one class, munching sweet biscuits and bonding amiably thanks to the indefatigable Miss Harper.

Her Halloween treat worked as well as her painless plan to raise *me* from the dead. Not only did I look better, I felt better and, by the look on Poppy's candy-coated face, so did she.

The class dispersed, some heading home, others heading to the pub for a celebratory pint—Halloween did come but once a year.

While I folded up easels, Poppy collected pencils and Harry discarded the packaging and put the remaining sweet treats into a bag for Poppy to take home. I reclaimed a tin of pencils off Poppy and set it down on my desk. "Thank you, Poppy, and thank you for the biscuits, Harry. That was very thoughtful of you. Let me give you some money toward them…" I nodded in Poppy's direction.

"Thank you, Harry," Poppy said, taking hold of Harry's hand. "I had a ghost for my supper."

Harry laughed and made a ghostly sound. "Yes you did, sweetie. Don't forget to take the bag home with you." She turned to me. "There's no need, Max. I know one of the girls who works at the cake shop near the college. She collected them up for me at the end of the day, so there was no charge."

Poppy dashed off to inspect the contents of the shopping bag, leaving us facing each other. "Even so, it was a nice thought." She nodded, accepting my acknowledgment. "And ... I'm sorry you weren't able to demonstrate your drawing skills tonight. You seemed distracted."

"Mmm. I was. The cup and saucer are lovely but it's just me. They remind me of something—a memory I would rather forget."

I folded my arms and sat back on the edge of my desk. "I'm sorry to hear that. I understand." *I better than anyone,* I wanted to say, but held my tongue.

She looked me in the eye with such intensity I felt the skin on my neck prickle and rub against my collar. "I think you probably do."

She had Googled me.

"You're famous," she remarked.

I tipped my head to the right. "Not any more. Maybe in a previous life." I offered a toothless smile.

"It's such a waste, you being here." She scanned the room, stopping to examine the easels I had leant up against the far wall. "How can you resist the temptation to grab a pencil and show us how it's done?"

"It's easy. I don't draw and I don't paint..." The conversation was becoming increasingly uncomfortable. She really *had* done her homework.

"Because of what happened to your wife?"

I looked down. "Yes. Partly."

She glanced over at Poppy. "That's so sad. You're a wonderful artist."

I had not heard anyone say that for a while. It did wonders for my ego. "Thank you, and you could be too, if you set your mind to it."

She smiled and shook her head. "No way. I take classes in the day and work at night. I barely have time to sleep."

Poppy appeared at my side, clutching a black bat. "Daddy, can I have this, please?" Her eyes were so wide and her expression so pleading, I had to say yes.

I stroked her hair. "Okay. Just remember to clean your teeth at bedtime."

She returned to the grotesque assortment. "I will."

I settled my eyes on Harry. "So, you work at night?"

"Yes."

"Doing what?" My first guess was bar work.

Her face softened as she seemed to relax. "What do you think?"

I scratched my beard. "Exotic dancer?"

She laughed for the first time in two hours. "Yeah right! I'm five-six with crooked teeth and no rhythm. Would *you* pay me to strip off and dance?"

I had an answer in mind but kept it to myself, deciding on a noncommittal, "I might."

"No, I'm not an exotic dancer. I'm a croupier at Hot Slots Casino in the city centre. I've been there for a couple of years."

"It sounds like a demanding job." I had no idea what it entailed but I wanted to keep the conversation going.

"It does? Counting chips, dealing cards, watching people lose their life savings on the toss of a dice or a hand of cards? Yeah, it's demanding, all right." She laughed, letting me know she was joking and not being belligerent. I was still learning to read her and appreciated her visual clues. "Anyway, it's my night off and I agreed to meet up with some of the guys in the pub round the corner."

"You meet up?" I had no idea.

"Yes, we discuss our creations and, well, *you* mostly." Her smile widened.

"Really?" I huffed. "They can't have much going on in their lives if *I'm* the main topic of conversation."

She pulled up her collar and threw her rucksack over her left shoulder. "We don't. That's why we come out in the pouring rain on a Tuesday night to draw."

She had me there. "Well, you certainly made tonight special for everyone." I tipped my head toward Poppy who was scrapping black icing off the bat with her teeth.

Harry twisted her mouth. "Sorry about that. She'll need a bath before bed."

"Yes. She'll go to bed happy after a quick shower." I slipped my right hand into my pocket and rocked back, trying to look casual. Inside I could feel my heart rate increasing and my free hand slipping on the corner of the desk. "We've arranged to go into town tomorrow for lunch. Why don't you join us? Payback for the biscuits."

She appeared genuinely surprised. "Will there be real food?"

I smiled warmly. "I'm hoping vampire bats *won't* be on the menu."

"In that case... What time?"

I was making things up as I went. "What about one o'clock?"

"Great. Where?"

I had no clue and shrugged. "The last time I ate out people smoked as they were eating."

"That long ago?" She laughed. "Where have you been?"

"Indoors mostly. Y*ou* might be better off choosing the place."

"Let me think..." She tugged on her bottom lip and racked her brain. "Are we talking pub lunch or something more up-market?"

I had no preference. "You decide. Just somewhere quiet where you can have a conversation without having to shout."

"Right. I hate places like that too. What do you like to eat?"

"Mmm... We'll eat anything ... without icing," I declared easily, checking out Poppy who was looking more like one of the black cats by the minute. "Why don't you have a think and give me a call when you decide?" I showed her my telephone number and she copied it into her phone.

"That's a good idea. I'll do that." Noticing the time, she zipped up her jacket. "I'd better get going or they'll think I'm not coming. See you tomorrow. Bye Poppy," she called out. "No need to give me a hug." She was chuckling as she left the room.

I grabbed a couple of paper towels, softened them with water, and darted over to Poppy. Her face was covered in grey streaks, her teeth were black and her hands were so sticky they had become webbed.

"Oh my God. Look at the state of you." The paper towel stuck to her face and quickly turned into a speckled beard. "I'm glad Halloween only comes once a year."

"Why, Daddy?" she asked, twisting and turning to avoid the paper towel.

I laughed as her cheeks became visible. "Because I think you've had enough sugar to last you for the next twelve months."

I cleaned her up as best I could but her hand still attached itself to mine as we crossed the car park. As I pulled out into the road, I noticed that her head had fallen and she was lurching against her seatbelt.

I reached over and touched her arm. "Are you okay?"

She nodded, but didn't answer.

"What's wrong? Why are you sitting like that?"

She raised her head and turned to face me; her mouth was downturned, and she was pale beneath the smoky streaks. "My tummy's sick."

"Sick how?" I asked. "Sick with a pain or sick with … sick?"

"Sick with sick," she mumbled.

I tutted. "I knew you shouldn't have had that damn bat." I patted her head gently. "Will you be able to hold out until we get home? We're nearly there."

She nodded and leaned against the door. "Will we have ghost biscuits next year?"

"I think so. But we're definitely not having black bats." She didn't disagree.

Relieved to have made it back, I turned into our driveway. Poppy flicked off her seatbelt, pushed open the car door and vomited. I dashed round to help but was too late. Without speaking, we both stared at what looked like an oil spill. Poppy looked up and smiled looking decidedly ghoulish: her eyes were watering and her teeth and gums were jet black. I returned her smile, lifted her out of the car and carried her inside.

With Poppy showered and tucked up in bed, I sat down with a neat scotch to consider how the night had gone. If it had not been for Poppy's projectile vomiting, I would have called it one of the best I'd experienced for a long time, not because it worked out well for me, but because everyone left smiling. I had to accept that the class was not about picking up pencils or dabbling in paints, that was the least of it. Lance had been right, and Harry had been right too—three weeks in and I got it.

Just because I used to be someone—a successful artist and a loving husband who had the perfect life snatched away from him—didn't give me the right to make their night out insufferable. They were good people, probably just as lonely as I was. I decided to try harder—that's what Hope would have me do.

It was eleven thirty when my phone buzzed. The number was not recognised and I let it ring. It danced around on the coffee table a second time, and only then did it occur to me that it might be Harry. I snatched it up and swiped it. "Hello."

"Max? I'm sorry it's so late. Did I wake you?"

I recognised her soft voice straight away. "No. I was just having a nightcap. How was your visit to the pub?"

"We had a laugh. I just got home, so I'm a bit tipsy." She giggled, seeming relaxed and carefree.

"Really? A pint of water and bed for you then." I sounded like her bloody father.

"Yes. I think that's a good idea." She paused. I waited. "I just wanted to say that I'm sorry for prying into your private life earlier."

She was sorry! If she only knew...

"I had no idea you'd been through so much. No wonder you seemed like you had a brush stuck up your arse in the first class." She giggled again. She really was tipsy.

I smirked visualising her smile. "Well, I don't ... I mean, I didn't get out much. I suppose I wasn't used to being around people." Why was I telling her that?

"I thought so. You seemed so sad, and now I know why." Her voice had become a caress.

"You do?"

"Yes. I'm sorry your wife died in childbirth. It's terrible losing a loved one, but in such a tragic way? Jesus! It must have shredded you."

"It did," I confessed, surprised by my honesty.

"Like I said. I'm sorry for bringing it up. It was ... insensitive of me, you starting to cope with it better, and everything." She was whispering and I had to listen extra hard to catch her words.

"Don't worry about it. I wouldn't have told you who I was if I didn't want you to know." It was my night for confessions.

"Well, thank you for trusting me. I suppose we all have things from our past that we'd prefer to keep private. I get that." She of all people truly did.

"Thank you. Hadn't you better get to bed?" There I was sounding like her father again. All that was missing was the 'young lady' part.

"Yes. You're right again," she conceded. "I'll read for a bit."

My curiosity was piqued. "What are you reading?"

"I'm reading *Enduring Love* by Ian McEwan and really enjoying it."

"I'll have to check it out." That would be my next task once I put the phone down.

"Some of the characters are sort of twisted, but it's well written. I think you'll like it." She yawned loudly. "I can't keep my eyes open. "

"I can hear that." I laughed briefly. "Did you have a chance to think about lunch tomorrow?"

Her mood brightened. "Yes! I did. What about The Bellhop Restaurant on Princes Street?"

"Okay. I don't know it, but I'll Google it and see you at one o'clock. Unfortunately, Poppy was unwell when we got home and she won't be joining us. She'll still be feeling a little under the weather, I should think."

"On no! I'm sorry to hear that." She sounded genuinely concerned. "I bet it was the black bat that did it."

"Yep. It was one bat too many, I'm afraid." I laughed at my own joke to conceal my nervousness.

She laughed too. "I really hope she feels better tomorrow. Tell her I said hi."

"I will." I ran out of things to say and filled the silence with a cough. "So, you'd better get some rest. See you tomorrow, Harry."

"Looking forward to it, Max. Night."

"Night."

I sat motionless and stared at my phone for at least a minute. The last time I had conversed on the phone with a woman was six months ago, and that was with my mother-in-law. Thankfully, my chat with Harry was much more congenial.

I turned off the lights and quickly got ready for bed, eager to return to Harry's journal. I had left her holding her breath in a hospital bed. I imagined her gasping, coming up for air and making for a safe haven away from Sam.

I turned to the next page.

HARRIET - DYING SLOWLY

THERE ARE THREE THINGS I remember about my post-hysterectomy recovery.

One: being woken by the smell of coffee on the ward at seven in the morning.

Two: Sam being conspicuous by his absence.

Three: finding out some news so devastating it had me counting down the days until I died.

I was healing well, they said. I would be out in no time, they said, but only until a cardiothoracic surgeon called Mr Parikh came a calling.

He was a tall, dark-skinned man of around forty. I imagined him sporting a golfing sweater and Ray-Ban sunglasses at the weekend. He was polished and well-spoken with a good bedside manner, but no less scary for all his attractiveness.

He sat on the side of my bed, flicked through my chart and settled his dark eyes on me. "You've had a rough time," I remember him saying. I nodded, unwilling to elaborate. He had read my notes; he didn't need me to spell it out.

"I have some difficult news to give you, and I'd like you to listen carefully before you ask me any questions. Would that be all right?"

I nodded. All kinds of deadly diseases ran through my mind like a fleet of runaway trains. I strapped myself in and listened as he delivered his news in a calm, considerate way. I can't remember his exact words but the crux of it was that during my operation I had flatlined and been resuscitated. He had been called in to see what had gone wrong once every other possible reason for my heart failing had been investigated.

He took hold of a brown folder from the bottom of the bed. Clearly, he'd been saving it for just the right moment. He asked if I'd had fainting spells or shortness of breath, if there was a family history of heart trouble, deaths in the family—that kind of thing. I told him about my father dying young of a heart attack and he jotted everything down.

His pronouncement that I had a congenital heart defect fell on deaf ears initially. He explained how I had been born with a defective heart and it was not until heart failure occurred in the operating theatre that it became apparent. If the same thing had happened anywhere else I wouldn't have survived, not unless someone with good knowledge of CPR had come to my rescue.

I didn't want to hear the details but listened anyway to the handsome doctor on my bed speaking in a language I could barely understand.

"Significant defects in the interatrial septum and the interventricular septum were allowing blood to flow from the right side of the heart to the left, reducing the heart's efficiency…"

Feigning optimism, I asked what the cure was. He said I would need to slow down, have a modified diet, have multiple operations, but there were no guarantees. I should resign myself to living a more sedentary life. In other words, I was destined to endure a life that was no life at all.

If that wasn't bad enough, it meant that my plan to leave Sam was out of the question. If I couldn't work, I would be housebound—a sitting duck.

I was tempted to dive out of bed and throw myself out of the window there and then. What was the point of living if all I had to look forward to was a slow painful death?

Seeing my horror Mr. Parikh, took my hand. "You're young, Jane, and other than your heart you're perfectly healthy and there is always the possibility of a heart transplant."

I don't know what shocked me more, being diagnosed with CHD or the idea of receiving a donor heart from a stranger.

After three weeks, I returned home to a bunch of flowers and a takeaway meal that Sam picked up on our way home from the hospital. We spoke very little; the loss of our child, and the circumstances that caused it, made it impossible for me to look at him. Any kind of meaningful conversation was out of the question. The chasm between us was turning into a vacuum; it seemed to suck the air from the room, leaving me lethargic and breathless. Some nights I would fall asleep on the sofa and wake up in the early hours with a duvet thrown over me. I didn't complain. I wasn't in a position to.

The doctors had explained to us both the seriousness of my condition. In response to it most people would feel regret, be compassionate, seek forgiveness—not Sam. It had the opposite effect; it made him feel as if he had been cursed and saddled with me. I became no more than an untouchable burden.

There was only one thing that would allow me to make my escape, and that was the one thing I had absolutely no control over.

My fate was sealed.

WHEN I PUT HARRY'S journal down and removed my glasses, I exhaled, feeling as if I'd been physically wounded. Going through everything with her had made me lightheaded and weak too, and more emotionally drained than I had been for some time.

I flicked off the bedside lamp and pulled up the duvet. The darkness encircling me with all its unidentifiable shapes and recollections became no more than empty space, a defiant demon making its presence felt.

To ease my torment, I placed my hand on my heart and felt it steady and rhythmic against my hand. I knew what it was to have a broken heart, but I had the capacity to heal mine: she was broken maybe beyond repair.

I sincerely hoped not for her sake, and for mine.

I liked having her in my life.

CHAPTER SIXTEEN

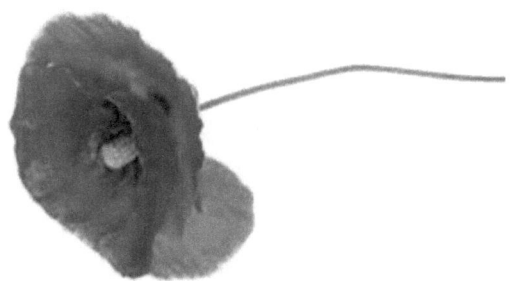

THE BELLHOP RESTAURANT WAS easy to find. The minute I walked through the door I was engulfed by a dense cloud of cordiality clinging to groups of cheerful diners. It was a cross between a traditional pub and a busy bistro.

I arrived early to check it out, only to find Harry sitting at a quiet corner table reading the menu. I wasn't sure whether I should shake her hand or simply sit. I waited for visual clues. She kept hold of her menu and indicated the seat opposite with her other hand. That was clue enough.

"Hi," she announced cheerfully. "You're early."

"So are you," I commented.

"I'm hungry," she said with a smile, not wanting to appear too keen.

"Did you sleep in?" I opened the oversized menu.

"No. I had a lecture at ten. Took some books back to the library and came straight here."

Of course, I reminded myself, *she's a mature student*. "Ah. Sorry, I'd forgotten you're studying. Psychology, right?"

"Right. See anything you like the sound of?" She called the waitress over.

"Are you ready to order?" she asked, taking Harry's menu from her. "Just to let you know, the soup of the day is minestrone and the special is lamb shank."

Harry smiled. "Thanks. I'll have the lamb then."

"With chips, mash or new potatoes?"

"New potatoes," Harry said after a couple of seconds. "And could we have some water for the table please?"

"Sure. And what about you?" The waitress turned her attention to me.

I was still deciding. "I'll have the same, seeing as it's the special. Do you have a wine list?"

She gave me a blank expression. "We serve it by the glass. There's the wine list." She pointed to another oversized menu. "Do you want chips, mash or new potatoes?"

"New potatoes, please."

"I'll come back when you've decided on your wine?"

I glanced at the meagre selection and put the menu back into its little holder. "No need. I'll have a pint of lager. What sort do you have?"

"What sort do you like?" she asked brusquely.

"Do you have Corona?"

"Yes. By the bottle but not in a pint glass." She adjusted her weight from her left to her right foot impatiently. "I can bring you a pint glass and two bottles."

"That would be wonderful," I replied, maintaining a straight face.

She returned to Harry. "And what about you? You just want the water?"

"I'll have a dry white wine—the house wine will do."

"Wonderful," she answered, mimicking me, I'm sure.

I rubbed at my beard and watched her leave. "She's a charmer."

Harry slipped off her leather jacket to reveal a pale lavender dress. "She was fine. You're used to fancier places than this, she could tell and got defensive."

I was so taken with her dress, I had not realised it was my turn to speak.

"Don't worry. She'll get over it. Just give her a decent tip." Harry made room on the table for the jug of water and two glasses, my two bottles, a pint glass and her glass of wine.

Instinctively, I started shuffling them around like pieces on a draughts board. "Does she think we're going to drink out of these or play checkers?" I tapped them with my knife, creating a tuneless serenade.

Harry started to laugh. "You're funny."

I felt my eyebrows rise in surprise. "I am?"

She removed her cutlery from her paper napkin. "Yes. Who would have guessed?"

"My mood tends to improve once I pull the brush from out of my arse," I stated, with a smirk.

She blushed at the recollection of her alcohol-induced comment. "I'm glad." She tried to conceal laughter behind her hand. "I hope it wasn't too uncomfortable for you."

I started pouring out my drink. "It being stuck there or me pulling it out?"

She laughed out loud. "Both."

I wrestled with the glassware, looking for table space. "It's not something I'm planning on making a habit of, let's put it that way."

She regained her composure and raised her glass of wine. "I'm very pleased to hear it. Let's drink to comfortable sitting and good food."

"Sure." I raised my glass and sat back into my chair. "So far so good."

When the food arrived, I was pleasantly surprised; the meat was tender and the vegetables nicely cooked.

Harry cut up her food and raised her eyes to me. "Do you cook at home?"

"God no! Toast I can do, and that's about it. I have a housekeeper, Mary. She doesn't live-in, but she takes care of us."

"That's good. I live across town, only a couple of miles away on Richmond Road. It's convenient for everything." She returned to her meal. "What about you? Do you live out of town?"

"Twineham. It's about a thirty-minute drive north on the A23. It's quiet."

"It sounds idyllic. How long have you lived there?"

I had to think. "Around four and a half years. We had a house built … my wife and I." The word *wife* caught in my throat. I wasn't used to discussing her—or myself for that matter.

"I'd like to have my own house one day. Property is so expensive in the Southeast. I just rent, but I'm saving up." She smiled, resignedly.

"Don't you have a partner?" I enquired between mouthfuls of cold beer.

Not bothering to raise her head, she explained, "No. I was involved with someone, but things didn't work out."

"That's a shame. Were you together for long?"

Like I didn't know.

"Yes. We met at school. I had a crush on him. It turned to love, and we lived together." She made it sound the most natural thing in the world.

I paid close attention. "You were very young when you met then?"

"Yes. I was fifteen and he was a few months older, so we grew up together."

I already knew the answer, but I asked anyway, "Where is he now?"

She glanced around the room. "I don't know. I left him three and a half years ago."

"Why? Did you stop loving him?" The question came out more direct than I had intended.

"No." She paused. "I still loved the boy from school, but he stopped being that boy. He changed and it was like living with a stranger who treated me... Well, let's just say that the boy never became a man; he became a monster." Her eyes welled a little with the recollection. "Everything I loved about him was overwritten. It was like the real Sam—that was his name—had been erased."

I knew exactly what she meant, but I couldn't show it. I feigned confusion and frowned.

She picked up on it immediately. "I'm not explaining it very well, am I?" She patted her mouth with her napkin and moved in closer, so close I could see the way her eyes had taken on the colour of a depthless blue ocean.

I nodded. "No need to explain. I get it."

She edged backward a little. "To cut a long, boring story short, things went from bad to worse and we became another statistic."

"Were you married?"

She shook her head. "No. We lived together for six years and then, one day, I just packed up my things and left."

"And you've not spoken to him since?" I raised my head to hear her answer.

"No." She returned to her meal having said everything she was prepared to say about the matter.

I could fill in the gaps for myself, but I played along. "What about your family? They must have been worried?"

"Not really. My dad died of a heart attack when I was seventeen and my mum remarried and moved to Australia. Frank—that's the guy she married—he has family there and so they emigrated. Last I heard they were very happy."

"Even so…"

"It's okay. We Skype now and again. She has a new family, grandchildren and the weather's better over there too." She forced a smile to cover her disappointment.

"No brothers or sisters then?"

"No. I had a younger brother, but he died of cerebral palsy when he was six. So I never really knew him. I just remember that he cried a lot." She shrugged away the woeful memory and took a gulp of wine. "Anyway, enough about me. You must be wondering what you've let yourself in for?" She raised her glass. "Welcome to my world, Max."

I tapped her wine glass with my pint glass. "Happy to be here—I think." I tipped up the corner of my mouth to reassure her that I was teasing. Her candour and easy conversation was like a tonic. Despite the misery her former life had brought her, she seemed to have put it all behind her. I admired her for that and began to relax—the half pint of beer helped.

"My wife left us almost four years ago…" I resorted to the same old line and began spewing out my stock response—she deserved better. "When I say left, what I actually mean is that she *died* almost four years ago." There. I said it and I hadn't gone up in smoke or been struck by lightning.

Already knowing that, she simply nodded and squeezed her lips tightly shut as if there was no utterance that could adequately convey her sympathy. I liked that she didn't gush or offer me her hand like so many people had done in the past. Nothing anyone did or said would make the slightest difference, anyway—my wife was dead.

She screwed up her napkin in one hand. "I've seen how you were together: the articles, the photographs, the pair of you at the opening of your exhibition. I've never seen a more devoted couple."

Her declaration struck home with the force of a baseball bat, leaving me momentarily winded. I exhaled, "We were."

"Then I remembered how you looked on that first night at our art class." She seemed exasperated. "I don't mean because of the wayward beard, the worn out clothes or how you didn't give a damn ... it was your eyes: you looked as if the spark had gone from your life." She looked down, suddenly self-conscious. "I recognised the look, Max. When I lost the love of *my* life, I blamed myself. I wondered what I'd done wrong to deserve that kind of punishment, and you know what?"

She did not need my reply to continue. The fact that I was listening so intently, and nodding was encouragement enough.

She leaned closer and stated, "It took me a while to figure out that I'd done *nothing* wrong; that there are bad people in the world who do bad things to people like you and me. Shit happens, Max." She shrugged her shoulders and finished her wine, unwilling to face me, fearing she had been too forthright or too opinionated.

I reached for my pint, using the seconds created by her silence to evaluate what she had said. "No one has explained what happened quite like that," I remarked coolly. For as long as I could remember, I had blamed myself for Hope's death, assumed that I had it in my power to somehow have prevented what had taken place in our house that day. The way Harry was describing it made it seem as if I had been a victim too.

She slumped in her chair. "I'm sorry. You don't need me telling you what you should be feeling. I know that losing someone you love is heart-breaking, and to lose them in tragic circumstances is even worse." She raised her arm to attract the attention of the waitress. "I'll get the check."

I reached for her arm and lowered it. "I'm not ready to leave yet." I snatched at the oversized dessert menu. "I can't wait to see what sweet delights they have on offer."

"I heard that the red velvet cake's really good." She suppressed a giggle.

I shook my head. "There you go again with the icing." I glanced up from the menu. "I know where there's the most amazing carrot cake."

"I love carrot cake," she announced, putting the dessert menu in the rack.

I waved our charming waitress over. "Can we have the bill, please?"

She appeared at our table in a flash. "No room for dessert?"

Harry shook her head. "No, thank you."

"My compliments to the chef," I said with a smile. "The lamb was delicious."

She stopped in her tracks. "It was?"

I nodded.

"I'll tell him you said so. I'll be right back with your bill." She smiled and disappeared with our glasses.

I paid the bill with my card, threw down a five-pound note and reached for my coat. When I turned to invite Harry to sample carrot cake at the Grant residence, she was a few paces behind, having been accosted by our smiling waitress.

Standing outside, feeling the cold air on my face, I threw my scarf around my neck and stuck my hands in my pocket. All around people were scattering in different directions like leaves caught up in the breeze. Neon signs and headlights appeared out of the afternoon gloom; blazing balls of white light creating an optical illusion. Looking left and right it appeared that the mid-week shoppers had ghostly halos—heavenly angels milling around, wearing winter coats and waterproof shoes.

There was one exception.

From my sheltered position, out of the wind, *I* was devoid of any light; my face was no more than a shadow. People like me who had stopped believing, those of us who had sinned, didn't get to be blessed. We sought redemption at best and justice at worst—or whichever came first in my case.

I waited for no more than five minutes for Harry to come join me on the pavement. "I wondered where you were."

She zipped up her leather jacket. "Linda, our waitress, wanted to ask me something."

I ventured a guess. "If your wine was okay?"

"No! What do *I* know about wine?" She looked left then right. "Which way's the carrot cake, then?"

I extended my arm in the direction of the car park. "Walk this way." We walked briskly, a forceful wind blowing her hair across her face when we reached a crossroads. Tiring of her vision being impaired she lifted a purple beanie out of her bag and pulled it down to just above her eyes. It suited her, made her look younger than her years, like she didn't give a damn.

She bumped my arm with her shoulder. "Don't you want to know what she asked me?"

I shook my head. "Not really. I can't see it having much to do with ending the conflict in the Middle East or whether you side more with Jung's or Freud's version of psychoanalytical theory…"

She grabbed my left arm and pulled me back. "Are you being purposely obtuse?"

We came to a stop so suddenly people had to slalom around us. "No. Not purposely," I replied innocent of any charge.

"She asked me about *you*." Her eyes widened on the emphatic *you*. "She asked if you were my boyfriend and if you weren't, to give you this." She placed a sheet of paper torn from an order pad into my palm.

"What is it?"

She rolled her eyes. "What do you think it is? It's her phone number. She wants you to call her."

I screwed up the piece of paper and placed it back in her hand. "And why would I want to do that?"

"Max, you're a good-looking guy, you dress nice…" She saved the best until last. "Not only that, you're a single dad."

"But she didn't know that, Harry," I said, holding up my left hand to reveal my wedding ring.

"She worked it out, Max. Single women looking to settle down have a sixth sense when it comes to available men." She took a step, I matched it and we moved forward once more.

"What made her think *we* weren't a couple?" It was my turn to ask the questions.

"She could tell."

"How?"

She shrugged, unwilling to answer.

I pressed her for an answer. "How?"

Her attention seemed to waver. "Because you and I don't match."

I heard the diffidence in her voice. "How do you mean? *We don't match*?"

"You have an aura about you that makes people look up to you. People notice you."

She smiled through her insecurity.

For all her ruminating, she wasn't completely healed after all. Sam had really done a job on her.

I turned her around to face me and took her face in my hands. *"I noticed you, Harry,"* I said unflinchingly. She was as surprised to hear me utter those words as I was. I lowered my hands, slipped them into my pockets and offered her my arm. "Carrot cake here we come."

Harry said very little when we parked up in front of my house. It didn't look its best. Of course, Mary had seen to it that the windows had been cleaned regularly and the drive kept in good order but the skittering leaves and absence of sunlight made it look more like a glass box than an actual home.

I closed the front door behind us and strode into the lounge. "Mary?" I called. "Anyone home?"

Mary peeped around the kitchen door once then twice, seeing Harry standing behind me. She dusted off her apron and came to greet us. "You're back early. Did you have a nice meeting?" She looked around me, waiting to be introduced.

The minute I saw her I regretted having told her I was going to a meeting, but how could I have predicted that I would have invited Harry back for cake? I only realised myself in that thoughtful gap between lamb shank and dessert. "Yes, thanks, Mary. We've had a very pleasant meeting. This is—"

"Harriet, I presume." Mary beat me to it.

"Hi, Mary." Harry shook her hand. "You keep this house immaculate. It's like a show house."

"Yes, Mary takes good care of us," I explained, determined to include myself in the conversation.

She batted me away. "Oh, away with ye. This man can take care of himself just fine. I'm here to make sure he doesn't poison his beautiful child—"

I interjected, "Talking of beautiful child ... where is she? Is she feeling better?" The house felt so quiet, I thought Poppy might be sleeping.

"She's in her room, up to no good I should think. I'll go and check." Mary departed, leaving a stream of floral scent in her wake.

"Can I take your coat?" Harry handed me her coat and I hung it up in the cupboard by the front door, leaving her to scan the room.

I stood back and watched as she silently fingered the plush cushions Hope had scoured the Internet for, caressed her face with the velvet soft drapes and inhaled the scent from vanilla candles—the only ones Poppy could live with.

She seemed perfectly at home.

As if sensing my eyes on her she turned and looked at me over her shoulder and smiled in such a way I was forced to take an extra breath. It was as if my most treasured picture of Hope—the one framed on my desk—had been recreated. It took me a minute or two to break free of my daydream, letting go of such a mesmerising recollection took sheer willpower—and a mighty distraction in the form of Poppy Grant dressed to impress in her favourite party dress—I knew why.

On seeing Harry, she called out her name and sprinted across the room. Rather than lifting her up, Harry fell down onto one knee to receive Poppy's enthusiastic squeeze. I looked over at Mary; she had seen many wondrous things in her life but Poppy's reaction when she saw Harry was enough to bring her to tears. She held her hand across her mouth to hold back emotion and shook her head in disbelief.

The way the scene played out came as no surprise to me. The more I discovered about Harry, the better I was able to see what Poppy saw, and feel what Poppy felt: an overwhelming desire to welcome her into our lives with open arms.

Poppy removed Harry's beanie and pulled it down over her own wayward curls. Using her fingers as combs, she gently straightened Harry's hair, stoking it, marvelling at the absence of curls. When Harry stood, what little light there was seemed to pool around her, turning the sleeves on her lavender dress into transparent wings.

I heard them chatting about Halloween biscuits and a sick tummy... Harry made Poppy twirl in her clumsy boots to show off her party dress. For a moment, I lost all sense of place and time. I would have been happy to stand and watch them for the rest of the day, or at least until the sun went down. If it hadn't been for Mary's hand on my arm, I probably would have done just that.

"She looks very young," she whispered uneasily.

"She's not," I assured her. "It's the hat. She's older than she looks."

Mary nodded. "Ah. I wondered when I would get to meet her."

"What do you mean?" I couldn't help but frown.

"She's all Poppy has been talking about for the past fortnight. Haven't you seen her drawings?" Her grip tightened on my arm.

I nodded.

"She's lovely, Max."

Mary returned to the kitchen before I could answer, "Yes, she is."

I beckoned Harry to sit down on the sofa, to make herself at home. Poppy took her hand and led her to the sofa where she climbed up and sat next to her, barely noticing me perched on the edge of the sofa opposite.

"How are you feeling, Poppy?" I asked. "Is your tummy feeling better?"

She nodded. "Yes. All better now. Is Harry staying for dinner?"

I smiled. "Sure, if she wants to."

She rested her hands on Harry's arm. "Daddy says you can. Do you want to?"

Harry could hardly say no, not after she had been on the receiving end of such a cordial welcome. "I'd love to, if you have enough."

"Mary always makes lots," Poppy gushed. "I'll set the table. She slid off the sofa and shot into the kitchen.

I called out, "It's only three fifteen, Poppy. There's no need to rush." I was wasting my breath.

She appeared with Mary in tow, carrying a white linen tablecloth, placemats and napkins. She skipped around the circular, glass table straightening out the sides, laying out placemats. Mary shot off to collect something else and returned with a shiny bundle of cutlery wrapped in a tea towel. She passed them over and Poppy arranged the correct setting, only three—Mary wouldn't be joining us.

When the glasses and candles were positioned just so, Poppy climbed onto a chair and kneeled up to inspect it. A proud smile played on her lips. "Harry! Come see what I've done."

Without a moment's hesitation Harry jumped up and walked over to the table.

"Wow! That's lovely. Did *you* do that?"

Poppy nodded so much I had to reach out to catch her as she wobbled on the chair. "Yes. I did it for you."

When Harry looked at me, I noticed that she was moved to tears. She bent over Poppy and kissed her head through her beanie. "Thank you, sweetie. That's very kind of you."

Feeling a hard lump in my throat, I headed for the kitchen. I had promised Harry carrot cake without even knowing if we had a single slice of it. I folded my arms and leaned against the door jam, noticing Mary was making tea. "Do we have any carrot cake left?"

She gave me a puzzled frown. "Didn't you just have lunch—at your meeting?"

I laughed, inwardly, holding back the sound of it behind a tight-lipped smile. "I'm sorry I called my lunch with Harry a meeting. I wasn't sure how it would go and didn't want you jumping to conclusions."

She turned her back to me to pour water into the teapot. "Now why would I do that?"

"Because—"

"Because you've not set eyes on a woman in four years, give or take a couple of weeks." She flicked me with a tea towel. "Now look at you with your dreamy eyes."

"I don't have dreamy eyes, Mary," I said, pretending to be affronted.

"Of course, you don't." She passed me a tray with the teapot, two mugs and a milk jug laid out on it. "Off you go. Let me get on with dinner and see what I can do about that carrot cake."

Following orders, I about turned and left.

"Tea, Harry?" I asked, returning to an empty lounge. It seemed the more I tried to establish a new kind of normality the more time I was spending on my own. I was beginning to feel side-lined, a strange feeling for someone who sought only solitude a month ago.

I guessed they were in Poppy's room, drawings would be scattered on the floor, books would be spread out on Poppy's bed, maybe her set of Polly Pocket dolls lined up like a welcoming committee.

I poured out my tea and strolled over to the enormous glass sliding door. Outside, the wind had dropped. The new plants and shrubs Mary and Poppy had planted looked like little islands sprouting up in a blue sea of slug pellets. Further afield, the trees were still, their drooping branches appeared to be relaxing, making the most of the respite. The lake was still, bar the occasional silver circle announcing the presence of a trout or a perch ascending from the murky depths. On the horizon, green merged into grey creating a muted autumn canvas desperately in need of colour.I remembered the boat.

Two pair of hands would be better than one.

After minimal persuasion, the three of us wrapped up warmly and ventured outside, remodelling the tableau with our cheerful chatter and colourful clothes.

While Harry and I dragged the rowing boat out of the workshop, down the cobblestone path and across the damp grass to the lake, Poppy regaled us with every boat story and song she knew and even with some new ones she had made up on the spot to commemorate the occasion.

All it took was a couple of heavy-handed shoves to launch the little boat into the uninviting water. We waited a couple of seconds for it to stop tipping over, and then sighed with relief when it became cradle-like, rocking gently from side to side.

We broke the silence with a noisy cheer, loud enough to scare birds from the trees, but not so loud that we couldn't hear Poppy's boots squelching in the mud as she danced on the spot. She gripped both of our hands and we swung her over the water. She screamed, giving voice to unadulterated delight.

"Well done!" Harry called out. "Good job, guys."

I tied the boat up on the wooden support at the far end of the jetty and joined Poppy and Harry on a slow walk back to the illuminated house. From our lethargic strides we must have appeared out of the fading light like weary travellers guided home by the reassuring brightness coming from our very own lighthouse.

As soon as we entered we became aware of two things: firstly, the pungent aroma of home-cooked food and the waiting towel that had been positioned on the floor by the door. I scooped Poppy up and Harry removed her boots, leaving her free to wander off and hang up her coat. We did the same; one hand on the wall, the other freeing our feet from muddied boots.

Barefooted, we sat down to dinner having washed up and served out bubbling moussaka. Before we could eat, we had to hold hands and say grace. This was something Mary had insisted Poppy do before each meal and I saw no reason to break with the ritual.

Poppy recited, "For all we eat, and all we wear, for daily bread, and nightly care, we thank thee heavenly Father. Amen."

With my left hand I held onto Poppy, and with my other hand I held onto Harry's nimble fingers. She had no reason to be cold, but they were almost icy, just like the last time. Her entire hand fitted into mine and felt so fragile that I lessened my grip, fearing I might injure her. While they both closed their eyes and dipped their heads, I took a visual snapshot: Poppy's cascading curls covering her face, the words of a blessing said with total conviction; Harry's hair falling in waves across her face, partially concealing her flushed cheeks but leaving enough for me to feast my eyes on.

The meal was delicious and our house guest equally as pleasing on the eyes and the other senses, reminding me of what it was to be close to a woman again and what it felt like to be a real family. Knowing did not make the not having any easier to bear. In fact, so profound was that realisation that I stepped away from the table on the pretext of fetching something...

Homemade carrot cake and a jug of custard.

We collapsed on the sofas, our faces glowing: one of the after-effects of our expedition—the other was fatigue. Too tired to make the walk to her room, Poppy crawled onto Harry's knee, rested her head on her chest and dozed.
Harry carried her to bed. I thought I detected a slight wheeze but thought nothing of it.

Harry loaded up the dishwasher while I made coffee. We carried our mugs into the lounge and sat opposite each other. She tipped back her head and yawned. "I'd better get going soon. My shift starts at ten."

Her having a night job had slipped my mind. "Of course. I wouldn't have asked you to help me drag the boat over to the lake if I'd remembered."

She held up her hand in protest. "Don't be silly, I've had a great day. Best in a long time, actually."

I nodded in agreement. "Yes. For me too. I..." The sound of movement in the hallway drew my attention. "Did you hear something?"

She nodded.

I was just about to investigate when Poppy appeared, barely standing, clinging to the wall for support. She was pale, her lips had a blue tinge to them. She was struggling to breathe.

"Oh my God!" Harry cried. "What's happened?"

I didn't bother answering. I picked Poppy up and ran with her to the kitchen. I sat her down on the counter and began to talk softly to her. "You're okay, Poppy. Daddy's here. Let's get your medicine." I attached the inhaler to her mask and placed it over her face, filled it up with the frosty solution and spoke to her in a quiet voice. "Now take a deep breath, slowly."

She gripped my hand and struggled to take it into her lungs.

"Just give it a minute. You're such a brave girl." I filled the mask. "And again." I breathed with her. This time she seemed to inhale more deeply. "Well done."

I took a moment to give the Salbutamol time to work before getting her to inhale another dose. She was still wheezing but not struggling, thank God. A tinge of pale pink was beginning to return to her cheeks.

"Okay?"

She nodded.

"One more puff and we'll get you a drink." I squirted the powder into her mask and she inhaled deeply. I felt her shoulders sag under my hands and the tension ease from her body. Panic over.

It wasn't until Poppy was breathing normally that I noticed Harry standing by the door, visibly shaking; tears streaming down her cheeks. "Are *you* okay?" I asked, cracking a smile.

163

She nodded. "What happened?"

I removed Poppy's mask. "Poppy had an asthma attack, but she's fine now." I brushed my hand over her bed head. "She's such a brave girl."

Poppy treated us both to one of her sweetest smiles. "I'm tired. Can I go back to bed now?"

"Sure." I slung her over my hip and she wrapped her hands around my neck. "Say goodnight to Harry."

"Night, Harry." Poppy stretched an arm out to give her a kiss on the cheek.

"Night, sweetie," Harry replied, sniffing and wiping her nose. She accepted Poppy's kiss and followed us, carrying a glass of water.

I pushed open Poppy's bedroom door and took a step back in horror. Curled up on the bottom of her bed was the kitten.

"How the hell did that get in here?" I yelled. "Did you let him in, Poppy?"

She released her grip on my neck to face me. "No, Daddy. No animals allowed."

I turned to Harry. "Will you put the cat out, please? That's what caused Poppy to have an attack."

Harry picked it up off the bed and disappeared. We could hear the glass door being opened then closed. I pulled off Poppy's top blanket and threw it out in the hall. When she was settled in bed, I pressed her again. "Are you sure you didn't let the kitten in? Because if you did, it's okay to tell me, I won't be cross."

She shook her head. "I didn't. I didn't see the kitten. I was just sick in my…" She tapped her throat.

"In your chest."

She nodded.

"So, you didn't know the kitten was here, in your room?"

"No. I would tell." She was too sleepy to be interrogated further.

I believed her. She didn't lie and especially not about something as serious as this. "Do you need to go to the toilet?"

She shook her head.

"Okay. Now go back to sleep. I'll see you in the morning." I kissed her forehead and edged toward the door but changed my mind and checked her window. It was closed but the lock was off. "Night, Poppy. Sweet dreams."

Harry left around nine thirty, having had a stiff drink, dried her eyes and smartened herself up. Seeing Poppy like that had scared her. It had scared me, but I knew better than to panic. She was still shaken when she left but did manage to force a smile as she climbed into the taxi.

I asked her if her day had been ruined because of it. She said it *would* have been if anything dreadful had happened to Poppy but as I'd handled the situation so well, she was just relieved to see her breathing normally again.

Finding the kitten lying on Poppy's bed had been a terrible shock. NO PETS was a house rule—one *someone* had broken.

I decided against calling Mary there and then, it was late, and she would probably be in bed, but I would demand an explanation in the morning as to how it had got into our house. Without thinking, she must have opened the glass door, maybe looking for us to wave goodbye when she left, or to assess the progress we were making in the launching process. Whatever she had done, it could never happen again.

Struck down by physical and emotional exhaustion, my shoulders stooped and my head ached. I fell into bed at ten o'clock with the haunting sound of Poppy's wheezing still in my ears.

Needing a distraction, I picked up my Kindle and began reading the copy of *Enduring Love* I had downloaded. A few pages in, and I was gripped but had to put it down. The thought of a tragedy appearing out of the blue served as a painful reminder of the night's events. The senseless loss of life brought home to me the possibility of losing a loved one unexpectedly, all because of a reckless act.

Letting that kitten into our house could have been catastrophic. If Poppy had not managed to drag herself into the lounge, I wouldn't have been able to save her. I was too busy enjoying Harry's company, good food and wine, engaging conversation, and music—components of calamity.

The one time I had lapsed into normality, something untoward had happened. My focus had to be Poppy—I was her father. I was responsible for her welfare and taking my eye off the ball was not an option.

I leaned across to the bedside table and took hold of Harry's journal, remembering her last entry. Her life was hanging by a thread and still she had fight enough to sustain her until a remedy could be found. As I flicked through the pages I had read, I pictured her across from me in the restaurant. Many times during our conversation at lunch I had been uplifted by the potency of her positivity; my heart pulsated with the healing power of genuine affection. I had received it and, more importantly, I wanted to reciprocate, not for Poppy's sake—even though that did cross my mind—but for my own. I had forgotten what it felt like to be touched, even platonically; so much so, the connection that arose when she placed her hand on my left arm caused a tingling sensation that started at my fingers and ended somewhere beneath my chin.

Over dinner, holding hands, I tried to dismiss the same sensation in my right arm, feeling as if I was being recharged and reanimated once more. Harry was raising me from the dead one limb at a time.

Returning to her journal, I was eager to find out if someone had done the same for her in her hour of need.

HARRIET - WITH EVERY BEAT OF MY HEART...

THE HOSPITAL HAD SUPPLIED me with an emergency beeper, not so I could call them, but for them to call *me* if a compatible heart was found. I slept with it under my pillow, I propped it up against my shampoo bottle when I bathed and set it down on the dinner table when I ate, just in case.

When it flashed and buzzed a few days before Christmas, I assumed it was a mistake. I remember those six words that would change my life:

We have a heart for you.

I tried not to build my hopes up and fought back tears long enough to write Sam a note—*gone to hospital, back soon.* I dragged my small suitcase to the front door, already packed and jumped into a taxi.

En route, I surveyed my neighbourhood, maybe for the last time: the shops, the new tattoo parlour, the recently refurbished pub on the corner—Sam's second home—and the single storey building on the edge of town that had become my place of work. I was tempted to call in to the surgery and say, "I'm off to have a new heart fitted, see you later." But it all seemed much too theatrical.

Instead, I texted my best friend Moira to let her know my news. She had offered to take me to the hospital many times, but she had her hands full with her mother who had been diagnosed with Alzheimer's and I didn't want to worry her.

I thought about calling my mother in Australia, but the time difference made it unlikely she would take the call. I left her a text she could read in the morning, by which time I would be out of surgery.

When I arrived at the hospital entrance, it was to a flurry of activity. I was placed in a wheelchair and whisked away to a private hospital bed, helped to change into a gown and given a pre-med to calm my nerves and lower my blood pressure.

A fleet of medical professionals paid me a visit: my anaesthesiologist, cardiologist and surgeon, who kept the description of the operation as simple as possible. He held my chest x-rays up to the window so the light could illuminate ventricles and aortic arteries which were no more than shadows and distorted shapes to me.

A senior nurse drew blood to cross-match the donor blood for the last time and inserted a cannula on the top of my right hand. In less than two hours, I was being wheeled to surgery, my hand in Moira's after she had ignored my text and come anyway. I was not scared. I was nervous, of course, but I had nothing to lose.

I counted back from one hundred, closed my eyes and put my life in the hands of a surgical team who became no more than a sea of green.

I woke up in a room surrounded by machines. I heard them before I saw them, metallic pieces of apparatus with wires, dials and flashing numbers barely visible in the subdued light of the Intensive Care Unit. I felt no pain, other than a dull ache that worsened when I inhaled too deeply. The ventilator eased my breathing and, although I was no more than a puppet on multiple strings, I smiled, feeling the trickle of tears and the dampness of my pillow either side of my face.

For the first time in my life I felt truly blessed.

Using my inner voice, I thanked my donor for their kindness and generosity of spirit and promised not to squander their gift of life.

Someone had died tragically, but they would live on through me.

CHAPTER SEVENTEEN

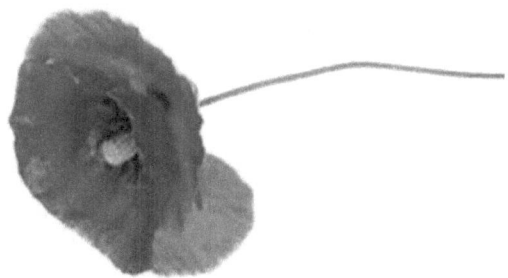

UP UNTIL I HAD invited Harry to our home, she had been a charming acquaintance, a novelty that I had found fascinating and was drawn to. After reading her last entry, I pictured her lying alone in her hospital bed, having endured hours on an operating table with a mountain yet to climb, and I was humbled by her fearlessness.

I squeezed the bridge of my nose, catching empathetic tears.

I was starting to care deeply about her; there was no denying it. Seeing her that afternoon with Poppy was the turning point. Every bone in my body ached for her, ached for her caress, her company and her undivided attention.

I was falling for her.

I had a decision to make, probably one of the most important decisions I would *ever* have to make. I could take a leap of faith and risk being irreparably hurt or die slowly in the dreary world I used to inhabit, where beautiful women in lavender dresses were no more than a fleeting fantasy.

I decided there and then.

Harry chose life.

I would choose life too.

Having come to a decision, I turned out the light, still experiencing the prickling sensation I had felt earlier in the day, though now it had spread across my chest, over my abdomen, and come to rest between my legs. It had been so long since I had experienced an erection that it came as a pleasant surprise to discover the equipment was still fully functional.

I closed my eyes and touched myself, and for the first time Hope's image blurred and Harry's came into focus, smiling; her hair swept across her face by a freak wind, her hands caressing my face, her breath steamy and sweet on my lips.

Dear God!

I crawled out of bed and showered, feeling scented suds and hot spray mixing to cleanse my satiated body. I towelled dry and headed back to bed to find I had received a text.

> *Sorry it's so late but I just got a break.*
> *Is Poppy OK? Are you OK?*
> *I was just thinking about you. H x*

I wanted to reply, *I was just thinking about you too.* But I didn't. I marked the text as unread, turned off the bedside light and fell asleep with the biggest smile on my face.

I was seated in the lounge when Mary arrived just before midday the next day, Thursday. She was her usual breezy self, humming an undecipherable tune and cursing the weather. She was used to my mood swings and paid no mind to my stern expression, assuming the previous night's meal, and whatever followed, had not gone to plan.

She had shopped for groceries and I helped her carry the bags into the kitchen, offloading their contents until almost every inch of countertop was covered. I folded my arms and positioned myself by the double drainer, waiting for her to ask what it was I wanted. It didn't take long.

"Will you be wanting anything special for lunch, Max?" she asked in her lyrical style.

I answered tersely, "Not really. I don't have much of an appetite after last night's drama.

She continued to open cupboards and drawers, unhindered by my irritation. "Ah. The lady left early then?"

"No. She stayed until nine thirty, until we got Poppy settled and back into bed." With that, I had her attention.

She stopped, my deadpan delivery triggering her curiosity. "What was she doing up after her escapade? She must have been worn out."

"She was," I agreed. "And she had an asthma attack."

She raised her chin "No! While Harriet was here?"

"Yes."

"Oh. Poor thing." Her expression softened at the mention of Poppy suffering. "I'll go and give her a hug. I thought it might be too cold for her, and that wind coming off the water…"

I shook my head. "It had nothing to do with the cold or the wind, Mary. That kitten she made friends with who sits on the deck on the other side of the glass … it was in her bedroom. She didn't know it was in there. It must have been under her bed."

She threw her hands across her ample bosom in horror. "Oh, Jesus, Mary and Joseph! How did it get in the house?"

I shrugged. "That's what I wanted to ask *you*. Did you leave the door open?"

"Of course not! Do you think I'm an eejit? The last thing I would do is let any animal in *this* house with the little 'un as asthmatic as she is. Perish the thought."

"Then *how* did it get in?" I unfolded my arms and held up my hands.

She massaged the skin around her neck and thought hard. "Did you ask Harriet? She wasn't to know…"

That wasn't the answer I was looking for. "Harry didn't let it in. She was with us the entire time. We left together. I closed the glass door. She took hold of Poppy's hand and led her down the steps to the garden. There was no kitten."

She returned to her unpacking. "Then I don't have an answer for you, Max. I swear on the life of my first born that I didn't let it in. I've been with you now for over two years, I know better than that."

I wanted to believe her. She seemed sincere, but there was no other explanation. "How do you think it ended up on Poppy's bed then, Mary?"

She glanced at the floor. "Did you ask Poppy? I said that if she tells lies, her tongue will grow and turn green, like a snake's."

I snickered. "Nice."

"I'll go and ask her myself. If she's fibbing, she won't open her mouth." She disappeared out of the kitchen, calling out, "Poppy! Come here, pumpkin."

I looked on.

Poppy appeared wearing her Wellington boots, a pale purple dress she had rummaged through her wardrobe to find, and a beanie, looking like a mini-Harry. I saw Mary's eyes widen. "You don't need to be wearing a hat in the house, Poppy. Take it off, please."

Poppy shook her head. "My ears are cold."

"Nonsense. It's eighty degrees in here." Mary held out her hand. "Come and sit down next to me." She patted the sofa.

Reluctantly, Poppy pulled off the beanie and passed it over, revealing a tangle of unruly curls. "What are we having for lunch? Can we have pancakes?"

"Hold your horses. We'll discuss lunch in a minute." Mary straightened her apron and took hold of Poppy's hand. "Your daddy was telling me that you had an asthma attack last night."

Poppy nodded.

"He also said that kitten was in your room."

Wide-eyed, Poppy nodded again.

"Now, it's a bit of a mystery how it got into the house and I was wondering if you felt sorry for it out there in the wind and the rain and let it in to warm up a bit..." She lowered her head pinning Poppy in place with a probing stare.

Poppy shook her head.

"Are you telling the truth? This is not the time for telling lies. " She inhaled. "Now, let me see your tongue."

Immediately, Poppy stuck out her tongue, and left it there for inspection. Mary jumped to her feet. "Okay. Good, now let's go make some pancakes, pumpkin."

Hand in hand, they strolled past me; Poppy smiling at the prospect of pancakes and Mary, having completed her interrogation, shaking her head.

The mystery of how the kitten found its way into Poppy's room would continue, but our vigilance was heightened as a result.

Come Friday, I prepared to swap an insulated existence, enlivened by fairy-tale creatures and Irish jigs, for a couple of hours in a workingman's pub with the self-effacing Samuel Reynolds, but not before I had answered Harry's text:

> *Sorry I didn't reply last night, went to bed early. Poppy is much better, so don't worry I'm catching my breath too! Do you want to meet up tomorrow in town? The three of us can grab some lunch and do some shopping. Let me know if you fancy it. M*

I told her a half-lie but hoped the lunch arrangements would make up for it and give me a chance to get to know her better.

I took pleasure from premeditation: speeding down the motorway at eighty miles an hour on Friday night at seven o'clock gave me the time I needed to think through my line of enquiry, to get the measure of the man whose belligerence and long record of bad behaviour was imprinted on my brain.

I was starting to break free of my self-imposed seclusion. The architect we had commissioned to design and oversee the building of our modernist house had followed our instructions to the letter and fashioned a refuge out of metal and glass that was perfect when it came to letting in light, but unhospitable when it came to welcoming guests. I had spent four years, maybe even longer, on the inside looking out, seeing little further than the end of my nose; meeting Sam made it possible to look inside, into the darkest corners of the human psyche.

Sam had become a fascinating examination of the sociopathic mind—or that's what I kept telling myself. I know now that I shouldn't have let curiosity get the better of me and concentrated on cultivating a meaningful relationship with Harry—but what is done is done. Instead, I went headfirst into the unknown unprepared, underestimating Sam's strength of character and aversion to common sense and decency.

I cut my cloth to suit the occasion. I became a mirror image of Sam: I dressed down, adopted a casual posture and relaxed into the role. I was about to order a second pint when I felt Sam's hand on my shoulder and turned unflinchingly.

"You've got good timing." I pointed two fingers at my empty glass and, Mick, the barman, followed my wordless instructions and began pulling pints.

Sam seemed on edge, a storm was brewing in his eyes; he drummed his fingertips on the bar and checked out the pub as a burglar might survey exits. His face appeared so freshly scrubbed, he had the look of a man who had come straight from the gym having lifted weights or run ten miles on a treadmill.

Even without further scrutiny I knew I was his antithesis when it came to physical fitness. I'd started taking better care of myself, but *my* body was not a temple—far from it—more like an abandoned shack that bore the marks of neglect and self-loathing. I had let myself go while he had remained lean and probably mean in the three years or so since Harry had escaped his clutches.

If I'm honest, meeting Sam for the second time was no hardship on my part. My delivery man persona needed no redress; it was accepted without question. In some ways I felt like I was reconnecting with the world, the world of men from my younger, carefree days. It felt self-indulgent, almost playful.

There were times when I relaxed, fell back into an old routine, engaged in witty banter, played pool. I had to remind myself of my mission, my objective: to see him up close and to find his Achilles heel and exploit it. One way or another, he had to pay for what he had put Harry through.

There were moments when Sam came across as decent and hard-working; a guy who was well liked by his peers and popular with the ladies who flirted shamelessly with him. Even without turning around I felt female eyes on us. I ignored their forthright advances, he batted them away as you would mosquitos, and still they came, drawn to him like he was fresh meat.

I broached the subject of lost love, explaining how my wife had left me four years ago; how I'd had the occasional fling but nothing serious, how I doubted I would ever find a replacement. Sam followed my lead.

"I met the love of my life when I was fifteen and twenty-four when she disappeared off the face of the earth. Jane Harper, she was called." I nodded. He continued. "She'd always been at my school, but I'd not noticed her. Well, you don't, do you, until they start having an arse to pinch or tits you can grope behind the bike shed." He snickered at his joke. I forced a smile. "But Jane wasn't like that. It was like she just appeared. Puff! And there she was…" He stopped to take a swig of beer and whatever it was that had him so wound up seemed to unravel and dissolve in the liquor.

"Where did you two get together?" I asked, curiously.

"At a New Year's Eve party. She wore a red dress." He expelled air. "You should have seen her, Max. My eyes nearly popped out of my fucking head and my dick out of my pants." He laughed with false embarrassment.

I laughed along and ordered a couple of shots to help lubricate his tongue. "Did you get to take her out?"

"Not straight away." He threw back the dregs from his second pint. "I had a way with the girls, you know? Those I hadn't shagged, I could count on one hand. I didn't have any trouble in the dick servicing department." He tipped his head, immodestly. "But Jane … she was different. I knew she was a virgin, so I waited … until I was sixteen."

"That was good of you." I remarked, hoping he was too engrossed in his recount to perceive the sarcasm. "What about her?"

He bounded on, galloping toward the climax like a thoroughbred. "She was a couple of months off and I was prepared to wait, but one night when my parents were out and we had the house to ourselves, she gave me my birthday present." He actually winked. "One I wouldn't forget."

"And what was that?" I asked.

Like I didn't already know.

He turned to face me. "Her."

"Nice," I lied. His comment made me want to christen his head with my beer, still in the glass.

"It *was* kinda nice. Took some doing, her being so tense and tighter than a fish's arse, but she got used to it. It got so she liked it." He laughed loudly, expecting me to do the same. A smirk was all I could manage.

"We're men of the world, Max," he went on, bumping my shoulder. "Some women do it to please us, others grin and bear it, and some women just like to fuck. Jane liked to fuck." He was determined to labour the point. "She liked it every which way." He threw back the shot and slammed down the glass. "Once she had me bend her over a park bench and fuck her in broad daylight. I was scared of being caught and almost didn't get it up, but one look at her legs spread wide and her sweet arse and I was in there like a rat up a drainpipe." He roared with laughter, it rumbled around in his throat and left his mouth like rolling thunder.

I swallowed hard, feeling ale regurgitating in my gullet. "Sounds like you had fun together."

Piece by piece, he was revealing his nature, one which would develop and mature into the monster Harry had described so vividly. I wanted to punch him there and then, but I didn't.

To give me some breathing space, I played pool. I was rusty at first, but it was like riding a bike and came right back to me. I partnered Sam against two of his buddies and we won easily.

By ten thirty, Sam was high on alcohol and in a celebratory mood. I sat by a side table and checked my phone—no emergency calls, only a text from Harry:

Sounds like a plan! I'll meet you at the merry-go-round at
one and we can take it from there. Looking forward to it. H x

I had no idea where the merry-go-round was, but it wouldn't be hard to find and wouldn't require the kind of investigative powers I was about to employ with Sam.

He appeared through the crowd with two pints and a bag of crisps, which he proceeded to tear open and share. "You're a dark horse, Max," he commented, stuffing a handful of crisps into his mouth. "You should join our pool team."

I reached for my pint. "Nah. I'm not much of a team player."

I felt his eyes burrowing into my cheek. "You should get back on the horse, mate."

"I'm not much of a rider either!" I smirked, pretending to misunderstand his suggestion.

He punched my right bicep. "You know what I mean. A good-looking guy like you needs to put yourself about a bit."

"I do?"

"Sure! When my missus fucked off it knocked me for six. I didn't see it coming." He wiped away droplets of beer with the back of his hand, becoming more animated with each mouthful. "Some of our friends thought she'd been abducted or sold into the white slave trade."

"Sounds a bit far-fetched."

"Yeah. I waited around for a couple of days, wondering what to do. I didn't call the police. Why would I? All that talk of abduction was bullshit. I knew that, and the reason I knew was because she took almost *all* of our savings, almost *all* of her clothes, and left me with almost nothing."

I shook my head and tutted sympathetically. Inside I was thinking, *you had it coming, mate.*

"I was the sad fuck she left behind, the one left to face family and friends when they asked where she was." He threw back his head and laughed. "And boy, did they ask! It was like facing a fucking firing squad."

His version of events were couched in such a way that he cast himself as the victim; no mention of his abusive behaviour. I pressed him further. "Wh y do you think she left?"

"Who knows?" He shrugged and offered a downturned smile. "Like I said, she was a strange one—a schemer. When I lost my job…"

I feigned surprise. "You lost your job?"

"Yeah." He turned away. "It's a long story…"

"I'm not going anywhere. I've got a pint in front of me." I held it up to make my point.

He did the same. "I did something stupid and paid the price for it. Still am."

"Go on…"

"I stopped a mate from driving us home from the pub. He couldn't even stand, and I offered to drive. I'd only had a couple, but I hadn't eaten all day. I'd worked through to get a delivery done before six. You know how it is, you set your mind on something…"

I nodded.

"It would've been okay but for some drunken bastard stepping out into the road from between parked cars. I had to swerve to miss him and hit a lamp post."

I felt my eyes widen. I was genuinely surprised. "Jesus! Was anyone hurt?"

"Yeah," he sounded contrite. "The three passengers in the back had whiplash and Terry in the passenger seat had to be cut free from the car." He bowed his head and rubbed his hand across his face. "He was okay, but he has a leg held together with nuts and bolts now."

"What a fuck-up!" I said, needing a couple of gulps to keep any additional comments to myself.

"You can say that again." He paused reflectively. "I lost my licence, lost my job and lost my girl because of it." He took a long sip of beer. "I had to move in with my mother." He inhaled deeply and exhaled noisily.

"But you got another job, right?" I was thinking about what Harry had said about his illicit money-making activities. What better time than right then to press him?

"Not really. I got work where I could and Jane, my ex, had a decent wage, so we stretched it out, thinking that once I got my licence back, things would get back to normal."

"But they didn't?"

"Nope. After being together for nearly nine years, I got dumped." That realisation seemed to hit him like a body blow. "Looking back, I should have seen it coming. But I didn't... Well you don't, do you? You think you'll carry on forever the way you always have until the day comes when you don't—end of story. She must have thought the grass was greener..." He shrugged away the comment with a twisted smile. "Without so much as a, 'See you later' the girl I fell in love with packed up her bags and left me." He sunk into his seat. "I'd have felt better if it'd been for someone else; if a mate had said, 'I saw her with another guy' I could have cursed her to hell and moved on, but the not knowing ... it chewed me up inside."

The noise in the room seemed to fade away, eclipsed by his despondent admissions. I nudged him in the arm. "I'm sorry I brought it up."

"It's not your fault. I try not to think about it, but I can't help it; it's an itch that won't go away no matter how many times I scratch it."

"Over time her memory will fade." I chuckled, not at him but my own situation. I was the last one to be giving advice, least of all to him. "I'm not laughing at you—at myself."

"You know how it feels." He finished his pint in one long gulp. "After three days I did call the police. They asked fifty questions and treated me as if I'd buried her in the garden. Two plain clothed cops sat me down, scrolled through an iPad and interrogated me for an hour—and when I say interrogated, that's *exactly* what it felt like."

"No way?"

He was on a roll. "I swear. There they were grilling me about our relationship, our sex life, where I was the night before her disappearance. And there I was thinking, *What the fuck? When did I become the bad guy?*" He was about to stand and fell back down. "I put them straight. I said, "'We were at school together—childhood sweethearts.'"

"And what did they say?" I asked, feeding him another question.

"Not much. They had nothing to go on. It was like she'd vanished. I had nothing to hide, except that she'd almost cleared me out." He finished off the crisps and screwed up the bag. "She didn't know I had another account on the side though." He winked. "She didn't take *everything*."

I smiled and cocked my head. "Smart move."

The alcohol was taking effect and he was starting to slur his words. "For six years we built a home together but in the last year, the year before she left, everything changed. We were living together but as strangers. I don't even think she loved me." His head drooped, and for a minute I thought he had dozed off.

He sat up with a start. "If I'd known then what I know now, I'd have let her go, let her spread her wings. But I can't... I need to know the truth."

I was so intrigued I turned to face him. "The truth?"

He rubbed out a dark beer stain on his jeans. "Yeah. I have to warn the guy she's with that she's not what she seems."

"She isn't?" My answer came as a reflex response.

"My darling Jane is more Russian doll than woman; no matter how many layers you think you've peeled away, there are still more to find—she has hidden depths and the deeper you dig, the less you recognise her."

I felt the hairs tingling on the back of my neck. "How do you know that?"

"How do I *know*?" he asked, blinking through blurry eyes. "I know because I'm the sad bastard who loved her, every single layer. And I won't rest until I find her."

I was lost for words. "Right," was all could muster. It was enough to pacify him in his drunken state.

He threw back his head and yawned. "I'm pissed."

I smirked. "You don't say."

He began fumbling with his phone. "I'll call a cab." He swiped his phone to reveal his screensaver. It was a photo of him and Harry together, arm in arm. She looked around eight years younger, not long out of school. They were both blond and beautiful and clearly in love.

"Is that her?" I asked, pointing to his phone.

"Yeah." He moved like a drunken sailor, his body lurching right then left and back again. "She was the love of my life."

"She's beautiful, Sam." After his confession I felt I owed him that and, besides, it was the truth.

He composed himself long enough to ring for a taxi. I returned our glasses to the bar. Mick ushered me over. "Are you gonna make sure he gets home in one piece?" he asked, leaning over the counter.

"Of course," I said. "He's in a bad way."

He started collecting empty glasses. "He always gets that way when he talks about her."

"Her?" I enquired, passing him a couple of pint pots.

"That girlfriend of his: Jane something or other, she left him years ago and he's never got over it." He turned his back on me and got to work, ending our conversation.

I had more questions for him, but he was calling last orders, rounding up patrons and creating a tower of pint pots. I missed my chance. I walked away, as far as Sam who was slumped against the door frame and led him outside. He stirred when the chill night air hit his face.

"Is my taxi here?" he asked, leaning into me.

A black cab pulled up against the curb. I walked him over to it, opened the door and pushed him inside, realising I had no idea where he was going. "Sam! Sam!" I called out. "What's your address?"

"Four Abney Drive, flat fourteen," he slurred, semi-consciously.

"Did you get that?" I asked the driver.

He nodded. "It's not far."

"Will you make sure he gets inside, please?" I asked, handing him a twenty-pound note. "That should cover it."

"Can do. Have a good night." He raised the window and pulled away.

I strolled in the direction of the bed and breakfast hotel I was staying in a couple of streets away, my hands tucked in my pockets and my collar up-turned against the wind tossing the clouds around in the starless sky. Only a few of the apartments and houses were lit, most were not, resembling dark squares on an enormous chessboard, flat and lifeless. I began to feel hemmed in by the darkness and quickened my step hoping to make it back to my overnight shelter before it caught up with me.

What scared me most was not the empty streets, but Sam's revelations. He had sown the seeds of doubt in my mind and I feared the approaching daylight would encourage them to germinate and drive out any preconceived ideas I had about him and his ex.

Were there things Harry wasn't *telling* me?

I found myself in deep, unchartered water and it appeared to have less to do with that drunken man mourning his lost love that I'd spent the evening with, and more to do with the woman Poppy and I were meeting at one o'clock the next day by the merry-go-round.

CHAPTER EIGHTEEN

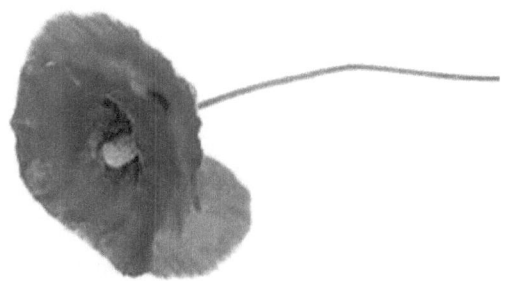

UNABLE TO SLEEP, I tiptoed out of the bed and breakfast early and was on the motorway by seven thirty. Google maps estimated the ninety-mile drive would take a couple of hours or less if I set off before traffic started to build. In a hurry to get home I put my foot down, cut over to the outside lane on the M40 and stayed there, doing eighty.

I arrived home too late for breakfast but early enough to catch the aroma of toast and porridge. Hearing the front door closing Poppy appeared wearing her PJ's and a beanie Mary had bought her in a pale pink colour. She rushed into my arms as if I had been away for a couple of weeks.

"Daddy!" I bent down to meet her, feeling her arms clinging to my neck like ivy.

I lifted her aloft and swung her around. "Hi, Poppy. Where's Mary?"

"In the other bedroom." She pointed down the hall.

"Okay. Did you have a good time last night?" I asked pulling down the beanie until it covered her eyes and lowered her to the floor.

She danced on the spot, wrinkled her nose and raised her beanie. "Yes, we had chocolate, but I'm not supposed to tell." She put her forefinger over her lips.

"Really!" I followed suit. "My lips are sealed."

She held out her little finger, and instinctively I wrapped mine around it to the covert sounds of her shushing. Eager to get back to whatever she was doing, she turned and left.

"What are you up to?" I called.

"Drawing. Don't look!" She pushed her bedroom door to.

I followed instructions and found Mary in the guest bedroom. "Hey. I wondered where you were. What are you doing in here?"

She looked startled. "Oh! I've changed the bedding and I'm freshening up the room a bit, just in case."

"Just in case of what?" I must have been tired because the reason didn't register until I'd asked the question.

She flung down a pillow and kneaded it until it fell into shape. "Just in case you have a guest stopping over."

I offered her a weary smile. "You mean Harry?"

"I do. Although, I hate to be the bearer of bad news, but you had a call last night from Mrs. Chambers. She asked me to ask you to call her."

I nodded. "Okay. I'll do that, but I can't see her wanting to stop over." Hope's mother rarely asked for anything from me, so I had to assume she had something urgent to discuss.

One final tug at the duvet and Mary was done. "You might want to clear a couple of drawers if you're going to be having guests," she suggested with a knowing smile. "Assuming your guest is stopping for longer than one night..."

As tired as I was, I picked up on the judgmental tone; it remained in the air long after she swept past me carrying the laundry before her like a deflated sail. I sat on the double bed, felt the soft, freshly washed duvet under my hands and braced myself for the task ahead.

Hope was not a clothes horse, but she did like to trot around barefoot in comfortable clothes: angora sweaters, warm scarves, wraparound cardigans, too large for her normal size but made to measure when she was eight months pregnant. Those were the clothes in the drawers I couldn't bring myself to look at, let alone throw away.

I set myself, as if about to run a marathon or attempt a high jump that appeared beyond my capabilities; I rubbed at my beard roughly and closed my eyes, waiting for my simmering courage to bubble to the surface. It came in the form of a small hand placed upon mine.

"What's wrong, Daddy?" Poppy asked softly.

She had found me, unmoving and downcast, and was looking up at me with those captivating hazel eyes of hers, framed in chestnut curls. Mary must have caught up with her and instructed her to reconsider her appearance. Gone were the PJ's and the beanie, back were the pink boots and flowery dress so well-suited to her inimitable style.

Slowly I opened my eyes and placed my other hand onto hers. "Nothing's wrong. I'm just sad because I have to clear out these drawers."

She wrinkled her nose, not understanding the problem. "Why? Don't you want to?"

I forced a smile. "No. I don't want to, but I know I have to."

"Did Mary say so?"

Wasn't that the truth!

I smiled at the implication. "No. Mary didn't say so. It's something I have to do. The time's right."

"I can help, Daddy." She nodded and moved toward the drawers. "What's inside?"

I opened the top drawer and placed it down on the bed. "These were your mummy's clothes."

Poppy's eyes remained focused on the sweaters. She was frozen to the spot and had no words to voice her surprise.

"It's okay, you can touch them. We need to put them in a pile so we can give them to people who have no clothes." I reached out for a bottle green cardigan.

She grabbed my hand with both of hers. "But they're Mummy's clothes."

When I looked at her, I saw tears forming in her eyes. "Oh, Poppy, I know. But she doesn't need them where she is and…"

Teardrops cascaded down her cheeks. "But what if she comes back and she's cold…"

I fell to my knees and took her in my arms. "She's not coming back, Poppy. Ever. She's in heaven." I enveloped her tiny, tear-stained face in my hands. "Remember? I told you she's a star in the sky now?" She nodded and squeezed her eyes tightly to stem the flow of tears. I kissed her forehead. "You know what we'll do? We'll sort through the clothes and we'll chose one each that we can keep to help us remember Mummy, or to wear when *we're* cold. Okay?"

She opened her eyes and smiled bravely. "Okay."

Discreetly, I wiped the tears from my cheeks and cleared my throat. One by one I told a story about the day her mother had worn each sweater, how she had wrapped herself in the cardigans when there had been snow on the ground and robins in the garden. Most of the stories were true and when I couldn't picture Hope wearing the item, I made something up.

Mary returned with a large, black bin bag and, seeing our pink-rimmed eyes, quickly departed, not wanting to intrude. Poppy made her decision toward the end of the sorting session. I was surprised that she put a purple cardigan to one side and opted for a navy blue sweater.

"Why that one?" I asked her.

"It smells like Mummy," she announced and proceeded to wrap it around her shoulders like a magic cloak.

I understood completely and chose a multi-coloured cardigan for personal reasons. Hope had worn it throughout her pregnancy, the cuffs were a little frayed and there was a button missing but it had to be my choice for the memories it evoked and—in Poppy's words—*it smelled like Mummy.*

I completed the task alone, but as I was sliding the top drawer into place, I noticed what appeared to be a small white envelope that had become lodged against the back panel. I reached inside.

To my utter surprise, on the front in my fancy, left sloping handwriting was my wife's name.

I slumped back onto the bed and looked at it, turned it over, put it to my nose and closed my eyes, willing her to return if only in the form of a hazy apparition. I hated that I couldn't see her face when seeing her would soften what was bound to be very painful blow.

Alone with the cardigan wrapped around my shoulders, I ran my trembling fingers along the flap but didn't open it. If I had, I knew I would be right back where I started before Harry came into my life—knee deep in misery; the road to recovery would become a quagmire of remorse dragging me down to the point of suffocation.

I couldn't risk that. Not when I'd come so far.

Rocked by that thought, my whole body sagged, and my head felt too heavy for my shoulders. I fell to my knees and hit the carpet with a thud, still grasping the envelope. Hearing the bump, Mary ran into the room and halted once she saw my diminished state.

"You found the envelope," she stated. "I saw it yesterday when I was clearing out the drawer and left it. It wasn't my place to…"

I held up my hand. "Give me a minute, Mary."

She backed out of the room slowly. "Of course. You know where I am."

I crawled onto the bed, gripping the duvet in one hand, and lay upon it in the foetal position, my vision too blurred with tears to reread the letter. I had written Hope one, maybe two letters in the entire time we were together. This one was dog-eared, worn from reading. In it I professed my eternal love for her.

The woman I had betrayed.

The only woman who had loved me unconditionally, and told me many times, "You have my heart. It beats for you, Max."

I don't know how long I lay there. It seemed like an hour, maybe two. The familiar sound of cartoons playing in the other room reminded me of what I already knew: I had a daughter, and a pinkie promise to keep.

I slipped the envelope into my back pocket, checked myself out in the en-suite, splashed my face and combed my fingers through my hair.

We had a lunch date.

Poppy skipped all the way from the car to the merry-go-round, doubly excited at the prospect of riding it and seeing Harry again. She let go of my hand with a few yards to go and made a beeline for our black-booted friend.

With no visual signals, I patted Harry's arm and said, "Hi. I think Poppy's likely to explode if we don't get her indoors pretty soon."

Harry looked down at her and yelled, "BOOM!" and Poppy pretended to fall over. We laughed and shoppers looked on with no understanding of our little pantomime.

With the ice broken, we headed in the direction of a small restaurant in a side street called, Bambi. Once inside it was easy to see why. The walls were plastered with stills from Disney films. Clearly, they catered for young diners and had a play area where they could interact with colourful toys and each other.

I had no idea such a place even existed.

Harry had reserved what must have been the quietest table tucked away to the side, but not so far away from the action that we couldn't keep an eye on Poppy. The table was bright yellow, the chairs were in red plastic, the menu comprised of burgers and an array of kids' food that I skimmed over en route to the sandwich section.

Poppy pointed at the pictures and opted for a cheeseburger with fries and a strawberry milkshake, despite me trying to persuade her to join me in a *delicious* sandwich.

With our order placed, Poppy and Harry strolled over to the play area. Initially, Poppy was apprehensive; she hadn't seen that many children in one place at one time and it took her a few minutes to assimilate.

Gradually Harry backed away and returned to our table. "There are kids her own age there. I think she'll have fun."

"I don't doubt it," I agreed. "What made you choose this place?"

Her smile faded. "Don't you like it? We can go somewhere else…"

I shook my head. "No. It's fine. It's just that I feel like a fish out of water."

"That's because you haven't been swimming for a while," she teased, rearranging the cutlery.

I held up a correcting forefinger. "Ah. I will have you know that you're almost wrong there!"

She grinned. "Almost?"

"Almost. I took Poppy for her first swimming lesson on Monday and we're going back next Monday."

"I see. I stand *half* corrected. But what about you?" She rested her chin on her upturned hand. "Did you venture into the deep end?"

I massaged my beard. "Are we still talking about swimming? I think I may have lost track."

She laughed and made room for our meal. My sandwich was on white bread and Poppy's cheeseburger and fries came on a plastic plate; I made a mental note not to order the fillet of fish as Harry had—it was overly cremated for my taste.

I put the noise, the food and the uncomfortable chairs down to experience, and when Poppy asked if we could come back again next week, Harry and I answered in unison with, "Maybe…"

Poppy and I returned home at six thirty to a note Mary had left explaining there was shepherd's pie in the oven and lemon meringue in the fridge. I wanted to kiss the woman on behalf of my digestive system. Poppy seemed to be on a natural high, probably from the chemicals in the food and the colourants in the sauce poured over her generous helping of ice-cream.

She wouldn't stop talking about her day: what she had done, seen, tasted, and she couldn't stop admiring her new leather boots. Harriet had explained how as lovely as her pink Wellington boots were, they were not good for her feet, not when they were worn every day. If she was going to wear boots, which was a given, they had to be in leather to let her feet breathe.

Poppy's feet breathed all over the house, as she tap-danced, jogged on the spot and waggled them beneath the dinner table. I declared that we had one rule, and it was non-negotiable. She could not sleep in them and, if that meant taking them out of her bedroom to allow her feet to breathe on their own, then so be it.

189

Sipping a tumbler of scotch and ice to dilute it, I paused to reflect. Twenty-four hours earlier I'd been throwing back shots with Harry's nemesis, listening to him wax lyrical about the love of his life, his childhood sweetheart.

In front of me I had Harry's journal—and that told a very different story, one that had moved me to the point of tears and produced in me a feeling of attachment—an irrepressible bond.

We had spent the day together and it was wonderful. I had looked down my nose at Bambi, and would return there under protest, but Poppy had loved it. The memory of the day would sustain her for an entire week.

Once again Ms Harper had opened my eyes to Poppy's needs and I had to accept that she was growing on me. She laughed at me and with me and made me laugh too, but ... something Sam had said about her being more like a Russian doll had hit home. The only way I was going to discover what he meant was to peel back those layers for myself.

I read on.

HARRIET - THE ROAD TO RECOVERY

TAKE IT FROM ME, after a heart transplant the road to recovery is littered with obstacles: getting my body to accept what is essentially a foreign body, being vulnerable to infection and, if that wasn't bad enough, the narrowing of blood vessels, osteoporosis and weight gain—side effects of immunosuppressant medication.

I wasn't fazed by any of that. As long as I had a fighting chance to start over, I would never surrender myself to the alternative.

Looking back, plotting my escape from Sam was handled with precision: my determination to be well prepared didn't wane, especially not when I had Trish to spur me on.

Nurse Patricia Barcus was a petite, softly spoken woman of twenty-nine from Lithuania. Once I was taken out of ICU and placed in a small side ward with one other person, I was fortunate to have her as my night nurse. She had two children under five and worked the nightshift while her husband, Lukas, worked as an electrician during the day.

It got so I planned my day around her shift: woke up for breakfast at eight o'clock, dozed until lunch; ate lunch and dozed some more until visiting time—on the days that Sam or friends would appear brandishing fruit or snacks. I tucked into dinner at five o'clock and then slept until eleven thirty. It was an abnormal routine but nothing about my life was normal—every day I was in training for the great escape.

To make that happen, I needed a new skill, something I could train for while I was recovering. While other patients slept, Trish and I worked on perfecting one. I tried to learn French but failed miserably. I signed up for a correspondence course for bookkeeping but didn't have a head for figures. I needed a sit-down job with minimal physical exertion, one that paid enough to cover the cost of a small apartment and general expenses.

I couldn't think of leaving Sam until I had a job to go to.

One night when we were chatting over tea and toast, Trish explained how her brother had started a job as a croupier. He'd had no previous experience but had taken to it like a duck to water. I asked what was involved and realised that I had found something I could train for requiring skills I could perfect in the privacy of my hospital unit.

Over the next couple of weeks, Trish brought in packs of cards and a selection of used chips. Together we read *how to* books and watched videos on YouTube. We tested each other on terminology—hers for a nursing course to increase her level of expertise and me on everything a croupier needed to know.

After four weeks, I was able to shuffle cards one handed and count and collect chips like a professional. Every night, before her shift ended, we would clear everything away, leaving no trace of my newly acquired skills.

Her brother offered to put in a good word for me at Hot Slots in Camden Town, but I wasn't planning on sticking around. The company had lots of branches and I made the decision to apply for jobs in Newquay and Brighton, seaside towns where the air would help to speed up my recuperation. All I had to do was complete an application form, send a photograph with a reference her brother had typed out on letter headed paper, and arrange an interview.

That's exactly what I did, using Trish's address and my new identity: Harriet Harper. Plain Jane Harper was about to breathe her last breath.

HARRY'S SINGLE-MINDEDNESS RADIATED OFF the page: it was almost palpable. It triggered my senses and rang out like a battle cry, a one-woman crusade against capitulation in any form.

Was this one of those layers Sam intimated about, lying dormant beneath her once malleable exterior? If so, he really had no idea of what she was capable of.

CHAPTER NINETEEN

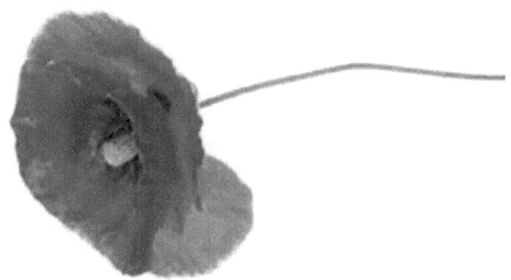

HARRY AND I WERE becoming good friends. Maybe she hoped for more. I know I did. We were good together, good for each other. She was one of life's survivors and—God knows—I needed someone with good survival skills in my camp.

Giving her time to sleep in on Sunday morning, I called her around lunchtime to invite her to dinner. I could visualise her rubbing her eyes or wrapping both hands around an over-sized mug of coffee. I knew she had Tuesday night off for the art class and was prepared to accommodate her any other night of her choosing.

As luck would have it, she was free *that* night. She explained how the second night off worked on rotation. Last week she had Saturday night off, that week, it was Sunday.

I felt fortunate in one sense, but with that initial feeling of providence came the realisation that I was on my own. I had limited time to prepare something with Mary taking her day of rest. It would be quite a task for one so culinary challenged as myself, but I was up for it, feeling confident that I could at least match Bambi when it came to gastronomy.

I flicked through a couple of cookbooks and couldn't find anything I liked that required basic skills. I did what anyone would do under the circumstances; I took one of Mary's signature dishes—labelled 'beef lasagne'—from the freezer along with a raspberry Pavlova and set about defrosting them. That left me with time enough to rustle up a salad and garlic bread while Poppy set the table and helped choose some music.

She appeared in her favourite pink party dress and black boots with one hand holding a hairbrush and the other two pink hair slides and a mirror. Giddy and almost speechless, her face had become one big cheesy grin; even her eyes smiled.

I sat her down on my knee and brushed her hair until it shone and her chestnut curls wrapped around my hands like silk ribbons, falling naturally to one side. I pinned her fringe in place with both hair slides and paused to receive her approval.

She raised the mirror, tipped her head left, then right and turned to thank me. "Good job, Daddy." A grateful kiss brushed against my cheek. "When are *you* getting ready?" She jumped down from my knee.

I looked down at my sweater, my jeans and my bare feet. "I wasn't planning on changing."

"But it's a party." She looked at my feet disapprovingly. "You have no shoes on!" She took my hand and attempted to pull me to my feet with a noisy tug. "You *have* to wear shoes."

She was right.

Leaving the delicious aroma of beef and tomato sauce behind, I followed instructions and selected some shoes and a fresh shirt. While I sat on the bed, tying the laces on a new pair of shoes, Poppy climbed up to reciprocate and brushed my hair, more determined than ever that we should make a good impression.

When the doorbell sounded at six thirty, we both jumped to our feet. Poppy beat me to the door and jumped into Harry's arms like a jack-in-the-box, testing her reflexes.

"Now that's what you call a welcome," Harry announced, laughter already sparkling in her eyes.

"Come in, Harry. Let me take your coat." I peeled Poppy from her torso and slipped her jacket off her shoulders. Beneath it was a purple dress with tiny pink flowers dotted about it in cottage garden colours. It was pulled in at her waist and clung to her figure, creating the kind of curves that turned heads—they certainly turned mine.

With Poppy skipping alongside she followed me into the kitchen.

"You've been busy. Something smells delicious." She scanned the kitchen.

"It's lasagne—"

I was about to play up my culinary skills when Poppy interjected with, "Mary made it."

I rolled my eyes. "Yeah. Thanks for that, Poppy." I pointed a thumb in the direction of the Pavlova. "I had nothing to do with dessert either."

"It's all in the serving," Harry said with a suppressed chuckle. "Need any help?"

"You could get a couple of wine glasses out of there." I pointed to the top cupboard nearest her. "I have red or white." I held two bottles of wine aloft.

"I'd prefer white, if that's okay?" She reached up for the glasses on her tiptoes, elongating her petite body.

I tried not to stare, but it was impossible. From only a couple of feet away, I watched her reach for one then two wine glasses, appreciating the fluidity of her movements, the arch of her back, the outline of her breasts, not as an artist but as a man who had not had any physical contact with a woman in four years. I turned away and occupied myself with the search for an ice bucket.

With Poppy's help I tipped out a bag of ice, lowered the bottle into the broken cubes with a crunch and carried it into the lounge. "Take a seat."

Harry followed me. "Great. I'm starving." She moved toward her bag next to the sofa. "Have we time for a gift?"

Poppy's head spun in my direction.

How could I say no? "Sure."

Poppy positioned herself next to Harry, invading her body space, but our guest didn't seem to mind. I sat opposite, leaning forward on my knees, prepared for anything.

From out of her backpack, Harry lifted out a shoe box. By its size I knew what the contents were. She handed the box to Poppy. "I know you have a birthday coming up, so I got you these. I hope you like them."

Poppy held the box on her knee as if it was sacrosanct and brushed her hands across it reverently.

"Aren't you going to open it?" I asked, encouraging her to lift the lid.

As if in slow motion she lifted up the corners to reveal a mound of pink tissue paper. As she peeled it back her eyes turned from hazel to agate in colour, wide and almost translucent. The moment of reveal was announced with a squeal, a solitary second before her chin fell and her mouth fell open.

"What is it?" I asked, leaning over to see.

"Shoes!" she exclaimed. "*Princess* shoes."

She lifted them out to a chorus of ooh's and ah's. If joy could be vocalised, then that is what it would sound like.

The shoes were completely impractical, of course. They were glass slippers decorated with two poppies on the front and on the tiny heel.

"They're dress-up shoes," Harry explained. "You can't go out in them."

Poppy nodded her head. "They're Snow White shoes." She fondled them, turned them over again and again, admiring the shape and the colours. She returned them to the box, placed it on the sofa beside her and scrambled up Harry's body. Their noses touched and she planted a noisy kiss on her cheek.

"Thank you, Harry. It's the best present!" She climbed down off the sofa, took hold of the box in both hands and disappeared down the corridor to her room.

I walked over to the ice bucket, poured Harry a glass of wine and handed it to her. "Thank you. That was very thoughtful."

"It was the only way I could think of, of prising her feet out of her damn boots for a couple of hours when she's in the house." She smiled and we toasted to her ingenuity.

"You nailed it," I acknowledged. "Now all I'll have to contend with is…"

We turned to see Poppy in her party dress and new dress-up shoes. The sight of her brought a lump to my throat; her looking so grown up and prettier than I had ever seen her before made my heart soar.

Harry touched my arm. "What will you have to contend with, Max?" she asked.

Before I could answer, Poppy approached us, visibly thrilled to be making an entrance in footwear that no longer landed with a thump but shattered the stillness of the house with resounding clip clops.

"Oh God!" Harry turned to face me. "I hear what you mean. Sorry." Her amusement belied her apology and caused a chain reaction in us both.

Poppy called out, "Watch me, Daddy," and proceeded to dance to the music, increasing the tempo of her heel tapping to that of a flamenco dancer.

As Harry, Poppy and I held hands and twirled in a circle, it occurred to me that the resounding echoes of our jovial jamboree were signalling the end of my silent isolation.

Not only was I laughing, *I* was dancing in new shoes too.

By ten thirty, Harry had broken her two-glass rule and was on her third glass of wine. She raised her eyes to mine. "Can I ask you something?"

I nodded. "Sure."

"Why are there no pictures of your wife anywhere?" She glanced around the room. "The artwork is fantastic but…"

I wanted to make up a story about a fire, unreliable removal men and lost photographs but I decided to come clean. "I don't need a photograph to remind me of what my wife looked like." That was not entirely true. "Anyway, it hurts too much to see her face looking back at me. It brings back the day when—"

She interjected, "You don't have to tell me. I wasn't trying to pry."

"You're not." I walked over to the ice bucket and returned with what was left of the white wine. I sat on the sofa, turning my body toward her. "I've only told a handful of people what happened."

She nodded and set her wine down. "I'm listening."

"My agent told me that I needed a new portfolio as soon as possible as all my paintings in the exhibition had been sold. I needed to, 'strike while the iron was hot,' he said. I'd never been in demand," I stated, making light of my success. "In the early days, we felt lucky if I sold two pieces a year."

I took a sip of wine, bolstering myself for what was about to come. "I was engrossed in my work to the detriment of my marriage. Hope became a housekeeper; she brought me food and drink and I barely found the time to speak to her. I painted when inspiration called—sometimes in the middle of the night. I slept in the day. We became ships in the night." I stopped, giving Harry time to follow my narration.

"In retrospect, she must have been so lonely. And pregnant too! What the hell was I thinking?" I hung my head in shame. "I was a terrible husband."

"She must have known how driven you were?" Harry's words were intended to soothe my tortured brain, but they only served as a reminder of what a selfish bastard I'd been.

"She did but that doesn't excuse what happened to her. I was tucked away in my studio and she was left to face the real world on her own, and when the worst example of it came knocking, she took it on." Needing something stronger than wine, I topped up Harry's glass and headed over to the drinks' cabinet. In my woeful state only a double dose of scotch would get me through.

Harry waited for me to sit back down before asking, "I read that you were robbed, and they beat you both up. Is that what happened?"

I nodded. "Yes. I called the ambulance and by the time we arrived at the hospital, it was too late for Hope but there was time to save Poppy."

She placed her soft hand on mine. "I'm so sorry."

Emotion stirred in my chest and ascended through my throat forcing me to choke and cough. "Yes. It was the worst time of my life."

"That's a sad story, Max, but you've left something out." She wrinkled her nose in a way I might have found endearing under different circumstances. Her grip on my hand lessened, but her eyes remained fixed on mine.

"Like what?"

"Like Hope having filed for divorce three days before she died."

My heart jolted in my chest. I heard one word reverberate in my brain.

Layers...

"She ... didn't." Not only did her knowledge of the facts floor me, it caused me to perspire to the point of combustion. I felt ambushed and tilted away from her. How the hell did she know that?

"We had a wonderful marriage," I mumbled almost inaudibly.

She was not buying it. "I don't understand. Why, then, did she file a petition with the court on the grounds of adultery?"

Layers...

My God! How much did she know? "What makes you say a thing like that?" I asked feigning incredulity.

"It's what I heard and it turned out to be true. It's a matter of public record." She seemed very well informed.

Was I about to be blackmailed?

"It's what you *heard?*" I wanted to pace, but doing so would have made me look as if I'd been caught out—which, of course, I had. With my heart rate decreasing, I asked, "You heard when?"

"When I was in hospital. I'd been in and out of there so many times I'd become part of the furniture. The nurses talked freely around me—and they *loved* to talk."

"I don't get it." My beard took the brunt of my agitation.

"The gossip in the hospital cafeteria was about a woman who'd died in childbirth and was married to an artist. When they sorted through her belongings, checking for medications, they found a copy of the petition. It was dated fifteenth December, three days before she died, so you must have received it?"

"What were they doing reading her mail?" I yelled, losing patience.

"I don't know why they read her mail, Max. It's just as well that *they* did and not the police. Don't you think?"

I buried my face in my hands. "I don't know what to think, or what you want from me, Harry." I pulled myself together and faced her, preparing for more questions.

"I don't want anything. Only the truth." She took a sip of wine and started over. "Were you unfaithful while Hope was pregnant with Poppy?"

"Frankly, I don't see how that's any of your business." I spat out my reply.

"It probably isn't, but it seems to me that you've been holding something back. Something about what happened that day, maybe?" She spoke softly.

I held her gaze. "Like I said, we were happy together."

Harry smiled knowingly. "Not happy enough to stay married though, eh?" She leant forward, intending to stand and probably leave. "I don't think you're being straight with me, Max."

I reached out and took hold of her wrist. "Look, *you* know how people can change…"

She sat back down. "I do?"

"Take you and Sam, for instance. Look how that teenage romance of yours went sour."

"How do you know that?" she snapped, her face contorted into a grimace.

I had to recover quickly. "You told me … last week in the restaurant, remember?"

She was still unsure. "I did?"

I was not entirely convinced that she *had* told me. Perhaps I had remembered it from her journal. Either way, I had to remain insistent. "Yes. How else would I know?"

"I must have mentioned him," she conceded.

"Right. Well you did, and it was the same with Hope and me…" I sighed with relief.

"So, you're telling me that you were happy to perpetuate the myth of your perfect marriage until someone—like me—called you out on it?"

"Is that what you're doing?" I tipped my head and waited for her reply.

"What's done is done, Max. I just think you'll be able to get on with your life once you stop beating yourself up about what happened. The way you've been acting, anyone would think you *let* her die. That's not true is it?"

"I loved her."

"That's not what I asked."

"I know."

"Could you have saved her?"

"I. Don't. Know!" I cried, close to breaking point.

She nailed me to the spot with a penetrating stare and I felt her hand on top of mine. "Don't worry, Max. I'm not going to say anything to anyone."

"That's very generous of you." I removed my hand from hers.

"Me knowing doesn't change anything. Max, I admire you, I really do. What I don't admire is your self-pity. Isn't it time you turned your eyes outward? Started seeing what you've been denying yourself all these years? Maybe then you'll be able to see what you've been missing."

"Like you? I see *you* more clearly now."

She laughed. "See, there you go deflecting. Let's not make this about me. What about Poppy? Your beautiful daughter…? She needs a full-time father, not a martyr."

"You think I'm a *martyr*?" I heard the intonation in my voice. She must have heard it too.

"Not exactly. I just wonder when you're going to step down and accept that you don't have to be another casualty of a terrible attack, just because you were being unfaithful."

I sighed, letting out a gust of hot air. "You don't know what happened?"

"Maybe not, but I can read. I can operate a laptop, check newspaper archives. It was all there in black and white," she said emphatically.

"And red..." I turned away, blinded by a crimson cast, taken back to that horrific day. The moment I dreaded had come about. The explanation I had tainted, too proud to tell anyone the truth—until then.

"I wouldn't know anything about that." She paused, sensing my brief departure. "Only you know what happened, and maybe one day you'll be able to tell someone; to free yourself of the burden of guilt you carry around with you like a sack of lead."

Her description was spot on; sometimes my body almost buckled under the weight of it. I was too ashamed to let it drop and too proud to admit I had failed my wife when she needed me—when her life was in my hands.

"I think you've suffered enough, served your time. It doesn't have to be a life sentence and it's only fair you should be let off for good behaviour but, there is one condition..."

"And that would be?" I asked, almost too vexed to contemplate what else she had up her sleeve.

She leaned forward, preparing to stress her point. "That you tell me what happened. What *really* happened."

"For that I'll need a drink. A real drink." I held up the bottle of scotch, offering her a shot.

"No thanks." She smiled sweetly and patted the space next to her on the sofa, looking like a child excited at the prospect of being told a bedtime story they already knew the ending to. On her knees, her hands ruffled her dress, drawing it up between her fingers. "I'm sorry if I make you feel uncomfortable. I don't mean to."

"You don't," I admitted, massaging my beard. "That's the problem."

Her eyes flashed. "It is? I don't see it that way." She reached for her bag. "Maybe I should leave, then?"

I turned to look at her, not so much as an adversary but as a man believing he had found a kindred spirit. I twisted my body in her direction. "You don't have to leave, you know. I won't touch you."

"I know, but that's…" She broke off.

"That's what?"

"That's what I want," she declared, drawing her bottom lip into her mouth nervously. "I want you to, or I think I do. But it's been so long I've forgotten how it feels to—"

"To want to be close to someone." I ended the sentence for her, when really I was speaking about myself. "How long has it been?"

She giggled. "Too long."

I forced a smile of resignation. "Tell me about it."

She moved closer to where I was standing, so close I could inhale her delicate perfume. I modified my breathing, kept it shallow and controlled. I'd been suffering from sensory deprivation for so long the faintest whiff would be more than enough to get my libido racing.

She cleared her throat to speak. "You loved your wife, Max, I get that. Just the same way I loved Sam, and now he's dead to me too. We're not perfect and neither are the people we love, but we love them anyway. The bad things we have seen or done don't vanish overnight, they're like weeds; no matter how hard you try to pave over them and replace them with more attractive memories, they pop up when you least expect them to."

I placed my forefinger and thumb under her chin and raised her eyes to mine. "What are you saying, Harry? You want to help me landscape my life; plant new memories and watch them grow?"

She smiled, allowing the slightest upturn of her lips to convey her intentions. "I suppose I am. At least they'll be real ones."

I huffed, still stunned by her powers of perception. We both had multiple *layers*, it seemed. She had seen through my cracked veneer and was still prepared to stick around.

"I was in love with the idea of love because I was lucky enough to be cocooned it in for fifteen years. It became a habit, something I couldn't do without. The unconditional love Hope gave me was like a force-field: it kept the world at bay. The trouble was, I used it to keep her at bay too."

As a gesture of affection, I planted a kiss on her forehead. "Sometimes when I hear you speak you remind me of my wife; not your voice but the honesty in your words— a glimmer of Hope." I took an energising breath. "She was an amazing woman. She made me smile for no reason other than feeling so damn privileged to be the one she was smiling at." I smiled reflexively.

"Once in our first home together a blackbird flew in through an open window. We ducked. I fell to the floor and watched it bouncing off walls, knocking over ornaments, crapping on furniture. I swore and screamed at it for invading our private space while Hope silently backed into a corner.

At first, I thought she was terrified, but that wasn't the case at all; she was giving it more room and time to catch its breath. It rested for a moment on the arm of a chair, its heart beating out of its chest, its eyes wild and demonic." I checked to see she was listening. "You know how they get when they're cornered?"

Harry's eyes became wide as she nodded. "What happened? Did you manage to get it out?"

"*I* didn't. Hope put on a pair of woollen gloves and picked it up. I'm not sure if it was the warmth of the gloves or her soothing words, but it settled. She had me open doors all the way down three flights of stairs into the garden where she placed it beneath a hedge. We watched it regain its balance, test its wings and fly away. 'There he goes,' she said. 'Back to his family.' She threw the gloves in the washing machine and went about her day as if nothing had happened: collecting feathers, picking up ornaments, wiping up bird crap.

That was the moment I realised that she handled me the same way. When I got lost or was beset by self-doubt and frustration, she wrapped her hands around my face, looked into my eyes and soothed me." I stopped, lost in the memory. "I miss that."

It was true, and the first time I had shared that recollection with anyone. "From day one she saw something in me, that thing the art critics called talent, perhaps ... or whatever it was. She never doubted me—not until the end." Disgraced, I hung my head, burdened by the weight of my eternal shame. "She deserved more, and when it came down to it, all I could offer her was less." I considered my words carefully. "You deserve more too, Harry."

"More of you?" she asked tentatively, with a directness that forced me to review my intentions.

"I'm not sure I have much to offer, not after—" Before I could finish, I felt her lips brushing against mine, her tongue pushing back the fears I had about being found out. I wove my fingers into her hair and kissed her softly, feeling the lush wetness of her lips against mine. Her entire body radiated heat, causing my hands to tingle as my grip tightened and my thumbs found the sculpted roundness of her cheeks.

"Harry," I gasped, walking her backward onto the wall, roughly pinning her against it with my hips. "If I carry on, I might not be able to back off. Stop me now if…"

Her palms found their way to my chest. "It's too soon, Max. I want to, but I can't…"

I pulled back, eased my weight off her, knowing the hardness of my erection had left her under no doubt as to my intentions. I would have taken her right there against the wall if she had let me.

She swept a stray curl from her face. "I'm sorry. This is more difficult than I thought it would be."

"I understand." I caressed her flushed cheek.

She offered a watery smile. "But it doesn't mean I don't want to…"

"You don't have to explain." How could I say, I know what you've been through, and it would be a miracle if you let a man lay his hands on you *ever* again? She was being honest with me and I was feeding her a line—the same line I had fed the police, the press, my family and friends, and even myself. I inhaled deeply and prepared to break my self-imposed code of silence.

"Harry, I've not been totally honest with you and you deserve the truth. When it came down to it on *that* day, I didn't do the honourable thing—far from it. I put my own reputation before my wife's needs and convinced myself and the rest of the world that everything between us was okay. It wasn't." I lowered my hands from her face.

"Hope stopped being my muse, she became my pregnant wife who looked different, acted differently with her hormones all over the place, and more worryingly, she saw *me* differently." Taking her hand, I led her back to the sofa and urged her to sit facing me. I rebuffed her comforting touch and settled my hands on my knees in a two-handed fist.

"I changed. The fame went to my head. The money went to my head. Hope didn't want to live in a house like this: it was *my* idea." I snickered, remembering how insistent I was. "She wanted a small cottage in the country, not some hi-tech designer home with glass walls and metal beams—an over-priced monument to materialism. She wanted roses around the door and a picket fence, and she got it, but only as add-ons that *she* created while I went about the business of painting and promoting myself.

When she said she wanted a divorce, I was devastated. And then, when I found out that it was on the grounds of adultery on my part, I realised what I'd done."

"Did you love another woman?" Harry asked quietly, her eyes never straying from mine.

"No. I fucked another woman, a younger woman from the gallery who idolised me and inspired me to paint, the way Hope used to." A torrent of words tumbled from my mouth as I confessed, purging me of my guilt a little more with every new revelation.

Harry was enthralled. "How did Hope find out?"

I shrugged. "She picked up my phone and read a text."

"That's all?" She leaned back into the sofa, saying nothing but inwardly questioning the reliability of my explanation. "It must have been a graphic text."

I shook my head. "It wasn't. It was the tone that had Hope checking out my studio while I slept and discovering Melody there exhibited in all her naked glory in intimate pencil sketches and painted in oils."

More disbelief was etched on her face. "And from that she assumed you were having an affair?"

I took a breath, priming myself for an admission. "No. She knew my insecurities." I licked my lips. "You see, I have an artist's heart, I need to be motivated by passion, not only for the person but by the project itself. Without it, I wouldn't have been able to tap into my creativity. She knew that."

"So, your marriage was on the rocks, you had a mistress and—"

"And the rest is history."

"But you didn't tell the police about any of this." Harry pointed out, looking troubled more by what I hadn't said rather than what I'd confessed.

"I didn't. I shredded the letter from her solicitor, covered up the paintings of Melody and haven't been in my studio since."

She shook her head, disbelievingly. "I don't understand how you still feel responsible for Hope's death, Max. You didn't know you were going to be robbed, that they would hurt her and that she would haemorrhage and go into premature labour..."

"No. I didn't. What I suspected was that they chose this house because it looked like there would be treasure inside: they must have viewed it as an open invitation; seen it as The Promised Land. Little did they know that most of the ill-begotten gains that came from selling my artwork had gone into the building of it. Look around, there's not much worth stealing here. Of all the things inside, Hope was the greatest treasure—the one thing they destroyed."

My confession was taking its toll on me. I was starting to feel empty inside, as if my soul had been seized, leaving nothing of substance, merely an empty shell of a man.

As the facts were being revealed, one piece at a time, I was losing face and losing the support of the one woman who could truly understand the meaning of doing whatever it takes to survive. When Harry resolved to save herself, it took bravery to see it through; when I opted to save myself, it took nothing more than dishonour and betrayal.

"So, what you're saying is that you insisting on having this house built, having an affair and being obsessed by your work brought about the death of your wife? Is that what you honestly believe?"

I nodded. "That's three quarters of it."

"And what's the final part?" she ventured to ask.

I closed my eyes. Saw Hope slouching against the upturned coffee table haemorrhaging, looking to me to save her. I opened my eyes and picked at the festering scab that would never heal. "I didn't fight for her. I saw how she was suffering, and I did nothing." I raised my head, as if facing a firing squad. "I knew there were two guys in there with her—"

"How?"

"I spotted their van outside. I heard noises and investigated. I saw the two sets of muddy footprints and I saw them reflected in the mirror above the fireplace when I entered the library. One was behind the door and the other was by the bookcase on the other side. They were smaller than me, younger. I could have beaten them both to a pulp."

"And?"

"And, I didn't. I didn't pick up a lamp or form a fist or even try to defend my wife. I could have been a hero, charged in, took them on, saved the day, but I had another agenda: one I have been using as an instrument of torture since that awful day." I shook my head and focused on the floor.

"Can you believe it? I even took a visual snapshot." I closed my eyes. "A side-table upturned, glass ornaments smashed, bookcases emptied, books tossed on the floor, their backs breaking, pages torn, cushions scattered, lamps shattered and Hope stretched out on the floor cradling her stomach with one hand—her hands and dress blood-soaked." My description had become a crescendo. "I leaned forward and took the bloodied hand she held out to me and waited to be knocked out, knowing she had been punched and pushed to the floor for fighting back. She still had her favourite paperweight beside her, the weapon she had grabbed to defend herself."

Harry turned away, visualising the scene, frowning as it took shape in her mind's eye. She inhaled and looked at me. "All that does is make you a coward, Max, not a wife killer."

"You think?" I sneered. "Who do you think called the ambulance in time to save our daughter?"

"I don't know," she whispered.

"Hope! She saved Poppy—not me. I was unconscious until the medics arrived…"

"But you told the police you called them." There was a tremor in her voice. "That's what it said in the papers."

"You shouldn't believe everything you read in the newspapers, Harry." I shook my head and locked my emotions behind a tight-lipped smile. "Hope was so close to passing out and bleeding to death all she got out was, 'Help me.' They traced the fucking call back to my phone."

I paused to catch my breath.

"The stories out there reported that we were devoted to each other, we had a wonderful marriage, we were looking forward to starting our life together with our baby girl in our new home; I was the darling of the art world—it was all bullshit!" I had to stop myself from shouting before I lost all self-control and scared Harry away for good.

With a softer voice I continued. "Hope was going to leave me after Poppy was born. I couldn't paint with Melody out of the picture and, if it wasn't for Hope's life insurance, I would be broke." I threw my head back and laughed but it was a hollow imitation of laughter—an audible expression of self-loathing and shame.

Harry looked away into the distance. "I don't know what to say."

"Call me a taxi?" I reached for my phone on the coffee table.

She responded by placing her hand over mine. "Give me a minute."

"Do you want a drink?" I asked, needing something with a kick in it to calm me down. "I have more wine in the kitchen if…"

She shook her head. "No thanks. Water would be fine."

Feeling like a man on the verge of collapsing, I hung over the kitchen drainer letting cold water gush into the sink. I threw a handful over my face, needing to feel its cleansing coolness on my skin, and patted it dry with a tea towel.

When I returned to the lounge, Harry was nowhere to be seen. She'd made her silent escape—she was good at that—but who could blame her? Why would someone like her want to have anything to do with a wife killer like me?

CHAPTER TWENTY

LEFT ALONE WITH MY thoughts, I slumped down on the sofa and sipped the water. Drinking hard liquor had lost the appeal it once had and no amount of whisky would wash away my sins, not now, not after I had confessed and they were out in the open and free to roam like unforgiving phantoms.

I swear I thought I was hearing things when the doorbell rang fifteen minutes later. I rushed to open the door, blood thrumming in my ears, thinking, *Harry has reconsidered. She got as far as the end of the drive and decided to return, needing to close the space between us: breaths blending, mouths colliding...*

I could taste her on my lips.

I pulled back the door to greet her, a zealous smile plastered across my face. "Did you change your...?" I did not get to finish the sentence.

It was *not* Harry.

I recognised him instantly, his blond hair soaked and lying flat on his head, wet tendrils crisscrossing his forehead. His petrol blue jacket had dark patches on the lapels where the rain had trickled down from his broad shoulders.

Sam.

I managed to edit the expletives before speaking. "What the hell are you doing here?" I asked, feeling my cheeks flush and my nostrils flare in response to his unexpected appearance. Even though we had met socially, it had been on my terms: *I* had chosen the when and the where. Sam turning up at my house was a scenario I was not prepared for. "What do you want?"

"I was in the area and thought I'd look up a mate and give him this." He handed me a twenty-pound note and took a step back to inspect the house. "Not that you need it."

I accepted the bank note and stuffed it into my trouser pocket. "Thanks. You didn't need to come all this way to pay me back."

"Anytime." He didn't budge. He was waiting for me to ask him in or, at least, ask *how* he found me.

I crossed one foot over the other and leaned on the door jam. "Okay, I'll play along. How did you find me, Sam?"

He laughed. "Your delivery man story just didn't hold up. You were just too … too fucking classy, mate. I've delivered shit since I left school and I've never come across anyone like you."

I folded my arms. "Is that so?"

"Yeah. So then, I got to wondering why you were poking around in my neck of the woods when you could be here in your fancy house." He tilted his head back in an exaggerated gesture.

I feigned disinterest with a shrug. In fact, I was hanging on his every word. "And what did you come up with?" While he was thinking through his answer, I tried frantically to come up with one of my own; one that had nothing to do with Harry.

He stuck his hands in his jean pockets and tapped his feet together. "Well, for starters, you're not gay," he stated mischievously. "You wouldn't be spending the night with little Miss Harper if you were." He nodded in the direction of the drive then refocused his attention on me.

And there it was: the crux of the matter. He had found me and watched Harry leave, or he had followed her here and found me through her. Either way, I was in deep shit.

"What's that got to do with you?" I ventured to ask, feeling the hairs on my arm beginning to bristle and having nothing to do with the night air. "Have you been stalking her?"

"Me?" He snickered. "Why would I stalk *her?* The way I see it, I had a lucky escape,

210

and if you've got any sense, you'll invite me in, offer me a stiff one and let me explain."

I looked out into the night. There was no sign of a car. "How did you get here?"

"The same way you do. I drove." He gestured with his thumb. "My car's down on the road at the end of the drive. I watched her get into a cab and walked up." He looked around me. "Look. I'm not here to cause trouble. I'm here to warn you."

Behind me there was the sound of movement. Poppy padded toward me clutching her blankie and rubbing her eyes. "Daddy?"

At the sight of her I felt my heart pounding in my chest. I knew what he was capable of and wanted her well out of the way. "Don't come to the door, Poppy. Go back to bed. I'll be there in a minute." I gave her a reassuring smile. "Off you go now. Don't catch cold."

Sam looked over my left shoulder. "Cute kid."

"Yeah." I eyed him suspiciously. I was in two minds: I could tell him to leave and spend the rest of my life wondering what it was he wanted to warn me about or let him in, annihilating any remnants of anonymity I had left. Either way, I had to handle him with care. Only a fool would take such a tenacious tiger by the tail.

I opened the door and beckoned him in. "Take a seat. This will only take a minute."

When I returned from Poppy's room, he had poured out a couple of glasses of scotch. "I hope you don't mind. I thought it might take the chill off." His damp, blue jacket was hung over the back of a dining chair.

I positioned myself across from him on the sofa, scotch in hand. The cushion was still warm from the body heat Harry and I had generated less than twenty-five minutes earlier. "Make yourself at home why don't you?" I tipped my glass and took a large gulp, believing it would help alleviate the unease arising from his impromptu visit.

It didn't.

"You're not an easy man to find, Max," he remarked coolly, leaning back into the sofa, outstretching an arm along the back as if he was settling in for the night. I felt the blood in my veins effervescing, making my skin tingle and flush. Sitting opposite him, I mirrored his behaviour, mocking his mood.

He continued. "But, I suppose if I'd been through what you had, I'd want to crawl under a rock too." He snickered, inappropriately. "Although, this is *some* rock." He raised his head to take in the high ceiling and the open space.

There was so much I wanted to ask him but, fearing I would appear too unnerved, I prepared to frame my questions in such a way that they were skewed in the direction *I* wanted them to go—away from Harry and focused on me. I crossed my right leg over my knee. "But *you* found me. How did you do that, Sam?"

He dug his hand into the front pocket of his jeans. I couldn't see what he had taken out—it could have been anything.

"I knew I'd seen you somewhere, but couldn't place you, then…" He stared off in the distance recalling a memory; a memory that conjured up an encounter that I had long forgotten, perhaps.

I waited to hear more, becoming aware of my breathing and the abnormal way my chest was rising and falling beneath my shirt. "Then…?"

"Then I remembered this." He unfurled what appeared to be a crumpled piece of origami. With a flick of the wrist, he turned it round to face me and flattened it out.

It was a newspaper article.

Feeling bile rising in my throat, I swallowed deeply, gripped my shin with one hand and leaned forward to pick up the cutting with the other. I knew exactly what it was: a sensationalised account of the break-in, Hope's death and the birth of our baby girl snatched from the jaws of death in my wife's dying moments.

The words merged as my eyes clouded over. I had made a point of not reading any news reports across any media channels: I lived it and didn't need to be reminded of my failure as a husband, not when I alone knew the truth.

I pushed it back to him, not about to deny that the clean-shaven man smiling broadly next to his beautiful wife at the opening night of an art exhibition was me. "Seems odd that you have a copy of a newspaper article about someone you hadn't met until a couple of weeks ago." I needed answers and fast.

He nodded. "True. I had to get a couple of boxes down from my mother's loft to get that."

"You kept it? Why? Out of some morbid fascination for pregnant women killed under tragic circumstances?" I reached for the scotch and took a galvanising gulp.

His mouth twitched as he held back a self-satisfied smile. He was unwilling to give anything away; he had his heart set on a game of cat and mouse, and we were going to keep racing round in circles until he grew tired of it.

"I'm not the one with a morbid fascination, and I didn't keep it, Max. Why would I?" He paused for dramatic effect.

"Then who the *hell* did?" I yelled, about to convert a fit of rage into a collision between his face and my fist.

He answered calmly, "Why Jane of course—or whatever she's calling herself these days."

A split second after he spoke, I recoiled. He hadn't put a hand on me, but his reply left me seriously wounded and lost for words. "Wh ... what?" I exhaled.

Without asking, he topped up my glass and his own. He held his glass aloft. "Cheers."

"What do you mean, 'Cheers?'" I didn't reciprocate; I was too busy downing the double dose of scotch to speak. Only after every drop had been supped did I smash down the glass and lean forward, focusing all my attention on him. "Tell me what the fuck's going on, Sam." I clenched my right fist reflexively.

He noticed. "You've been had my friend. I did warn you…"

I was so hot tempered, I was close to igniting. If he didn't come clean soon there was no telling what I might do. "Warn me about what?"

"Not what—who. About our darling Jane—or should I say Harriet? For argument's sake let's call her that. It does have a nice ring to it: Harriet Harper." He nodded and considered its alliterative quality. "What do you know about her?"

"Never mind what *I* know…" I hissed. "Where did you get that newspaper article?"

He sighed. "When she left and I had to move into my mother's, remember I said I lost my job?" I nodded. "I cleared everything out, bagged what she'd left and gave it to our local charity shop. The overnight case she'd used when she was taken into hospital was still there, in the back of the wardrobe." He picked up the article and returned it to his pocket. "I checked the inside and outside pockets for cash but only found that tucked away in there. She must have forgotten to take it out when she left."

He reached for the bottle of scotch. I beat him to it. "Leave the fucking bottle where it is and start talking. I've played this game of yours for long enough."

He shrugged his shoulders. "What do you want to know?"

"For starters … how long you've known Harriet?"

He exhaled loudly. "We met at school. Like I said last week, she turned up at a New Year's Eve party in a sexy red dress and caught my eye."

I urged him to continue. "Them you *were* childhood sweethearts, like you said?"

"Yeah. That's what I told you. The Golden Couple we were called, more like fool's gold as it turned out." He chuckled. "But, to be honest, I gave you the edited version, you being a romantic and all." He paused and then thought better of it when I didn't take the bait. "I thought you'd want to hear about true love and all that bullshit. And … I *was* pissed. I see everything through rose-tinted glasses when I've had a few."

"Spare me. Tell it to me straight," I insisted.

"Okay." He folded his hands behind his head and stretched out. "Like I said, once I broke her in, she couldn't get enough. She was permanently on fucking heat." Entranced by a vivid memory he smiled to himself. "She wanted it every which way and I wasn't gonna be the one to rain on her parade." He tossed me a knowingly look. "Don't get me wrong. I didn't take advantage—I didn't have too. There *were* rules though. I had to wear a condom and had to promise not to tell anyone: it was our dirty, little secret. To the rest of the world she was Miss Fucking Perfect when, in fact, she was the perfect fuck." He laughed at his joke and pulled on his bottom lip with a forefinger and thumb. "I could tell you a thing or two about Harriet that would keep you toasty at night—if you get my drift."

I rolled my eyes. "Don't bother."

He finished off the remaining droplets of amber liquid clinging to his glass, "Anyway, I'm only telling you what you already know, right?"

He perceived my silence as a negative response.

"Jesus! Don't tell me you've not tapped that yet?" Now he was the impatient one. He leaned forward. "When you do, just make sure she doesn't get wind that you're not totally into her!"

Feigning indifference, I asked, "Who said I was into her?"

He shrugged. "I'm just saying… She made me pay bigtime for just looking at another girl. She wouldn't let me fuck her for a week. I had to jerk off in front of her while she played with herself." He exhaled. "Longest week of my fucking life."

He regaled me with crude anecdotes from their misspent youth, and the years that followed. I didn't recognise the Harry I knew in a single story. So convincing was his delivery, I found it hard to believe that he wasn't making everything up. "How old were you when all this was happening?" I asked, curiously.

"We were both sixteen. She went off to college doing typing and stuff, and I got a job at Dash Deliveries, in the office at first and then as a driver once I got my licence. Later we moved into a place of our own."

"Then why, if you were living the dream, did she leave you?" I asked bluntly.

"I told you. With me out of work, she must have thought she could do better and went fishing for a replacement." He stopped suddenly. "Someone like you."

"I'm hardly a catch," I huffed.

"You've had some bad luck, that's for sure, but look at you… You've got your own home and a kid…" He glanced over in the direction of Poppy's bedroom. "You're a meal ticket *and* a ready-made family rolled into one, my friend."

"Is that what you thought when you saw Harriet leaving?" It was time for truth or dare.

"I thought, seeing as you looked out for me last week, I should do the same and warn you." He laughed. "I've known where she was for almost two years, Max. I know this area well. I even went into Hot Slots Casino in town once and watched her working."

"She doesn't know that…"

"And I want to keep it that way. I'm doing okay without her, thank you very much. It's you I'm worried about." He stood and took the ten paces over to the dining chair where his jacket was drying off. "I do wonder, though, what she said that made you come looking for me." He shrugged on the jacket. "It can't have been good."

I stood preparing to show him out. "It wasn't."

"I thought so." He reached out to shake my hand. "Watch yourself. Don't let her play you, my friend."

I shook his hand. "She won't. See you around."

He seemed to remember something and spun around. "They're running a comp in the pub on Friday. If you're making a delivery in Camden that is…"

We both smirked at the absurdity of my failed pretence. "I doubt it."

"No worries. Just remember what I said about that Russian doll. She's not the kind of person you want your kid to be playing with … that's all I'm saying."

"I know what you're saying."

I watched him zip up his jacket and make the trek down the drive, measuring his progress by the volume of footfalls on gravel, the whirr of an engine and the speeding away of a fast car.

It had stopped raining, but heavy clouds still covered the moon with inky gauze through which only the brightest stars could be seen. It seemed like the sky above my head and the world beneath my feet had become impermeable. I truly believed that if I looked more closely and delved more deeply into those twin realities, the truth would find a way to shine through.

I felt blinded and blind-sided by Harry *and* Sam. I had invited them into my home and been privy to their secrets but three weeks in and nothing was as it seemed. A virtuous man might have closed the door on them both and left them to their disquieting duplicities.

I was not that man.

I allowed their versions of the truth to cloud my judgement, reshape my reality: it came naturally to me. Like them, I too had fashioned my own warped version of the truth to preserve my reputation, and I was more like them than I dared to admit.

CHAPTER TWENTY ONE

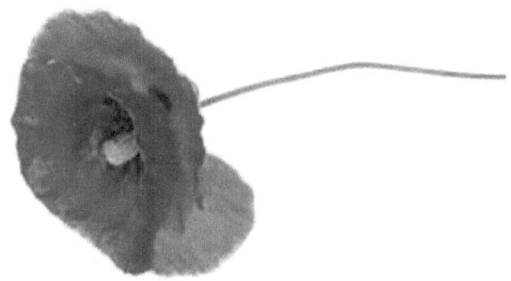

I WENT TO BED with a headache; one of those headaches that feels like your skull is in a vice. Finding it hard to concentrate on anything, I turned to Harry's journal, though I was beginning to think of it not so much as an autobiographical account but as one person's version of events.

Robert Evans once said,

"There are three sides to every story: my side, your side and the truth. And no one is lying. Memories shared serve each one differently."

To my dismay I was starting to question everyone's memories, even my own.

HARRIET - STARTING OVER

HAVING SURVIVED EVERYTHING LIFE and death have thrown at me, I get to spend my nights making it possible for people with more money than sense to gamble away their savings. What the hell … it's a job. The pay isn't that bad and the tips make it worthwhile.

From my very first shift at Hot Slots, I started as I meant to go on: I arrived early to change into my tailored uniform out of sight of my colleagues: white shirt, navy skirt with matching waistcoat. I still make a point of avoiding the full-length mirror, turning away from my reflection when I catch sight of familiar blue eyes, eyes that have seen way too much.

I had hoped that as I moved into the healing light of a coastal hideaway I would not only be able to reinvent myself by means of a new name, a new job and a new home, but physically too. I prayed that by some miracle my body would be rejuvenated and remodelled—but no.

Over time emotional scars have healed but physical scars remain like lines drawn in sand with crimson war paint; indelible traces of battles lost and won that cannot be erased, only camouflaged or concealed.

I think that has a lot to do with me becoming a creature of the night. In the first few months, working the night shift at Hot Slots did take some getting used to—it's much easier now.

For two years, I've headed home in a taxi at six fifteen in the morning, blinded by insistent sunlight, reminding me that I'm living a back to front life. That's why I love the winter months; diving into bed as the rest of the world is rising is easy when there is frost on the ground and snow in the air.

Since working there I've made friends and, more importantly, made money, enough to fund my education. I figure that if I can blend potential with opportunity, I just might make something of myself, and who knows, one day someone might actually look at me and see beyond the scars. Maybe then I'll be able to see myself through another person's eyes and like what I see.

When I started this journal, I did so to free myself of my past, to write it out of me, to see it in black and white then tear it up, burn it and scatter the ashes to the wind.

That's exactly what I'm going to do...

I CLOSED HARRIET'S JOURNAL for the last time and placed it on the bed next to me. It was a bitter pill to swallow after all she, and indeed we, had been through: a stark reminder of my treacherous behaviour not only as a friend but as a potential lover.

More positively, it denoted closure; it was her way of freeing herself from the nightmare that was her past life. I realised how she never intended for it to be read by anyone, certainly *not* by me. Essentially, it was a cathartic exercise; she was exorcising her demons and tracing the steps she had taken to reinvent herself.

She had come a long way. I couldn't help but admire her, and yet, my perception was tarnished by what Sam had described so vividly: her promiscuity, her vengeful nature and more worryingly the speed with which she turned on him when he was down on his luck.

And what about all those layers…?

I set myself a task—to press them both further. I was not prepared to turn my back on a kindred spirit or walk away from a friend who had taken the time to warn me about his ruthless ex. I owed it to myself to find closure.

That newspaper clipping Sam had produced had me questioning Harry's motives. Had she been dead-set on getting close to me for years?

In the absence of pencils and paints, she had become the project into which I had thrown myself with wild abandon. Her world had become my world. Had I been too quick to invite her into mine?

I hoped not.

I needed to know, one way or the other. More importantly, I owed it to Poppy. Keeping her safe was my priority, and if that meant exposing a sadist abuser of women or a vengeful woman with a perverse sense of injustice, I was prepared to do it.

CHAPTER TWENTY TWO

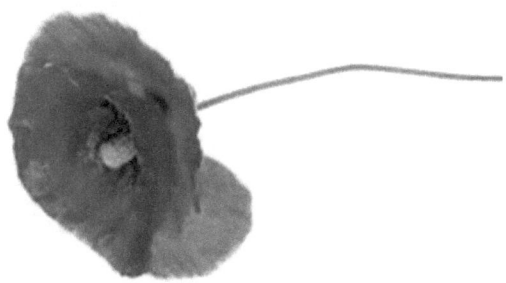

MONDAY MORNING WAS SPENT readying Poppy and myself for our lunch date with Grandma Chambers and her swimming lesson later in the afternoon. For Poppy, it was all about the dress, the boots and matching hair slides. My preparation was more of a psychological nature.

Constance Chambers has never been enamoured with me. From day one she thought Hope could do better. I had to agree, but the fact remained, Hope chose *me* as her husband. No matter what she said, or what I did, her reproachful mother disapproved. Even when I won the prestigious Richmond Artist of the Year Award and had a much acclaimed exhibition in London; not even when all my paintings sold and I was commissioned to paint more did she accept that she may have been a tad judgemental.

To her shame, Constance had taken no interest in Poppy. In the four years or so since her only granddaughter had been born, she had seen her four times. Poppy barely knew her, and when I read her third birthday cards out to her, I had to explain who she was and make up a story about Grandma Chambers living far away, and how nice it was of her to send a card and a ten-pound note.

It's the thought that counts…

She had sent us a mass-produced Christmas card featuring a studio photo of her and Hope's father, Bruce, standing by an enormous Christmas tree. The message printed inside read: *Best wishes, Constance and Bruce.* No distinction was made between work colleagues, family or friends. I tore it up. Who needs that kind of impersonal bullshit?

When I spoke of her to Poppy, I took all necessary measures to conceal my disgust: I bit my tongue, swallowed my pride… I did whatever necessary to keep her happy and misinformed. When the day arrives for her to come to her own conclusions about Grandma and Grandad Chambers, I'll be able to supplement her observations with my own.

I had seen Constance six months ago when my mood was still melancholic and mournful, when neither of us was able to forget or forgive me for what happened to Hope. We faced each other across a dinner table, separated by a chasm of fine cutlery, porcelain and empty pauses. When the forty-minute reunion ended, the abyss was still there.

I was feeling good about myself as Poppy and I walked into Chez Pierre at twelve thirty looking like a pair of new pins: polished, nicely preened and ready for inspection. We were shown to a table positioned in a quiet corner where Constance was sitting with her back to the window, pretending not to have noticed us approaching.

Poppy's eyes were everywhere: the urchin in a floral dress and boots with tumbling ringlets greeting sophisticated diners with a smile they couldn't help but respond to. Her stride didn't falter and her grip on my hand was not overly tight, which was a good sign under the circumstances, given that she was about to meet her condescending grandmother for the first time.

Bar the diners, everything was white and shiny, extravagantly adorned and perfumed—that included Constance sitting bolt upright as if about to receive royalty.

"Constance," I acknowledged, holding out my hand to her.

"Maxwell," she replied, quickly shifting her gaze to Poppy.

"This is Poppy, your grand-daughter."

The waiter helped Poppy remove her backpack, pulled back her chair and lifted her onto it. "Thank you," she said cheerfully. Mimicking my behaviour, Poppy held out her hand. "Hello Grandma. I like your necklace."

Constance took hold of Poppy's hand across the table. "Oh... Thank you. It was a gift from my husband." She fingered it and patted it into position on her décolletage. "You look lovely too."

Poppy placed the napkin on her lap. "Thank you. Do you like my hair slides? These are my favourite ones. I've worn them because Daddy says this is a *special* day." She wiggled them into position.

"It is," Constance agreed. "They look lovely too. You have a lot of hair," she remarked, providing me with my cue.

"She takes after her mother," I commented, knowing perfectly well what she meant: Poppy's lack of grooming, her wayward hair, her non-standard attire, her forwardness...

I called over the waiter and asked him to remove the large vase of flowers near the table. I whispered in his ear about Poppy being asthmatic and he was quick to oblige.

"So, how have you been, Constance? You look well." I picked up the menu and passed it to Poppy even though I knew she would only be able to read a couple of words.

She ran her fingers over the embossed cover. "It's pretty."

I nodded. "It is. What would you like to eat?"

She shrugged and turned to Constance. "What are you going to eat, Grandma?" she asked unselfconsciously. "I can't read very well, so will you tell me what I can choose?" She sat back with her hands on her lap.

Somewhat caught unawares, Constance began scrolling down the menu with a freshly manicured nail. "Let me see. The lamb's good here and the fish too..."

Poppy listened attentively, waiting to hear the list of options before making her choice. I smiled inside, loving how she wouldn't be rushed or forced to eat whatever was put in front of her.

Constance continued, "There's pork with mushrooms and white wine, steak tartar..."

"What's that?" Poppy asked stopping her in her tracks.

"It's raw steak..."

Poppy's eyes widened. "Not cooked?"

Constance shook her head, making her earrings swing. "No. Not really."

"Yuck!" She leaned over to me. "Don't have that, Daddy. Mary will be cross."

I laughed. "Why's that?"

"She says we have to wait until dinner is ready." She turned to Constance. "I don't want not-ready steak."

Constance chuckled and returned to the menu. "I don't want not-ready steak either," she stated. "What about pasta?"

Poppy nodded. "I like pasta."

"Good. Do you like penne, ravioli, spaghetti, lasagne...?"

Poppy turned to me once more. "Which one do I like, Daddy?"

"You like ravioli with extra parmesan cheese," I said, still making my own choice.

"Can I have ravioli with extra *parmesam* cheese please, Grandma?" She looked very pleased with herself.

"Of course, you can, Poppy." She raised her eyes and settled them on me. "And what about you, Maxwell?"

"I'm having the steak, medium rare with a side salad." I lowered the menu. "What about you?" I asked maintaining civility.

"I'll have the mushroom and lentil pappardelle Bolognese." With our decision made she signalled the waiter and gave him our order while I poured water into Poppy's glass.

She drank it nicely, grasping the glass in both hands. Holding it up to the light, she looked through it. "There's a rainbow in my glass!" she stated, her voice full of wonderment.

"That's because it's a crystal glass. Be careful you don't drop it." Constance took a sip of water, straightening her vanilla coloured suit as if preparing for an interview and began. "Something has come up, Maxwell, and I thought it only fair that I make you aware of it."

"Oh?"

"Yes. Hope's grandfather died recently, and she was named in his will. He had a large estate and most of it goes to his siblings, obviously, but he did bequeath these to Hope."

She removed a small, crimson box from her handbag and passed it across the table to me. I had no idea what it was. I speculated that it might be jewellery.

I wasn't wrong. Inside the small, padded box was a set of diamond earrings in platinum. They were exquisite.

"Can I see?" Poppy asked stretching over to take a look.

I lowered the box so she could see. "They're earrings."

"Earrings? They're pretty. They have rainbows too!" she exclaimed. "Look, Grandma."

I tipped the box up for Constance to see, even though she knew perfectly well what they looked like.

"They'll be yours one day," Constance said, rather surprisingly. "Your mother always remarked on them when her grandma wore them. That's why her grandpa left them to her in his will."

Poppy looked at me for a translation.

"Your mummy's grandma wore them, and your mummy used to say how pretty they were so, when she went to heaven, she left them for your mummy as a present, and as she's not here…"

Poppy turned to Constance. "Mummy's a star in the sky," she said plainly. "We look up at night and see her sometimes. Don't we, Daddy?"

I nodded. "Yes. We do."

I ran my hand over her hair. "You'll be able to wear these when you're older." I slipped the box in my jacket pocket. "Say thank you to Grandma for bringing them for you."

She smiled so wide her face almost split in two. "Thank you, Grandma." She blew her a kiss across the table.

Constance put her hand to her mouth and for a second I thought she might blow her a kiss back. But she did not. From the way tears were filling her eyes, I saw that she had her hand to her mouth to cover her trembling lips and was too emotional to return Poppy's kiss.

"Look! Here's lunch," I said, drawing Poppy's attention from her grandma to the aromatic food.

"Yay!" Poppy leaned forward and smelled the ravioli, taking big breaths. "It smells yummy."

"That's a good sign," I said, doing the same with my steak and caught the waiter's attention before he left. "Can you bring me a whisky on the rocks, please, and a gin and tonic?" I looked over at Constance. "Isn't that what you drink?"

"It is." She nodded to the waiter.

"And a glass of orange with ice for the young lady." I glanced down at Poppy who was too happy for words. "You can start eating now," I said, picking up my fork.

She held her hands together. I lowered my fork and did the same. She waited for Constance to follow suit. "For all we eat, and all we wear, for daily bread, and nightly care, we thank thee heavenly Father. Amen." Quick as a flash she grabbed her fork and started eating the ravioli.

"So," I asked, adding salt to my meal. "How's Bruce?"

"He's doing fine. He's about to take up a new post in some God forsaken place in the Far East, so I expect we'll be moving over there some time in the Spring."

"Sounds exciting."

"It's only for a year or so until they find a suitable replacement. They needed an experienced member of the diplomatic corps, and you know what he's like...? Bruce to the rescue." She tipped her head from left to right unimpressed by his devotion to duty.

I knew exactly what he was like: browbeaten and probably wishing he could leave her behind. Listening to her talking after such a long time I was reminded of her idiosyncratic style. She did not have so much of an accent as an affectation; she spoke with received pronunciation; a regal tenor accentuated by a lisp causing her to hiss when the letter 's' slipped out.

As I ate, I amused myself with an image of her vocalising some of the songs Hope and I had bopped around to when we discovered we were having a baby: fast paced, sing-a-long pop songs. Although my movements were imperceptible, I was moving to the beat and anyone looking under the table would have seen my feet tapping. Constance was too focused on Poppy to notice but, if she had looked under the table, she would have seen that we were *both* moving like a pair of ducklings beneath the waterline.

"What have you been up to?" Constance asked Poppy, feigning interest.

"I go to the big school with Daddy." Poppy was happy to volunteer information. "I like to paint but Daddy says I have to learn to draw first."

Constance stopped eating to listen. "Is that so?"

I interjected before she could conjure up a derogatory comment reflecting my lack of parenting skills. "I teach a night school class on a Tuesday and Poppy has been coming with me."

"Ah. I see. And do you still have a housekeeper?"

"Yes. Mary's still looking after us." I smiled, trying to figure out where her line of questioning was going. It had to be going somewhere.

"That's good."

Thankfully, our drinks arrived. "Are you still living in Hampshire?" I enquired, crunching on an ice cube.

"Yes. It's the family home."

I wanted to say, *Not quite. Poppy's never been there* but chewed on a piece of steak instead and focused on my food.

"I must say, Maxwell. You seem significantly more ... composed than when we last met, more approachable... Thank you for bringing Poppy along." She lowered her eyes.

"I thought you might like to meet her—in the flesh, so to speak." *And not behave as if she doesn't exist,* I wanted to add.

She spoke without raising her eyes. "Indeed. So, what has changed, to bring about this transformation?"

I pushed my plate to one side. "I've grieved for long enough, Constance." I took a sip of whisky and felt its reassuring warmth in my throat. "A friend said recently, 'There are bad people in the world who do bad things to good people. S-H-I-T happens.' And she was right. Poppy and me, we're a team and we'll be okay. I'll make sure of that."

She patted her mouth with a napkin. "I believe you, Maxwell." She turned to Poppy. "You look just like your mummy when she was your age. How old are you now?"

"I'm nearly four. How old are you?"

Constance laughed. "Add fifty to that and you'll be nearer the mark, my dear."

"Fifty-four!" Poppy exclaimed.

"That's right."

We laughed.

"You know, Poppy, when your mother was your age, she was like a magpie…" Poppy struggled to grasp the analogy. Constance explained, "She was drawn to sparkly things: jewellery, paper weights, even shiny surfaces. She just had to touch."

Poppy stopped eating to listen.

"That reminds me of someone around this table," I said, brushing my hand over Poppy's curls.

Constance found her stride. "When she was twenty-one, I bought her a bracelet just like those earrings, and when you're twenty-one, it will be yours."

Poppy turned to me. "Is that true, Daddy?"

"Yes. I have it locked away at home." I held back on the sentimentality.

"Can I see when we go home?" she said, keeping her voice at a conspiratorial level,

I nodded. "Sure. But we'll have to put it back. Okay?"

"Okay. Just to look at and touch…"

"Exactly."

I remembered when Hope received the bracelet. It was at her twenty-first birthday party Constance had arranged at their family house. She was not into expensive jewellery but wore it to please her mother.

"I think I've a photo of your mummy wearing it. I'll have a look for it when we get home. Now finish your ravioli before it gets cold." We shared a loving smile.

I could almost hear Constance's brain ticking. "It's good to see you smiling again, Maxwell. Do you have someone in your life who's helped with your makeover? You looked like you'd been sleeping rough when I…"

"Harry!" Poppy called out, almost bouncing in her chair. "Harry makes Daddy smiley."

Constance's eyes widened. "Harry?"

"Not Harry…" I assured her. "It's short for Harriet."

"Ah." She looked relieved. "I thought it might be. Is this someone you've known for a while?"

I allowed the waiter to clear our plates before continuing. "No. She's a woman we've become friendly with from my art class."

"I see. A student," she ventured, no doubt picturing a post-pubescent woman in a mini skirt and high heels.

"Not at all. She's a mature student, Constance. An adult," I asserted, browsing the dessert menu. "She has a real job too."

"Good for her," she said, sardonically, unable to conceal her amusement behind the desert menu she was clearly using as a fan to cover her face.

"I'm assuming you want the ice-cream, Poppy?" I asked, hopefully.

She nodded eagerly. "What colours do they have?"

"What colours do you like?" Constance enquired, settling her menu on the table. "I bet it's pink." Hardly a lucky guess considering Poppy's attire.

"Yes!" Poppy exclaimed with glee, already reaching for her spoon. "What other colours do I like, Daddy?"

"Erm, you like chocolate and vanilla."

She turned to Constance. "I like chocolate and *banilla*."

Constance laughed. "I like banilla as well. Let's order that."

Poppy ate the ice-cream in a delicious daze, vocalising her childish delight through a series of unconscious noises, head nodding and leg swinging.

"There's nothing wrong with her appetite," Constance observed, scraping thin slivers of ice-cream onto her spoon.

"Nope. She'll eat most things." I threw back the remains of my drink.

When the bill arrived, I placed down my card and a decent tip on the tray. Constance took out her purse. "Put your purse away. It's our treat."

Her eyes met mine briefly. "Thank you. That's nice of you."

We left the restaurant and made our way to the lounge where Poppy shot off to a window seat, opened up her backpack, emptied out its contents and started to draw. We waited for our coffees in silence.

Constance cleared her throat. "She's just lovely, Maxwell."

"She is. I'm very lucky—"

"There's no luck involved," she interjected. "You've proven me wrong. You've raised a fine daughter, all by yourself."

"I had help," I conceded.

"Not from me."

"No. Not from you."

She reached over for her coffee and gave it a stir, playing for time. Conceding defeat did not come easily to her and I was not about to make it stress-free, not after the things she had said and done.

She hung her head. "When we lost Hope, I said some cruel things…"

"Like me being unfit to raise a child?" I returned fire reflexively.

"Yes, I'm sorry. I regret having said that now." She bit her lip nervously.

"You were grieving," I conceded, with a shake of my head. "We all were."

She raised her head like a cobra about to strike. "We were, which I found surprising in view of your infidelity."

I tried not to allow the shock of hearing that word to show on my face. It didn't, but my heart took the brunt of it and pounded in my chest like an electric current had been fed through it. "That was between Hope and me, and it was something we would have worked through."

"She didn't seem to think so, Maxwell," she snapped. "She filed for divorce."

"How do you know that?" I asked, sharply.

"She asked me to recommend a lawyer. I did. And when I asked why, she broke down and told me that you were in love with a young woman from your gallery. That you were having an affair."

I hated that the truth was coming out, first Harry and then her. Who was next? The press, the police? I had spent almost four years covering up and denying the truth, even to myself, and there I was stripped bare in front of Constance, my guts hanging out. I hated that she, of all people, knew. It seemed like finally, her disapproval of me was founded on real evidence and not mere supposition. I had been playing at being married; I treated our marriage as a sketch when it was the *Mona Lisa* of marriages. I had become a self-fulfilling prophecy.

And there I was thinking she had come to meet her granddaughter, to offer an olive branch, to take an interest in us both, but that had never been her intention. She had come to scold and gloat and walk away, back into her pristine world of fine dining and perfume scented ice-cream.

I called over to Poppy, "Get your things we're leaving…" I don't think she heard me above the clatter of the waitress collecting glasses on the other side of the room.

Constance took my arm. "I blamed you for everything…"

I shook my head. "You were right to. It was *all* my fault: the house, the obsession, the affair, her dying—everything!"

"That's not true, Maxwell." She lifted a ragged sheet of paper from her bag. "I've had this for a while. You can tell by the date on the email. I should have given it to you before now, but I was too embarrassed, I suppose."

She handed me a standard sheet of plain paper folded into four. It was a print out of an email, dated almost four years ago, in fact a month after Hope passed away. "What is it?" I asked.

Seeming flustered, she rearranged her hair. "Just read it, Maxwell."

Dear Mrs. Chambers,

Firstly, let me offer you my deepest condolences. I was a friend of your daughter and I cannot express how devastated I was to hear about her passing, especially as it was in such tragic circumstances.

"It's a letter of condolence…" I remarked. "We received lots of them."

"Not like this one we didn't." She tapped the corner of the sheet.

I read on.

You may not remember me, but I recall having met you at Hope's eighteenth birthday party at your family home. Hope and I spent a lot of time together that summer, the summer before she went off to university.

To say that I adored her would be an understatement. I believed that we would spend the rest of our lives together. So, imagine my horror when she called me to tell me that she had met Maxwell Grant, a second-year art student, and that she was going to marry him. It took me the best part of six months to get over her—perhaps I never will.

I used to spend hours scrolling through old photographs. In fact, I have attached one. Perhaps you will remember me?

Constance nodded and handed me the photograph. Even though it was printed on standard paper, Hope was clearly recognisable. I even remembered seeing the cardigan in the Goodwill pile Poppy and I had made.

I searched Constance's face for answers. "Is this guy for real?"

"Please read on." She sipped her coffee, and it was then that I noticed her hands were shaking.

I looked down at the sheet of paper and saw that mine were trembling too.

I assumed Hope had found her soul mate and, while I was happy for her, I felt a sense of loss, knowing I would never love anyone the way I had loved her and she had loved me. I had to accept that we were young, and love was something that came and went with the seasons for some people—not for me.

Last year when she contacted me just before Easter, I had to pinch myself. Naturally, we met and I was overjoyed to see her, but less enamoured with her husband on finding out that he had been seeing another woman—a younger woman—and neglecting her, leaving her alone for days at a time, not speaking to her, forcing her to live in that God awful metal box in the middle of nowhere. She was like a prisoner and I did all I could to comfort her.

"Comfort her!" I yelled. "What the fuck does that mean?"

"Maxwell," Constance muttered. "Please..."

We became lovers once again, Mrs Chambers. What we had was not in the least bit sordid. It was more spiritual than that. The coming together of two lost souls...

And this is why I'm sending you this email. I believe that Hope's baby may be mine.

Floored by the last line, I gasped and looked over at Poppy, clutching my chest. Thankfully, she was busy drawing and didn't witness my panic or see the flash of tears in my eyes.

Too overcome with emotion to read, I reached for my coffee, not even trying to stop the cup from rattling in the saucer as I lifted it to my lips. I turned to Constance. "You've known about this all these years and said *nothing*?"

"I ... I didn't know what to say. How to tell you... Not when I had been so set on making you r esponsible for everything and then there was the prospect of losing Poppy to a stranger and I..."

"No!" I cried. "That will never happen! Over my dead body." I sniffed back tears and flattened out the paper.

> *I have no wish to impose on you at this most wretched of times, but I think it only right that paternity over the child is established, and we find out if she is indeed my daughter. I will be in touch.*
>
> *Once again, my deepest condolences, Mrs Chambers.*
>
> *Yours,*
> *Spencer Ferguson*

With his words still buzzing around in my brain like white noise, I called over the waiter and ordered us two stiff drinks.

"What am I going to do?" I asked my pale-faced mother-in-law and former adversary. "You could have sorted this out a long time ago, once and for all. Did you think better the devil you know...?"

"Of course not. Hope loved you and if you hadn't put your damn work before her she would have continued to love you and not fallen back into the arms of— "

"Spencer Ferguson."

"Exactly."

I looked into her watery eyes. "But all this time ... I was thinking that it was me who..." I hung my head and raked through memories looking for that solitary moment when Hope turned from me, falling willingly into the arms of a former lover.

I couldn't find it.

In my mind she personified all that was right with the world; her name alone spoke of optimism and promise. I was the sinner, the home wrecker—not her.

What troubled me was the knowledge that I had not become infatuated with Melody until much later, not until Hope was at least three months pregnant.

She left me first.

I looked more closely at the photograph. "*Did* you remember him when you saw the photo? Did it jog your memory?"

She nodded.

"And? Was he a knight in shining armour?"

"No." She pinched her lips as if tasting something tart. "He was a weasel of a boy who had bad taste in clothes and a sister who laughed like a horse."

I scrutinised the photo. "Was he dark like Poppy? Did he have dark eyes? I can't tell from the photo." I was desperate to know.

"Yes. He had dark hair and dark eyes." She studied me closely. "Like you."

When the drinks arrived, I threw mine back in a single gulp. "I'll have a paternity test done. If it turns out Poppy is mine, then we have nothing to worry about. If … if not, then I'll sell the house and disappear where weasel boy will never find us." I shook my head and wrestled with my beard. "I can't risk him turning up and taking her away."

Constance nodded. "I understand. If that's what transpires, I'll help you. Like I said we're going to the Far East in the spring. Bruce will be able to set you up there and, better still, I don't think China has an extradition treaty with the UK."

I laughed sardonically. "I hadn't thought that far ahead."

"I've had longer to mull it over." She finished her drink and patted her mouth with a napkin. "I'm sorry for bringing you this news and ruining a wonderful day. When I look at Poppy, I see Hope, even the curls." She began to cry. "You're not the man I thought you were, Maxwell."

I held up my hand. "For God's sake, Connie. Will you call me Max? We're not in some American soap opera."

She laughed through her tears. "I hope the woman you've met is good for you. "

"She is—or at least, I think she is. We've got a couple of things to iron out, but…" I shrugged my shoulders. "She makes us both smile."

"I'm glad. Let's hope you've been through the worst of it and your life will continue to get better." She looked over at Poppy wistfully. "I always wanted the best for Hope."

"She deserved the best—in everything."

"Yes. And for most of the time you were with her, that's exactly what you gave her. I believe that included Poppy." I felt her hand on my arm.

"Oh, dear God! I hope you're right." I called Poppy over. "Poppy! Come and say bye to grandma."

"She's such a dear." She reached for her handbag. "Thank you for allowing me to be part of her life ... part of *your* life, Max. I've been married long enough to know what it feels like to be second best, to come runner-up in the race for the perfect career. Hope was used to having all your attention and when she didn't get it, she found solace elsewhere."

I shook my head, unwilling to allow even her mother to deface her memory, pausing to regain some semblance of composure. Stepped back I bowed my head, carrying the burden of regret once more.

"We have both sinned in one way or another, Max." She patted my hand. "Hope was no saint, I can accept that now. She had such a big heart and she filled it with love for you and your beautiful daughter—"

"The one she never got to see," I interjected, my voice breaking on the last word.

"Oh, don't you be so sure. If I know my daughter, she'll move heaven and earth to be with you both again."

I concealed my sadness behind a smile. "I'd like to think so." I stood and took hold of Poppy's backpack while Connie helped her put on her coat. Our taxis were waiting outside.

With little regard for her expensive suit, Connie knelt and began buttoning Poppy's coat. "It was so nice to meet you. Maybe we'll get to spend some time together over Christmas and you can meet your grandpa."

Poppy looked across to me for confirmation.

I nodded. "Sure. I'll give you a call and you can come round and open your presents."

"That sounds wonderful." She pulled Poppy in close and hugged her. "Goodbye, my dear." Her lips brushed Poppy's cheek.

"Bye, Grandma." She kissed her cheek quickly and about turned to the window seat, her boots making a familiar rattling sound on the wooden floorboards as she ran. I was just about to call her back when she returned holding a sheet of paper. "I made this for you."

Connie held it up and I watched her expression change. The steadfast woman with sharp features and darting eyes appeared to deflate to such an extent I thought I might have to catch her. She fell down onto her chair and reached into her handbag for a handkerchief. "I don't know what to say, Poppy…" She was too overcome with emotion to speak.

"Say thank you," Poppy said cheerfully.

Connie's face brightened. "Yes, of course. Thank you." She dabbed at her eyes. "It's a wonderful gift, and I will treasure it." She blew her nose before standing.

Poppy moved around to my side of the table and slipped her fingers around mine. With my free hand I reached out for her drawing, not knowing what to expect. What I saw made me want to close my eyes, to take a moment to process what I was looking at.

I was the bearded man; she was the little figure in black boots next to me. On my other side stood Connie, apparent by her bright yellow necklace and reading glasses. On Poppy's other side was Harry, as plain as day. Then I saw what had moved Connie— it struck an agonizing chord with me too. It was the simplicity of the message; we were holding hands and all around us were tiny pink hearts. It was an expression of pure affection, not only between Poppy and me, but all four of us. We were linked intrinsically by our love for each other.

My intuitive daughter had cut through the drama, all the heartache and drawn our family as she saw it—how it should be: standing together, united in our grief and in our belief that we were strong enough to live through anything.

Anything.

I looked at Connie, sensing she and I were sharing the same thought. We both doubted we *would* be able to live through losing Poppy. I tightened my grip on her hand, leaned over to kiss her grandmother on the cheek and left the restaurant with Poppy skipping all the way to the taxi.

As it pulled away, she kneeled up on the seat giggling and waving through the rear window. I placed my open palm on her back, preventing her from falling, as the driver played stop-go with the afternoon traffic. The throng of people wrapped up in scarfs and knitted hats went about their business, shopping, clutching cups of coffee, greeting friends … while I rocked back and forth to the irregular rhythm of my fractured heart.

CHAPTER TWENTY THREE

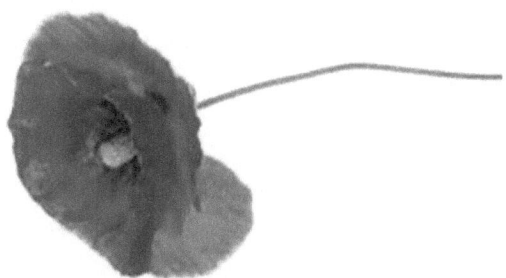

TUESDAY MORNING, I DARTED into my office first thing. The November sunshine illuminated the dust motes daring to dance on top of my desk. As I picked my phone off the desk, they scattered like miniature fairies in the early morning rays. I paused to organise my thoughts before making an urgent appointment at a private clinic in Harley Street.

They were very understanding when I explained the need for a paternity test—I had to know one way or the other.

After I made the call, I pulled Mary to one side. I needed to tell someone, someone I could trust knowing that, if the worse came to the worst, she would have to get involved and provide a character reference if a custody battle ensued, or, God forbid, take care of Poppy while I fought tooth and nail to keep her.

Mary grew pale throughout our conversation; I say conversation, but it comprised of me talking gibberish and her punctuating my sentences with gasps. She held onto the doorframe and lent forward so obviously shaken by my news that I thought she might faint. Only when she had pulled herself together and blown her nose could she go about her business, her heart seemingly breaking at the prospect of losing our little girl.

As requested, she placed Poppy's toothbrush into an envelope, which I had her seal. I did the same with mine and dropped them both into two separate, plastic bags before leaving for the clinic.

I shouted goodbye, trying not to make a show of my departure, but Poppy heard and came sprinting to the door before I could make my escape.

I heard her before I saw her and didn't have the heart to close the door and bolt.

"Daddy!" she called out. "Where are you going? Can I come?"

"I have to go to a meeting in the city," I explained. "I'll be back for dinner." I picked her up and planted a kiss on her cheek. My focus shifted to Mary. "Anyway, I think Mary needs you to help her this afternoon."

I saw Mary take an invigorating breath. "I do indeed, pumpkin. We've apple pie to make and that pastry won't roll itself out." She held out her hand.

I lowered Poppy, becoming conscious of her proximity. She was leaning against my leg, using extra sensory perception to tune into our anxiety. Perhaps it was the happy-go-lucky tenor of our voices, or the way our glossy eyes seemed to be holding back tears… Whatever it was, she had noticed a change in the air, in our demeanour, and it worried her.

"We can make pie another day," she answered. "I want to go with Daddy." Her grip tightened around my leg.

I peeled her off me. "Not this time, Poppy. We'll be going out later, remember, to the art class? Won't you need to get ready for that?"

Just as I knew it would, my casual reminder caused her to rethink her decision. "Okay." She let go of me and moved away to stand by Mary.

As a reflex action, Mary placed her hand on Poppy's head. "Now be off with yer. We have women's work to do."

There was a time when Mary saying that would have irked me: the thought of Poppy being trained in the domestic arts, but on that day of all days, I found her words reassuring. Poppy was in good hands.

The technician in the clinic explained that they would check both samples for DNA and if a match was found then that would confirm parentage. My legal position would be more transparent and defensible; I could get on with my life—our lives—knowing weasel boy had no rights with regard to Poppy, regardless of what he claimed had taken place between him and my wife.

If the results came back and there was not a match, then it would be a case of taking evasive action, whatever that meant. The tone of the email, and the fact that he had even sent it, was disturbing, there was no disputing that. But the fact he had not acted upon his suspicion and not bothered to make contact for what would amount to four years would go against him.

How committed *was* he?

Until it could be proven *who* the actual father was and if *he* was even interested in taking possession of his child—a child he had never known—Poppy *would* remain with me. I didn't care what anyone said, she was, is, and will always be my daughter regardless of the result.

As I drove from the clinic I looked about me in a way I had not before, making a mental note of possible hiding places: multi-storey hotels silhouetted against cumulous clouds tumbling over each other in their desperation to escape something sinister; out of the way bed and breakfast hotels where no one would notice us as we skittered back and forth between a bathroom and unmade beds; street signs with railway symbols, overhead signs with an airplane directing me to Heathrow, high-speed means of escape to places where we could remain together as father and daughter.

I had time to think things through, a week the technician had said—time enough to make plans. I was not a wealthy man. Most of what I owned was invested in bricks, mortar, glass and metalwork—our home. But I would find a way: sell paintings collecting dust in my studio, sell the house, sell my story to the papers, if need be.

Hope had believed that where there was a will, there was a way. I had always been a willful man and it would take more than weasel boy to come between Poppy and the only father she had ever known.

I turned up early for class that Tuesday evening, grasping a shopping bag of items for the evening's composition in one hand and Poppy's nimble fingers in the other. The ride over had left me feeling perplexed; my beard itched, my head ached, I was irritable and in no mood for playing teacher—not the *nice* kind.

Poppy had no way of knowing that I had more important things to think about than Grandma, her Christmas Day visit and our need to shop for presents. How could I say I wasn't sure if *we* would be spending Christmas together, never mind adding her grandparents to the mix?

Harry and I had not spoken since Saturday night and I feared she might not even turn up, having had time to consider how I had fallen short and behaved disgracefully, as a husband and as a protector. The closer we were becoming, the more the truth seemed to bleed out of me, like a wound that would not heal. No matter how many times I wrapped it up in bandages it leaked through, visibly staining my character.

What would she make of my news? She adored Poppy, so who better than her when it came to lending an empathetic ear when I needed it? The fact of the matter was, I felt I might have burnt too many bridges between us, even before we had ventured across them.

I held on to the notion that recent events had made me overly susceptible to the possibility of failure and disappointment. I had courted pessimism for so long that it followed me around like a shadow. Hopefully, Harry would be able to look to the future—our future together—with optimism and no small amount of affection, even after our heart to heart and her vanishing into the night.

The contents of my shopping bag spilled out onto the small display table at the front of the class. Poppy helped to arrange the seashells and pebbles around an enormous conch, but not before putting it to her ear.

She held it out to me. "Listen. You can hear the sea."

I raised it to my ear, still holding onto a smooth grey pebble with the other hand. She was right, I *could* hear the sea. I closed my eyes, taken back to Brighton Beach, tightening my grip on the pebble, using it to intensify the experience and amplify the sound. In the echoing waves, I heard Hope's ghostly voice, no words, just an impression—a soothing whisper.

I opened my eyes and placed it on the display table, completing the composition. When I looked up, I saw Harry by the door. I had no way of knowing how long she had been standing there, but from her kind smile I would say a while. Poppy shot over to her and leapt into her arms.

"Hi, Harry," I said, returning her smile. "I wasn't sure you'd come."

"*Why* wouldn't I come?" she asked, putting on an affectation. "Where else would I go on my night off?" She winked at Poppy who chuckled, not understanding what we were really saying but enjoying the banter.

The evening followed the usual pattern; my students drew to the best of their ability. I offered praise and advice and announced Alison as the most improved student—which she clearly was. I didn't have a prize so offered her the shell which Poppy was eager to present in her unique way. She accepted it with good grace, and we all applauded.

They left for the pub and I invited Harry back to join us for tea. We both knew tea was the last thing on our minds but with Poppy within earshot, Harry was happy to play along.

CHAPTER TWENTY FOUR

WHILE I MADE TEA, Harry got Poppy ready for bed and read her a short story.

In less than half an hour, Harry was seated on the sofa in a familiar pose, her legs tucked under her, sipping tea. "She was exhausted. Fifteen minutes in and I realised I was reading to myself. It would take an earthquake to wake her up." Harry laughed, but the laughter faded quickly and was replaced by a serious expression. "I want to thank you for being so honest about the circumstances of Hope's death. I've been thinking about it ever since."

"I don't want you to worry. Talking about it has made me feel much better about what happened." It really had.

She smiled warmly. "I'm glad. I didn't want you to think you had come clean and there I was holding onto my secrets."

"You have secrets?" I feigned surprise.

"I haven't always been Harriet Harper," she confessed easily.

"Is that so? If I bribe you with wine, will you tell me about the *real* you?" I winked and waited on her reply.

She laughed softly. "Of course. Pour away."

I grabbed a bottle of white wine and two glasses. "Come with me to the interrogation room." I led her down the corridor to the library. I hadn't been in there for a couple of weeks, and then only for a flying visit, but Mary had seen to it that it was dust free and every surface was gleaming.

Harry's eyes grew wide and expectant as she entered. "Wow! I had no idea you had a room like this; all these books…" She walked around picking things up and putting them down. "A real fire too."

"Yes. This was Hope's favourite room. I'm sure you can see why."

She nodded. "It's very cosy." She spun around. "Not that the rest of the house is a shambles or anything … but this room has a different feel to it."

"Yes, it does. I don't come in here often because it's where, you know…" I indicated that we should sit down.

She covered her mouth with her hand in an expression of horror. "Oh, Max. I'm sorry. Don't feel you have to come in here for my benefit."

"I don't." I set down the bottle and fiddled with the screw top. "I have to come in here for *my* benefit. Better that I do so with you than on my own."

She sat on one end of a tapestry style sofa and I sat at the other; we faced each other like a couple of bookends soaking up the ambiance.

I passed her a glass of wine. "So, Miss Harper. Who are you?"

"Well, you may be surprised to know that for most of my life, up until I was twenty-three, I was known as Jane Harper…"

I nodded, offered words of encouragement and listened to her recount what I already knew. It wasn't until Sam started to feature that I really tuned in.

"Sam was patient with me. He could have any girl he wanted, but he was willing to wait for me, and that made me feel special. It meant I wasn't like all the others."

"He was a good-looking boy, then?"

"Oh, yes. There was a permanent queue of girls just waiting for him to move on after me." She laughed, but it seemed forced, as if she was making light of something far more meaningful than a schoolgirl crush.

"When we made love for the first time, it was because we were ready. He didn't pressure me at all. We'd been together for over six months. I used to tease him and say he was like a firework; when I touched him I felt as if I was lighting touch paper; if I didn't stop and move away quickly, he would start to burn and BANG!"

Again came the nervous giggle. It was growing on me, so much I felt myself waiting for it as a kind of provocative parenthesis controlling the pace of my pulse. "I assume you got your private moment?" I held up my hand. "By the way, you don't have to tell me, you know."

She nodded. "I know, but I want to, it will help you to understand the person I've become. Why Jane became Harriet."

I knew exactly what she meant. I'd already been treated to Sam's vulgar version of events. The least I could do was let her tell it her way.

She continued. "When his parents went away for the weekend, we told them we were going to a party and stopping over. It was a lie." She focused on the fireplace. "When it happened it didn't feel sensual, not even slightly. We were both distracted, listening to each other's noises, too preoccupied with the act itself to enjoy it. Afterward, we grinned, wide toothy, teenage grins that split out faces in two. I told him that I loved him, and I meant it."

I smiled, encouraging her to continue.

She turned to face me. "To hear me tell it, it seems innocent enough: young love, first sexual encounter, school sweethearts... I thought so too. That's why I understand what it's like to lose someone. Sam moulded me into the person he wanted—he defined me. We were the Golden Couple. It was like he had the Midas touch: everything he touched just seemed to go his way. I couldn't see a way forward without him. How could I have known that touch would turn into a slap or a punch?"

I grimaced. "I'm sorry to hear that. But you got out and saved yourself? That was a brave thing to do."

"Not really, I had no choice. I would have died if I hadn't—I almost did."

I appeared shocked. "What happened?"

"He came back from the pub drunk. I refused to have sex with him and we ended up on the landing. The next thing I knew I was at the bottom of the stairs." In an involuntary gesture, she touched her stomach. "I lost our baby and had to have a hysterectomy because of complications."

"My God! I'm so sorry." I didn't dare tell her about the way he had befriended me, appeared at my door making all kinds of accusations about her. I felt like a phoney friend—an imposter. Hearing her tell *her* story made it all the more believable. He was the disingenuous one, set on blackening her character.

I took her hand in mine and stroked it; her fingers were nimble and the palm of her hand soft, almost squidgy. "I understand. I was young once too. You invest so much in a relationship that you lose sight of what it's doing to your character, your potential." I leaned across and topped up our glasses. "I had a thing with an older woman when I was seventeen, just before I left for university. She taught me a thing or two but nearly buggered-up my examination results in the process." I smiled at the memory. "It's not as serious or as tragic as your experience but there are similarities."

She nodded politely. "I was naïve. I mistook domination for love and accepted his insistence as a sign of him wanting to take care of me. That wasn't his game at all. He used me, sexually, made demands on my body no sixteen-year-old should have to endure and then told his mates about it."

"That's shocking." It truly was.

"I can't tell you the abuse I got off the other girls. They were jealous to start with, me being the least likely candidate for his attention, but when they heard what we were getting up to, they called me all kinds of horrible names."

I shook my head. "What did you do?"

"I went away for a week to stay with my cousins and when I came back, Sam was so desperate to get our relationship back to how it was, he got rid of the girl who had started the rumours."

"Got rid of?" I asked disbelievingly.

"I don't mean he killed her." She grinned. "Nothing as bad as that. He put glue on her chair and when she got up her skirt tore. Everyone laughed, except me."

"Why?"

She sighed. "Because I knew she'd blame me, and she did."

"What happened?"

"She went running to the Headmaster and I got summoned to his office." She shrugged. "What *could* I say? I hadn't done anything."

"Did he believe you?"

"I think so. I was a straight-A student, and he couldn't believe all the things she had been saying about me and Sam. I can't believe them myself when I look back." She hung her head. "But Sam wanted to keep me sweet and compliantm so he killed a cat and left it in her locker."

"Jesus!"

"I know. He hates cats." She took a sip of wine and pictured the memory. "I heard that it was only the head, not the full cat: just enough for her to recognise it. It must have been horrible."

"You think?" I huffed, vocalising my disgust. "So that was it? Sam scared her off and she left?" I reconsidered my question. "I'm *assuming* she left?"

"She did and no one said anything nasty about me after that. They all knew *Super Sam* had got rid of her." She took another sip of wine. "Even as a boy he had two faces; he could be really loving and generous, but if he didn't get his own way, if you said *no*, then he would get physical. He talked me into having sex lots of times: in storerooms, science labs, in the changing room at the back of the gym..."

The more I heard, the more I hated Sam. He really was a manipulative bastard. "Couldn't you have ended the relationship, found someone else?"

"That was never an option. He would have killed me. I would have ended up like that cat." She shook her head. "He was the devil, he offered me something I had never known and could never experience on my own—to be popular, to be envied, to be desired. I was his, his favourite toy, and I blame myself. I was always runner up, second best at everything except when I was with him. I was his first choice. I felt powerful."

Overwhelmed by the intensity of her confession, she stopped to compose herself.

"Over time, when he couldn't do without his daily fix of me, I would withhold it: stay behind after class, attend extra lessons or claim I was having my period, just to make him wait. If I wanted something, I would promise him sexual favours in exchange for it. Even at sixteen, I used it to my advantage." She shook her head in disbelief. "I'm ashamed of myself, ashamed of what I let him turn me into—that wasn't the real me."

I gave her hand a squeeze. "Harry, I dare say there are hundreds of young girls who have been in a similar position and done what was necessary to get by."

"Maybe? But all that changed and there was a shift in power. It was as if losing his job triggered a chemical reaction inside his brain and the playfulness no longer existed. I became the enemy. An enemy with orifices…"

I closed my eyes, considering her blunt description. I moved closer and looked into her eyes. "All that's behind you, Harry. You've come so far. You don't ever have to go back to that."

"I know." She gazed dreamily into her glass of wine. "I miss the sex though." She glanced up at me through dark eyelashes, gauging my reaction. "When it was good, it was very good."

I squirmed on the cushion and let out a blast of hot air. "I think we've both been saving ourselves for the right person." I pressed her hand against my lips. "I can't guarantee to match Super Sam in the bedroom department, but I'd like to try."

Her cheeks flushed. "I'd like you to try too, Max."

I removed the wine glass from her hand and pulled her to her feet. "Come with me." I led her along the corridor.

My bedroom was clean and tidy thanks to Mary; glossy white furniture polished, reflecting what little light there was in the room. I turned on the bedside lamp, letting it drench us in soft light as we stood facing each other by the bed. I began unbuttoning her dress; my clumsy fingers struggled to undo the tiny buttons.

"Let me," she said, giggling. "We'll be here all night." There was no concealing her impatience.

I unbuttoned my shirt and threw it onto a chair; my shoes and jeans went the same way. I stood before her in boxer shorts and waited for her to join me in my nakedness.

Her fingers halted on the last button. "My God, Max, you're a handsome man." She ran her hands down my collar bone, circled my pectoral muscles with her fingertips and wove them into my chest hair. I could feel my arousal increasing, my skin tingling and becoming over heated. While she circled my body scrutinizing every inch, I opened my mouth, gulping in air as her heated breath swept over my shoulder blades.

Having come full circle she stood before me, significantly smaller than I had imagined without shoes, and utterly desirable. I reached over to remove her dress, but she flinched and I held my hands aloft.

"I'm sorry."

"Don't be," she whispered. "You're so perfect, and I'm so flawed. I don't want to disappoint you."

I kissed her gently. "Harry, you could never do that."

"Can we have the light off?" It was more of a plea than a question.

I leant over and clicked the switch. "Better?"

"Yes. Thank you." She slipped out of her dress and stood in her white underwear.

I threw back the bedding and invited her in, detecting a flash of indecision, which lasted no more than a split second.

We cuddled under the covers, skin against skin, reminding us of what it felt like to be close to someone—no words were needed. We separated and let our hands say what needed to be said as we explored and caressed each other to the sound of fevered breaths.

Lengthy foreplay was unnecessary; we had been ready for sex for years and simply speaking about it had served as an arousing aperitif to the main course.

Harry's impatience peaked quickly, and she rolled on top of me to feel the hardness of my throbbing erection against her. She straddled me, pinning me in place with her knees, arching backward, grinding against me until I was delirious with desire.

I reached up and gripped her chin in one hand and followed the line of scars between her breasts, underneath, down her abdomen and along the narrow space between her hips. She was a shapely silhouette, a composition that had been taken apart and put back together again—a living, breathing piece of art.

As hard as we tried to keep the noise down, we found ourselves vocalising the ecstatic sensations pulsating through our bodies. When I entered her, she let out a rapturous scream so loud, I had to smother it with my mouth.

"Stop!" I called out, holding her in place, savouring the intimacy of our union: our bodies fused together by a powerful bond. "I want to feel what it's like to be inside you," I whispered.

She mirrored my smile and locked her body in place on top of mine. Together we found our rhythm; a gentle rocking at first, increasing to a pounding, throbbing ache—there was no holding back. She elicited every ounce of pleasure from my body, rode me, wrung me out and made me climax with a delicious agony, the likes of which I had never experienced before.

I had the distinct feeling that I had been claimed and that added tenfold to my pleasure. There would be time enough to reciprocate.

Too tired to chat, we dissolved into a pool of perspiration and fell into a glorious repose wrapped in each other's arms. For the first time in four years, I didn't notice the darkness, reach out to find cold, empty sheets or torment myself with drink-induced dreams—I slept.

Harry and I had not *fallen* in love. Having fallen so hard in the past and had to pick ourselves up off the floor we knew better than to lose our heads and take a tumble without first erecting a safety net. But, after that night, all safety nets were down.

Seeing the love she had for Poppy and experiencing it for myself, I felt sure that she was the one person who could mend the broken pieces of my heart, turning them from a jumble of misshapen shards into a fully functioning, pulsating organ.

I wasn't wrong.

As a new day dawned, sending wedges of filtered light through the blinds, so did my appetite for sex; it stirred and I woke with a startled yawn. Harry, sleeping next to me, was bewitching and beautiful, all the nourishment I needed.

I kissed her neck to rouse her and nibbled on her earlobe. Giggling, she rolled over, allowing me to peel back her arms like petals on an exotic flower and descend her body, kissing, caressing, tasting. She wriggled and writhed and tugged at my hair, raising herself off the bed, craving my touch. She knew what she wanted and made sure I followed her direction, rewarding my dedication with a breathless orgasm that escaped her mouth in a throaty growl hot enough to have me fighting off my own and crawling up her body like a maniacal mountaineer.

Positioned between her legs, I took her in her semi-conscious state, thrusting hard and deep as she responded ardently to my early morning lovemaking. The combination of her internal clenching and the vibration of her muted moans on my neck was enough to send me into an ecstatic oblivion.

We lay side by side, watching golden shapes form on the ceiling: a mystical mirage that briefly held our attention. As she dozed I took delight in her presence; traced the shape of her nose with my eyes, thought I saw the hint of a scar on her brow, at the corner of her left eye, but it might have been no more than a delicate crease.

Feeling satiated, we slept in the lap of the gods.

The percolator bubbled and fizzed on the countertop, easing me slowly out of a restful slumber into wakefulness. I'd risen early, around seven thirty, and padded into the kitchen in a pair of sweat pants in the hope of beating Poppy to breakfast. It had been a while since I'd had a woman in my bed, and I wasn't sure of the correct protocol. I'd not woken Harry but slipped out like a forbidden lover to prepare coffee, croissants and a dish of fresh fruit for three.

I was opening cupboards in search of a tray when the ear-splitting sound of a high-pitched scream took me away from my task. I dashed to the lounge fearing the worst: a cut, a burn, a fall … a jet-propelled daughter?

Poppy charged into me looking startled but intact.

"Daddy, Daddy! Guess who's in your bed!" she yelled, a vision of tumbling curls and bright, amber eyes.

I wanted to laugh, or at the very least smile, but something held me back—a sense of responsibility. Had I not sworn to be the best father I could possibly be? Had I not made a pinkie promise? I had, and yet there I was having sex with someone in our home the first chance I got.

I quickly swept away any semblance of guilt. She was not *someone*—she was Harriet Harper.

I did what I thought best: I played dumb.

"Someone's in my bed?" I asked feigning surprise.

In a jumble of excited words, she explained, "I … I went in to wake you up and she was there!"

"Who?" I pressed her further, lifting her onto the countertop, hoping her reaction was the result of excitement not disapproval. As young as she was, she was used to having me to herself. She hadn't had to share and hadn't been confronted by a naked woman wrapped in a sheet before.

"It's Harry," she beamed. "Harry is sleeping in *your* bed. How did she get there?" she asked, picking at a warm croissant.

I thought on my feet. "She, she must have been too tired to go home after class and thought, 'I'll stay with Max and Poppy, they won't mind...'"

She continued to eat the croissant, taking it all in. "I don't mind. And you were asleep all the time?"

I cleared my throat, preparing to lie convincingly. "Yes. Fast asleep. I thought something was wrong when I heard you scream."

"Oh, Daddy." She started giggling. "It was a surprise: a happy surprise." She smiled widely.

I kissed her forehead and lifted her off the countertop. "I'm happy too. I'm making us breakfast."

Poppy tugged at my jogging pants. "Daddy ... do you think that if Harry gets tired, next time she'll sleep with me in my bed?"

I glanced down at her lovingly, moved by her generosity of spirit just as much as her need for human contact. "We can ask her."

She had another thought. "I'll take her a drink."

I poured steaming coffee into a mug.

She took a step back and shook her head. "Mary says I can't carry hot drinks." She opened the fridge and took out a carton of orange, set it down on the counter and clambered up onto a stool. I placed down a glass but she gave me a look that said, 'wrong again,' and replaced it with a plastic tumbler with a Polly Pocket transfer on the side. I shook my head. I was getting a lesson in child safety from a three-year old.

With the precision of a tightrope walker, she began the long walk to my bedroom, holding the beaker in both hands.

Having covered every inch of the tray with breakfast treats, I halted by the door, not afraid but flushed with nervous anticipation. I need not have worried.

Harry was sat up in bed wearing one of my dark green T-shirts, sipping orange juice. To the right of her, beneath the covers, was my daughter, chatting, laughing, unfazed by the situation.

I announced my arrival with a cough, playing the pantomime waiter, tea cloth over my arm. "Can I interest you two ladies in some breakfast?"

"Daddy!"

Poppy's face was a picture. I found it amusing that she was more taken aback by my role play than there being a woman in my bed.

I moved closer and placed the tray down on the vacant side of the bed. "We have fruit, croissants and coffee. Please help yourself. I was telling Poppy how you were feeling tired last night and thought you would sleep here." I gave Harry a wry smile.

Her eyebrows lifted, her eyes shifted left then right as she thought through a credible response.

"Are you feeling rested?" I asked, passing her a mug of coffee.

She couldn't contain a giggle. "Rested? Oh, yes, thank you. I got lots of rest, eventually."

With her mouth full, Poppy nodded and reached for a croissant. "Will you make breakfast *every* day, Daddy?" she asked, distracted by the feast.

I shook my head and headed for the shower. "No. I've done it because today's a special day."

"Because Harry's here?" she asked pointedly.

I looked back at them snuggled up together in my bed, Harry swathed in my oversized T-shirt; the sunlight diffusing through the blinds creating a haze of happiness so harmonious it warmed my heart and made me smile. There they were, two red-lipped leprechauns with bed heads, sporting hopeful expressions and gleaming smiles, hanging on my every word.

"Yes," I said throwing caution to the wind. "Because Harry's here and because *you're* here too—my two favourite girls."

Poppy reacted to my heartfelt declaration by wrapping her arm around Harry, who reciprocated by kissing her hair. The dark cloud that had hung over Harry seemed to have dissipated and, in response, she had blossomed overnight.

253

In that moment I saw our future together; it was vibrant and colourful like a paint pallet, full of promise and potential—a masterpiece in the making.

CHAPTER TWENTY FIVE

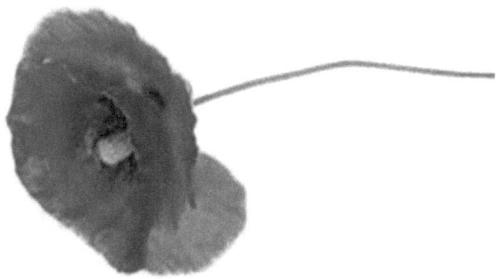

LATER THAT WEEK, I retraced Sam's steps for the last time, all the way to The Prince of Argyll pub, and sat alone at the bar. The weight of responsibility had become a millstone around my neck. Returning to the world of men—and women—had been hard enough without having to come face to face with a *monster,* insisting he tell me candidly about what happened between him and Harry—the real reasons for their break-up.

There would be no more warnings and talk of *layers,* I had to know the truth. All I had to do was contain my revulsion long enough to listen to what he had to say without us coming to blows, but I was under no illusions…

I was well and truly in the lion's den.

Images of Harry and I naked, entwined in the darkness flickered across my mind like a flaming candle, causing my chest to flush and my buttocks to clench. I wasn't a novice when it came to lovemaking. Hope and I had had a healthy sex life, but four years of abstinence and limited contact while she was pregnant had turned me into a lascivious lover with a voracious appetite for sex.

The same could be said about Harry—she was ravenous too. I had never felt more desired than when I was with her.

My sensual musings were ruined by the arrival of a young woman. Looking slightly startled by my bearded appearance, she positioned herself on the stool next to me by the bar.

"Hello," she said with a wide, cherry-coloured smile. "You must be Max."

I raised my eyes from my phone. She couldn't have been more than thirty, but she had the ravaged look of an older woman, a woman who had seen more than most, and lived to tell the tale. Her hair was bleached blond, hanging about her shoulders in man-made waves that didn't move freely but shifted with her head like a frosted helmet. Her eyes were fringed in mascara and false eyelashes which stuck out above her eyes like spiders' legs.

Her face and hands were the colour of burnt caramel, thanks to fake tanning, but her most striking feature was not her vivid lipstick or her ample bosom protruding from her bra like two over-ripe melons, it was something much more disconcerting. She had a three-inch scar on her neck, partially covered by a thick, gold chain. In the powerful spotlights positioned around the bar it looked silver, frayed in parts and, as hard as I tried, I couldn't take my eyes of it.

"I'm Kirsty," she announced confidently. "Sam sent me to make his apologies." She slapped her bag down on the bar. "Are you gonna get me a drink, or what?"

I was tempted to say 'or what' but thought better of it. "What would you like to drink, Kirsty?"

She looked me up and down and fluttered her eyelashes, making me feel as if I was being stalked by a lioness who could quite easily chew me up and spit me out. "A vodka and orange, please, Max."

I signalled to the barman and ordered another pint for myself. "What are you apologising for?" I asked, slipping my phone into my pocket.

"For him being a no-show," she giggled. "Looks like you've been stood up." She gave Mick a smile and took hold of her drink. "He's told me all about you."

"Has he?" I put my empty glass to one side. "Not all good, I hope?"

"Not ALL good," she grinned and slid two straws into her glass. "He said you're an artist."

"An ex-artist."

"How come? Do you have artist's block?" She was deadly serious.

256

I laughed. "Artists don't get that. It's what writers get when they can't write."

"I see. That makes sense." She took a long pull on the straws. "So, you *can* paint then?"

My unwillingness to paint was about to become common knowledge. "Yes. I could, if I wanted to."

She tutted. "Then why don't you?"

"I've decided to take a break from painting." I shrugged. "It's something that artists do from time to time." I lied, hoping that would be the end of it.

"Okay. I get it." She swivelled around to face me, so close I could feel her breath on my left cheek and inhale her perfume. I leant away as far as I could onto my right forearm. "Then what are you doing instead?"

I had no answer, not one she would understand, so I improvised. "Boat building."

"Boat building?" Her face folded into a frown. "What kind of boats?"

I fought off a smile. "Rowing boats."

She was aghast. "No way! Is there any money in it?"

I raised an arrogant brow. "Have you been to Hyde Park lately?"

"No. I can't say I have. I don't get to visit Kensington that much." She stirred her drink with the straws, tossing ice cubes around. "I hear Windsor Castle's nice."

I spun around to face her, preparing to give her a geography lesson. "Isn't Windsor Castle in Windsor?"

"Nope." Her eyelashes fluttered once more, shifting the air between us. "Not The Windsor Castle pub." Her laugher drew the attention of almost everyone in the bar. "You should see your face," she cried gleefully.

I could picture my look of astonishment and laughed along, feeling embarrassed and slightly humbled. There I was playing it cool, only to be out-witted by a young woman seemingly less sophisticated than myself. "You got me there."

"Yep." She edged closer to me, as if about to share a secret. Her bare knees rubbed against my left thigh. I wanted to edge away but I had nowhere to go, not without looking like a scared rabbit balancing on a stool.

"Sam says you're a millionaire." She licked her lips, until they were the colour of a ruby red post box caught in a shower.

I returned to my pint. "Sam says a lot of things."

"Well either you *are* and you don't wanna say, or you're not and you want people to *think* you are. Which is it?"

I faced her head on. "It's none of your business." I checked my watch.

She saw me clock watching. "Don't fret. He'll be here in fifteen."

The word *fret* irked me. It implied we had some kind of bromance going on. I had to put her right. "I'm not fretting."

She shrugged and took another slug of her drink. "Don't you like the ladies?" she asked candidly.

I was tempted to play the cad and turn around to look for one—a lady, that is. Instead I swallowed my pride along with two mouthfuls of beer. "I'm here to have a couple of pints after a busy week, if that's okay with you?"

"Sure. It's no skin off my nose." Her drink took the brunt of her annoyance and was on the receiving end of a good whisking.

"Anyway, won't you be busy when Sam gets here?" She was more *his* type than mine.

She sucked the vodka off her straw. "Busy? How do you mean?"

"You're his girlfriend, aren't you?" I asked, assuredly.

"Me?" She laughed out loud. "I'm not his girlfriend—not anymore."

"Oh. Sorry to hear that," I answered, assuming *he* must have found a replacement.

"Don't be," she huffed, leaning into me. "I'm not into that kind of thing."

I edged backward an inch. Had I missed something, misread a clue? "What kind of thing's that?"

She swivelled in her chair and tapped my elbow with hers. "You know."

I really didn't, and unless I asked more questions I never would. "No. I *don't* know."

She crossed her legs, revealing more of that burnt caramel skin, now rippling around her thighs. "I thought you two were mates…"

"We are, sort of," I stated, lacing my answer with as much sincerity as I could muster.

"Then you'll know that he can get a bit … rough." After checking we were not being watched, she lifted her gold chain to reveal the silver thread of the scar on the left side of her throat.

"How did it happen?" I asked, keeping my voice as controlled as was possible with my heart racing. I tightened my grip on my glass.

She appeared to struggle to vocalise what had happened and lowered her eyes like a naughty child about to reveal a secret. "He didn't mean to do it, or that's what he said after I got it stitched up."

"So, it was an accident?" I ventured, quietly.

She looked at me demurely through spider legs that appeared to be resting. "If you think that holding a knife to my throat while he fucked me, and slicing open my neck was an accident then, yes, I suppose it was." She took two noisy slurps of her drink.

I signalled for Mick to give her a top-up, prolonging the conversation.

She pushed away her empty glass. "It's not that noticeable and he bought me this gold chain to cover it up. Anyway, I don't like to talk about it." She ran her fingers along the chain in a rocking motion.

I didn't know what to say other than, "I understand."

When it came to Sam, it would appear that flattery and accolades were in short supply. In the way Kirsty spoke, I detected fear so pronounced it eclipsed her flirtatious banter: for a young woman who seemed to have gone to great lengths to appear sexually available, she spoke irreverently of the best-looking guy in the neighbourhood. Beneath those false eyelashes and crimson lipstick was a much maligned woman.

As if waking from a dream she sat upright, having rediscovered her concentration. "But I will if you want me to…"

Another drink and she was putty in my hands, putty that had been badly mishandled. "No. It's all right," I said. "But thanks for your candour."

She rocked back and forth on her chair. "That's a nice word. I'm going to steal it." She inhaled. "Thank you for your *candour,*" she mimicked playfully. "No worries. I just thought, with what happened to your wife, you'd want to … you know?"

I was baffled. What had Sam told her about my wife? "No, I don't know."

She checked her nails. "Didn't she get attacked or something?"

I nodded. "Yes, she did and died in childbirth because of her injuries." The words left my mouth in a splutter. She was the first stranger I had told, and I was surprised at how willing I was to confess, to tell her the truth when my entire persona was built on a lie.

"Fuck!" she announced, almost sliding off her stool. "That's terrible!"

"It is."

I felt her hand on my arm, her grip tightening. "I'm sorry. Did your baby make it?"

My mouth upturned into an involuntary smile. "Yes. Thank God."

"Christ, you've had it rough, haven't you? And there I was thinking I was the one with bad luck." She ran her forefinger along her scar, unselfconsciously.

"That's not bad luck, Kirsty, that's physical abuse. Assault!" I couldn't conceal my abhorrence.

Her eyes widened in surprise. "Isn't that what you guys get off on? The power thing?"

"No," I stated, shaking my head. "Not *all* men like that kind of thing."

"All the men *I* know do." She laughed weakly, removed her hand from my arm and set about stirring her freshly poured drink.

While she played with the straws, I scrutinised her more closely. She was younger than I had first thought, maybe late twenties—Harry's age. She had a good bone structure and blue eyes that had become lost in the spider's web of lashes. Her teeth would have benefited from her wearing a brace as a kid and she could do with losing a few pounds but, underneath the war paint and the peroxide, I sensed there was a good person who lived in a world populated by *bad people:* male monsters who had taken delight in inflicting pain upon her and left their mark like a calling card—Sam was one of them.

"Look, Kirsty. I have to go but promise me you'll take better care of yourself. No one has the right to hurt you or to take advantage of you like that," I implored, offering her a smile she couldn't help but reciprocate.

She stood, wriggled into her pale blue dress and finished her drink. "Sam will be pissed that you left. He'll blame me for being such an airhead." She expelled air. "Oh, well ... it was nice meeting you, Max. You're a nice guy. You don't belong here. Let me give *you* some advice." She stood on tiptoes and kissed me on my cheek. "Get the fuck out of this place and don't ever come back."

The painted smile faded from her lips, leaving a thin, determined, crescent of crimson. She threw her bag over her shoulder, raised her chin and walked away in the direction of the pool table. "See ya."

That was the second piece of advice I had received in less than a week and I was not about to ignore it. I left my pint on the bar, headed for the door and didn't stop until I had reached the bed and breakfast hotel, two streets away.

Once inside, I packed my overnight bag, eager to leave. Kirsty had explained how Sam was a dominant man, he liked rough sex. If that was the case, did it automatically follow that he had it within him to brutalize the *love of his life* in *and* out of the bedroom?

I left ruing the day I had heard the name Samuel James Reynolds.

SYDNEY JAMESSON

CHAPTER TWENTY SIX

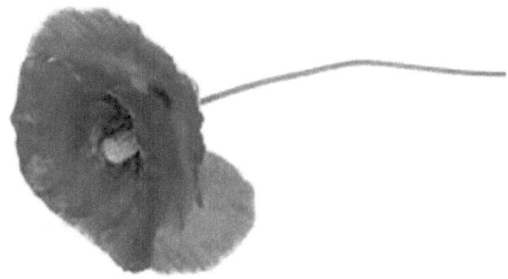

I RETURNED HOME THAT Friday night consumed by an irrepressible sense of discovery. A chance meeting with one of Sam's former lovers had been the evidence I needed to come to a decision, a decision that would determine my fate and the fate of my daughter. My moral compass had been restored, enabling me to see, finally, in what direction I should go.

Mentally, I began charting a course.

Monday presented itself as a prism of sunlight appearing from behind a cloak of opaque clouds, bright and illuminating. I waited until lunch to call Harry, to invite her to come over for dinner on her night off.

Taking her role very seriously, Mary spent an hour shopping for ingredients and another hour preparing an Irish stew, with dumplings that floated on top of the rich gravy like mini moons. If it tasted half as delicious as it smelled, I knew we were in for a treat. Poppy helped out, clip-clopping around in her new shoes and laying out the table without instruction.

Over the past month, a change had befallen us, befallen me, for sure. It was undeniable, palpable, in the way I walked around the room with a spring in my step, as if I had been given a new lease of life. Rather than focusing on myself, I had turned my eyes outward, and what I had witnessed had come as a revelation.

Poppy and I, with help from Mary, were falling into a relaxed routine and I longed for Harry to be a part of it, to view our budding relationship as I did—as something special, something worth pursuing.

I had come to a decision. I wanted her to become a permanent part of our lives: friend, lover, mother … wife. The idea was radical, but it was what I wanted, not for myself alone, but for Poppy too.

That night I planned on telling her exactly that.

Harry arrived at six thirty brandishing a bottle of white wine, a sparkly hair slide for Poppy and a modest bouquet for Mary, as a token of her appreciation for her slaving away in the kitchen. Both receivers glowed with delight and reciprocated with hugs—they were becoming a frequent feature of Harry's visits.

Not wanting to advertise the intimate nature of our relationship, I kissed Harry's cheek and she kissed mine but we lingered to look at each other, our eyes locked together, our bodies stirred by the memory of our passionate lovemaking.

I rested my hand on the small of her back and led her over to the dinner table, remembering the heat we generated as our bodies writhed: the friction, the orgasms. I poured out glasses of chilled water and downed mine before Harry was comfortably seated in an attempt to dampen down the visceral response I was having. After being dormant for so long I felt as if my body was overly sensitized, my libido on overdrive. I threw a napkin onto my lap and willed myself to calm down.

Mid-meal, Mary left to tend to her own family: a husband and a cat called Marcus. Her children were grown-up and living their own lives and, I suspect, that is what made her such a good mother figure to Poppy—she loved her as she would her own child. That night she bid us farewell, sensing my need to move things along with Harry.

While I was dressing for dinner, I noticed she had left extra towels in my bedroom and a new toothbrush in the holder next to mine. Had she smelled the sheets, noticed the extra glasses in the dishwasher or had Poppy kept her up to speed on breakfast treats and Daddy's *sleeping* partner? I found it amusing and endearing, her way of giving me her blessing.

By nine o'clock Poppy was settled and sleeping. After the swimming lesson and our dinner party, she had become overly excited and had to take her inhaler to prevent her wheeze becoming a full-blown asthma attack. I had given her some linctus too, knowing it would help her sleep.

With our privacy assured, I took Harry in my arms. I threaded my fingers through her hair, found her lips with mine and kissed her deeply. She matched my fervour, and our tongues mingled and danced to the beat of our hearts.

It felt unashamedly natural.

Suddenly, using both hands, she shoved me away. "Make love to me," she gasped through hot breath.

In needed of no prompting, I reached for her hand and, barefooted, we began our brisk walk to my bedroom amidst unabashed smiles and suppressed laughter. I pushed back the door in an elaborate gesture and beckoned her inside, offering her more than casual sex, more than a lust-filled encounter, much more—I was welcoming her into my world.

But for the sound of the doorbell, that welcome would have been fulfilled.

At first, I thought I had imagined it; my mind had fabricated a kind of subconscious alarm, a wake-up call, but no. It *was* the doorbell.

Harry heard it too. "Are you expecting anyone?" she asked, the mood ruined by the interruption.

I answered with a frown before speaking. "No. I don't have visitors." I checked my watch. "Especially not at nine thirty at night."

It rang again—continuously, insistently, loud enough to raise the dead.

"I'll see who it is. I won't be long." I charged off down the corridor, past Poppy's bedroom to the front door.

His finger was still on the bell when I swung back the front door. "What the hell do you think you're playing at?" I yelled into Sam's face. "Do you want to wake-up the whole fucking house?" I had not intended to swear but my heart was racing, I had a head full of sex and I was too fired up to deal with an intrusion.

Coming face to face with my rage, Sam backed away. "Woah! Keep your pants on, mate. Did I come at a bad time?" His mouth formed into a sneer; he could tell by my manner, my dilated pupils and my creased shirt that he had come at a *very* bad time.

"What do *you* want?" I asked brusquely.

His eyes skittered and rested on the space behind me. "Is she here?"

I exhaled, feeling my breathing returning to a regular rhythm. "Who?"

"You know who. Jane, or should I say, Harriet? She is, isn't she?"

I folded my arms. "What's it to you? You said you were well rid of her."

He shrugged his shoulders nonchalantly. "I am," he stated. "Just wondered how you're getting on."

"No need. I can take care of myself." I kept my responses short and delivered them with an air of confidence. I was not like those women he could intimidate and scare, poke fun at or brand with a knife.

"You might think so, mate," he scoffed. "But you've no idea who you're dealing with. Why don't you let me come in and I'll put you straight?" He looked me up and down. "What have you got to lose?"

Seeing him there, having come so far to speak to me, I wondered what he could possibly say about Harry that I didn't already know. Looking back, I suppose curiosity must have got the better of me, that or the smallest speck of doubt about Harry's sincerity still remaining in my mind like a pebble in my shoe. I opened the front door a little wider and watched him cross the threshold like an unwelcome spirit who could alter the temperature in the room by simply showing up.

There was nothing for Harry to fear, he had no hold over her and I wouldn't let him hurt her. In facing up to him, perhaps she too would be better able to move on—to cast out her demon, once and for all.

Having said that…

I confess to making many mistakes in my life, welcoming Sam into my home that night was probably the worst of all.

Not being drenched, as before, he had no reason to raid the drinks cabinet. Instead he selected a spot on the sofa, close to where Harry and I had been embracing less than ten minutes before and tossed his keys onto the coffee table. He ran his fingers along the material left and right of his knees and looked about him. "I thought there'd be books," he announced.

His observation took me by surprise. "Books?"

"Yeah. Don't rich guys like you buy books, first editions as investments?"

I shook my head. "I really wouldn't know." I sat across from him. "Anyway, I'm not a rich guy." I needed to prompt him but didn't want to appear too desperate for information. I had one eye on him and one on the corridor, hoping Harry would stay out of the way.

That hope was not fulfilled.

The moment she saw him she gasped and recoiled as if she had been struck down, almost losing her balance. I shot up and dashed over to her.

"Are you all right? Come and sit down." I took her by the elbow.

She shook off my hand. "What's *he* doing here?"

He grinned wolfishly. "Nice to see you too, Jane. How've you been?"

Too focused on me, she didn't answer. Her eyes raked across my cheeks, searched my eyes for an answer. "Max?"

How could I say that I'd been visiting the man she had run away from for the past three Fridays? That he had told me all about her—that I had led him to her?

I moved away from her and faced Sam. "Look, this was a mistake. We both know what you did to her. It's no wonder she's upset…"

"Upset!" The 's' sound was no more than a hiss. "Oh dear. Have you been telling tales?" He eyed her with derision and enunciated his words as if talking to someone with impaired hearing or learning difficulties. He rolled a dark blue chip around his fingers, not so much as a party trick or to show off his dexterity, more as a mind game; showing Harry that he knew her secrets, even where she worked. That silent message was conveyed, loud and clear.

Visibly wilting, Harry turned away, her hands clenching, her head falling in submission. When she raised it to face me, her eyes were swimming in tears. "I can't take this," she whimpered.

"This is going to blow your mind, Max." Sam said, relishing her suffering. "Go ahead, Jane. Spit it out." He stood, folded his arms and rocked back on his heels impatiently. "No? Has the cat got your tongue? You had a change of heart?" He chuckled, sending an icy shiver down my spine. He really was a piece of work.

She shook her head and pleaded, "Don't, Sam. Don't do this."

"Don't do what?" he snapped. "Prove to lover boy here that you're a fucking liar and an imposter?" He glowed with a sadistic satisfaction, preparing to tear apart any shred of integrity she had.

I reached out to her. "Look, I don't know what he thinks he has on you but just tell me, okay? Then we'll be done with it." I swallowed deeply. "I've not been entirely truthful with you either, Harry." Her journal was locked away in my office drawer; it would only be a matter of time before I had to confess *my* deception.

She turned to me, searching my face for clues. "Nothing like this, Max," she said, biting her lip.

Sam couldn't hold back. "You ready for this?"

I didn't answer. I was too focused on Harry to pay him any attention. "I know what he put you through, you told me—"

"I told you the truth, mostly… He did abuse me—"

"Don't believe a word of it, Max," Sam snapped, pointing an angry finger in her direction. "She's a compulsive liar."

I cautioned him with a fierce look. "Shut up, Sam. I've listened to you. It's her turn to speak." I softened my voice. "I know you left a good job and a nice house and started over…"

"A what? She was a fucking receptionist, and we had a two-bed flat on Camden High Street over the Bookies…"

That wasn't what I'd read…

"What did she tell you? We had a cosy house with a garden, and she had a fancy career?" He scoffed out loud. "Oh, this is going to be priceless."

I urged her to continue. "Harry?"

"It's true, I was a only a receptionist at the surgery, but sometimes I used to cover for Louise when she was on holiday…"

"Then you weren't a medical secretary or a PA?"

She shook her head.

"That's okay. You're studying now…"

Sam coughed. "About that… I called into the office at Eastwick College and said I was working for a debt recovery company. I asked if they had a Harriet Jane Harper on roll, taking a course, any course. Guess what they said?" He grinned. "You want to explain that, Jane? How you're not a student there, never have been and never will be?"

I waited for her to correct him.

She didn't.

"Harry? Is that true?"

Reluctantly, she nodded, keeping her eyes downcast. "Yes." Harry pursed her lips and grimaced; her suffering sharpening her features.

I couldn't disguise my surprise. "So, all this time you were lying about being a student, wanting to be a psychologist?"

She lifted her head boldly and prepared to explain. "Yes, I pretended to be a student so I could attend classes. It took me *two* years to save up enough money for the fees, and then, at the last minute, I lost my nerve; I didn't think I was smart enough to follow the course. I've been attending classes and lectures, trying to build my confidence. No one ever checks. I'm the most reliable student: I'm never late. I hand in essays…" Amid her rushed explanation, she sniffed back tears. "Now I know I can do it, I'll stop going and sign up for real next year, pay the fees and get qualified."

Her explanation seemed plausible, taking into account how Sam must had rocked her confidence, but it was lie number two and I was starting to wonder how many more there would be. "Anything else?"

"Not really…" She took a deep breath. "Everything I've said and done has been for you."

Sam chuckled. "See? What did I tell you? Now she's making out it's *your* fault that she's a fucking fraud."

I didn't answer. I wanted to take Harry's side, to dismiss Sam as a vindictive ex with an axe to grind, but so far the things he had said were true—he was unravelling her one lie at a time.

Sam was so fired up I thought he might strike her. I moved closer, ready to put myself between them if necessary. He bombarded her with flying spittle and more insults, stuttering words that left his mouth in rapid fire.

She withstood his verbal assault bravely, but there was only so much she could endure; her emotional fortifications began to visibly crumble and, with her defences down, it would take him no time at all to demolish what was left. She tried to speak, to offer a counter argument, but he shot her down, pointing a finger in her face, curving his body into hers.

"You disappeared without a trace, leaving me to pick up the pieces, face the police and explain to everyone what had happened—*even* your own parents." He puckered his lips angrily until they resembled a dried-up rosebud. "You crucified them, you selfish bitch!"

"That's enough," I said, holding up a hand to quiet him. "You've said your piece." I turned to face her. "How can you justify your lies? Saying you lied for me? Is that another lie?"

"No." Her lips quivered. "I knew you wouldn't give me a second thought if I was the woman I used to be—plain Jane. You're so talented and smart, you've done things and been places—"

"So have you," I announced, recalling her diary entries. "You've visited famous landmarks, galleries, museums…"

"When?" interjected Sam with a baffled look. "In the last three years?"

I was confused too. "When you were together…"

He presented a downturned smile. "Nope."

"You visited Rome, took a tour of the Coliseum…"

"I—"

Before she could answer, Sam interjected. "We went to see the Gunners play AS Roma. We stayed in a shitty hotel just outside Rome."

Harry and I faced each other like a couple of marble statues. "What about the Uffizi Gallery in Florence?"

Sam scratched his chin. "Is that near Pisa?"

I nodded.

"We saw Arsenal beat Juventus three two after extra time." He raised his arm in a celebratory salute. "What a result!"

I began sifting through memories, places Harry had 'escaped' to in her mind when he had forced himself on her. "What about The Rodeo in Turkey?"

"Galatasaray. An away win. We lost in the next round."

I was running out of locations. "The Louvre in Paris?" She had to have gone there, surely.

"Disneyland? That's in Paris, right?"

I didn't bother answering. Harry had *gone* to the cities, but to watch football matches with Sam, and had lied about visiting famous museums. I spun around to confront her and took hold of her forearms, not to intimidate her but to confess. "Harry, I've read your…" I hesitated, finding it hard to finish the sentence, to own up to my treachery. "I've read your journal. The one you lost. I found it on the floor in the art room after the first class. It must have fallen out of your bag … that's how I got to know you. Now I find out it was all lies!"

"She wrote a journal?" asked Sam, unable to contain his amusement. "And it didn't cross your mind that she might have *left* it there for you to find?"

His suggestion left me speechless. Not for one minute while I had been reading it had I considered that might be the case. But now … after the lies and her duplicity, that was a real possibility. I tightened my grip on her arms. "Is that true?"

The seconds it took her to find her voice stretched out between us. "Yes," she whispered, but her single word reply seemed so far away, I could barely catch what she had said.

"Don't mumble!" Sam shouted, making us both flinch. "At least have the balls to confess when you've been caught out." Sam shook his head and laughed. "What did I tell you? Women! Can't live with 'em. Can't fuck without 'em." His laughter died on seeing the colour fade from my face. "You alright, mate? Better sit this one out." He pointed to a nearby chair.

I collapsed into the chair, allowing my head to fall into my hands. "For the love of God, Harry, why did you lie about *everything*?" From the very first page, I had read her all wrong; she'd taken me for a fool and played me, just as Sam had warned me, she would.

"Harry," I spoke quietly, or as quietly as the raging furnace inside me would allow. "Will you at least tell me why?"

She knelt down before me, wrapping her trembling fingers around my fists. "I'm so sorry, Max. I couldn't stand the thought of being plain Jane, not anymore. You deserved so much more, and I had to create that person for *you.* " She pressed her free hand against her chest. "Inside, in here, I *was* so much more. I wanted you to see that—to see my potential. You made me feel special, special to *you! Li*ke I was worth a damn." She bit back tears. "If I was the old me, I wouldn't have met you. I wouldn't have written a word. How could I? I'd become a ghost—I was dead inside. I wanted to live. Is that so wrong?"

With words sticking in my throat, I raised my eyes to meet hers.

She apologised through tears that were not so much of a trickle but an inconsolable outpouring of emotion that stained her cheeks and made her eyeballs swell. She wiped her nose on the back of her hand. "I wanted you to *see* me."

She turned to look at Sam standing over her. "You treated me badly, Sam. You made me afraid of everything, especially you." She got to her feet. "But I'm not afraid anymore."

He didn't believe her. That was a plain as the sneer on his face. "Is that so? You think that because you've changed your name and dyed your hair you can just walk away and hide from me?"

"I did," she stated defiantly.

"Then it's time you came home and faced the music like I had to. Can you imagine what people said—?"

"They would have had a lot more to say if they'd known the truth about *you*." Her voice was so full of malice, her declaration sounded like a threat.

They exchanged glances like caged animals in a dogfight; bearing teeth, barking insults and tearing into each other. His smirk became a malevolent sneer. "Oh, yeah. You making up more stories, Jane?"

"No. You stopped loving me, Sam. That's the truth." She aimed her assertions right at him, increasing volume and pitch as she got into her stride. "I was no more than your punch bag. Every disappointment you had, you blamed on me. Every failure, every fucking let-down, you took it out on *me.*" Unshakable, she bent forward like a tree bowing in the wind. "You made me responsible for *everything* that was wrong in your life. None of that's fiction. You hurt me so badly, Sam. And *you* killed our baby."

Surprisingly, he seemed unprovoked by her outspokenness and shrugged away her reprimand: it had no impact on his intention. He had his own agenda and I wished I'd known then what it was.

"All that's behind me now," he stated in a measured tone that was so uncharacteristic it was disconcerting.

Harry picked up on it too but carried on regardless. "I'm glad. Now you can get on with your life and let me get on with mine."

He tilted his chin. "I want you back..."

"That's *never* going to happen," Harry snapped.

He eyed me sideways, still perched on the edge of a comfortable chair, and dismissed me with a condescending look. "Is it because of him?"

"Yes." She nodded her head. "But mostly it's because of you. I don't love you anymore, Sam."

He flinched. "And you love *him*?"

I held my breath. Up until that point I had not suffered his wrath. Fearing I was about to, I clenched my fists.

She looked across to me. "I could love him if he'd let me." A smile brushed across her swollen lips.

I reached for her hand, but she shook her head and resumed her conversation with Sam. "Just go." She wiped the mascara from her eyes and stood her ground.

I admired her courage; even though he was much larger and physically stronger than her, she held her nerve and never took her eyes off him. "You've done what you came here to do," she stated, drawing on an inner strength, the result of years of surviving a barrage of insults and personal tragedies.

Although he must have been inwardly combusting, Sam gave off an unnatural aura of composure and asked, "Tell me … what's that, Jane?"

"You've introduced Max to Jane and now he's met her, that's the person he'll always see, not Harriet—the person I created in the hope he would fall in love with her." She looked at me longingly. "More than anything, I wanted what Hope had and to have that I had to reinvent myself."

"But I loved *you*," I whispered between frenzied breaths.

She shook her head, dislodging the flow of tears cascading down her cheeks until her face was glistening and wet. "No. If you'd loved me, you wouldn't care about the journal. You'd see it as the ramblings of a lonely woman, wishing she could change things, be someone else—"

"While giving me what *you* thought I wanted?"

"It's what we *both* wanted, Max. What we needed," she sobbed. "To escape the suffocating grasp of our pasts. We both lost something precious: you lost Hope and I lost myself. We couldn't move on being who we were. Don't you see… We've set each other free?"

Sam turned his attention to Harry. "Free! You think you were so hard done by. I gave you everything, even at school when you were nothing, I turned you into someone. You were so fucking needy. It was like looking after a kid. I pitied you." He spat out the consonants and put his right foot forward: she took a step back in response. "I had my pick of the crop, *I* was the golden boy. *I* had everything going for me, and like a fucking idiot I got landed with you … and what did you do? You left me with nothing, not even my pride." His words were delivered with venom, intended to inflict further suffering.

Harry didn't flinch an inch. Minus her glossy veneer, she had nothing to hide—and nothing to lose. She seemed to inflate, rediscovering the stoicism that Sam had chipped away at over the years. "You know what, Sam? If thinking that helps you sleep at night, then go ahead. But we both know the truth. That New Year's Eve when you asked me out, you did it for a dare. I was young and innocent; you corrupted me, made me vain, and selfish. I became your biggest, sexual conquest, the one you bragged about to your mates. You pretended to love me; fucked me for fun and when the going got tough you took out your frustration on me. I have the scars to prove it." She wiped leftover tears from the corners of her eyes. "The thing is, I don't need you to turn me *into someone.* You made me think I was nothing without you and I believed I had to reinvent myself to be truly loved by someone, someone like Max. I'm leaving. You should do the same."

I stood and barred her way with my arm. It was a standoff. "Is there anything else you've made up for my benefit?"

She shot me a fierce stare. "No."

"And what about our relationship? Is it built on a lie, or a series of lies? Have you been pretending all this time?"

Her body visibly sagged. "Max, when we've been together, I've never pretended: not when I've laughed at your awkwardness, read bedtime stories and made love to you. That was all me." She kissed my cheek. "You loved Hope, and even when I knew I was nothing more than a stand-in, I tried to *give* you hope, in your arms and in your heart." She made a move to pass by me.

Struggling to imagine my life without her, I asked, "But how can you expect me to ever trust you again after what you've done, after all those lies?"

She forced a weak smile. "I can't."

I was so emotionally shaken I didn't know who to believe; so many untruths; tributaries to an ocean of deceit into which I had fallen headfirst. Once more Fate had played the worst trick of all on me. What better way to make me pay for breaking my vows, for abandoning my wife and failing as a father, than to snatch away the woman I had dared to love?

Sam raised his chin and followed her with his eyes. I watched a small, mean smile form as he glowed: he was triumphant. "Looks like she fucked us both over, mate." He pulled the zip up on his bomber jacket. "I'll leave you to it."

I didn't respond. I was not convinced I'd been *fucked over*, and I certainly was not his mate. "Do you feel better, having got her to feel what you felt?"

He huffed. "Nah. She took me for a fool. Thought she could be rid of me, but your past has a habit of catching up with you when you least expect it."

I eyed him with derision. "And here you are." Regaining my second wind, I approached him. "You should leave."

He glanced around the room. "Yeah, there's nothing here for me."

"That's right," I agreed, unwilling to be baited. It struck me as odd that he was willing to leave without arguing his case. In his eyes, he had been wronged; his character had been denigrated by the 'love of his life,' and he was about to leave just like that?

He had said that he wouldn't give up until he had found her, and yet there he was allowing her to slip through his fingers like trickling water. I couldn't believe he had it in him to be that forgiving.

"I've got a long drive back," he stated. "Can I take a piss? You don't want me making a nasty patch on your lawn, do you?" Casually, he threw his weight onto one leg and faked a smile.

Before I could direct him, he was off down the corridor on the left. "Make it quick," I called out.

I ran shaky fingers through my hair and paced, feeling the aftermath of a confrontation *I* had brought about. I had made the mistake of getting involved and, in doing so, allowed their war of words to turn my home into a battleground. I was still mulling over my miscalculation when Harry returned to the lounge, her jacket over one arm and her overnight bag in her other hand.

"I've packed." She scanned the room. "Look, I'm sorry it's..."

"Me too," I said before she could finish. "You'd better sit down. I haven't called a taxi yet."

She moved to the single chair by the window and flopped down onto it. Her petite frame was reflected in the glass, coat across her knee, hands twitching, looking as if she had come too early for a dental appointment.

I watched her press a rolled-up pair of jeans into her bag and struggle to draw the zip, forcing her to remove items. On the floor was a toiletries bag and a paperweight that looked shockingly familiar.

"Where did you get that?" I asked, feeling blood rushing to my head.

She raised her eyes. "Get what?"

I pointed a finger in the direction of the glass object. "That! The paperweight."

She picked it up nonchalantly. "It was a gift."

"Off who?"

She shook her head. "What does it matter? I was going to give it to…"

I strode over to her. "It matters because Hope had a paperweight exactly like that."

The skin above Harry's nose drew together. "What are you saying, Max?"

"I'm saying it looks like the one that was taken from this house on the day she was attacked." I snatched it from her hand. "Shit! It's the same one."

I placed it within inches of her nose. "See that little tear in the petal, that's what Hope loved about it. How it wasn't perfect but still beautiful." My breathing became shallow. I struggled to make sense of it. The wound I had thought was healing had opened up as if prodded by a sharp implement of torture. "Who gave it to you, Harry? Tell me!"

"Sam," she confessed, chewing on her lip nervously. "He came home one night just before Christmas and handed it to me as a gift."

I looked down toward the hall. There was no sign of him. "He's been here before," I stated. "That's how he knew about the break-in and found me so fast."

"I tried to tell you." Harry started to cry. "He's a dangerous man. All those things he said about me…"

"Never mind about that now." I rammed the paperweight into my pocket.

"At least he's gone…." She sighed, patting away tears with her fingertips.

I shook my head and felt the icy hands of fear gripping my throat as I whispered, "He hasn't."

Her head turned so quickly I thought she might injure herself. "Where is he?" Her eyes flashed and turned sapphire in an instant.

I tilted my head in the direction of the washroom. "He asked to go to the toilet and I—"

"On the way to Poppy's room?" She sprang to her feet and stepped over her bag. "How long has he been gone?"

I sprinted in the direction of the washroom. "Too long!"

Harry was less than a step behind me. "They kept souvenirs," she called out.

I flung open the washroom door. It was empty.

277

Poppy's bedroom door was ajar down the hall. We tiptoed inside. Her merry-go-round lantern was revolving; fairy-tale figures were dancing on all four walls. Seeing the child size mound beneath the duvet I let out a deep sigh of relief.

I crept around the bed, my feet landing on discarded drawings as if they were fragile stepping-stones or pieces of a jigsaw puzzle. I caught sight of a couple and bent to pick them up. On the periphery of each one was a strip of blue: a streak between the trees, a flash of something outside Poppy's window... The most recent one was a hand sticking out of a blue sleeve.

"What the fuck!" I said in a half-strangled voice. "See these streaks of blue? They're not my car. It's Sam! He's been stalking us: the kitten in the house, the open window..." I reached for the kitten's diamante collar placed on Poppy's bedside table. "And this! More fucking mind games." He had been watching our movements, peeping through windows; he had entered the house and had probably tortured and killed the kitten.

In the seconds that followed, I saw the truth, a truth that transcended my deepest, darkest fear. I'd been swinging like a pendulum between two versions of the same past, too preoccupied with establishing my parentage and Poppy's future, and lost sight of the present. The one person who *could* take Poppy away from me was not weasel boy—it was Sam. He'd been under my nose the entire time, in my house, and Poppy had been within touching distance.

Fear gripped me and wrapped around my heart like a boa constrictor, making breathing difficult. With shaky hands, I pulled back the duvet and didn't stop until the cover was off the bed, revealing not my sleeping daughter, but two teddy bears.

I gasped.

Harry gasped.

I turned to her. "I'll fucking kill him." Pushing past her I ran for the door yelling, "You take the back door! I'll go round to the front."

CHAPTER TWENTY SEVEN

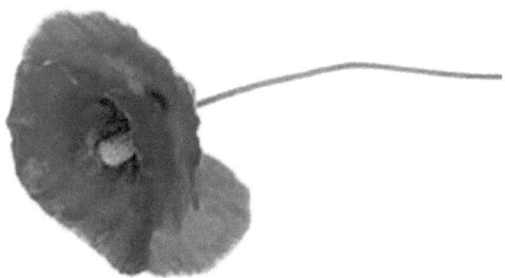

I SPRINTED DOWN THE drive to where Sam had parked his car, silently praying he had not driven off and taken Poppy to … God knows where.

I stopped abruptly. A solitary car was parked in a layby on the main road. It had to be his. Breathing heavily, I ducked into the undergrowth and approached it, fists clenched, eyes wide.

He was not in it.

He was back at the house with Poppy and Harry.

In the hazy light of a November sunset, I looked out into the violet horizon where the demarcation between forest and sky became a jagged line above the lake. I saw two figures on the jetty: one female, peering into the rowing boat; the other had to be Sam.

He stood closer to the bank with his back to me, a black chess piece silhouetted against the sky—a dark knight or a rook, always one move ahead of me. Even as I looked on, I had no idea what he was about to do or what he was capable of. All I knew was that he had Poppy wrapped in a blanket flopped over his shoulder like a ragdoll.

Instinctively, I stepped forward, feeling my right foot sink into the mire; it caused a squelching sound that made me duck for fear of being heard. I had to get around the back of him. If he saw me coming, he might panic and do something crazy—like throwing Poppy into the cold water to be swallowed up by branches and reeds. She wouldn't stand a chance and, without a torch, finding her would be almost impossible.

I couldn't allow that idea to clutter my thoughts; I needed to be clear about what I had to do. If that meant giving him whatever he wanted, money, Harry, I would do it. She would understand.

I signalled my position to Harry by raising my wrist and reflecting the light of the moon on my watch face. We stood a better chance of overwhelming him if we worked in unison, but every strategy had to be considered.

As long as he had hold of Poppy, we were powerless.

I sensed by the gap in their exchange that Harry had seen me and felt relieved—two against one had to be better odds.

Feeling a crunch beneath my left foot, I bent down to pick up a branch; its bark was slimy but the wood was good, solid enough to make a good cosh with which I could strike him. I considered the prospect of combat like a man who was actually used to it—that couldn't have been further from the truth. At that moment, I was without fear: the blood of a warrior ran through my veins and would be spilt if necessary. If it came to killing him, I had no doubt in my mind that I would do that too. The choice would be his: walk away and live, stay and risk being beaten within an inch of his life.

I watched him take a step further along the jetty. My courage wavered. Realising I couldn't hit him while he was holding Poppy, I froze and dropped the branch.

From where I was crouched, I could hear them speaking in hushed tones, the sounds melding into a continuous hum that carried on the wind in my direction. As the clouds flittered across the moon, I edged nearer, catching their words like night flies, stringing them together into sentences.

I picked up on the initial panic in Harry's voice, until it was replaced by a sultry tone, almost seductive. In response, Sam's body sagged. He shifted the weight of his bundle from one arm to the other. My heart fluttered at the possibility that he had already killed Poppy—she seemed unnaturally still. But, surely, he was more cunning than that. He had a plan, and Poppy was part of it.

I drew his attention and made myself visible.

He didn't change his posture. He knew he had the upper hand. "I wondered when you'd show up." His manner was genial, but his traitorous eyes gave away his thoughts; those flecks of fiery blue were no more than a distraction camouflaging his insidious intentions.

I raised myself to my full height. "I'm here now. What do you want?"

"I want to set the record straight."

I snickered. "I thought you had."

"Not really." He shook his head as if finding a thought amusing. "I swear I've never come across anyone as easily fooled as you. Can't you see how you've been played?"

"Played?" I laughed smugly. "You're hardly in a position to point the finger at anyone. You've kidnapped my daughter."

"Nah. I'm willing to make an exchange." He tipped his head in Harry's direction. "I'll take her off your hands. That way you and the pink princess here will be a lot safer."

He had *been watching her.*

"It doesn't look that way from where I'm standing."

He jerked Poppy onto his shoulder, and I took a step forward. "It's a bit radical, I admit. But needs must, and all that."

"Okay," Harry said, drawing his attention. "Give Poppy to me." She swept back strands of hair from her face. "Let me put her to bed and then I'll leave with you." She held out her hands in supplication. "That's what you want isn't it?" Even though he was giving her a look that anyone in their right mind would back away from, she was willing to leave with him to save Poppy.

He tipped his head. "It's *one* of the things I want."

"What else?" she asked, as the wind caught hold of her words and carried them across the lake.

He sneered at her question. "I want *you* to tell *him* the truth." He jerked his head in my direction, revealing the relentless nature of his intent.

She frowned. "I have."

"Oh please. You just don't know when to stop, do you?" He turned to me. "Did she happen to mention she had a bad heart?"

I nodded. She hadn't mentioned it, but I had read about it.

"And did she explain how she received a donor heart?"

"Sam!" she yelled. "No!"

I shook my head and took a step nearer to him. "What of it?"

"She got her heart on the nineteenth of December. Ring any bells?" He laughed contemptuously. "I do believe my old mate Max is finally seeing the light, getting to the heart of the matter, you could say."

I swayed, almost losing my balance, teetering on the edge of oblivion. If my feet had not been full of lead, I would have fallen off the jetty.

Sam laughed. "Your lovely wife died in childbirth on the eighteenth, right? But there wasn't a damn thing wrong with her organs, was there? She donated them, didn't she? Lungs, liver, kidneys—*heart?* Your wife died and hey, presto! Goodbye, Jane and Hello, Harriet." He looked over at her contemptuously. "Like I said, you've been had, mate."

I turned in Harry's direction, utterly stunned. "Is this true? All this time you've had my wife's heart beating inside your chest?"

She closed her eyes and lurched forward, covering her mouth. Her nod was barely perceptible, but it was there.

"Here. Take her," he instructed Harry. "*She* belongs here but you don't. Put her to bed."

For a split second, I came between them. "Give her to me."

"No." He twisted his body until Poppy was hanging precariously over the water. "I want *her* to do it."

"It's all right, Max," Harry insisted. "I'll put her to bed and get my things together." She lifted Poppy from Sam's arms and held her close.

Her things—her small bag of possessions scattered on the floor in the lounge, bar one: Hope's paperweight.

I held up my hand. "Wait a minute. Stay there."

Misunderstanding my concern, Sam spoke out. "She won't hurt her."

I shook my head. "I know she won't."

"So...?"

I nailed him to the decking with an intense stare. The tension between us became elastic, it stretched out between us—him pulling away, me pulling him back, keeping us attached. "Tell me what you know about my wife."

"Your wife?" He shrugged. "She was a good-looking woman—"

"And..."

A cloud of menace hung around him, foreshadowing something sinister. "Tough, a fighter..."

At that moment everything started to fall into place, the most treacherous truth of all came to me slowly and took shape in my mind. "You came here four years ago? When you lost your job, you used your experience as a delivery man to pass information on, to provide leads, didn't you?" He didn't deny it. "Is that what Hope was, just another lead?"

I lifted the paperweight out of my pocket, my throat tightened, and the mudslide of memories came flooding back, dragging me under. I struggled to remain lucid. "This was Hope's and you gave it to Harry as a fucking souvenir, didn't you?"

He shrugged his shoulders. "Sure. You were this bigshot artist with your fancy house and your pretty, pregnant wife. When I asked her if she wanted me to lift the parcel inside, she said, 'Yes, if you wouldn't mind. The man of the house isn't around much these days...'" He used a high-pitched voice to mimic Hope.

His words were so sharp, and so well aimed, I recoiled. "And how much was my wife worth to you?"

He wrinkled up his nose. "Worth?"

"Yes. Your thieving buddies paid you money for info on easy targets, didn't they? Isn't that why you spent so long rummaging through your old job lists and checking satellite navigation equipment for addresses?" My face became a grotesque grimace. "How fucking much?"

"A ton," he shouted. "That's the going rate for a good tip-off!"

I scowled and screamed, "She's dead because of you!"

He sneered and shook his head. "Not me, mate. You! I was never there, but *you* were." He stood tall, puffing out his chest, challenging me to verbal combat. "You had everything to fight for but—from what I heard—you chickened out, you froze like one of your fucking sculptures. She was the one with the balls." He prodded my chest with a forceful finger. "Now, if that was *me* and *my* family was in danger, I'd fight like hell, but *you* didn't, did you?" His eyes were blazing. "Beats me how you slept at night."

"I didn't," I confessed. "But I will from now on." I swung my right arm and hit him across the head with the paperweight. He staggered backward and landed in the water with an enormous splash. Harry staggered backward and Poppy stirred.

I was frantic. I scanned the water for any sign of him, looking for ripples and bubbles.

Nothing.

Behind me there was the sound of breaking water, right where Harry was crouching, holding Poppy. The two people I cared most about were huddled together on the jetty as a monstrous hand stretched out, grasping Poppy's ankle, dragging her into the water. Harry held fast but he was strong and determined to take them down with him

"Keep hold of her!" I screamed, turning about.

"I'm trying! I'm trying!" Harry yelled, kicking at his hand with her feet, her heels scuffing the decking, moving closer to the edge of the jetty.

I launched myself in their direction and stood over him panting, my heart racing, hatred burning in my lungs and my throat. I turned to Harry, not seeking approval for what I was about to do, but as a reminder of what I was fighting for. I was not distracted by her petrified stare, her tear-stained face or Poppy's terrified screams, not when I saw the scar on the left side of Harry's throat—a streak of silver illuminated in the moonlight. Sam *had* left his mark on Harry, just as he had on every woman he had tortured, abused and raped over the years.

He looked up at me with wild eyes, his face streaked in blood.

"You were right!" I yelled. "I wasn't there for my family then. But I am now. You bastard!" I raised my right foot and landed a powerful kick just below his chin, on the left side of his throat. The upper cut caused his head to jolt backward. I heard a crack. It could have been the decking beneath my feet or bone—a jaw bone or vertebrae…

He let go of Poppy's ankle and slipped slowly backward into the dark water, his face fading, his eyes staring, his arms outstretched like a man being crucified, laid to rest in a watery grave—reparation for a lifetime of sin.

Poppy was weeping. Harry was rocking her back and forth in her arms, soothing her with words of comfort. "It's all over now. The bad man's gone."

I pulled them both to their feet, took Poppy into my arms and headed back into the house, not stopping to look back.

Harry and I put Poppy to bed, insisting over and over that she was safe. What had happened had been a scary dream and when she woke up everything would be all right. Poppy only believed us when she linked her little fingers in ours and we made a pinkie promise. She slept with the reassuring fairy-tale figures circling her room, her innocence restored.

When Harry appeared in the lounge, she was carrying Poppy's drawings. We lay them out on the dining table like a storyboard, using our clothes and activities to arrange them in chronological order.

As far as we could deduce from Poppy's illustrations, Sam had been stalking us for almost a month. No one had noticed, and even if they had, they would have assumed the reoccurring flashes of blue were my car or a figment of Poppy's imagination.

"We'll have to call the police," Harry said, collecting up the drawings with shaky hands.

I hung my head. "I can't. I can't risk all this coming out."

"But what if … what if someone finds him?"

"Like who? The lake and the field beyond is private property, it's fenced off—it belongs to me."

What we had done was morally wrong, but I couldn't allow her to be caught up in this ill-fated crime, even if she *was* complicit. If the truth came out, I would confess everything.

I poured out a couple of glasses of scotch and handed her one. She took it and moved over to the sofa. I did the same.

She paused before speaking, noticing the small mound of keys on the coffee table— Sam's keys. "I'm scared, Max. Not for me, for you and Poppy. I'll say I hit him. I brought all this on…" She lowered her eyes unable to face me.

"No, you didn't. If I hadn't gone looking for him, he wouldn't have been so set on taking you back. He knew where you worked. He could have got his hands on you at any time."

Her mouth fell open.

"He could handle not having you, but not someone else having you." I spelled it out for her. "That's what set him off."

She closed her eyes tightly. "And all this time I thought I was free of him."

"He wouldn't rest until he found you." I massaged my temple, easing my aching head. "Tell me, Harry, was it true? What he said about you having Hope's heart?"

She nodded.

"And you planned everything just to get to me?"

She nodded again, drawing her bottom lip into her mouth, fearful of my reaction.

"Why?"

She scraped her hair behind her ears, revealing her pitiful face, her tearful blue eyes. "Because it didn't matter what I did, or where I went, I couldn't stop thinking about you. Before I was given Hope's heart, I was dying, literally, and not only physically but in my mind—a little every day. After I received the transplant, I wanted to know more about your life. You being well known, finding out about you wasn't as difficult as I thought it would be. I even visited one of your exhibitions." She smiled at the memory. "I couldn't afford to buy anything, but I bought a programme and fell in love with you through those paintings, and through your words…"

I raised my head. "We spoke?"

"No. I read your interviews and saw you on TV. It wasn't hard to see what Hope saw in you. I saw it too. I was drawn to you." Her eyes filled with more tears. "You're a good man, Max."

"A double killer."

She shook her head. "That's not true. We've both done things we're not proud of, like leaving my journal for you to find." She swallowed deeply. "But through that journal, I found my voice. I revealed myself to you in those pages."

"But you lied, Harry."

"Not about myself," she asserted. "Not about what happened to me, only my job and the course, and the travelling and I even did that, virtually. I had to. Where else could I go?" She placed down her empty glass. "When I was little, my mother asked me what I wanted to be when I grew up, half expecting me to say, a model, a singer, a teacher..." She smiled, remembering the conversation with fondness. "I told her I wanted to be loved. She said I would be one day, but it isn't until now that I think she might have been right."

She rested her hand on her chest. "I fell in love with you a long time ago. Don't you realise? You have my heart. It beats for *you*, Max." She stood and moved listlessly intending to collect her coat.

"Don't leave, Harry." I patted the sofa, and she came and sat down next to me. "You have a good heart, there's no denying it. Not because it was Hope's but because you've made it your own; it's *your* blood being pumped around your body, and your empathetic nature that has drawn you to me."

She looked so bewildered I ran my hand across her hair as I had done so many times with Poppy. She closed her eyes and rested her tear-soaked cheek in the palm of my hand. "You saw a fellow sufferer, a kindred spirit, and you came to my rescue."

She forced a smile.

"In my way, I've tried to do the same. The more I read about you—the real you— the more I fell in love with you: your tenacity, your determination, your love of life. And then, when I got to know you, experienced your kindness, your humour, saw the way you were with Poppy, I knew you were the one we were holding out for."

Harry's head fell and she sobbed, her tears falling like silent raindrops.

I meant every word. Harry had brought about a change of heart in me too. In my own mind, I would never be vindicated, but the best I could hope for was clemency for time served. I wanted to live too—with her by my side.

I held onto her hand and squeezed it tight with Hope's words, the same words Harry had said five minutes earlier, ringing in my ears like a miraculous reprise: *You have my heart. It beats for you, Max.*

I was filled with wonder.

I raised Harry's eyes to mine and found myself gazing curiously into her face, and there it was; the one thing I had longed to see, wished for with a need so desperate and deep I thought it would never be fulfilled by anyone—the glimmer of unconditional love.

Without shifting my gaze, I traced the scar on Harry's throat with my forefinger, the ultimate proof of her legitimacy. She was the victim—she had *always* been the victim; her body was a map upon which a lifetime of suffering had been drawn in pale pink and silver.

And I loved *every* inch of it.

If I had drawn my soul a month ago, I would have used chalk and produced a white outline on the floor without features, feelings or a future, a dead ringer for the man I had become. Harry had helped me erase the legacy of shame I had been living with, showed me how I had been grieving the loss of the perfect woman—a woman who didn't exist.

There was no two ways about it, I couldn't conceive of a future without Harry. Her face was tear-stained, her eyes bloodshot from crying. She looked pale and drained of all emotion. I held her face in my hands, wiped away her tears with my thumbs and kissed her softly. I pulled her close, feeling her damp cheek against my own, her warm fractured breath in my hair, and the sentient synchronicity of our hearts, and our minds.

EPILOGUE

17th December

Hope rises like a phoenix from the ashes of shattered dreams.

~ S.A. Sachs

IS THERE AN EASY way to disentangle Christmas tree lights?

The reason I'm asking is because we've bought an artificial Christmas tree and I'm in charge of sorting out fairy lights. Poppy has been hanging baubles, chocolate coins and fairies for the past three hours and now, exhausted, has found refuge on Harry's knee. Together they are humming along to carols and making multi-coloured paper chains to decorate the house.

Poppy is comforted by the beat of Harry's heart, I'm comforted by the knowledge that we are a real family about to celebrate Christmas, as well as Poppy's birthday tomorrow, and that it will *not* be the usual half-hearted gathering with Mary and a grieving father. We have a party planned. Friends from Poppy's swimming club will be arriving at two o'clock, Mary and her husband at three and Grandma and Grandad Chambers at four, all expecting to see Christmas tree lights … hence the initial question.

Up until three weeks ago, Christmas held little significance for us. With the result of Poppy's paternity test still unconfirmed, Harry and I were living on a knife edge. The worry that came from not knowing took its toll on us; we had trouble sleeping, lost our appetites, we were irritable and hard to be around. So, on a fateful, Friday night I had Harry unfold the letter and read it aloud. We huddled together, held hands and there was a quiver in her voice right up until the line when the result appeared like a dying wish. It was positive.

I *am* Poppy's father.

We fell onto each other like ragdolls and cried until relief took hold and transformed our tears to thankful smiles.

A lot has happened since the *incident* on the lake. The night after, I donned a baseball cap, a pair of jeans, an old zip-up jacket and a pair of gloves and drove Sam's car to Camden. I parked it a few cars down from the Prince of Argyll pub and caught the train back. As far as anyone is concerned, Sam was there a month ago and has not been seen since.

My hair is short and styled now; I'm clean-shaven. I have rediscovered my cleft chin and cheek bones which Harry, my future wife, cannot help but caress. I look nothing like Sam's old drinking partner, and we are convinced that there is no way of connecting us to him.

Harry and I are of the opinion that some sins are excusable, and others are not. We have pardoned each other for the lies we have told and the secrets we have kept. We accept that we are responsible for the biggest sin of all and are united in the clandestine belief that in eradicating a monster we have made the world a safer place.

The weather has been unpredictable lately, making it impossible to take the boat out. They say snow is on the way and we may have a white Christmas. When we look out onto the lake, we can see ice forming: an opaque layer between the past and the present becoming more impermeable every day.

I'm draping lights over our tree with fingers that are daubed in paint. A fortnight ago we threw back the dust sheets in my studio. Reluctantly, Poppy wore her facemask and arranged tubes of paint on a dust-free table while Harry and I over-painted portraits of Melody with shades of green in preparation for spring—an indication of the changing scenery, signifying a fresh start.

In need of no muse, I have started painting again. No portraits, not yet, only landscapes as a way of rediscovering my talent, reacquainting myself with the feel of a brush and the satisfying sensation of creating something of beauty. I'll be doing portraits by Easter—I have the perfect models.

Harry is turning this glass house into a home. Hope's paperweight sits on the coffee table polished and pristine, paired with the painting hanging over the fireplace that I completed three days ago.

It depicts the view from the lounge, looking out over the garden, the forest and fields beyond broken up by an expanse of water: a rippling carpet of grey streaked with silver and petrol blue, reflecting pockets of light in passing clouds. The jetty stretches out into it, a wooden platform onto which a small rowing boat is attached.

Among the greenery is a single indomitable burst of colour, reaching up from the reeds like a lifeline—a bright red poppy. It's beautiful, unforgettable … a beacon of hope.

If you have enjoyed reading THE DARKEST CORNERS, please be so kind as to leave a review.

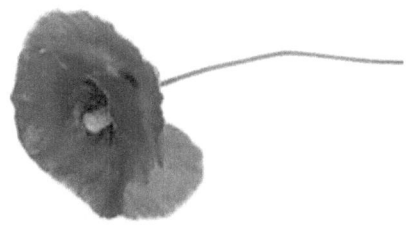

'Hope' is the thing with feathers—
That perches in the soul—
And sings the tune without the words—
And never stops—at all—

And sweetest—in the Gale—is heard—
And sore must be the storm—
That could abash the little Bird
That kept so many warm—

I've heard it in the chillest land—
And on the strangest Sea—
Yet, never, in Extremity,
It asked a crumb—of Me.

EMILY DICKINSON

SPECIAL THANKS

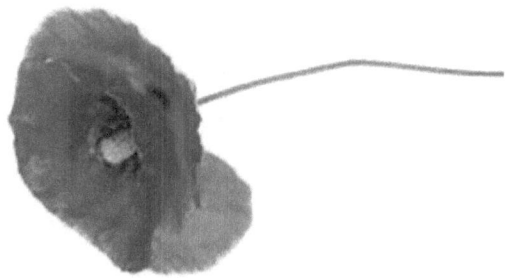

Thank you to those who work tirelessly to keep the wheels of the publishing world turning: the bloggers, the reviewers, the formatters, cover designers, proof readers, editors and publicists who continue to wave the flag for both traditionally published and self-published authors sharing their stories. Where would we be without you? Thank you Michele for your patience, also Marie for your intuitive editing, proofreading and encouragement and, more recently, Ava, for your formatting wizardry.

Likewise, my appreciation goes to fellow authors who go out of their way to support each other; doing so in such a competitive industry is a reflection of your generosity and sincerity.

My most sincere thanks to the many friends and readers from around the world who have been on this creative journey with me from the beginning, discovering new worlds and meeting unforgettable characters along the way. You know who you are: Kim, Susie, Judith, MJ, Karen, Lisa, Annette, Joyce, Ilona, Sam, Donna, Sharon, Elizabeth, Sarah, Carrie, Elaine, Jennifer, Jackie. Mary, Tasha. Also to readers and friends who have shown their support and helped to make this venture into new territory a little less daunting: K.L., Tracie, Jenn, Lisa, June, Amber, Candice, Robin, Sandra, Tanya.

My two sisters in arms Julie and Alice have been with me from day one. You never fail to amaze me with your loyalty and devotion. My gratitude goes out to you and to my beta readers for finding time to read something very different from me, offering insightful comments and advice. Without your encouragement, The Darkest Corners wouldn't have been written.

What an exciting time this is for us. We are about to delve not only into the hearts of new characters, but their minds too, allowing our emotions to run wild and our hands to grip our kindles just a little tighter as they tumble toward a dramatic climax.

I hope you enjoyed reading **THE DARKEST CORNERS** as much as I did writing it. If so, please take a moment to post a review, share your experience and get ready for more soul-stirring stories that twist and turn in who knows what direction…

Much love

Sydney Jamesson

ABOUT SYDNEY JAMESSON

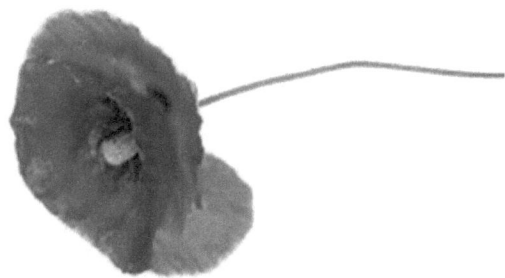

Sydney Jamesson is an English teacher by day and a USA Today Bestselling author of romance, suspense, psychological suspense by night. She is nocturnal by nature and loves nothing more than staying up late, listening to music and being inspired to write. She has always scribbled things down; in her home is one enormous wastepaper basket full of discarded phrases, opening lines and pieces of dialogue that have hit her like lightning in the middle of the night.

Her bestselling trilogy, The Story of Us is available worldwide. Due to popular demand, she was thrilled to continue Ayden Stone's and Beth Parker's epic love story in The Story of Us Series: Into the Blue, comprising: Blue Genes, Blue Hearts, Blue Moon.

The Darkest Corners is a departure from romance suspense and an exploration of the human condition; dealing with loss, domestic violence, forgiveness, learning to love again and what happens when the darkest of secrets surface, putting those you love in serious danger.

Following on from this novel, Sydney has continued to captivate her readers with more psychological suspense thrillers. In DUTY OF CARE and THE CARETAKERS - THE DUTY BOUND DUET - readers explore the seedier side of the Dark Web; witness abduction, human trafficking, and a devoted sister's willingness to do whatever it takes to safeguard the wellbeing of those in her care. It's a real page turner, filled with incidents which are heart-breaking and heart-stopping in equal measure!

AFTER READING THIS BOOK...

CONNECT WITH SYDNEY JAMESSON ON:

Email Sydney Jamesson to discuss this book or
film rights: sjpublishing@virginmedia.com

Twitter

Facebook

Goodreads

Instagram

Join The Darkest Corners Collective on Facebook

ALSO BY SYDNEY JAMESSON IN PAPERBACK &

IN KINDLE FORMAT

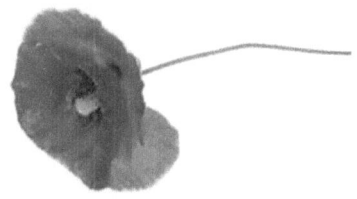

PSYCHOLOGICAL SUSPENSE

THE DUTY BOUND DUET

DUTY OF CARE #1

THE CARETAKERS #2

ROMANCE SUSPENSE

THE STORY OF US TRILOGY – USA Today Bestseller

TouchStone for play

Touchstone for giving

TouchStone for ever

THE STORY OF US BOXED SET

THE INTO THE BLUE SERIES

(following on from TSOU)

Blue Genes

Blue Hearts

Blue Moon

www.ingramcontent.com/pod-product-compliance
Lightning Source LLC
Chambersburg PA
CBHW032207190626
46810CB00019B/2172